A FOREST BURNING

A FOREST BURNING

A NOVEL

CAROLE GIANGRANDE

CORMORANT BOOKS

Cormorant Books gratefully acknowledges the support of the
Canada Council for the Arts and the Ontario Arts Council for our
publishing program. We acknowledge the financial support of the
Government of Canada through the Book Publishing Industry
Development Program (BPIDP) for our publishing activities.

The marching verses — "Napalm, napalm," etc. — were
documented by Carol Burke of Johns Hopkins University
in "Marching to Vietnam," *The Journal of American Folklore*,
v.102, #406; Oct.–Dec. 1989. Reprinted with permission.

Printed and bound in Canada.

Canadian Cataloguing in Publication Data
Giangrande, Carole, 1945—
A forest burning
ISBN 1-896951-25-2
I. Title.
PS8563.I24F67 2000   C813'.6   C00-900672-9
PR9199.3.G46F67 2000

CORMORANT BOOKS INC.
RR 1, Dunvegan, Ontario K0C 1J0

for Brian

Why do you look for the living among the dead?
— Luke 24:5

❧ *Fire I* ☙

One

Lorne jumped into the goddamn fire! — the voice in Sally's headset was like static from a lightning storm. With her back to the cabin, with the roar of the wind, she had no idea what had happened, who'd spoken. *Those macho jerks are pulling my leg,* she thought. It was only when she banked that she saw the figure of Lorne Winter, small and frail as a scrap of birchbark, swept by the air to the flames, to the blazing tops of spruce and jack pine. She imagined him catching fire as if he'd leapt down to chase it, to catch it with his hair, his sleeve, to embrace it with his arms and legs. *Got you!*

Camera One — her name for the man who'd told her, she couldn't remember his real name just then. An agitated voice. A TV reporter here to shoot the Conlin forest fire, a man who'd covered Haiti and Somalia, who thought of Northern Ontario as peaceful country. *God help us,* he whispered. Sally heard him, imagined the lens of his camera zooming in on Lorne, as if it were a giant hand that could sweep him out of the flames.

Lorne — what the hell, I've got work to do. She had to ice her mind with thoughts like this, she had to stay calm. It must have been a camera angle gone wrong, a miscalculation. He couldn't have planned it, she felt sure. Chilled inside, her thoughts were skidding on ice. *What I saw was a heat mirage. I didn't see Lorne on fire.*

Jimbo, sitting next to her, was talking into the mike. He spoke with his lips, his teeth pressing into the soft first letter of a word as if it were breakfast, *Fucking fruitcake.* Jim Bodan the Morning Man, on CJQT, most days wired on glazed doughnuts and double-double coffee and traffic reports of dead moose blocking Highway

11 northbound, but not today. He'd seen it too, a human filament flashing into light, into trees that were blackened wires, darkness. "Fly, don't look," he said. "I'll talk to the newsroom."

My own damn fault I let him come. She called the control tower, reported the accident. "I'm back to fly-ins after this," she said to Jim. "Float planes, fishermen. No more news jobs. Ever."

Lorne's jump was far too easy to imagine. The chopper door removed for the cameras, Lorne crouching in front with his Hasselblad, the video guy standing behind him, sighting over his shoulder, *We're moving up on it, Jesus Christ, look at 'er rip,* and Lorne springing up on his feet and, right in front of the video lens, pitching his body forward into the wind.

A voice buzzing in her headset, Camera One again. "Hate to have to ask you for a second pass. Blew my shot, I'm sorry."

No problem, she told him. It was what she did on shoots, routine to give the cameras whatever help they needed. Camera One had missed a nice, slow pan of a fire burning for a week now. The poor guy had pulled the lens in, then zoomed out for Lorne's descent to earth. He'd given the world a gruesome shot, the only photo that Lorne Winter couldn't take himself. Maybe that was why Camera One was sorry.

Sally turned the plane around, heading back towards the edge of the fire. *You can feel yourself dangling in a chopper,* she'd said to Lorne. *Over the treetops, bobbing up and down like a toy on the end of a string, God's toy.* He'd laughed and kissed her neck. *I have faith in God the pilot,* he'd told her.

Lorne below her, burning to death. Married, one son.

Jimbo in her headset. "Guy's nuts."

"I shouldn't have let him on board," she answered.

"Take it slow." Jimbo opened his mike and started broadcasting his news bulletin, but Sally tuned out his channel, listened for the tower. *Hang in there, over,* the tower said.

After twenty-five years, Lorne Winter shows up last fall on my fly-in to Windigo, all cameras and lenses and what-a-surprise-this-is. Right out of nowhere, how he does things, the way he's throwing his death at the world.

A voice in her headset, *We're done back here, any time you wanna head back,* and she said *Roger,* not even thinking *OK* or

Sure thing or any other human word.

Sally guided the chopper down, letting herself vanish into the noise and throbbing of the plane. Too small was how she felt, her body encased in the cockpit like a seed in a metal husk. Her frozen thoughts were melting into the fire, into the crackle of jack pines burning, heat springing their seeds from the cones, Lorne springing loose from the plane. A large man. She, much smaller, felt unprotected by her casing, her jumpsuit and boots, her helmet, her skill in the air. Clearance to land at Timmins, yes. She gripped the steering bar.

Lorne Winter dead, spat out of his own life. She couldn't bear to think it.

She felt as if she were a bird, a flying thing, her hair short and black, spiky as the feathers of a crow. Yet she knew that her dark eyes were a sentry's, steady, moving. Sure of herself, she kept her mind on landing, touched down. She did this well, her hands recalling her first flying lesson, her instructor helping her up into the cockpit, and her not realizing until that moment how large a thing a bush plane really was. *Big or small doesn't matter when you fly*, the pilot had said. *Only good judgement.* She had none, letting Lorne on the plane. She would turn in her licence, never fly again.

Sally sat in the cockpit, her face in her hands. She felt Jimbo's hand on her shoulder.

"You all right, kid?" Sally told him yes. She sat up, dazed.

"That shitbag, who was he?"

"Lorne Winter, the photographer."

Jimbo snorted. "Artsy-fartsy. What the hell's he doing on the news chop?"

"He asked me to let him on. My fault."

"Your fault, nuthin'. Ego. Everybody famous for fifteen seconds, right? He died for CNN, the prick."

She nodded, stared out the Plexiglas. Police and emergency crews all over the tarmac; reporters. She climbed out the door and down the cockpit stairs, limp, exhausted, hardly ready to talk to anyone, a mike thrust in front of her, a videocam. Behind her, poor frazzled Camera One was now himself in the camera's eye. *Hell isn't fire*, Sister Frances had told them years ago. *Hell is the worst that can happen, only forever.* Sally remembered searching for images of hell that fit this definition, imagining a hall of endless reflections, mirrors inside mirrors, light bending back on itself. She glared at the lens.

"What did you do when you heard he'd jumped?"

"Kept flying," she said.

"You saw him, though, when you banked the plane. What did you see?"

Sally paused, took a deep breath — breathed in the smoke of twenty-five acres burning, her lover, Tim Gabriel, high as a top C, the two of them running from the flames, him screaming, *Charlie Cong is after me*, the last time she saw him. It was 1966, her family's land, not far from New York City. Still no one understood the fire, why it happened.

Even now, years later, Sally wasn't prepared for tragedy. She took assignments like Conlin when they came her way, took comfort in the forester's knowledge that fire, while dangerous, was not an extraordinary thing. This was her third trip to Northern Ontario's burning woods. A hot and terrible June for fires, and she would have work until the flaming trees lost interest for the cameras. This was not only work but a tax she levied on herself, one that had bought her relief, serenity. Until today the tax had not been an onerous one.

She told them that she had seen the forest burning. It was summer, she reminded them. Fire season.

꧁꧂

Later Sally thought of Gabe, her son.

She tried to remember his face, frail and wrinkled as thrown-away Kleenex — an infant wet and squalling as a gale — his father sailing out of the hurricane of Vietnam. Tim Gabriel's child. Twenty-eight years old, raised by Lorne and his wife, Ella, adopted long ago, when Sally knew them, when the world was strange with incident and trouble, and with friends who shared joints and marriages and children. Now her son was a young man watching TV in a brittle glass ball of a world, a house with no curtains to draw across its windows, one where he'd witness his adoptive father's death, a million viewers with him. Gabe Winter, a nineties kid who had lost one of his mothers, both of his dads. She wondered if he'd gotten on well with Lorne.

Sally told the media none of this, had no need to tell the police. She answered their questions, said she was fine, really, she'd make it back home OK, then drove her pickup into the forest, to her cottage on Gold Dust Lake. It was an isolated spot outside Timmins; past the outfitters at Big Lake, where a few times a week she picked up mail and groceries and shared the talk of neighbours about snow or fishing tackle or flying alone in the wilderness.

Gold Dust was too small a lake for hunting or fishing lodges, too close to the echo of northern mining. It owed its name to the early part of the century, when Timmins sat on the largest store of gold on earth, and miners, their pockets full of cash, came here to fish. Old-timers said that they left behind the dust of their boots, that the lake sediment was powdered with gold. Now the lake looked ordinary, the land almost deserted. After giving up her son, Sally had come here, moved by this place and its tiredness, its shapeless trees, left to shelter nothing more than wind.

She had picked a shack as humble as a plate of beans, where the shoreline was knifed with pebbles and beer-bottle glass, where effluent foamed in the water. A lean-to, a nest in the woods, a thing to abandon and flee if she had it in mind to do that, but instead she fixed it up, made it a winterized cabin, a warm, comfortable place. Walls painted cream, no pictures, as if the walls were raw and couldn't bear the touch of things, of a simple crockery plate or hanging plant. Skittish as a deer, she felt incapable of more than this.

Flying, reading, sleeping, chores; her life. Sometimes a visit to North Bay or Ottawa or Montreal, to see friends who reminded her that she needed a holiday, a weekend off, a Christmas away. There were men also; some shared her bed for a while, then drifted on, as she did. Now and then she thought of her mother and father, how desperate they had been to vanish, the unsolved mystery of why they had fled; how much happier their lives might have been if they had lived alone as she did. Yet she accepted their lives as they had been, knowing they had shown her how to live inside of silence, within its walls, under its roof, warming herself by its hearth. In this dwelling she felt solace, comfort.

Lately she had begun to wonder how long it would take to forget the sequence of the spoken word, the thoughts on sleepless nights, the long, lonely trains of them that clattered through the tunnels of her mind — how long? Too much time alone, that was what brought on thoughts like these. Sally liked her solitude in spite of that. She remembered that, as a child, she had prayed a ridiculous prayer to God, one fed by too many tales of Catholic saints and martyrs, a prayer for the loss of speech in return for the enhancement of a different sense, of sight, of inner seeing. Silence, she knew, was her parents' language, so nuanced and articulate a form of speaking that, by comparison, the words of life at school and play were crude devices, crumbling bricks, rubble that fell on the ears and left her choking, coughing in the dust. Alone the night of Lorne's death, she sat and stared at the dead eye of the tube, felt Lorne's finger resting on her lips. Wanted then to hear real voices, words.

Two

Which is why I have to speak.

We met again last September, Lorne and I. It was late summer, fall in the north, the days getting shorter, the night air crisp as blue ice. Lorne was one of my passengers on the float plane, a tall, fair man, city-dressed in slacks and soft leather, wearing the uncertain look of businessmen who've never flown in a four-seater, who think of it as a toy, an insect, a lumbering water-strider on pontoons, not a serious plane with phones and headsets, peanuts and booze. I've flown those kinds of guys from time to time, but I didn't recognize Lorne. I wouldn't have expected to see him with fishermen and hunters. His eyes were far away, looking at nothing. And then he looked and saw me.

Lorne was twelve years older than me, just over sixty, a celebrity, his camera gear swinging from his neck, lenses gleaming all over him like mirrors stitched on Indian dresses. I hadn't seen him in almost thirty years. *Sally Groves*, he said to me. *It's been a long time.* He shook my hand, didn't smile much, looked tired. I had work to do, other passengers to check in on my regular run to Windigo Lodge. Lorne fiddled with his camera, took some pictures, asked for the front seat, next to me. That was fine. In the racket of the plane we wouldn't hear each other, wouldn't talk.

I gave the throttle a push and we were off, skimming the lake, the glassy look of it sheared apart by spray, the silence of the wilderness cracking like a china plate. I like my work. It reminds me I'm human, the only noise in the stillness.

Lorne I forgot for an hour or so, until I began my descent and started banking over Windigo. I could see that, with this beautiful sideways view of the bush, he was taking pictures of everything until the plane hit the lake, its pontoons slicing water. I steered it to the dock, cut the engine. Lorne got out first, then the other passengers. He offered me a hand down from the plane. He said he was there for a shoot, two nights.

"Is this your job now, Sally?" he asked.

I nodded. "Anything I can fly, I fly."

"I wondered where you'd gone," he said. "Told Ella that."

He checked his gear in the lodge and invited me to go for a walk with him. I didn't mind a stretch, I always go hiking after a flight north. Besides, I knew the trails; Lorne didn't. Shield country, three billion years of stone underfoot, the chill air hard as a slap. Lorne was wearing warm enough clothes, a leather jacket lined with fleece. He kept his hands in his pockets, eyes cast down. We walked in silence. After a while, we came to a wreck of a log, a spruce tipped over long ago by lightning. He sank down on it, patted the spot next to him.

"Sit," he said. I sat, looked at his worn and fine-boned hand at rest on the wood, age touching it with detail, with lines etched into skin, a mottling of freckles, gold hairs white with time. Meticulous, his nails still filed with care, the tips of the fingers squared, the strong, eloquent hands of someone who might have played an instrument or moulded clay. Eighteen years old — potter's clay I was then, I could feel it, his mark still on me. I asked him how Ella was.

"We're still married," he said.

"That's good news."

Lorne laughed. "That's a legalism. We haven't lived together in years."

He shrugged, kicked hard at a pebble on the ground. On his feet were dark brown leather boots, fine men's wear. He leaned over, pulled up a pant cuff, straightened a silk sock, then brushed some gravel from the grooves on the soles. We'd walked a kilometre of dirt trails, and his boots were streaked with mud. He pulled out a handkerchief and began to wipe them.

"So let's hear about your staid and happy life," he said.

I laughed. "So staid. You should fly in winter."

"Dear God, Sally. Pilots are so *fit*, so *dull*. No booze and early to bed."

He smiled, but his smile was a cut in his skin, like acid burning through cloth. I looked at him hard, saw how the years had worn away the sculpted edges of his face, the cold stone eroded by exhaustion, ageing, tears. His hair was thin and wind-blown, platinum white, and his blue-black eyes were opaque as berries — no longer meditative, more troubled now, more distant. It was the face of someone who had suffered, who could make no sense of what he had endured.

"You're staring," Lorne remarked. "Don't say it, I'm getting old."

"It's nothing to be afraid of, getting old."

He didn't answer. He finished dusting his boots and put the handkerchief back in his pocket.

"Do you hear from your brother?" he asked.

"Mike's going west in the spring," I told him. "They've sold the place to Jake Nolan." I asked Lorne if he remembered Jake. Something wavered in his eyes; hesitation, fear.

"That hack."

"He always wanted the house, Mike said."

And I was glad. Groves Island bore my family's name, pinned me to a place the way a string on a fence-post tethers a balloon. I'd been back once or twice, but I had no need to go there any more, and in my heart I thanked my big brother for wanting to sell the property.

And as for Jake Nolan, he'd do no harm. He was my age, a pal of Mike's, a digger and dredger of island lore, a local guy who used to own the *Island Banner*. Mike said our family was Jake's hobby. Jake had taped him, Mike had told me; he'd no doubt chase me with a videocam if I showed my face, since we were the last of the family, the island's first settlers. Jake felt we deserved an archive on our own land, maybe some kind of monument. Lorne grimaced.

"Some tacky statue, I'll bet."

I looked at him, puzzled. "What's it to you?"

"I knew your family better than he ever will," he said.

"You should call him."

He sighed. "Too much, is what I know."

"Lorne, it's years ago."

"Jake Nolan, fucking stoned and higher than the jet-stream."

"You watch what you say about him."

"You watch what you say about me."

"To Jake?" He took a deep breath, kicked at a lump of dirt. When he looked at me again, his eyes were glittering like rough seas. I wasn't even planning to speak to Jake, but Lorne gripped my arm with the desperate hold of an old man unsteady on his feet. His grip hurt. It was the first time he'd touched me since the day years ago when he had grabbed my arm in a cold rage, tried dragging me off in his car, away from Tim. He felt remorseful afterwards and apologized for his cruelty. Maybe the fear in my eyes now made him remember that day. He let go.

"I'm sorry," he whispered. "I'd forgotten. You were never one for casual talk, I'm sorry."

He looked confused. For a minute he sat with his face in his hands. Then he felt for his handkerchief and wiped off the dirt he'd kicked on his boots. We walked back to the lodge in silence.

Toronto
8 September 1994

Dear Sally,

I'm writing to apologize for my rude behaviour. I know you'd never compromise my privacy and I'm sorry that I assumed you might. Arrogance dies hard, doesn't it? Mine, at least. I neglected to mention that your son's turned out well. Gabe's a freelance journalist and, unlike me, a whiz at the computer. He works at whatever he can.

Will you be kind enough to write to me, Sally? How good it was to see you again after all these years.

Lorne

Gold Dust Lake
20 October 1994

Dear Lorne,

I'm glad your son turned out well. I hope you'll understand that when I gave him up, I did it for life. I don't want to talk about him further.

Jake Nolan has written to me and asked for your address. He's putting together a TV documentary and he's looking for photos. I bet he's thinking back to your days at the *Island Banner* in the fifties, and this would be a good chance to fill him in on whatever you know, but I won't give him your address without your permission.

Sally

Toronto
28 October 1994

Dear Sally,

Feel free to pass my address along to Nolan. Just don't imply I might have something for him, please. He has no taste in photography; strictly the "local colour" sort of thing. I won't venture any more opinions, only to say I appreciate your kindness, that you wrote back. I'm getting old, but I'm not afraid or regretful. My mistakes have followed me, I accept that.

Lorne

Gold Dust Lake
12 December 1994

Dear Lorne,

...Jake was happy to get your address. He'll be back in touch in the spring, he says, since his project's on hold. Mike's let him on the property to do some cleaning up. Mike and Adele head west in June. All the best for '95.

Sally

Toronto
1 February 1995

Dear Sally,

I'm sorry I didn't answer your card. On Christmas Eve, Ella came to visit, arrived early and found me with a young kid. I'd given her a key, it was bound to happen. She's on TV now, could finish me off if she wanted to. You could almost say I set her up to do that. I'm telling you this because I've never managed to fool you. You know me from before. I'm resigned to the fact that I deserve what's coming.

Lorne

Gold Dust Lake
22 February 1995

Dear Lorne,

...Sex will cure what ails you at thirty, but at your age maybe you should think about iron pills or two weeks in the sun instead. It sounds like you're throwing your life out the window. I'm glad you don't feel sorry for yourself because I don't either. We all end up paying for the wrong we do, that's fair. Write after you've taken a few weeks off.

Sally

Toronto
30 March 1995

Dear Sally,

You give good advice, and I appreciate your honesty. I'm rested now. Would it be possible to visit you? I'll be coming up north in the spring to work on a shoot. There's something I'd like to give you, a small piece of art. Our trek in the woods made me think of it.

Lorne

❦❦

Curiosity kills, Sally thought later that spring. Lorne is not a man to sit around and unravel the past with you, yank out the loose threads, stitch up the holes, string bits of meaning on a loom and weave a new cloth of all that came before. She saw that he was lost instead, and that their common past would not be gracious, would not reveal design to him. Except that he had loved her once, and he'd made amends for the trouble he caused by giving her son a father. Because of Lorne, her life was good, better than his. For these things, she had to show him gratitude, forgiveness.

She met him at the airport. On the drive into the bush, he didn't say much. He seemed troubled by something, preoccupied. He sat with his camera grip on his lap, staring ahead, his dark eyes as far away as planets. She knew he would find it unpleasant that her dirt road into the bush was as chewed up as an apple core, that the beach was encrusted with tin scraps and bits of glass, that her cabin was so without loveliness, plain and un-adorned.

Lorne said nothing when he walked inside. He stood in the door, well-dressed in leather and fine wool, taking in what he saw before him with the silence of a pilgrim.

"Simple is best sometimes," he said.

"It's what I needed."

She felt his eyes on her. He didn't speak at first as he glanced around the bare room. "I envy you," he said.

She took his camera bag, got him a beer. After he drank it, he looked at her.

"Sally?"

"What?"

"I miss you. I hope you don't mind my saying that."

"I don't mind." Only that Lorne looked desperate. He hid his face in his large fine hands as if they were a mask. He spoke from behind them.

"Tell me what's going on," he said.

"I don't understand."

Lorne sat up and stared at her. "I came to find out why Jake Nolan is snooping around my business."

"I don't know why."

"He wrote to you, didn't he?" Sally felt afraid. Yes, Jake had written. *I'm a witness*, his letter said, *to your family's life, to all the misfortune that surrounds it. You are my friends and your lives are mine. But because I'm a journalist, I have to understand what gives. I was there the day your father vanished, I was at your mother's funeral, I saw your woods burn, I and half of Long Island Sound.*

"He never mentioned you," Sally answered.

"What did he say?"

"None of your business."

"He wrote about Tim, I'll bet."

Sally was aghast. "Why would he write about Tim?"

"Maybe something new the police found out."

"Lorne, dear God."

What was there to find out? She knew that long ago they'd found Tim's remains, checked his dental records. There was nothing new to find, and she told Lorne that his comment made no more sense than his sitting with his hands in his face, his whisper. Yet he didn't look up. He didn't seem to hear her.

"Jake wants me in New York," he went on. "Some goddamn TV show about your fire."

Sally was puzzled. "Can't you tell him no?"

A thought fluttered through her mind like a bat in an attic: *He's carrying more unhappiness than he can bear, years and years of regret. That's Lorne. Nothing's changed.* She took his hands, pulled them away from his face and held them.

"I forgave you long ago," she said.

Lorne looked grateful. Still on his knees, he grabbed his pack, pulled out a large padded envelope and handed it to her.

"Here's what I want you to remember," he said.

Inside was a framed copy of a picture he'd taken in Algonquin

Park in the late spring of 1965, not at all like the work that had made his reputation: the stark planes and angles of the human form that hung in galleries in New York and London and Montreal, the work in which sculpture had it backwards, and the body was a lump of stone imprisoned in the flesh. *It's only one level of depth, that stone,* he used to tell her. *Think of hard ore rich in gold.* Sally couldn't, can't even now. Yet this photo she loved in its ardent depth, its strangeness.

It showed what looked like a huge wooden object lying on the ground, part tree, part imagine-what-you-like, a wonderful tactile thing, wood rich in the detail of bark, its veined leaves curling like the fingers of a dead man's hand. It was a form that was hard to make out in the undergrowth — likely two trees that had fallen one across the other, the upended roots and tendrils visible. In his camera's loving eye for the wood, its scars and markings and striations, there was an intimacy, a warmth that was missing from most of Lorne's work. She remembered seeing these fallen trees. It had been in Algonquin Park, south of here.

"It made me think of a plane," she said. "I remember." Remembered and felt him, his hands on her shoulders, his mouth on hers.

"You were good," he told her. "But it wasn't a plane."

"What did I see then?" They had always argued about this.

"What you imagined," said Lorne.

Sally laughed. "'Beware of false witness.' Your line."

"A good line for historians," he said. "I should tell Jake Nolan that."

Sally heard the words on his lips as he kissed her mouth and drew her close, and then he was on his knees, his head in her lap, and she held him. *Sally, Sally, I came back to tell you I did you so much harm* — he kept repeating words that asked no forgiveness, words that after twenty-five years or more she didn't know how to interpret, a babbling in a foreign tongue, a language of absence, senseless. It was years ago, she had outlasted any harm, she said again that she'd forgiven him, then clamped her hand over his mouth. *No, Lorne. Stop.* She wanted his tongue inside her, wanted silence.

How brittle time had made him, and how frail, a scuttling leaf in the wind. *Don't forgive me*, he said in his sleep.

A week later, Lorne called from North Bay when he heard about the Conlin fire. He wanted shots for his book on the north, had heard from his media friends that CJQT would be out there. *Sally, will you take me up?* he asked.

She told him yes.

Three

On the night of Lorne's death, Sally was alone, her TV black as a shade pulled tight. The phone began to ring. *Sally, my God, we saw you on the news, are you all right?* Her old friend Riva, who lived in Montreal. *You come out for a weekend and rest,* as if they were still students. The guy down the road at Big Lake Outfitters, *you OK out there? Who was that creep, high on something, wanna bet?* Mail pickup, lumberyard, gas station, her neighbours in the bush, their nerves strung out on CNN. An inchoate roar, as if she were holding a seashell to her ear.

She listened, heard human voices, pilot friends. *Sally, are you OK? Who was that jerk?* Sometimes she wondered who they were talking about. Later she couldn't remember how she answered. Ashamed to say she knew Lorne, knew that he was a good man once. Enough that they held the phone to their ears, heard there the roar of the fire.

Another call, a strong voice, as far away as May dogwood — *Jesus Christ, Sis, I can't believe what I saw on the news.* Mike was on the island, packed and ready to leave for a job on the coast. He told her with big-brother moxie that he always knew the guy had duck-shit for brains. *Sis, you think you need a rest, you call, the house is yours. Whole summer, if you need it.*

"There was a fire," she told him. "Lorne went and jumped in the fire."

"I know, I know. You talk to me."

"A fire, Mike, the bush was dry, hot for June in the north, and the woods went up in lightning, and Lorne got hold of me and said, 'Sally, can you take me up?'"

"You're an ace, Sal. I saw you on TV."

"The video guy said he jumped." Sally wept.

"It's OK, Sis. Fran's on her way to the funeral. She'll look you up."

Lorne's big sister. Sally hadn't seen her in years. She shivered.

"You OK?" her brother asked.

"I'll be all right."

Sally hung up, exhausted. When she lay down on the couch and shut her eyes, the fire exploded in front of them, the sleeve of Lorne's jacket in flames. Jarred awake, she got up, turned on the TV, flipped around to an old late movie, watched it till she fell asleep. It was a romance, moon-and-June. Nothing she'd remember.

🦅🦅

The following morning, Sally slept late. When she got up, she found a message on her answering machine.

Sally dear, it's Fran. It's a terrible thing to speak into thin air about my brother's death, but I feel so badly that he did this to you. I'll do my best to stop by your place on my way to Toronto.

I'm out of her way, Sally thought. *By eight hundred klicks.*

Three hours later, Fran called her from the airport in Toronto, said she had a late-day connection to Timmins. She'd be with her sometime tomorrow; she wouldn't leave her troubled, alone.

🦅🦅

Sally was about to make a run in her truck to Big Lake when Fran Winter showed up at her door. For a moment she felt weak, afraid. She was startled by Fran's presence, by the strangeness of seeing her out here in the wilderness. For years she'd believed that no one from Groves Island, New York, was meant to come here, or wanted to come, least of all this woman who'd sent her north to live. She whispered hello. Fran put her arms around her, held her.

Sally stepped back, felt Fran's eyes holding her as cupped

hands hold water, gazing at her with compassion that teetered over into regret, sorrow. Fran, Sister Frances, her guardian, her oldest American friend, her mother's confidante, one who knew Canada well enough to come north in June in a turtleneck, windbreaker, jeans and hiking boots. Fran had never come to see her, not even in Toronto, not since Gabe's birth. On her trips south, Sally had visited her, but she couldn't remember when she'd seen her last.

Fran was five years older than Lorne, white-haired, her eyes grieved, her face rutted with suffering. Sally took her backpack and her sleeping-roll, asked her why she hadn't called for a lift. Fran said the mail truck had picked her up, the driver had known she wasn't from around here, guessed who she was here to see.

"Guy said you need looking after," said Fran. Sally offered her tea, plugged in the kettle, asked her how she was feeling.

"Like Job," Fran answered.

"You didn't have to come this far."

Fran looked about to weep. "I owe you that much," she said.

"You don't owe me anything, Fran."

"It sickens me to think Lorne raised your son. I shouldn't have sent you away like that, I shouldn't have let it happen."

Sally took Fran's hands in hers and held them. What terrible doubt and confusion Lorne's death had prodded loose in Fran, and at that moment Sally hated him. Poor Fran; Sally was old enough now to accept that those had been the days when parents felt shock about sex, when nuns felt a heaving and rocking of the earth, and Fran had been both these things to her in 1966, a year of hash and careless fire, stupidity and grief. Fran had sent her north to finish her studies, to take up flying, to start her life again in her mother's country. There had been years of awkward silence between them, pain that time had eroded into small, hesitant gestures of friendship, a timid reaching out. Sally told her it was no one's fault.

"I was doing sit-ins," Fran said. "I should have kept an eye on you."

"I grew up just the same."

Fran grimaced. "Lorne didn't."

Sally agreed, unplugged the kettle, poured the boiling water into the pot. Fran had been a teacher once, then a principal; now she was tending to the street kids and the homeless of the coastal towns that yawned and stretched their lazy way along the waters of Long Island Sound. She should retire from the world's mistakes, Sally thought.

"Lorne came by," she told Fran.

"He was after you again," Fran remarked.

"He asked for a seat on the plane."

Fran looked at her, hard. "Same thing."

Her look chilled Sally, made her wonder if Lorne had planned for reasons of his own to chase her down. The fall flight to Windigo, the letters, his aerial shoot and his death; he'd never been spontaneous, was what Fran meant. Sally felt afraid. She had to get out in the fresh air, had to shake Lorne's rustling and skittering through her head like a squirrel trapped under a roof. She told Fran she'd been about to make a run to Big Lake for supplies.

When Sally got back, she heard a chopping sound from the woodpile. For a moment she had the bone-cold feeling that Lorne was here, that he hadn't jumped, that the leap into the fire had been an illusion, that her house was burning. She wanted to thrash at the air, to run. A deep breath, then another as she carried in the groceries and went outside to look for Fran.

Fran had hauled out logs from the shed. She'd found an axe and was swinging it over her shoulder and down, *ka-chunk* into the wood, a clean split, the wood under the sharp blade cleaving, breaking. One after another she quartered logs with a rhythmic swing, the sharp blade slicing through wood, and she didn't stop until she was done. Then she stood, her eyes lowered, her hands folded over the handle of the axe. Not grief or acceptance, just a staring down at what the axe had opened in the wood, the places it had broken.

Work is prayer, she had told Sally once. Two-fisted prayer, work is.

Sally watched her put down the axe and sit on a tree stump, her hands clasped together, her head resting on them. She was like some great bird gazing at broken eggs, at the slight bones of her unborn young. Then Fran was up on her feet, hoisting an armload of wood, walking towards her. Sally started to back away in fear. It was nothing she could explain.

"This'll keep you warm the odd cool night," Fran said. Sally gripped the wood, tried to push Fran away.

"No fucking fire."

"Hey, cut that out," said Fran.

Sally kept pushing. Fran dropped the wood, grabbed Sally's arms and pulled her inside the cabin. "It's OK. Look at me," she said.

Sally looked. It was Lorne's face she saw before her.

Fran grabbed her shoulders, gave her a shake, as if she were trying to wake her up. Sally looked at her again.

"Lorne's in your eyes. I saw him floating down. His sleeve caught fire."

"Dear God."

"Like a big fucking leaf he was burning." Sally wept.

"Come to the island," Fran told her. "Stay a while and rest." *I should never have sent you away* — Sally heard this too.

Fran offered her tea, but Sally couldn't stop repeating, *there was a fire, Lorne died in the fire.* The words gripped her, made her shudder with the taste of him. She spilled hot tea on her lap, but Fran saw only that she wept. She held Sally in her arms, dried her off, took the tea away, found her some Scotch. Lorne's sister, her oldest friend, a voice in the roar of the ocean.

Four

Sally crossed the Sound on the ferry. It was a warm June day and, remembering that summer here meant summer, she had left behind her pullover, her lined and hooded anorak, her padded boots. She found it disconcerting, this doffing of clothes, shedding layers of a country that for so long had kept her warm. She looked at the water. Long Island Sound; the years had made this place unreal to her, no more than a stylish foreign name. Even more remote to her was the island that bore her own name.

Groves Island — *More a sailor than an island*, this was what her mother had told her once — a home of wanderers. It had become in Sally's mind a ghostly ship adrift and lost, all rotting clapboard and frayed American flags, an island as weathered and distant as grief understood. *Groves Island* — once she'd spoken the name with salt on her lips, but the years had left her reconciled, not bitter. She'd been back for Mike's wedding, another time to observe the twenty-fifth year of her father's disappearance and her mother's death. If Lorne hadn't ended his life, if Mike weren't selling his land, if Fran hadn't come north to embrace her, she might have felt that there was no need to return, no grief left to understand.

Only there was.

It was time to revisit the island fire, to absolve and forgive what it had done to her life. It was a task she'd never undertaken, having never felt a need. Yet the Conlin fire had reignited hers, as if its embers had never been doused, as if time had collapsed and Lorne's death belonged to the death of her forest. She had to find rest here, if this was rest.

Because of Lorne, she couldn't fly a plane. Her concentration had been jarred by her body's fear of looking down, her bones and muscles alert to the knowledge that catastrophe, in all its forms, would jump her from behind. Alone in quiet moments, she would breathe, try to be calm, then feel Lorne moving through her body, beyond it, as if he were a breeze and she were a screen door and this was all there was to forgetting, a cease-less movement of wind over earth. Relief came then, but flying troubled her.

The couple who ran Windigo Lodge understood, told her to take a few weeks off. CJQT said likewise, and sent her a basket of wine and cheese with a note *to one helluva flier from a grateful crew, for bringin' 'em all back home*, signed by Jimbo and the camera team on the Conlin fire shoot. Two weeks after Lorne's death, the fire was still burning, half the north was burning. It was a hot, dry summer and, far from habitation, a blaze might go raging on that way for days, for weeks, would be left to burn itself out, to end in a good rain. This was common practice in the north, and yet the thought unnerved her: Lorne as fuel for a spreading con-flagration, as if he'd had it in mind all along to pursue and destroy her serenity.

Alone in the wilderness of Gold Dust Lake, she had begun to lose her invisible hearth, the roof and the walls of her silence. There were calls and questions from the media, from strangers behaving like friends because they'd seen her on TV, even a nosy call or two from friends of Lorne's — enough to trouble her when she was still upset about his death, affronted by his use of her in dying. She wanted to be far from this, away from the north. Anywhere but here.

Her brother's home was set on the island's headland, a lump of trees and hilly ground protruding from the water like a fist. It had been their family's property years before she and Mike were born, all twenty-five acres of it, the forest of oak and sycamore climb-ing the slope of the hill, their spectacular lookout on the east point of the island, where her dad had built a treehome, a beloved landmark, now gone.

A da Vinci of the woods, one magazine called Glen Groves when he wired it for light and heat. *An eccentric*, Con Edison retorted. Her father had been matter-of-fact, shy about his feat, and it was left to Mike to be proud of him. *It's an ordinary house, son, only in a tree. The high point of the island, worn down now. It was the top of a mountain once.* Their home was an accident of time, their dad would say, like the other islands strung along this rich and lazy coast, a remnant from the ice age when the glacier melted, flooded the mountains and became the Sound, the ice pulling back, chiselling and scraping out the mainland coastal inlets, grinding its stones into sand.

The thought used to comfort Sally in her lost and parentless teens, that the sand owed its shapeliness to a glacial tongue, that the beachside mansions and country clubs of Linden and Meredith Point, their stone backs turned on the island, would all in time erode. They would not stand forever, those cold, mute things. They would not last longer than her parents, their frailty, their absence, their history in a family of soldiers and merchants, builders and artists who brooded here like nesting birds and then, like every living thing before them, left.

Sally felt the ferry bump and bang against the rows of tires lashed to the piers, heard the ramp clanking down on the lower deck. A stevedore with a Popsicle-orange vest waved the cars off the boat, then beckoned the pedestrians to follow them. Different now, she thought, from years ago.

This stevedore wasn't dressed in olive-drab fatigues, wasn't a soldier. Groves Island had shrugged them all off: the base where everyone worked, the recruits shipping out, the shabby wooden backsides of the old bars and cheap hotels: flotsam. Sally stood on the top deck thinking, watching, the June air around her white and sweet as milk. Hungry and thirsty, she opened her mouth, breathed in the whole sky.

꩜꩜

From the upper deck on the ferry, Sally could see the Shore Road, the old waterfront, docks and boats, old clapboard bars and clam shacks, a few tumbledown cottages, sails in a good breeze flapping like gulls — a mess of a place, as comfortable as old clothes. None of it had changed much. There was still an

American flag by the dock, as if the rickety heap of an island were about to weigh anchor and sail out to sea. She scanned the dock, looking for a taxi stand, then went below.

On shore Sally waited for the crowd to thin out, then sized up the traffic tie-up on the pier. Before she could wave for a cab, another crowd began to surge in and lock itself around her like a giant pair of handcuffs. Videocams, mikes, *Excuse me, Sally Groves? ABC, would you mind answering a few questions? Just look this way, please, I'm with Cable 10 and maybe you could tell us....* Whose damned idea was this? She glared at them.

"Would you get the hell out of my way?"

Red rover, red rover, let Sally come over. She'd been good at that game: a line of hands gripped together, you had to smash through the line running. One, two, three, she went crashing through the scrum, felt her elbow connect with the mike in a reporter's hand, didn't notice the stunned look of the man as he snatched the mike out of the air.

Up ahead someone was beeping his horn at her, a guy in a jeep with the engine running. It was Jake Nolan. He opened the door as she ran over and jumped in beside him. Jake made a sharp turn, hit the gas, left the dockside crowd in the dust.

"I'm so sorry," he said to her.

She looked at him. "How the hell did they know I was here?"

"ABC called your TV station. The one you fly for."

Jake Nolan offered her a lift home. He was a man who wore the sombre, careful look of a judge weighing evidence, one who ponders and listens day after day. She imagined his hand propped up against his chin, his fingers kneading thoughts into the folds and wrinkles of a tired face. Stocky, grey-eyed, his hair a faded brown. He watched her with too much consternation.

"I didn't know I was news," she said.

"You come from here," he answered. "They don't forget."

Fran, he told her, was away on a retreat, exhausted. Her damn brother's funeral had taken it out of her, she wasn't well, she was too involved in everything, too busy, too goddamn *upset* right now. He wondered out loud if nuns had retirement savings plans. He was thinking of packing it in himself.

Good old Jake, as mellow as a strummed guitar, was how she

recalled him before his army days. She could sense that he was not as happy now. As she climbed into the front seat, she heard a low growl behind her.

"Sarge," said Jake, patting the Doberman. "He wanted to help you bust through the line. I had to hold him back."

"Do you need a watchdog?"

Jake shook his head. "He's company."

Jake's marriage must be over, Sally thought. Stuck in the sun visor was a snapshot of a young girl in camouflage gear and an army helmet. She asked him how his daughter was.

"Fine, but you're looking at Carla," he said. "My gal."

"In the army?"

"Haiti. Back soon." He paused. "Don't see all that much of her."

He scratched his head, pulled his safari hat out of his pocket, put it on, ordered Sarge to sit and behave. Jake seemed embarrassed, and for no reason, Sally thought. There were things you needed sometimes, sexual comforts that weren't the same as love or friendship, even if they led you there.

"It's good you have a friend, Jake."

"You by yourself, Sal?"

"Not always."

He nodded, smiled a little. "So you know how it is."

"Yes."

He'd been taking time off to do some outside work on her brother's land. Mike had told her once that Jake had taken on landscaping work to shake off Vietnam, had planted a lot of saplings and shrubbery for rich people, had taken a liking to work outdoors, until he cast his eye across the water to Manhattan and found a job with the *Post*. He did well, got tired, lost his marriage, came home. He'd always wanted a small-town place back on the island, Jake told her now.

"You wanted my family's place."

"Yeah, Sal. A good place. Best there was."

Jake drove left on the Shore Road, which took a bend north to Washington Street. The main drag had been cleaned up since the army left the island. Gone was the Brigadier Hotel, along with the strip joints and most of the hookers. Like the waterfront, Wash Street was a friendly clutter of rundown things, antique shops and espresso bars, second-hand bookstores and bars and walk-ups, a street that grew steeper as it crossed Lincoln Road, meandering eastward.

There was no order to this end of the street at all. It looked like an earthquake in progress, as if the earth were swelling, lifting, about to send the whole unruly mess tumbling downhill into the sea — all the clapboard Victorian houses with rambling porches smack up against fake-brick dwellings carpeted with roses, the stucco houses with Spanish-tile roofs, the stoops flush with the sidewalks, the sidewalks buckled and cracked by the upward push of sycamore roots. It was a narrow street with too many cars, too many people, too many weather-vane daisies and plastic-bathtub shrines to the Virgin, too much reckless life. Exuberant and silly as a good cartoon, yes it was, and the soul hankered for a place like this, now and again.

It's so alive, she had said to Lorne once, years ago. *Yes*, he'd answered. *Alive, a culture all its own, like something you'd grow in a Petri dish.* She thought of Timmins, a frontier town in the wilderness. She thought of the silence of the north, the Conlin bush that was still on fire.

Jake drove up across Washington Street, made a left on East Shore Road, then headed out to her brother's place, two miles by the longer route that curved along the Sound. It wasn't a large island, Groves — only three miles long, an irregular turtle-shaped body of land, the turtle's head tilting west. At the northernmost point was Fort Travis, once part of her family's forest, sold by her granddad to the government, now closed and abandoned. To the south of it was Groves' woods, Mike's land.

Sally could see water, blue light through a sieve of oaks and beeches, then a few houses climbing the slope. Stone houses, one or two of stucco, most of brick or glittering gneiss. Sensible dwellings, none of them like the home in which she and Mike had lived, a gracious old wooden handcrafted house, shuttered and gabled. Their granddad had modernized it after World War I, and as he grew up Mike had lived in mind of that old man, Benjamin Franklin Groves, who installed the island's first electric lights, who drove its first Model T, who cleared trails through the woods and tended his trees with a farmer's patient love. In Vietnam it had given him hope, the thought of this ancestral home, waiting.

The house had burned down in the fire, and for a while Mike had felt bereft. Home from the war and bitter with disappointment, he'd thought of where he'd been, remembering the effects of fire on thatched roofs and patient villagers. He had built again.

His new house was situated farther east on the land, an aluminum-sided split-level home, safe and dull. Yet the blaze was family lore now. It would not lie down and sleep; it kicked and howled like a phantom child, hungry and crying for attention. At first he and Adele did fire drills, later worked out the evacuation route on the south fork of Lincoln Road. For a while he was a volunteer fireman. Last year he had done a reno, put in cream-coloured siding, fan windows, brass fittings, sundecks, central vac. He'd added smoke detectors, heat sensors, phone hookups to the fire station, until he realized how weary he'd grown of this ghost of a blaze, this delinquent kid, the last Groves to be born here. He was tired of what it had done to his family's land, his soul. He had to leave, and Sally understood.

Jake pulled up the long gravel drive through the eastern edge of the woods to the house. In a clearing it stood, forlorn and sunny, too new, the window glass sparkling like fine crystal in a TV ad; the raw ground in need of shrubbery, of Jake's attention.

"Mike's done a job on this house," said Sally.

"You noticed." Jake pulled his jeep up to the front steps, helped her with her luggage. She didn't hear him. Her eyes gazed across the clearing, to the side of it, beyond the house, through thicket and cattail, wetland clotted with reeds where the pond used to be. She told Jake she was looking for the remains of a huge split oak where there'd been a slatted staircase once, a wild spiral of a thing fanning upward through the trees.

"Mike had a man pull out the stump," he said.

Connected to the house was a new deck constructed in steps with the downward grade of the land. It covered the spot where the oak had been. Years ago the treehome had nested in its vast limbs. It had been the island's pride, and the *Island Banner* had called Glen Groves "the kind of quirky genius unique to America." *Better Homes and Gardens* and *The Times* had done feature stories on her dad's creation. Her mother had poured tea for the Garden Club ladies under this oak, and Sally remembered her mother's awkwardness, the seismic rattling of china in her hand. Sally had slept with Tim for the last time here.

"Jake," she said, "I'd like to go into the forest."

He looked at her. "Now? Why?"

"Not now. Sometime. I'd like to see Old Smoky."

That was what Mike called the place he had loved once, a carbonaceous lump seeded with dogwood and mountain laurel by errant birds and wind — their childhood home, a ruined house in leaf. He'd left it there, a monument.

Jake looked troubled. "Get a rest first, huh?"

Earlier he'd told her that he was going to clear some paths in the forest, but he was anxious to get at the pond first, dredging, cleaning, refilling it. The pond was close to the new house, yet Mike had abandoned it after the fire. Gone to weeds, the pond disappearing into the thicket, the land sloping down to their small beach and the waters of the Sound. *Tim leapt into the water and I followed him beyond the thicket and down the slope of the bank, down to the beach, Sound-water there.* Sally hid her face in her hands. The touch of memory, how the body ached for it, even when the mind said no; she hadn't been prepared for it. She felt a hand on her shoulder.

"You want to be by yourself," Jake said. She nodded, heard Jake's quiet footsteps as he left. The dead, her father and mother, Lorne and Tim, the relentless sound of their taking leave like a rolling of waves away from the shore, a tide that had for years been moving out to sea. Yet she had returned. *Times change,* she thought. *If time can take everyone away, time can also bring them back. In good time, anything can happen.* High tide, the wind had come up, the surf was hammering the beach like a fist.

Five

When Sally went into the house, she noticed an envelope on the table. *Sally*, the note inside it read, *I hope it won't be insensitive to ask if we can talk on tape for your family archives at some point in the future. It doesn't have to be this summer. Jake.*

Yes it does, Sally thought. At some point this summer, she'd have to talk to him, as if the note were reminding her of a thing she'd always meant to do. What a relief that she could tell Jake things she'd never tell Fran, that she'd been fool enough to sleep with Lorne and now she was grieved by the death of a man she hadn't seen in years, who'd whispered *Don't forgive me* in his sleep and then asked for a seat on the chopper to jump to his death. She wanted to tell Jake that Lorne was afraid of him, that when Lorne had tried to say more, she had covered his mouth, sure he was drunk, stoned.

If she'd listened, Lorne might still be here.

In need of solace, she unpacked and settled into the house, a spare clean place with more light than she was used to in the woods. Mike had left behind a TV and VCR, a computer he'd given Jake, cutlery, bedding and all she'd need for a restful stay. She began to feel grateful for the work her brother had put into his house, for the light in the clearing, for the pristine look of the place, for walls of window glass that drew together his home and the forest. Later she'd draw the curtains, hide from this seamlessness, this light that made her so visible. She'd sleep then, pretending it was a place she'd never seen. Turning on the TV, flipping channels for the local news, she was relieved to find no mention of her name.

❧❧

Sally slept, ran errands, walked on the beach and read, remembering to check Mike's roadside box for mail. She spent time with Jake's parents, visited her dad's monument and her mother's grave, called the sisters in Fran's house to ask how she was. She had no more calls from the media. After a week of rest, she felt compelled to visit the ruined forest. From far away in Northern Ontario, the darkness of this place had pulled at her. She could feel its gravity even there, waiting to disturb the orbit of tranquillity in which she moved.

Jake wasn't around that morning, so she went alone down the trail winding past the new house, to the old woods that, for many years after the fire, had been a meadow. Mike had sent her pictures of scarlet asters and goldenrod, blue chicory and Queen Anne's lace, tiger lilies and royal-purple iris. The meadow was changing, the forest was coming back, although it would take at least a century before tulip trees nudged the sky again, and the neck ached from staring straight up the trunks of beeches fat and grey as elephants' legs. For now there were smaller trees and bushes: slender dogwood, azalea, mountain laurel. She welcomed the sight of them, their return long after she had fled.

She was stunned by how little she recognized. Signs of the fire, still: charred trunks riddled with woodpecker holes; twigs dangling, useless and broken. Underfoot the newer life, roots that formed steps in the slope of the land. Light darkened here as it does in the nave of a cathedral, streaming through leaves and branches, falling to earth. Then, without warning, the light blinked, went out. Sally looked.

It was the old house up ahead of her, great and black as a lump of coal, a soft sculpture of steps, front porch and shuttered windows, their formless contours caving into darkness. A shipwreck, as if her forest were an ocean and she'd sunk to the bottom with no diving gear, no air. She gasped for breath, afraid, resting her hand on the wooden rail. It crumbled at her touch like a crust of burnt toast. Her foot on a step collapsed it into ashes.

There was no door, no entry, no repairing any of it. No need to; it was changing, growing on its own — a house of vines, scrub oak and ailanthus, the charred timber seeded, watered by rains — a house taking root in the forest. She sank down on her knees, leaning her body against the soft structure as if it were vegetation, a living thing. She didn't hear the footsteps behind her.

"Just me, Sally. Jake."

Sally turned around, stood up. "Were you following me?"

"Saw you heading out. Just came to warn you it's not safe." He looked concerned, touched her sleeve with his hand, showed her the soot on his fingers. "Got the house all over you," he said.

"Not a house any more," she answered. "Birds are starting to nest in it."

"It's why I told Mike, leave it alone."

Sally stared at the dark form in front of her, a lost home that had drifted away into another life. "I hardly remember the fire," she said.

"You want to?" Jake asked.

"I have to make peace with it," she said. "I'm not coming back."

"Conlin's still burning, I hear."

Sally took a deep breath. "Lorne came out to see me in the bush, Jake. He asked for a seat on the plane."

Jake stared at her. "You're kidding."

"I went and let him stay." Sally felt ashamed.

Jake looked at her, his eyes sad. "It's not your fault he killed himself."

"I don't know why he did," she said.

"All due respect, Sally, I don't care."

Sally opened her mouth to speak, but couldn't get herself to say, *Jake, he kept bringing your name up, something you wanted troubled him,* but she saw he knew already.

"Lousy spot on Cable 10 was all I asked," said Jake.

"What did you want to ask him?"

Jake paused, his eyes far away. "Lorne talked to the police," he said. "They thought he had pictures of the woods after the fire." Quiet Jake was, as if his voice were drifting away from his words.

What did he see? she wondered. *Did he come from Toronto, did he fly over the ashes? Like an Air Force scout when they dropped the bombs on Japan?* She remembered reading that a single plane was all it took to level each of those towns. Behind came reconnaissance, cameras.

"So what the hell made him die like that?" she said.

"It had nothing to do with you."

"He asked to fly in my fucking plane."

Sally shouted it. She hid her face in the bark of an oak and screamed into its hollowness, felt herself choking on ash and acrid smoke. Jake grabbed her shoulders and shook her hard.

"Stop it, stop," he said.

"Please, he didn't have to die like that." Sally wept. *Go easy on yourself*, his touch said as he softened his grip. *You don't know the half of it.* She felt the weight of his thoughts. He handed her his handkerchief.

"God knows why he did it," Jake said.

"Fucking spite." She dried her eyes, felt Jake's hand on her arm.

"Old Smoky's off limits," he said. "You need a rest, soldier."

Sally nodded, wiped her face with his handkerchief, handed it back. Jake folded it and put it in his pocket as if the cloth were fresh, as if it had not been stained by ash and weeping.

❦❧

Jake walked her out of the woods, then drove off in his truck. Alone, Sally went back to the house, remembered to go out to the road for the mail. In the box she found a handful of flyers and a letter addressed to her. Puzzling, mailed in Toronto two weeks ago, postmarks stamped all over it, circles, as if it had been used as a coaster for a drinking glass. It had been sent to her post office box at Big Lake, then forwarded here. It looked like a man's writing, no one she knew.

She opened the letter, read it, then leaned against the wall as if she were afraid it might tumble down on her if she moved away. She read the letter again.

Dear Sally Groves, it began. *I hope this letter will not come as an intrusion or cause you any hurt. My name is Gabe Winter and I am your son....*

❧ *A Witness I* ❧

One

Gabe saw his father die twice. The first time live on CNN, the next at the mall, both on the same day, when once was more than enough. He was working out of his digs in the west end, High Park, had just finished his *Toronto Weekly* write-up, just faxed it off. On his coffee break when Lorne went and leapt into the flames, live before millions of TV viewers, then a hop, skip and jump by satellite to every newscast on the continent.

Oh God, he thought, *what about Ella*, she'd be getting ready to go on air herself, watching this shit on a live feed. *The guy couldn't just do himself in, end up with a dinky little back-page obit, found-dead-in-his-apartment kind of thing. Had to go live on CNN, like a goddamn meteor smashing into the earth.* Questions, reporters, police at his door. A hot June day and Gabe was shivering. He felt for his baseball cap; it was there, right on his head, where it always was. Somewhere he read that, in cold weather, the body lost most of its heat through the head, which was why you were supposed to wear a hat in January. Or when you were frozen scared out of your skull, whichever came first. He poured the rest of his coffee down the sink, went for a walk.

"Who knows why he did it? He didn't exactly warn us," Gabe told reporters. "Something on his mind, who knows?"

"And what would that be?"

How would I know, Gabe thought. *Lorne never said a word to anyone.* He was outside his house, out on the sidewalk, didn't know where he was going as he pushed his way through a nest of mikes and videocams and flailing arms. Hands were grabbing at him as if they could pull words out of his body like splinters that had to be tweezed out with questions. Gabe broke free of them and ran. Reporters followed him down his street until he jumped in his car, slammed the door, then leaned against the steering wheel, his clenched fists hiding his face. They left him alone then.

His dad was in Northern Ontario, he had known that much. Flying around the edges of a forest fire way the hell north of Timmins, a real sizzler, burning for days. Lorne, a still photographer, a guy who went nowhere without a camera — why didn't he stick to his celebrity portraits and coffee-table art books, but no, life is about *risk*, son, he was shooting this incredible fire as a study of postmodern wilderness, whatever *that* meant. He should have *asked* Lorne what it meant, got the guy talking, ignored his own snide observations, the ones that elbowed past his common sense like those damn pushy reporters, knocking over pedestrians to reach him. The truth was that he knew Lorne was nuts, he could *see* it. And what did he do? He made fun of it, he smirked. *Precious old fart*, Gabe remembered thinking that. Maybe if he'd stuck with him, Lorne would've thought twice, wouldn't have gone. Gabe's face hurt under his fists. Everything hurt.

Three hours earlier, Gabe had been flipping channels when he caught the logo of the burning spruce, remembered his dad and began to watch. What a way to pass the time, he thought. Gabe Winter, human moth, dumb enough to get pulled into a TV conflagration. He began imagining the heat on the fluttering membrane of his wings, felt the singe and crackle as it ripped through the threads of his legs. *Gimme a break*, he said out loud, turning off the horror flick that was spinning out of his brain, pulling back from it at exactly the same moment that the cameras pulled back, so that he could watch as they panned across a charred forest of spruce and jack pine, the whole line of trees swaying and crackling and falling apart like a bunch of cadavers in hell.

Above them, Gabe spotted a huge fly of a news chopper way over the fire, eight hundred metres up, he guessed. He watched as a tiny figure leapt out of the plane, flinging an object ahead of him into the flames, then tumbling down after it. The man's body flared into light that was brighter than fire itself, the way a match does if you light it on a candle. Then it exploded like a small, frail cinder. Then it fizzed out into nothing.

That was what he thought he saw. He took off his glasses, cleaned them, looked again. It didn't occur to him just then that the man might be Lorne. He thought of everything else, including the fact that humans were full of carbon and weren't we supposed to smoulder and burn like wood? Maybe this guy was visiting from outer space and didn't know about fire. Some chemical made him go like that, pure magnesium, that flash. Anyway, that went live to air, and the whole world saw this human being do this incredibly dumb thing, and it wasn't that long before they cut away to the local news, where they said some nut had dropped his camera out of the open hatch of the plane, reached out to get it and fallen. No, an eyewitness update from Jim Bodan the Morning Man on the CJQT news chopper confirmed that Lorne Winter, one of Canada's most notable photographers, had jumped into the flames, tossing his camera down first.

Lorne *Winter*? Mister Excitement, the guy who photographed the Governor General shaking hands with the Pope? This is a joke, right? No, world, Gabe realized, this is not a joke. This is the Big Bang for a guy who's put it everywhere. That flash, that was his dick exploding.

The phone started to ring, inane and terrible questions crawling out of it and into his ears. Gabe thought ridiculous things, remembered Ella's cat with ear mites, felt like scratching himself, rolling on the floor, anything to get rid of the stupid itch of those questions. He slammed down the phone, turned on the answering machine and poured himself a beer. Then the police came and this time he had to talk, to tell them that Lorne Winter was his adoptive father, that he and Gabe's mom were separated, they'd been on and off like a lightswitch for as long as he could remember, maybe that was what pushed him over the edge, and maybe they should be talking to her, not him.

Yeah, he told the police, his dad had been all excited about going north, said he was shooting a fire, and no, he was an OK guy, I don't know about depressed. He was just, well, *Lorne*. He could've been stoned or gone on crack, right? I don't have that much to do with him, he didn't have that much to do with me. He has a sister in the States, my aunt. Friends? You mean people you could talk to about my old man? Officer, I have no idea. Maybe you should go down to Yonge Street, chat up anyone turning tricks. The officer was making notes.

"Scratch out the last part. I'm sorry."

"No need to be," the officer said.

Only he knew he shouldn't be taking Lorne apart. The guy helped bring him up and then he killed himself, so he must've been in rough shape, right? He felt as if he couldn't breathe, as if his chest were caving in under the weight of Lorne's death, like a building pounded by mortars, and under the rubble of irritation and snide remarks his pissed-off heart was about to break. Gabe slumped over. The cop put a hand on his shoulder.

"Rough," he said.

"My second dad. Both from the States. Maybe it's genetic." The cop nodded.

"You're American."

"My DNA is."

"You got someone you can call?" Gabe was puzzled. He thought of the U.S. consulate, the FBI.

"I mean a friend," the cop said. "So you're not by yourself."

Gabe told him yes, his friend Dawn.

It was after this that Gabe went for a walk, then had to escape from the media swarm. Once they'd cleared out, he left his car and went back into the house again, thinking that the clip of Lorne Winter jumping from the chopper to his death would be played and replayed, diced like carrots into a stew of hand-wringing and dumb prognostications (*Fire-Jumping Next New Craze, Police Fear*). Everyone he knew — and didn't know — from his J-school days would bug him for weeks, until the next crazy thing happened. He could always hope for another Chernobyl or *Exxon Valdez* to get them off his back, or maybe the country would break up and kick Lorne right out of the news loop on his flaming butt, and was he in shock to think a thing like that, or what?

One crazy feeling on top of the next, Jesus Christ, now he wanted his *mother*. Wanted her the way a kid does, a little kid who still sees Mom as part of him, feels a chill in the limbs when she's gone, as if he's lost a mitt in a blizzard. Only Ella kept reminding him that she wasn't his real mother, even though she'd done the mother thing, and that the term *mom* was generic, like those grocery bags and buckets with bar codes and big black letters spelling out DINNER FOR DOGS or ICE CREAM. *I have a name, Gabe,* she told him when he turned sixteen. *You're old enough to use it.*

Ella Rhodes-Winter, alias Mom — she had a point, not to mention a helluva famous TV mug, that short white feathered cap of hair and bald-eagle face, black-diamond eyes behind round-rimmed glasses. You couldn't miss her on *Midday News,* chewing out half the country. He wouldn't watch, though; not today. He'd call her after her show, try to say something helpful. *Ella, go to the funeral with me and I won't do anything to embarrass you. I won't wear my baseball cap, I promise.* He doubted she'd go.

Tired, Gabe stretched out on the couch and dozed. He remembered being five years old, when he could sense that Ella's care for him was a defiant act, a will to fight that only by chance involved her son, a clasping of him to her body in the same impersonal way that a seat belt holds a passenger in a car. *Stay here. Don't leave the house.* It was her parents she was fighting, rich Ottawa bigwigs who hated Lorne.

And now she was a witness to his death. Maybe she knew why the guy had jumped, Lorne Winter, also known as Dad, which was kind of generic too, almost meaningless, now that you mentioned it. Lorne, his face sombre, pale as the marble in some cracked old ruin from Roman times, the features etched into it, those deep blue sea-bottom eyes that must have knocked the girls out once; a look that got sadder as the years went by, more remorseful and distant.

🐾🐾

Over the past year Lorne had been zipped into one jammed-full appointment book, which more or less explained to Gabe why his father hadn't been around to see him much. On the few occasions when his father dropped by, he was polite, formal. He never touched him, never slapped him on the back, buddy-buddy. This had been Lorne's way with him since his teens, and Gabe sometimes wondered if his own looks were the cause of his dad's remoteness. A tall, lanky, dark-haired kid; maybe he was Ella's by another man. It wasn't something he could bring himself to ask, yet it troubled his mind enough that the thought was always there, hissing like a venomous snake, flicking its tongue.

That was how it had been two weeks ago, when Lorne came over. He'd stood rigid in the doorway, arms folded across his chest, pensive, eyeing him. Gabe had stared back, puzzled.

"I'm not contagious," Gabe said.

"I beg your pardon?"

"So come in." Lorne took one step into the room.

"You look at me like I'm bad burger meat," Gabe remarked. "E.coli bugs."

"Really," said Lorne.

"What's wrong?" Gabe asked.

Lorne said nothing, didn't move. Gabe got up and walked towards him.

"So who the hell do I look like, you want so goddamn much to blow my face off?"

The words were out of his mouth before he realized that he'd insulted Lorne, that the guy might get mad enough to slug him. Only Lorne stood there like a punching bag and took it. He seemed to crumble, a dry clay shell smashed open, shoulders slumped, face lowered in defeat, defenceless against his kid's dead aim, and for half a second Gabe saw a man in the depths of suffering, a man he didn't know. He wasn't sure what to say or do. Only he saw that Lorne felt chastened, as if that crack was punishment deserved. Gabe felt ashamed.

Yet it was Lorne who apologized, who said he was tired, who excused himself and left.

Gabe hadn't seen him again until today, on TV.

༄ ༄

Gabe needed to distract himself, so he counted up the family dead. Lorne, who came with deceased grandparents, so that was three right there; plus his grandparents on Ella's side, and his own real parents, all of whom were as good as dead, for a grand total of seven. After that it got nebulous, more troubling. His birth parents had had parents too, so he had four sets of grandparents and, beyond them, hidden relatives, phantom aunts and uncles, vanished cousins, first and second, once and twice removed, like stars strung out across the cosmos, clusters of stars so far away from him that he could only see them with a telescope, see the light they'd left behind a million years ago, before they turned to dead, cold rocks.

Families were like this, he felt it. All that remembered light, a chain, an endless gravity, a tugging of moons at some unseen ocean, a thing too large for him to name. He was part of it, though. He pulled this huge ghost-family after him. He cast their shadow.

He got up from the sofa, picked up a rock from the shelf, a lovely Precambrian granite, warm and pink. *Watch where you walk*, Ella had told him as a child, and so he did. He took these words as directions, and when they went north for holidays he would kneel and look at the ancient Shield beneath his feet, three billion years of it, the beginnings of the continent, the oldest stone on earth. Now Gabe held the rock to his cheek, let it rest there, the rough flecked surface against the warmth of his skin.

Touching it, he felt sad for the loss of all that was beyond him, of the family members he had never known, of larger things that he sensed belonged to him by right of birth. He thought of the places this rock had been in a million years of lonely travel, of continental drift across vanished seas with names like Tethys and Iapetus, rock that had drifted through the moment of the first conifer and white-petalled flower and seed of grass, through a giving birth, and no one, not a human soul, to see it.

He thought of his mother bearing him alone, thought of a nameless place he carried inside him, a time before he had language. Out in the cosmos there were pinwheel galaxies, their beginnings veiled in storms of gas and dust. In the warmth of his cheeks he could feel the body's memory of sunlight, he could feel but not see back to his own creation, to the still moment where he had begun.

Two

Gabe decided to call Dawn. Even if he couldn't get her, he could listen to her voice-mail, the items on the menu, all the stuff you could access if you just stayed on the line, if you just kept pressing buttons. *Dawn, please talk to me, anything so I won't feel like I'm freezing to death in outer space.* Scared, damn scared, it was starting to hit him now, a fright that knifed his guts whenever he stopped to think what had happened. He tried to relax and breathe, letting his imagination tumble into grade-B scenarios of Lorne as an alien from outer space, Lorne called back to the planet Zenon, Lorne who didn't die, who had to jump into that fire in order to melt, to reconstitute himself in liquid form like frozen orange juice defrosting, poured back into the fiery cosmos to live his life again. *Oh Christ, don't I wish.* He picked up the phone.

You have reached Wayfarers' Church-in-the-Mall, said the message. *Our ministry is available to you during mall shopping hours or by phone. If you wish assistance with your spiritual needs, press One.* Gabe did. When Dawn answered, he could have cried. He told her that it was an emergency, that she'd never believe what had happened. Dawn sighed.

"I'll believe anything. Just had a kid in here, does fries at Burger King. She has apparitions."

"Oh, yeah?"

"She's seeing Jesus congealed in the grease. He talks to her."

Gabe took a deep breath. "It must be the weather."

"What's wrong?"

"My old man jumped out of a chopper. Into that bushfire. Up in Conlin, I saw it on TV." Gabe felt his throat tighten, hard and aching, as if he'd swallowed marbles. Dawn said nothing. For a minute he thought he'd lost the line.

"You there, Dawn?"

"Sometimes I wish I weren't."

"My old man's history, I can't believe it."

Dawn sighed. "He jumped? Didn't fall?"

"*Jumped*, Dawn. That's right, made the whole damn planet watch him burn, didn't have the decency to keep his shit in his asshole where it belonged. You know what I think? I think he wanted to be the fucking first on earth to blow himself away in front of a billion people, is what I think."

"Maybe he left a note?"

"What the hell, Dawn, he could have *said* something."

Gabe took a deep breath, felt his head sink into his open hand like a basketball into a net, only it stayed there, didn't drop from his shoulders. He was shaking. Something wanted out of him, an earthquake, six point one. He wept. He half wondered if you could get electrocuted crying into the phone. There were all these microchips now, and for all he knew, every damn one of them was jam-packed with water-sensitive information. So let the little buggers drown, why the hell should he care? He heard Dawn talking on the other end of the line, *I know, Gabe, I know. Go ahead, cry. Come down, OK? You shouldn't be alone*, and he thought to himself that he couldn't work any more today, he might as well blow a few hours wandering through the shopping mall. No one was ever alone there.

In the heat of the subway, Bloor headed east, Yonge going south, Gabe was icing over with shock. His body was slippery-cold with it, like a car left out in a sleetstorm. *Just think about Dawn*, he told himself. *She didn't get that name for nothing.* So he warmed himself up with the thought of her, how they'd met, the funny story he told himself over and over on blue days when free-lance work got scarce or the *Weekly's* assignments were idiotic, or his computer crashed and lost everything, even the garbage. It was a story meant for today.

He remembered how he couldn't believe this funky chapel, a tall, skinny chrome-and-metal place that made him think of a rocket ready for launching, pushing right up through shopping levels One and Two, through cheapo and ritzy, as if it were saying, *God doesn't care what you wear, how much you spend in the end, friend.* What a corny slogan, dumb things just came into his head like that, but Dawn said, *Hey, not bad. Gabe, you'd be surprised what brings 'em in.*

He'd been doing his weekly mall-crawl for the arts-and-entertainment rag, deciding to tease out a story from this narrow, light-filled space. Nobody there, just him; the chapel had been open only a week. He sank into one of the sleek black leather couches, two rows of them making a semicircle facing the glassy nave of the church. Up above him was a wire-thin metal cross hanging against the glass. You could look right past it and see shoppers strolling by, lugging their bundles, kids eating junkburgers and greasy chips, a sign for ice-cream cones that spelled out *Lick It, Baby* in twinkling lights and, inside the church, the letters etched in silver on the glass, *Where two or more people are gathered together, there am I in the midst of them.*

And then her leaning over him, her corkscrew curls the colour of sweet caramel, and her Attention-K-Mart-Shoppers smile, so he was ready for the sales pitch that never came. Instead he let her blue eyes draw him close, a gaze as mirror-calm as a northern lake at sunrise, so intense that he could feel the splash of his hot and tired body in the water. She told him her name was Dawn, pointed to the flyer on the couch with the list of services provided by Wayfarers, said, if he needed anything, to ask. He stared at her.

"Like what the hell kind of place *is* this?" he asked.

"Something new for the nineties."

"What, a *church?*"

Dawn started to laugh. "The name of this place, that's what's new," she said. "Wayfarers, which means we don't really know where we're going, right?"

Gabe looked around. "It's different."

"We have services," she said. "I don't go. My job's to hang out." She modelled her T-shirt, bright blue with *Wayfarers' Church-in-the-Mall* on the front and *Would you like to talk?* in gold letters on the back. "It's how I meet people," she said, "I buy them coffee and doughnuts, I listen."

"You mind sitting here, talking to me?" he asked.

"No, not at all," said Dawn. "Should I?"

"I don't have anything to say."

"You don't have to say anything," she answered. "I'll listen to that too."

He should have told her right off that he was chasing a story, didn't, and later wondered if he should have. Didn't tell her because he wanted to get a sense of who this woman was before he rated her MMMM on *Mall-Crawl Deals 'n' Steals*. He watched Dawn. Serenity ebbed from her, towards him, draining him of weariness he didn't know was there. Gabe drank her in and couldn't stand his thirst. He felt afraid. She looked at him.

"Are you all right?" she asked.

He wasn't. He was fucking awful. "I'm fine," he said. "Gotta tell you something."

"What?"

Gabe smiled. "Place caught my eye. I'd like to write you up for the *Weekly*."

Dawn looked at him again, this time a careful scrutiny, as if she were reading a map. He could feel her pull away from him, then feel in himself a tangled knot of relief and sadness. He told her he was a *Weekly* staffer and she told him she recognized his name. Dawn had been on Ella's TV show when the Mall Ministry project got started. She knew his dad; everyone did.

"Should have told you first," Gabe said. "I'm sorry."

"Your mom thought Wayfarers was part of NAFTA, something Canada got stuck with from the States. She grilled me on TV. Then your old man came by, wanted to take a picture. He tried to pick me up."

Gabe made a face. "Then I came by."

"Yeah. I worry about heredity."

"I'm adopted. Made in the U.S.A."

Dawn started to laugh. "How did you end up with Ella?"

"Devalued dollar? I dunno."

Dawn told him that her parents were from the States, ex-hippies, they hated the place. They thought as Ella did, but that was their generation, their hang-ups from the sixties; he shouldn't worry, it had nothing to do with now. Gabe listened and felt as if her voice could mend a fraying soul with care and gentleness. It took the breath out of his body, that another human being could touch him in this way.

He stopped, wary as a dumb rabbit with its ears up, its nerves and muscles alert. He wondered how she did that, how she coaxed and nudged that tender feeling out of the tight steel trap of his bones. He wondered if she did this with everybody, men and women, every day. In any case, he was supposed to be here on business.

"Will you let me do a story?" he asked her.

"Just what do you know about this place?"

"Zip," he said.

Dawn laughed again, a cool liquid sound, one he could feel in the knot of sadness in his throat. "You're better than your parents," she told him. "You know when you don't know."

She told him that he could write her up if he spent some time there, but he'd have to do it soon because she was moving west to Alberta, to a new Wayfarers in the Edmonton Mall. Maybe he could observe her, help her a little, get a feel for how the place ran, how she worked. For a week Gabe trailed along behind her, watching and making notes while her eyes unlatched the hearts of strangers. He got so he could enjoy watching her work. He would pretend to be one of her clients, and feel the kindness of her gaze on him.

He decided that he was falling in love with her and, worse, that the whole thing felt ridiculous. He'd never been to church in his life, and here he was, doing a write-up for a cheesy tabloid and wanting to go to bed with a *mall minister*. A woman whose next job was way the hell out in polar bear country, the winters in Edmonton so goddamn cold that speed-diallers froze and mice wouldn't click. Besides, no hint of feeling came from her; either that, or he was missing it. Still, he was drawn by the look in her eyes, the tenderness she lavished on everyone, including him. He didn't know what to make of it. He couldn't imagine asking her out. She had two degrees, theology and psych. She hated TV.

That was only a month ago.

Downtown, Gabe got off the subway, passing through the yellow-tiled catacombs, down the escalators, through the swinging doors and into the sizzling lights of the mall. A triple-levelled glass enclosure, an arched cathedral ceiling in glass, light so red-hot and cold at once that it made you dizzy, shards of daylight splintering on leaves of ex-trees, *Ficus benjamina* bound and chained and doing time in huge clay pots. Careless light splattered like spilled paint through the central promenade, pouring down a cascade of escalators, trickling on the heads of shoppers strung out along the moving stairs like metal sprockets on a conveyor belt, prodigal light dumped into fountains, shining from banners, shimmering on video monitors announcing displays and specials. Gabe wished he had dark glasses, too damn much light. He found a bench, sat staring at the ground. He had no idea how long he sat before he felt Dawn's hand on his shoulder. She asked him how he was.

"My brain's doing wheelies," he said.

"Do you want to go inside and talk?" Wayfarers was just across the pedestrian walkway, but Gabe couldn't move. His eyes were drawn to the TV screen, a huge one at the opposite end of the mall. The news was on, it was pulling him into the screen, he couldn't believe he was actually *looking* for proof it had happened — no, worse, he was stuck there, trapped, his whole body glued to that horrible moment like an insect caught on flypaper. He was sinking into the giant imprint that Lorne Winter had made in the dust of the earth, he was going crazy. That damn clip, they were showing it. He wanted to see it again, no, he'd be sick. People were gathering around to stare. Dawn jumped up, stood behind him, her hands covering his eyes.

"We're going inside, you look away. Come on."

He got up, let her walk him across the shoppers' promenade, tried not to look. Only he could just about feel the heat, the breath of fire snuffing out air, see smoke and flame and hear the crackle of timber snarling and spitting at mesmerized shoppers all along the north end of the mall. The screen wrapped the fire around them, spat out Lorne's camera, then Lorne as he hurtled from the chopper to his death, a huge red cinder floating down towards Eaton's and The Gap and Hudson's Bay. All the while, people were running down the aisles, streaming out of the shops and towards the catastrophe like ants in the direction of a picnic.

"This has got to be crazy," Gabe said.

"It'll be quiet in here, poor Gabe," Dawn answered. She led him into Wayfarers', then put the *Back in Fifteen Minutes* sign out in front of the glass door, locked it and walked him to the rear of the nave. There she drew back a curtain hiding a storeroom door.

"In here," she said. Gabe followed her, let his eyes adjust to the dimness, relaxing after the light. Quiet, he thought, no more fire. Something else moved inside him in the stillness, and he heard himself whisper, *I'm going crazy, help me,* and Dawn put her hands on his face and stroked it and said, *Like this?* He felt his tongue flicking inside her mouth, flailing like a trapped bird while she opened his zipper and felt, and all the while she was whispering, *It's OK, Gabe.* What was it about fear that made him want her so much, and in a closet, for chrissakes, the two of them cushioned by bags full of Styrofoam chips, walled in by corrugated boxes. *Who's going to hear us,* she whispered. *They've got that damn TV on.* Afterwards Dawn held him, stroked his hair.

"I've never done that to anyone here," she said.

Gabe touched her cheek. "You told me I shouldn't be alone."

"You've done this before?" she asked.

"No." Gabe was shaking. Not like this, he hadn't. Until now, he hadn't known how hard it was on him, a human touch. He was breaking up inside, like ice floes in April. He couldn't look at her.

"Don't be afraid," she said.

Gabe grabbed a huge carton and dropped it down over the two of them. "Should've done it under this," he told her. "Security guys in the sub-basement, TV monitors. You could be fired."

"Scaredy-cat." Dawn lifted the box off, climbed out, kissed him on the lips. "Let 'em watch, it's all most people do in the mall."

"You're not scared you'll lose your job?"

"This *is* my job. Right this minute, anyway."

Gabe said nothing. He could feel her hand on his shoulder, but he pulled away. She was clamping jumper cables on his soul and he was stalled, stuck, icing over. He felt hopeless.

"Stop thinking about Lorne," she whispered. He turned his face to the wall, slammed his arm flat against it, as if he were trying to keep it from falling down on him, trying to stop his body from throbbing and shaking with the rotor of the plane, with noise and wind and low sobs, with the urge to shove himself out the door and down through a hole in the sky. Something else he felt: Dawn's arm around him, pulling him back from seeing too much, from staring down.

Three

Lorne had left Gabe a letter to be opened upon his death. A few years earlier, in a moment of conscience, he had detailed his funeral arrangements, named Gabe his executor and told him where in his Avenue Road condo he could find the letter and his other papers. He had left Gabe his duplicate keys, each one labelled, and Gabe had wondered at his dad's exceptional sense of order, at the number of things you could fit with lock and key: Front Security Door, Condo Entrance, Garage, Swimming Pool, Fitness Room, Bar, Strongbox, Desk And File Drawers, Wine Cellar (in his *apartment?*) and Fridge (he locked his *fridge?* Did he stock beluga caviar? It seemed irrelevant now).

Upset as he was, Gabe was grateful for his dad's fastidiousness, his decent behaviour in putting the mundane things of life to rest. It made death look like something normal people did, and not just Lorne. Shaken by his loss, he was also touched by Dawn's kindness, her offering him help in going through Lorne's papers. Gabe had never seen Lorne's condo, and he was jarred by the marble foyer, the art deco sconces, the motion sensors, by the number of things that had to be buzzed and keyed, pressed and spoken into in order to enter. Jesus Christ, the place had more damn locks than Kingston Pen, he *knew* Lorne had to be crazy. He hoped he'd find a note to tell him more. Only Lorne had left nothing to explain why he'd killed himself. Gabe searched everything, then turned on his father's computer, only to find the files scanty, the software out of date.

"Lorne's death was so fucking avant-garde," said Gabe. "I wanted to print out his suicide note."

Dawn frowned. "Check your e-mail. Later."

"Would you believe?" he said. "Lorne didn't have a modem."

Gabe decided to settle for Lorne's letter of instruction. It was dated 1993. *Gabe,* it read in part, *whenever and however I die, please know that I cared about you and that I regret my own lapses in being a father and a friend. Transgressions catch up with one over the years and there is sometimes no way of overcoming them. Yet there is the hope that our children will do better.... So here is something I want you to know.*

Your real mother's name: Sally Marie Groves. Address, General Delivery, Gold Dust Lake, Ontario. I am told she is there now, by my sister, your Aunt Fran, although I haven't seen her in many years. The two of us were renegade Americans. A girl of eighteen when we met. I was thirty. You may imagine what you like and it's probably true...

This jerk brought me up, Gabe thought.

...but I'm not your father. Please write to Sally on my behalf when I'm gone, and tell her I've never stopped caring for her.... I've left you some things of hers in the Eaton's box in the bottom drawer of the right-hand file cabinet. Also, some belongings of your father's that she left for you.

Dawn saw his face turn pale as drywall. "Gabe, what's the matter?"

He handed her the note. Shit, this was weirdness hopping the fence and landing on the third rail; it made his insides smoke with fury. It was *indecent* fucking weirdness. Wondering how weird it got, Gabe crossed the room, started unlocking the file cabinet. He found the Eaton's box and opened it.

There was a coiled and very long lock of hair tied with a black ribbon, labelled *Sally's*. He let his fingers stroke the coarse, brittle locks, a texture that made him think of a wild horse's mane, nothing human. Gabe wondered how Lorne had got it. He wanted to hold it against his cheek, couldn't let himself do it. It felt like something Lorne might do, Lorne alive in him. He felt afraid. "Dawn, check this out," he said.

Dawn was still reading the letter. She looked up. "Sally Groves," she said. "That name."

"What about it?" he asked.

"She was on the news last night."

"Go on."

"We can tape *Newsworld*, don't worry," said Dawn. "They're doing a recap."

"I've seen enough," said Gabe. "Lorne saved some of her *hair*."

"Real sixties," said Dawn. "Check for dime bags."

Gabe did, found instead a photograph of his mother, the first he'd ever seen. He picked it up. She was a slight, frail-looking woman, black hair falling to her hips, a fringed shawl wrapped around her tie-dyed dress. There was a troubling look in her eyes, a disturbing tranquillity, as if she didn't understand the camera, or where she was, or what was happening to her at the moment her picture was taken. She was too vulnerable, too quick to abandon herself to the probing of a man's eyes, lost in a stillness that no one had any business seeing. He put the picture down. He wished that Lorne hadn't left him this.

"My mother," Gabe said.

Dawn touched the photo. "Poor soul."

Gabe sat down, face in his hands, fingers spread wide like the slats of blinds letting in light. He spotted a glint of metal, something in the box he'd missed. He looked again, and picked up a small American flag on a stick. It had been attached with a rubber band to a rusted object that he warmed with his hand, a Zippo lighter. *Your real dad's*, the note read. *Sally passed it on.*

"What is it?" Dawn asked.

He didn't flick the lighter open. He squinted, looking at the inscription on the front as you might glance at a tombstone's epitaph, hoping to glean some history of the dead. Rusted out now, the words, what he could make of them: *Nothing's as sweet as the smell of death in the morning.*

That's too cute, Gabe thought, except that he'd seen this lighter, read that epitaph in a magazine or heard it on TV. He scratched his head. Trivia time.

"Dawn?"

"Yeah?"

"Catch."

She caught the lighter, looked at it, puzzled.

"Comes with a flag," said Gabe. "Where the hell did I see this thing?"

"Vietnam," said Dawn. "GI war junk. They sell these lighters over there, American booty from the war."

"How do you know that?"

"I read it at my mom's. In *The New York Times*."

"That's from the *States*," said Gabe. "Your parents let it in the house?"

"It was in the cat-litter box."

Oh great, Gabe thought. *How I found out my old man went to war.* His heart turned over in his chest and he could almost hear it sputtering, running out of gas. A stupid fluke, the garbage-dump way he's finding out about his real dad. Couldn't Lorne have written something out? Given the guy some dignity? No big deal, just *Gabe, your real dad went to Vietnam.* This was disrespectful, like everything else that creep had left. He said this to Dawn.

"Maybe Lorne didn't know your dad went," she said.

"You think he came back?"

Dawn stared at the lighter, letting it rest in the palm of her hand, as if she were afraid to touch it. Gabe lifted it out of her hand with care, as if it might break. He felt her eyes on him.

"Sure he came back," she said. "You wouldn't have this otherwise."

"They could have shipped it back," Gabe answered. "To Sally."

There were lists of names for the dead and missing of Vietnam, Gabe knew. All he needed was his father's name. Yet he was beginning to think he'd had it with fathers, dead, missing and otherwise. For what seemed the longest time, he held the lighter, then flipped it in the air like a coin. Heads said his dad got killed, tails said nothing. It came up heads. Gabe closed his eyes. *It's easier this way*, he thought.

🪶🪶

Forty-eight hours after Lorne's jump, his embers were still floating across video monitors and TV screens, caught in updrafts of horror and fury, spiralling down in a gust of questions. Having a few of their own, Gabe and Dawn sat in Lorne's apartment and taped the *Newsworld* special, including the one clip Gabe hadn't seen, the bright yellow chopper with CJQT NEWS painted in red on the side. There was a nice shot of it landing, cops and reporters staking out the airstrip, radio host Jim Bodan stepping out of the cockpit followed by a small woman in a helmet and jumpsuit, her face blank as a soldier's in combat, her dark eyes like two bulbs shorted out. Her name came up on the screen.

"The *pilot* of the fucking *plane?*" Gabe whispered.

Dawn shook her head. "I'll never complain about my parents again."

Gabe stared at the screen, thought of the photo Lorne had left, only now Sally's eyes were no longer young. He felt dizzy as Sally explained how she had had to keep flying the plane, how she'd seen Lorne Winter tumbling towards the fire, seen him when she banked the plane and made her turn, had a good view of the fire below her and him falling down. All this in speech as flat as a tin can crushed by a ten-wheel-drive, the toneless language of police detectives talking to the media, describing homicides in voices as stunned as the dead they speak about, *Yes sir, he fired fifteen rounds, turned the gun on himself, that's correct, sir.*

Sally Groves saying she'd arranged to get Lorne a seat on the plane, her lost eyes saying more. *Because he asked, is why. Lorne Winter was a professional, did lots of aerial shoots. Of course we take the doors off for the cameras; yes, it's legal, standard procedure. No, my job's to fly. Yes, I am responsible for the safety of my passengers, but not for deliberate acts of self-destruction, no sir, I am not.*

Gabe sat with his head in his hands. The woman was in shock, had to be. He looked up at Dawn. "I don't believe it. Lorne asked *her* for a seat on the plane?"

"Do you think she sensed anything, Gabe?"

"Who the hell knows? Her job's flying. You heard her."

"Yeah, but — " Dawn stopped talking, stared at the screen.

Lorne Winter spoke to you beforehand, the reporter said. *Any clues to his state of mind?*

No, sir. None.

"Poor woman," Gabe said. He reached out and patted the TV.

How the hell can I write to her? What'll I tell her, "I saw you on TV?" Gabe picked up the channel changer and clicked his way to the Stanley Cup playoffs. Dawn put her arm around him, and before he sank his face into her shoulder, he thought that this would be a story for his own kids, if he ever had any. How he turned on the TV and saw his mother, heard her voice for the first time, the top story on the evening news. A helpless witness to her suffering, like everyone else in the world.

❧❦

Toronto
25 June 1995

Dear Sally Groves,

I hope this letter will not come as an intrusion or cause you any hurt. My name is Gabe Winter and I am your son. I am writing to you because I was left your address by my late adoptive father, Lorne Winter. He asked me (in writing) to tell you he never stopped caring for you. He didn't leave a note saying why he took his life. I feel terrible that you had to go through so much on camera, in front of strangers. Including me.

Lorne and Ella never talked about the past. So I know zip about how I came to be, only that you and my dad were Americans. I realize you gave me up, and Lorne never told me he knew you. Still, he went and left your name and then I saw you on *Newsworld*, and now everybody on the planet knows you knew him, so I guess it's getting harder and harder to butt out and mind your own business.

I really don't know much about Lorne, and now that he's gone, I know less. A part of me went with him, the part that used to put two and two together.

I would like to meet you one day, but if the answer's no, I promise not to call or bother you. I would be happy just to write.

Thank you for giving me a good life.

With best wishes,
Gabe Winter

Salt Rain

One

Sally read Gabe's letter, then read it again, touching and smoothing the page as if it were a tired face. She slumped down on the raw wood steps, her head bowed, her body folded as if it were itself paper. He was her son, she had borne him, after all. She wondered at her knack for trouble, at the untidy matting of snags and pulls in the weathered cloth of her less than fifty years. She put Gabe's letter in her pocket and stared out into the trees towards the Sound. She wished he hadn't written her.

When she and Mike were children, their parents would take them walking there, down to the beach through the high grass. Later, Sister Frances would find the low point of the embankment, hitch up the skirts of her habit, take Sally's hand and walk along the rocky shore with her. *A good place for finding shells,* she'd say. *A little harsh, though. You feel marooned, shipwrecked.* Nine years old, still young enough to steal one of her father's handkerchiefs, tie it to a stick and plunge the makeshift flag into a pile of rocks. She took Fran down to the shore once to see this.

"I got washed up on the beach," she said.

Fran smiled. "Who'll rescue you?"

"No one," Sally answered. "No one knows I'm here." She showed off her pail and shovel, saying she'd eat well, she'd dig for clams when the tide was out.

"The water's salt," said Fran. "You can't drink that."

"I'll drink the rain," said Sally.

Remembering this, she got up and went for a walk. *Will you go to Mass with me tomorrow?* asked Fran, who'd called her this morning. She'd sounded tired, wanting no more than a shared observance of her brother's death. In the evening they'd have supper at Jake's, the two of them and Jake's parents. Sally had agreed to go with her. She'd tell Fran about Gabe's letter, how she felt like flotsam cast on the beach in a gale of remembering and sorrow. She cursed Lorne, that he had caused this to happen.

After a while she found her way through a field of wild grass where the pond had been, then down the embankment until she was stepping on stones, grey pebbles, wet and glittering like fish eyes. Above her the sky glared, wrinkled with clouds, hard and white as a clamshell. She glanced upward, wanted the sky to be hard, reproachful. She gave it a voice, Fran's. *Don't kid yourself. Tim's dead. You gave up his kid. Drop it.*

She remembered other words, real ones. *You're in trouble*, said Fran. *What else would you call it? You are very much your parents' child.* Sally felt in her pocket for the letter, felt instead Tim's death, saw the tide moving out, the past moving away from her. She crumpled the letter.

We suffer because we do not learn — Fran's words, bracing as salt air.

Sally stopped, picked up a shell, thin and sharp — a razor clam's — began to scribble in the moist tidal sand. ABC's, no words. When she was pregnant she couldn't speak at times, as if the child in her belly were swallowing her whole. In the hospital they'd show her objects and name them, the names of things slipping off like the labels of jars when you soak them underwater, a nurse, a patient woman, putting them back. *A comb, Sally. Food, water.*

Later, learning that this had happened, Fran insisted that Sally write down notes and family recollections. In Toronto Sally did as she was told, having no idea what else to do to redeem herself in the eyes of a woman who'd tried to be mother and aunt, who'd become a magnetic field drawing the shards of Sally's life into a pattern, a grip on sanity, the only one the young woman had. She felt desperate to win back Fran's affection, even if she never returned to the island. *Take some time to sort things out*, said Fran. She told Sally to work and ponder alone, to take her whole life, if she needed it. *The hardest thing is sometimes the best thing*, she added. *I'm sorry, dear, but I've had enough. I cannot be of help.*

Sally finished her studies, grew fond of her mother's country.

She felt close to Katherine, the mother she had lost as a child and met again inside herself in wandering and trouble. Forgiveness came as slow as weather, a light snow falling, small drifts that gathered in the hardness, forgiveness for terrible loss. Her mother had ended up far from Canada, adrift and frightened, her husband vanished. She was pregnant when the police found her upstate, on the highway, walking.

I cannot live through that again, Fran said to Sally.

Now she pulled the letter from her pocket, ripped it up, tossed the pieces into the outgoing tide. How grieved she felt, as if she were giving birth again. *You have to fight this*, she told herself. *You have to weed this out or it'll kill you.*

Kneeling in the sand, she scooped up water and drank it, drank more, thirsty from drinking it, salt on her lips, or tears, she wasn't sure. She and Mike had done this as kids, testing themselves against their parents' warnings. *You'll be sick, the water's a toilet, you could get polio, you don't know whose germs are here.* A victory, her face in the water, the salt of it a desert. She made herself drink. She was used to the bitter taste of it, she'd live.

🖋🖋

Fran stood in front of Holy Rosary Church, her hand gripping the stair rail like the talon of a giant bird, an eagle with a magnificent sweep of feathers. She was dressed in black, a silver cross on a chain around her neck, her white hair tousled in the breeze. There was something of Lorne in her appearance, her straight-backed conviction of rightness, her blue eyes intelligent and mischievous, benevolent and firm. Sally felt out of focus by comparison, tepid, insubstantial. She wondered if Fran had ever had lovers, women as strong as herself. The wind flapped at Fran's black skirt, at the fringe of her knitted shawl, a wind that had no strength compared to hers. Gone was the friend on a northern visit, raw with doubt and regret. This was an ageless teacher and guide, the Fran her mother had known.

"You look ill, dear," she said.

"Lorne's son wrote to me," Sally replied.

Fran looked bemused. "Whatever for, I wonder?"

"Lorne asked him to," said Sally.

"Poison. Throw that letter out," said Fran.

"I already did."

Fran took a deep breath. She seemed poised inside her own thoughts, like a swimmer on a diving board, about to leap. Then her thoughts shot forward into words, broke into Sally as if she were the water. "Gabe mustn't speak to you. I'll have a word with him."

Sally felt slapped. "He's not a child," she said.

"Even so. He never would have written. Lorne put him up to it."

"It's none of your business."

"More so than yours," Fran retorted. "I've known him all these years."

Sally hadn't thought of this — that Fran might have taken advantage of her loss, that she yearned to care for a child. She tried to look away, but Fran's eyes insisted on meeting hers.

"Gabe and I get on very well," Fran said. "Why, are you surprised?"

"It never crossed my mind."

"What, that I'd get to know him?"

"Once I was out of the way? No."

"Being an aunt isn't among my regrets," she said.

"You and Lorne. So damn sure of yourselves."

"Drop it, Sally."

She strode up the church stairs and Sally followed, wondering what had become of their northern conversation, of Fran's humility, her doubts. It must have been her mention of Gabe's letter that chilled the woman. Bowing her head, Sally tasted a familiar sorrow, the salt water that for all these years she'd been drinking, the residue of her own mistakes. Yet when she looked at Fran again, she saw that her face was streaked with bewilderment. A moment ago she'd been standing like a statue on a solid ledge of conviction. Now she looked dazed.

"Forgive me, dear," said Fran. "We mustn't hurt each other."

Sally turned her back to her, walked off.

Unsure where she was headed, she found herself down at the ferry dock, waiting for the crossing to Linden. She later disembarked and kept walking, not knowing the Linden docks at all well, wandering past the bars and rundown eateries. She was facing west, the sun dazzling her eyes, when she saw a dark-haired man by the side of the road with a bent nose and a small tattoo on his forearm. The years vanished; the man's look was familiar enough to fill her with a wild grief, an impossible longing.

Sally trailed him down to a shore road bar, Captain Kidd's, Rooms Upstairs. She didn't follow him in; kept walking, imagined herself going inside, meeting the stranger, who'd offer to buy her a drink. *I was in Vietnam*, he'd say. *You see the tattoo.* She'd touch it, then tell him how she had lost her man, how years later the ash of his death kept sifting down on her. Only she'd think of the son she'd given up, the hard slap of Fran's conviction, the bitter taste of the fire. *We're all vets*, the man would say. *I know how it is.* He'd buy her another drink, then take her upstairs to his room.

By the docks she stood weeping. Gabe's letter had brought Tim back into the world, had done her harm. Fran was right. Even so, she needed comfort. *The dust of the fire has settled into everything*, she thought as she dried her eyes. She walked back to the bar, went in.

Two

She returned to the island, much later in the day.

Exhausted, she'd drunk until her thoughts swerved and veered away from her, until she felt crushed into flyweight, into air. She'd found some company, couldn't remember who. At least she was over the shock, as if Tim and Gabe had never been.

There was Jake, Tim's friend. She was supposed to have dinner with him, with Fran.

I'll tell Fran she was right. Tell her I'm sorry.

When she drove up to Jake's house, she saw him in the doorway, his face strained with worry. "Fran's gone wild looking for you," he said.

"I gave her a hard time. My son wrote."

Jake looked stymied. "I didn't know you had a son."

Sally lowered her eyes. "Tim's." She told him what she could. "I wrote from Nam, I asked about you. No one said a thing."

"Lorne adopted him."

"Fuck."

"No, Jake," said Sally. "Lorne did a good thing."

Jake frowned. "You gonna write back, Sal?"

"No."

She watched his face, its furrows ploughed and seeded with trouble. He shook his head. "One tough grunt, you are."

I'm no good for Gabe, she thought.

Jake dropped the subject, told her he wanted to show her his obsession, the room where he housed her family's history, disks and documents, photocopies and *Banner* clippings, news-morgue photos and tape cassettes, wall maps, a land survey and a satellite photo of the Groves' property, a picture of her father's plane.

It felt like a forensics lab. She half expected scraps of metal, jars of formaldehyde, specimens of flesh and bone.

"Your legacy," he said.

"Does anyone care?" she asked. *Gabe does*, she thought. His letter shredded, his questions floating out to sea.

Jake's eyes were sad. "I care. You were my neighbours, Sal."

"Wild ones."

"Founders of the island. Think of Rome, Romulus and Remus. Nursed by wolves."

Sarge lifted his ears, came trotting over, rubbed his head on Jake's knees. While Jake went to let him outside, Sally looked at the maps, the photos, thinking again of her son. She picked up the phone, called Fran to apologize for running off.

"You've learned something," Fran replied. "Lorne was behind that letter of Gabe's."

"What's done is done," said Sally. "It's years ago."

"It never pays to cling to the past," said Fran.

Sally winced. "Neither does rudeness," she replied.

"You'll have to explain," said Fran.

Sally wondered at the woman's arrogance, admired it more than a little. Still on the phone, she picked up a photo of her mother and father, looked at it. *These are your grandparents, Gabe.* Wasn't this knowledge his by right?

"It's rude not to answer mail," she said to Fran.

"Rudeness," Fran answered, "is better than looking for trouble."

Sally hung up. A few minutes later Jake's phone rang. Fran was calling to tell him that she wasn't feeling well, that she wouldn't be coming for supper.

☙☜

8 July 1995

Dear Gabe,

Thank you for writing to me. It was a surprise, and also a shock; I have to say that. It must be a great sorrow to have lost Lorne, but

I hope your father's death won't make you think you missed out on a better deal. Life would not have been better if I had kept you, believe me. Lorne and Ella were my friends years ago and I was grateful to Ella that she would adopt you. I was very young, and her kindness gave me the chance to start over. I didn't keep in touch with your folks because I wanted them to raise you free and clear of me. They were generous to take you, Gabe. I still feel that.

So about Lorne and what was on his mind, I don't know. Lorne was the third or fourth photographer I flew in to the Conlin fire. It was no big deal, or so I thought. Now I wish I'd said no to him. On the other hand, if he was that unhappy, he would have found a way to take his life without any help from me.

As far as your roots go, maybe I can tell you a little about your American family. Groves Island, New York (where I grew up), was named for my great-great-grandfather, William Titus Groves, a trader and provisioner who gave a chunk of his land to the government as a hospital for the wounded during the Civil War. He became a wealthy man, and he bought property that stayed in the family a long time (this provided the income for our education when our parents were no longer with us). We had a beautiful forest, and the oldest home on the island (built in 1860). The land has just been sold to a family friend.

Your grandparents were a pair of loners. They loved their kids, but once we finished childhood, that was it. We were on our own. They vanished — my dad, Glen, in a plane, my mother, Katherine, on foot. She's dead and he's never been found. When we were children, they took us under their wings, nuzzled us close the way a wolf does with her cubs. They sheltered their young, but once we were bigger they couldn't abide us, in the real sense of that word. We made our own home, our own abode, as best we could.

My parents' restlessness is something I share, so I learned to love and forgive them. I gave you up because I had nothing to give you. So let's not meet. I don't mind questions, but what's done is done.

Sally Groves

❧❦

Toronto
15 July 1995

Dear Sally,

Thank you for answering my letter, and for being candid. I really appreciated getting so much information, and also that you're so truthful. It meant a lot to me. Lorne's death was a pisser, you'll excuse my language. He never talked a whole lot, never got close. Even so, it was like dynamite blowing a hole through the wall, and every time you turn around, you see that hole. I never thought of him as brick and mortar, if you know what I mean. He was more like a snapshot of a dad, not a real one. But he did bring me up, and I guess, as you say, it was a generous thing to do. And then I get to see him die on CNN, live. Go figure.

The damn fire's still burning, by the way. They're not even trying to fight it because, as you know, there's no one nearby to evacuate. A thousand hectares and counting, a fire burning for a month, this is a stinker of a fire season, trees popping like corks. They stopped reporting fires on TV, except they said there were maybe eight hundred new ones in June, lots still burning. And that's just Northern Ontario. All over Canada, the bush is more or less in flames right now. Sooner or later it'll rain.

I'll drop that because I know you're feeling just as bad as I am, if not worse. So maybe it will cheer you up if I tell you about myself, and let you see the good results of what you did. If you'd rather not read about me, you can recycle or reuse this paper and I won't feel bad. Just rip it off where I drew the line, right down there. Yeah, that's it. I'll sign off here.

Best wishes,
Gabe

So if you're reading on, I'm tall, with black hair and eyes, very sharp knees and elbows (as my girlfriend tells me) and what I would describe as a chipped clay pot of a face, not from fistfights or anything like that, but because I don't like clichés about bones sticking out. I wear glasses, because I spend too much time in front of my computer, which I really enjoy a lot. Also, I have a Baseball Cap Problem (Ella's term). I wear mine backwards and all the time, which is not exactly original, but Ella says it's incurable. It's in my gene-machine, she's sure of it. Sally, if there's anything else you want to know, just ask. I'm enclosing a photo. Lorne took this.

Best wishes,
Gabe

It was a cruel thing, this photo Lorne had taken of young Gabe, his dark-haired son. She closed her eyes, felt Tim beside her, all limbs, all sharp angles, his arm looped over her shoulder, his mouth sweet and aching on her breasts. She looked at the picture again and the memory faded like an echo. Gabe's body was his father's grave, the bones were Tim's. She wondered how it had felt for Lorne to look on Gabe's face, to see in his son a man he so distrusted.

She sat down and started a letter to Gabe. *I'm returning your picture. Please don't write to me again.* She left it and went walking on the sand, barefoot, the ache of pebbles and broken shells less painful than her humiliation. She should not have written to her son, no. Fran had told her before he was born, *a child can be redemption for a parent, but not always. Not for you.* She'd believed her. A few weeks back, she'd slept with Lorne. Dead now. Gabe hadn't saved him either. *You can't afford to be weak* — such grief and austerity in Fran's words, such harsh abstinence from life. It had done so little good, and yet Fran had survived. Sally went to see her, told her about the photo, waited for the woman to upbraid her. What happened was far worse than this. Fran said nothing. Then at last she spoke.

"Lorne wanted that child so much," she said.

"He got what was left of Tim."

Fran's eyes were downcast. "He wanted a part of you. I'm sure of it."

"I should never have answered that letter," Sally admitted.

"Sally," said Fran, "we suffer in this life by our own hands. You're a grown woman. I cannot tell you what to do."

Only it was Fran who wept.

❧❦

Groves Island
21 July 1995

Dear Gabe,

Thank you for your letter and your photo. You look a lot like your father, at least from the picture you sent. You have his tall build, even his slouch. Your sense of humour is all yours; you didn't get it from either of us. I knew your dad when kids our age were scared about the war, when none of us laughed enough.

Your eyes are like your grandfather Glen's. His look was so intelligent, so curious and alert to everything. He was a first-rate builder and a wartime pilot, what they used to call a man's man. You would have liked him.

You said you enjoyed computers. I'm writing to you on my brother's, which is a squat little house of a thing, but home is where you find it, I guess. So maybe while you're feeling rough, you can find some comfort there, make yourself a small home in the world.

Enjoy whatever home you find....

Sally didn't finish the letter, not just then. She gazed at the limpid blue of the screen, thought of it as an ultrasound. She felt pregnant with herself. What she carried would flutter before her into the light.

❧❦

Sally's dream: 21 July 1995

Young Gabe is sitting before a computer, keying in stories as I tell them. *They're all the same, every one of them*, he says. *They hang in the air like frost on your breath. Bits about Granddad, some good American stuff about the Second World War. Only, Jesus Christ, they don't go anywhere.* Where should they go, I ask him, as if stories were back roads, bridges to an island. *Honey, these are anecdotes, little sketches, one-liners. Things to know about your family, that's all.* Gabe looks troubled. *I need to know more*, he whispers half to himself, eyes lowered, fists clenched. *What do you need to know*, I ask him, but he doesn't answer. I put my hands on his shoulders until he relaxes, opens his hands and lets them rest on the keyboard.

Tell me about the fire, Gabe says. *Let me write everything that happened.*

He looks cold, in need of a jacket and scarf and gloves, as if he were afraid that my stories would freeze at the tips of his fingers, die like a cloud of humid breath, vanish into Canada, into the cold air he breathes.

❧ Glass ❧

One

1953

Gabe, you should know what happened then.

A flowering in the trees (as Sally Groves would tell her son), her father's most lavish indulgence, his only one, a home close to the sky. Glen Groves built it in the largest oak on his property, hammering and sawing away, facing the wooden stares of the neighbours as if they were rough boards he could plane down to a gentle, good-humoured chiding. His daughter was seven years old when he completed his project, and by then Sally knew what an oak tree was, knew because her mother, Katherine, had taken her hand and walked her down the path towards the clearing where her father worked his off-hours high up on a scaffold. There she'd told Sally the name of this tree, pointed it out, among others.

Katherine was learning tree names with her daughter, tulip and beech, sycamore and dogwood, which ones had serrated leaves, which leaves had edges that were smooth, which had a scent when you crushed them with your fingers. She carried with her *A Guide to the Trees of Southern New York State*, along with Sally's picture book, *Let's Walk in the Woods*. In her part of Canada, she explained, only *les pins*, the pines, grew as tall as these.

Sally remembered how her mother had looked on these walks, her black hair a criss-cross of plaits, her water-lily skin, a queen's touch of gold in her ears; a woman who even on walks wore white silk blouses, tailored blazers and slacks pressed to a knife-edge sharpness. Her mother, who could turn her gaze inward to a stillness quite beyond her daughter's understanding, would reach out to Sally with hands as soft as butterflies, as quick to move away. Dressed in her play clothes, a flannel shirt, a cotton blouse, dungarees, Sally would feel with wordless conviction that her own presence was a blighted thing.

Sally's dad was a carpenter, and his treehome was a single-storey cottage with hardwood floors and windows made of glass. She never asked him why he'd built it, and she felt no need to ask. He'd made their real Victorian home into a cheerful place, gabled and shuttered and screen-porched; he coaxed life out of wood. Her girlfriends joked about Jack and the Beanstalk, and she began to imagine that her dad had tucked a bean in the ground, that the stalk had grown, that a mystery was swaddled in its topmost leaves. High up with the birds, carried by wind, her dad had been a flier in World War II; he wanted a home in the trees.

Glen Groves had come back from the Pacific the year before she was born. Her brother, Mike, was five years old, and he had hoped his dad would bring him a souvenir, some child's idea of booty, a Japanese coin or medal, a small flag with a rising sun. *I didn't bring anything back*, his dad told him. Although he'd been a child, Mike remembered the look on his dad's face. Like opening a closet door, he told his sister, and seeing that all the clothes were gone.

Glen was a quiet, grey-eyed man, his glances quick and intelligent, as if he were a driver who had to be intent upon the farthest light, the closest vehicle, the safest way to get where he was going. His hair was light, as tawny as autumn grass. He'd grown thin in the war, her mother said, never gaining back the good, sturdy weight of his youth. Behind his ear was a pencil and in his breast pocket he kept a small pad, as if he was afraid of being seized by a thought he couldn't shape with hammer and saw, one he might have to sketch, to write.

It was after Sally's birth that Glen began to sketch the shape of a house in the branches, a human nest, drawing as if his arm were a branch and the drawings were pushing out of his fingers like leaves from twigs. He did this many times. Just as often, Katherine stood by the kitchen table watching him, and when he looked up and saw her there he stopped, put his arm around her waist and then around Mike's, and sat holding the two of them close. It always felt the same, said Mike; always as if he were just coming home from the war.

Evenings and weekends he spent hammering and sawing, setting a scaffold thirty feet up the twin trunks of the huge oak, so that the little house would be wedged at the widest point of the trunks, at the top of the V they made. V *for victory*, Mike said once, pointing at the sky with his fingers raised. He wanted to put an American flag up there when the house was built, but his dad said no. It was a home he was building, not a fort; a human nest with barnboard walls, glass windows on every side, wide on top and tapered at the bottom, like an air traffic controller's booth. Sally thought that perhaps her dad had meant to sit up there watching over the migratory paths of swallows and thrushes, guiding those small creatures home to safety, telling them when and where they could take off and land.

Glen added window boxes, planting them thick with impatiens and begonias, then secured his haven with a childproof fence. He fashioned a beautiful wheel of a staircase, a wild spiral up through the branches. In leaping up the stairs, Sally rustled leaves, pretending they were feathers, imagining herself as an eagle chasing the sky. Years later, the staircase made her think of a ziggurat, a spiral temple, a holy place where the ancients talked to God. It was then that she began to wonder if this was why her father had built a retreat, as a place for inner speaking, for naming things he had to settle with himself before he could live in the world again. A lot of men were like that after the war, she knew this.

Her father used the treehome for his own pursuits, for studying geology, rocks and minerals, aviation science. Here he collected maps that he read alone, and when he was done he locked the door, as he did when he left the family house. Sally and Mike were allowed to play there with his permission. At other times he took them up to the tiny porch, told them to look through the green fanning-out of treetops, down the hill to the beach and the water of Long Island Sound, its inner harbour a calm unblinking eye. *Pretend you're that eye*, he'd say to them. *Pretend you're water*, *look up, see how big the sky is.* And then he would quote the Bible, *No eye has seen and no ear has heard, nor has it entered into the heart of man...*he never finished the quote, letting the words dissolve into air.

༄༅

Gabe, I've written notes for you about these things, recorded the rest for a family friend. In a dream, you asked me to do this.

As I write, I'm wondering what this story means, why we have to capture and hold it on tape when its beauty is its evanescence, like a season's, like the world's. And does it matter what I forget, what's lost? Think about ancient ruins, think of how we've conjured up lost worlds on the scant evidence of buried potsherds and scrapings on stone. Out of a seed a tree is born, every cell in your body carries a program for the whole of you, the world is contained in every part of itself. It must be some law, I think, the conservation of matter: stories echoing stories we will never hear, calling out to our lost and missing loved ones, reaching for their outstretched hands as if they were alive.

What hope we put in stories, what mindless, loving hope.

Listen and I will tell you.

Two

1950

Around the time that Glen was sketching his treehome, Katherine, an artist before her marriage, picked up her brushes and began to paint again. Not on paper or canvas this time, but on clear glass cups and saucers. These she adorned with white trilliums and lavender thistles, soft enough that you could almost smell the scent, as if the flowers were tea in the cup. Katherine painted lakes and boreal forest, the Gatineau hills and Rideau Canal of her childhood, holding Canada like water in a glass, hinting at trees and shrubs that were not in Sally's forest: the northern spruce and maple and lodgepole pine, lowbush berries and mayapples and saskatoons. The gentle suggestions of wildlife, these she painted too: wolves and beavers, snowy owls and geese, and the human forms of tiny skaters, hunters, farmers, evoking them with little more than a quick line here and there, a drift of colour.

It would have been no more than a hobby, nothing exceptional, except that this was expressive, unusual work, and even as a child Sally knew this. Even more intriguing were the objects her mother chose to paint. One by one she removed all the white porcelain doorknobs in the house, returning each to its door with a shimmering lake, a miniature forest, a trail on the edge of a meadow. Next came stray objects she found around the house: stoppered perfume bottles, a brandy snifter, an old glass dinner bell, a cup or saucer or wineglass that didn't belong to a set. At Christmas there were clear glass balls frosted with northern pines and at Easter blown eggshells covered with violets and forsythia.

It felt like a kind of magic to Sally, that trees and flowers could take form like this, that lakes could be made to float on the handles of doors, that budding vines and tendrils would suddenly appear on the rims of glasses, almost a taste to the lips.

Her mother worked in a glassed-in porch at the side of the house that caught the morning light, her sleeves rolled up with care, her small gold earrings gleaming like coins. She wore a look of grave composure, an attentiveness to a cup or a plate that Sally envied. Sally thought of the glass as newborn children, frail in her mother's hands, in need of her.

If she came home from school when her mother was busy, Sally went into her parents' room and stared at her mother's photographs. On the wall were shots of her mother and father, their courtship framed in the noiseless white of an Ottawa winter. Katie and Glen skating on the Rideau Canal, wrapped in toques and mufflers and woollens, arms outstretched, gliding transfixed into silence. Another more sombre photo showed her parents standing by the wing of a small plane, its propeller visible on the left. *We were about to take a trip*, her mother told Sally, before she was old enough to read the photographer's note, the date.

In the picture, her parents had doffed their goggles and Glen had his arm around Katherine, squinting as if into the sun. Katherine was wearing an orchid corsage on her jacket. Their smiles were the kind of good-natured grins forced out by the photographer's voice saying *cheese*, as if the friend who took these pictures was afraid they wouldn't smile without a prompt. There was fear in Katie's eyes, a troubled look of surprise and foreboding in Glen's. *Our Wedding Day*, the caption read. *Buffalo, New York, 10 September 1939.*

She must have imagined that her mother, so calm, so poised, was nervous on the happiest of days. *We were in a hurry*, Katherine answered when Sally asked her why she had no wedding gown, no veil. *We were worried about war breaking out.* It never occurred to Sally to doubt her mother's words. At the age of nine she was beginning to think about weddings, as she watched her mother seated at her vanity brushing her hair. On the mirrored tray in front of her were abalone barrettes and tortoiseshell combs, glass and crystal bottles.

"Mom, may I brush your hair?"

Her mother smiled, handed Sally the oval brush, its silver back engraved with the letter D from her maiden name, *Duval*. With each stroke Sally smoothed her mother's hair with her hand, felt its silk grow pliant and alive. She draped the tresses over the palm of her hand like cloth. She rested her cheek against it.

"It's so *pretty*."

She wanted to wear her mother like a coat, to sleep in her arms. Afterwards Katherine thanked her, patted her cheek.

"*Tu as très bien fait*, you've done a good job. Now go." Sally felt a pang of sadness.

"Can't I watch you pin up your hair?"

"If you like."

On her mother's vanity were painted glass containers, brittle, almost papery, like ancient moths. Katherine picked up a crystal-stoppered bottle more solid than the others. It seemed to weigh on her hands as she held it, as she cupped it with reverence like a jewel. She pulled out the stopper, dabbed on some perfume. Sally sniffed it.

"That smells like *grand-mère*'s," she said.

Her mother looked surprised. "What makes you say that?"

"From Ottawa. I remember it."

It was lilac, a scent from a place she'd been when she was too young to recall much. She had saved pictures of her mother's hometown from *The National Geographic*, used them for a project at school: the steepled buildings, a tall clock tower, the Château Laurier near the Ottawa River and, on the opposite bank, the sugar-white hills of Quebec in early spring, none of which she remembered seeing. Yet she recalled the flower of this woman's scent.

"You've never been to Ottawa," her mother said.

"Mom, I *remember*."

"You remember me wearing it." She put the stopper back in

the jar, then turned towards Sally with a movement as graceful as a bird's, a sweep of silk and lace the way a wing unfolds before it flies. She put her hands on Sally's shoulders.

"Maybe you dreamt your grandmother then. *Oui?*"

"*Oui, maman.*" Katherine pulled the stopper out of the perfume jar, dabbed some behind Sally's ears.

As she left the room, Sally saw her mother sitting on the bed, bent and limp as a dead flower, head bowed, face in her hands. Later she wondered if she had imagined everything, even this.

***

1957

"Mom got knocked up," Mike said." I was there on her wedding day."

Booted, ducktailed, seventeen and buckled up with maleness, Mike was trying to help her clean out the basement. He stared at a copy of their parents' photo taken in front of the airplane. "Married the day the war began," he told his sister. "For Canada, at any rate." He dug into a box, pulling out his mother's skates, the laces tied to his dad's. "The junk in this place," he said. "Jesus."

"Are you mad at Mom?" she asked him.

"Nah. What difference? Got married, didn't she?"

"You think they loved each other?"

Mike shrugged. "Mom broke an engagement, sis. Some rich guy."

Sally picked up one of the skates, imagined herself whizzing along the Rideau Canal.

"I remember going to Ottawa," she said.

"You and Mom went."

"Not you?"

Mike shook his head, lit a cigarette. "Mom took a walk," he whispered, his eyes sad.

Three

1954

Katherine's glass was well-known on the island. Neighbours noticed it, and church parishioners also, remarking on the ethereal painting, how the objects that she adorned seemed to lose their ordinary shapes, to float in the hand, to give solace. Her bowls and vases sat in living rooms all over the island, including the home of the mayor's wife, and of her friend whose husband owned Shore Road Gifts and bought some on consignment; in Marjorie Nolan's sun-porch windows, squeezed between scented geraniums and African violets; in Van der Meyers' China, where visitors from Manhattan came to shop on weekends. Even in church, the vigil candles glowed in the soft rose shadows of Katherine's glass, so that, wherever she went on the island, Sally felt the air alive with the quiet hand of her mother.

One day Katherine gave Sally a gift, a small glass bowl in the shape of a flower, amber, gold and green. It glowed with light, as if it held a candle. Sally was afraid to touch it.

"This is for you. *Je l'ai fait pour toi*." Her mother stooped down beside her, stroked her hair and kissed her on the head.

"You made this for me?"

"Yes."

"How come?"

Her mother laughed. "Because it's spring." She handed Sally the bowl. Light seemed to spill out of it and dance around the room. Sally thought of the giddy joy of fireflies in darkness. Yet nothing could describe this gift, no words contain its life. In it was sunlight, a match lit to tinder, the making of some nameless, holy thing. She kissed her mother and thanked her. She wanted to make some wonderful gesture, to raise the bowl to her lips and drink the light. Her *thank you* felt too shrivelled up, too foolish. *I love you*, she said, but even love couldn't embrace the mysterious light of this gift.

Katherine's arms drew her close and Sally breathed in her lilac perfume. She could feel the round warmth of her stomach, her breasts like suns.

✺✺

A few weeks later, Katherine went to an antique shop and bought a plain set of glassware: six of everything, wine cups, water goblets, tiny cordial glasses, soup bowls and dinner plates for every course. On them she began to paint her life. She worked from photographs and memory, did strange, elusive renderings of familiar things, of her childhood home on the Ottawa River, her cat, Minou, crouching on the roof, her own mother, Marie-Claire, writing in her study, her father, Henri, a professor at a lectern, his hand gesturing to hills and trees. Glen in his two-seater aircraft, their wedding day. More than this, she painted the shifting haze of memory, the texture of leaves dissolving into faces, the touch of a hand moving through trees, her soul afloat in glass.

Bertram's Fine China, in Linden, asked to put the set on display. After this, there were calls about the offbeat work from galleries in Greenwich Village, and then an offer from a Manhattan art collector to buy the set for a thousand dollars.

"I wouldn't sell it, no," said Katherine.

"For one grand?" said Mike. "Mom, holy Jesus."

"Don't swear, Mike."

Glen smiled at his wife, a thousand-watt grin. "Katie, you'll be *famous*. Hey, gal." Still she wouldn't sell it, *jamais*, never, not for the crown jewels, not for a dozen Fabergé eggs, a Renoir in the treehome. *Two* Renoirs. *Non. C'est impossible.*

"You can make another one like it," said Sally.

Mike grabbed her hand, raised her arm in the air. "Sally's got *brains*," he said.

"No."

Katherine packed the glassware for mailing, wrapped each item in tissue paper, encircled each glass with a cardboard sleeve. Her dishes, she explained, were a gift to her parents in Ottawa. No, there was no reason, no birthday. Did there have to be a reason? she asked Sally, who remembered her mother's gift to her and said nothing.

"Will they even eat off it?" asked Mike, but Katherine smiled and said, "Kids, it's a gift. Once you give it, it's out of your hands."

Sally's grandmother wrote a note of thanks. "No more than that," Katherine said to her husband. "But thanks from her is more than enough." The note was written on onionskin, embossed with a pale pink rose. To Sally the envelope paper felt warm, alive. She wondered if words written on it would read like poetry, and then she imagined a drawing room in a foreign place, a gold-tipped fountain pen, letters swirling in a gracious hand from a writing-desk with pigeonholes and slender legs. She tried to picture her grandmother's skin, a soft rose blush to it, as beautiful as her penmanship, a touch that her cheeks remembered.

Her mother took the note to her workroom, read it in the sunny window until her hands fluttered, the letter falling out of them like a leaf escaping the wind. With time, paints and brushes began to tremble in her fingers, then fall, as if a storm were shaking a tree bare of its leaves.

One day a piece of glass fell and broke. Sally heard it and came running. A glass serving bowl lay in shards on the floor. Katherine got down on her knees and swept it up with a bright, fevered grimace of self-denial, a look that made Sally fearful, as if her mother were one of the shards, a broken thing.

Without knowing why, she felt the loss of something irretrievable. In her room, she went to the shelf where she kept her amber bowl. She reached out to touch it, but pulled her hand away.

❧❧

After that, her mother stopped painting. *Battle fatigue honey*, Sally heard her father say. *Just like a vet*. He put his arm around his wife, held her trembling hands. Katherine was remote, stiff as a mannequin, as if she no longer fit into the kindly bending and curving of his arms. Sally wondered if the shaking had caused her parents' love to crack and fissure like the glass, if it explained her father's sleeping in the guest room. Katherine told Glen she didn't need to see a doctor. "If it's meant to pass, it will," she said. On sunny afternoons she'd sit on the porch of the treehome, staring into the distance. "You can be too proud," she said once, when Sally asked if she missed her painting. "Maybe God is trying to tell me something."

Sally was young enough to wonder if her mother was a saint, a seer of visions, a woman trying to humble herself to prepare for the painting of a beatific Face. It began to feel as if Katherine wanted this.

❦❦

That May, the treehome made the cover of *House and Garden*. Sally's dad carried pots of mums and impatiens up the high stairs, sitting them on the platform-porch inside the fence. This stop was new on the Island Homes Spring Tour. They had visitors, Garden Club ladies in pastel suits, veil-hatted, eyelet-gloved, floating down the paths like dogwood petals.

All day long they sifted through the forest, the Garden Club ladies. Sally's mother set out damask and china on the picnic table, pouring tea from her grandmother's silver service, her nails manicured and polished in a shade called Oh-So-Pink, the first time Sally had seen them painted. Her hands were shaking as she poured, as she lifted cups and saucers that chattered like teeth in bitter cold. It was the photo on the magazine cover that made her mother nervous. Mom didn't like publicity, Mike told her.

Sally's mother dressed her in a starched white pinafore printed with roses, an outfit set off by a pink hair ribbon, white socks and patent-leather shoes. Old enough now, she was allowed to offer the ladies a small dish of petits fours. She was careful, polite, afraid of everyone — afraid with her mother's fear, the hot, sweet taste of it pouring into her as if she were one of the teacups, one whose life would always teeter on the edge of breaking.

🦜🦜

When the open house was over, Sally went up to the treehome porch to read. Quiet as the air itself, she sat and watched and listened.

Sister Frances had come to visit her mother. It was her striding up the path that made Sally close her book and squat by a crack in the floorboards. Sister's brusque school-corridor step and the edgy rattle and clatter of her beads were out of place here, her serge habit a flash of black and white in the green.

Her mother's friend. Younger than Katherine by some years, she taught Sally and Mike, talked their mother into volunteer work at the school library. "These pious books are an embarrassment, I apologize," she said to Katherine. "Here's what I read off duty," and she pulled a novel out of her habit pocket. On its cover was a man, his worldly gaze fixed on a beautiful woman. "Relax, Graham Greene's a Catholic," Sister said to Katherine's astonished look. Later her mother shared the novels of Mauriac, along with translations of La Fontaine's fables, the ones she read in French to Sally. *Le Corbeau et Le Renard*, the Crow and the Fox.

They hadn't met today to read.

Sally watched as her mother pulled out her grandmother's note, read it out loud. '*Whatever Glen's behaviour, you cannot come home and live with us. You must consider your family.*' Her shaking hand bunched the letter up, stuffed it in a pocket.

"She's right, of course," said Sister Frances. "Is it so bad, what Glen told you?"

Katherine spoke, her voice almost too soft for Sally to hear. What she heard, she didn't understand.

"We haven't had a marriage. Not in years."

"So he stayed in touch with a woman," Sister said.

Her mother's voice dropped again. "He did more," she replied.

"Sally needs a dad. Mike too," said Sister Fran.

"Sally stayed with my mother once." Sally listened.

"Yes, but you were exhausted then."

She lied. It weighed more than Sally did, the bone-breaking rock of her thought. It was more crushing than whatever troubled her parents. She watched Sister Frances as she squeezed her mother's hands like an iron pressing wrinkled cloth, its warm pressure hard on trouble, imperfection. Maybe Sister's hands could smooth away untruth, relieve the trembling in her mother's body. Yet no one could remove a lie and, worse, what Sally had heard here. Not even God could do that. Sally was alone with knowing more than she wanted to know, with wishing she hadn't stopped to listen. Below her she heard Sister Frances, more words she didn't understand.

"Have you forgiven Glen?"

"I'm not that brave," her mother answered.

"You'll have to be."

Sally watched her mother's hands shake like leaves in a hurricane, wind ripping the leaves from their branches. She could feel how her mother envied those leaves, their spiral down, their fall.

Wayfarers I

One

1950

Sally, four years old, stood at the kitchen table, staring up at her dad. It was June and there was a newspaper spread open on the printed oilcloth. The pattern on the cloth repeated over and over, teapot, creamer, sugar bowl, an unrelieved stuck-in-a-groove design, like the sound of a needle caught in a scratch of a record. The newspaper covered the oilcloth, as if it wanted to be one too, wanted to cover a table with soldiers and airplanes, huge black headlines, words.

Her father ripped the front page out of the paper, crumpled it into a ball, sat with his elbows on the table, fists clenched, white knuckles pressed into his forehead. Her mother put her hands on his shoulders. "Glen," she said, "don't let every little thing remind you."

"Korea is not a 'little thing,'" he answered. Her mother shrugged, then walked away, making a clatter of dishes in the sink. When her dad sat up straight and lowered his arms, Sally could see on his forehead the red print where he had pressed his knuckles, his fists.

❦❧

1953

At Holy Rosary School's weekly assembly most of the older kids told war stories, while Sally, too young and shy to stand before an audience, sat and listened. Some of the boys had fathers who, like hers, had been in the Pacific, who'd fought in the Marshall Islands or the Philippines. One or two girls spoke because their dads had medals from the landing at Normandy, and there was one lucky kid named Tom whose dad had been a Marine at Iwo Jima. Not that he'd raised the flag or anything, but he'd landed on the island with the guys who did, and they were buddies. He'd bummed an Old Gold cigarette from one of them, said Tom.

In Mike's class there was James, a brainy creep whose father hadn't fought at all, but he bragged anyway because his folks hailed from Oak Ridge, Tennessee, where *his* dad had helped build the atom bomb. Mike called him Mushroom-Head, told his little sister to ignore these kids, most of them were just a bunch of show-offs. "It's their dads who were heroes," he said to Sally. "Not them."

"You could talk about Dad," she answered.

"It feels so phony," Mike said.

☙❧

"Dad was a pilot in the Air Force," said her mother. "He has no stories."

"How come?" Sally asked.

"He was too high up to see much."

That spring, while her father was finishing the treehome, her mother stitched up café curtains for the windows. "For privacy," she told Glen.

He smiled. "Katie, hon," he said, "an acre on the high point of an island and no neighbours, who'd spy on us?" His body was as hard as a metal trap, and he shook as he laughed, as if laughing would spring an invisible lock and free him. Still chortling, he picked up the panel of a curtain and said, "They're not exactly bulletproof," and then his laughter shattered, as if the sky were breaking glass. Her mother's eyes were glittering with pain. This is a *home*, they said. Her dad kept laughing, his grey eyes full of tears.

☙❧

He'd served his country in the war, *before you were born, honey*, words he spoke as if nothing of consequence had happened before Sally had come into the world, nothing, in any case, that would interest her. Except for his going to the Coral Sea — she'd heard that beautiful name from him, imagining rock-pink islands and the fronds of palm trees waving like hands in the breeze. Guadalcanal he mentioned too, although it wasn't clear to her that he had been there, only what he thought of it. His tongue couldn't get rid of the word fast enough, *jungle*. To her child's mind, that was the home of elephants and tigers, two of every kind, like in the pictures in her book at school, *Noah's Ark*, with its forty days of rain on a terrible world. As a small child she had thought that the war, with its moist, rotting jungles, had something to do with Noah, with the punishment of rain.

In that dreadful war her father went wandering still. Sally knew it in the light-quick movements of his eyes. She saw how empty his hands were, his arms that reached out to embrace the air, as if he were the parent of a murdered child.

Glen Groves worked his hands as hard as he could. He prospered as a cabinetmaker after the war, remodelling all the kitchens on Groves Island and half the snazzy shore homes on the points of Beaches, Linden and Meredith, ripping out ceiling-high glass-paned cupboards and kitchen washtubs, replacing them with enamelled cabinets, Formica countertops, stainless-steel appliances flush with the walls. Everything *modern*, he said, his lips polishing the word to a high shine. *Stainless, spotless, scientifically proven safe, no one could set the torch to them, never again in the life of the world*, Sally felt these thoughts in the relentless gleam and lustre of his work.

At night, when she should have been asleep, she heard her parents talking in bed, her mother saying, *So it was good then, what you had*, and he answered, *Katie, there was a war, I love you still*, and her mother said, *But it wasn't the thought of me that kept you going*, and he answered, *I came back to you. Forgive me.*

He slept, but sometimes woke up shouting in his dreams. Sally heard him say he was tumbling from the cockpit, down through the jagged glass, the hole in the sky, words she couldn't understand, words that were tossed, clanking into her body like coins in a beggar's cup, incoherent words. *Oh God, where's the bottom of this? Let something stop me, trees and branches. Let me throw out my arms, let the glass snag me, like a hook in the mouth of a fish —* words she didn't hear, but felt.

She knew she was not to ask about the war. So she asked.

"What was it like in the Coral Sea?"

Her dad was busy remodelling their kitchen, installing a cabinet housing the sink. He said nothing for a minute, then smiled. "Warm," he replied.

"No, Dad, what did you *do* there?"

"We sent the Japs home."

"With your plane?"

"Uh-huh." He was hammering nails into the wood.

"Did you get shot?"

He put the hammer down, his face as grey as road salt. "Sally, hon," he said. "All these questions."

"Did you?"

He took a deep breath. "Not in the Coral Sea, no." He went back to his hammering.

"In Okinawa?" She took her time saying the unfamiliar word.

Glen stopped. "Where did you hear that, Sally?"

"In my sleep," she whispered.

Glen, who was kneeling on the floor, put down his tools and boosted himself up into a squat. He reached out, pulled his daughter into his arms and held her.

"You had a bad dream," he said. "But it's true."

"Where is Okinawa?"

"Near Japan."

When she looked at him, she saw his face pitted with desolation.

"Will you show it to me on the map?" she asked.

❧❧

Glen did his family's kitchen and put in a dishwasher, the first one on the island. For the first few evenings, after her mother loaded it and turned it on, he would bend down, kneel on one knee, hand pressed against the locked metal door, a hopeful look on his face as he listened to the swish and rumble, the tireless ritual of making clean. Then the cycle would move from wash to rinse, from a vigorous chugging to a waterfall. He would get up then, reassured.

Crouch and listen, what men did, just as she had *duck and cover*, air-raid drill at school. It was something she'd seen her father do often: stooping, hand on the hood of the car, listening to the engine; crouched before the furnace, the new one, after they took out the coal bin and put in oil; *She's kicking in*, he'd say. It was how she'd think of him, on one knee, hand on a locked door, any door, listening through the twisted metal wreckage, cries for help she couldn't hear.

❧❧

"It was the worst battle in the Pacific," said Mike. "We lost twelve thousand men in Okinawa."

"Dad came home," said Sally.

"Dad had it rough."

Their father had been wounded, shot down. It wasn't his fault, yet it felt shameful to Sally, just as if it were. It puzzled her that she felt this.

❧❧

"The law allows a single-family dwelling on this land, only one," said Glen. "Katie, I wasn't thinking."

She giggled. "Down the road they have a birdhouse. A doghouse also. No one's arrested them."

Glen looked at his half-finished work, despondent, "This is a *home*," he said. Katherine's laughter fizzed out into stillness, fear.

He called in the building inspector, Eddie Nolan. During the war they had called him Ready Eddie, dependable, quick and alert, a stocky, red-haired engine of a man who talked with a cigarette dangling from his lips, his words chugging out between the puffs.

"You want a *permit* for this, Glen?" he asked.

"Need," Glen said.

"You're not pulling my leg or nuthin'."

"It's a *house*," said Glen.

Eddie folded his arms across his chest, then smiled a slow grin, the cigarette holding still. "Don't need no permit."

Glen frowned. "Law says you gotta have one, you know that."

"Law says you should ask before you build," said Eddie. "Only City Hall don't care about no treehouse." He started to laugh, his baton of a cigarette beating time. Then he stopped, seeing in Glen's face whatever had frightened Katie, whatever had turned Sally's eyes into radar screens, tracking, picking up signals. Eddie put a hand on Glen's arm, lowered his voice when he spoke.

"Whaddya need this for, pal?"

"Huh?"

"Piece of paper don't change nuthin'."

Glen looked dismayed. "I'm breaking the law."

Eddie snorted. "You're watching too much *Dragnet*."

Sally's father gripped the man's arm hard. Eddie's cigarette fell out of his mouth. He bent over, picked it up. "Jesus, Glen. You'll live, relax."

"It's because I wanna live up there," said Glen.

"You tell Katie yet?"

Glen smiled a little. "Told no one."

Eddie pulled out his clipboard, filled out a predated form and gave it to Glen to sign. Then he put an arm around his buddy's shoulder, walked him out of earshot, talked to him. *Peace and quiet, way to get up in the sky again, that's what you want, huh?* The words drifted away from his lips.

After that Eddie dropped by more often, asked Glen how he was, scared up a game of poker with some friends, took him out for a beer. Now and again he'd go out in the woods and stare at the treehome with wary eyes, his arms folded across his chest, his cigarette unlit.

This is my father's story, said Jake. *The best and bravest story of the war.* Straight as a flagpole he stood at assembly, nine years old, his eyes as brown as good soil, his look grave. Ed Nolan had been a gunner on a fighter-plane, shot down, Jake told the school, in the last major battle of the Pacific war. Wounded though he was, his dad had saved the pilot, pulled him out of the wreckage. The rest of the crew had been killed. For his bravery, he had received a Purple Heart and the nickname Ready Eddie.

More important was the fact that his dad wouldn't allow him to bring in the medal, or to mention the names of his war buddies, living or dead. His dad respected the privacy of others, didn't like showing off. *Lots of men did the same, more*, he told his son.

Jake held up a photo of Eddie getting the medal pinned on him. He noticed Sally Groves and Mike, their lowered eyes.

☙❦

Notes written by Sally Groves in recollection of her father, Glen, in 1971

My father began his treehome at Eastertime, on a pleasant weekend in 1952. A perfectionist, he took that summer and the following spring to complete the finishing work. When he felt it was presentable, Mom made a picnic for thirty guests. Dad called the man at the *Island Banner*, who came and took pictures. The clipping is in my scrapbook — *Former Airman Takes To The Trees*, the outside of the treehome covered with weathered barnboard, four-sided, curtained glass windows on every side. Quaint and charming, yet wide on top and tapered at the bottom, a rustic fantasy entwined with branches and leaves.

In this newspaper photo, we are up in the treehome, smiling, Mom and Dad and Mike and I. Caught and held there forever, smiles pressed into our faces like the ancient marks of leaves etched in rock, a fossil record, life on earth before the meteor hit. A foreshadowing, trouble to come, devastation. On a late July Sunday in 1953, we couldn't see it coming.

Shortly after the photo was taken, I was standing next to Dad on the fenced-in platform of the treehome. He was holding my hand, and Mom was there too, arranging a pot of geraniums on a small table with a punch bowl and pretzels and potato chips. I could see straight down through the spaces between the leaves, thirty feet down. How lovely it was, like green crochet, light sifting to the ground through the airy leafwork, a dusting of light on what Mike called the serious food. *Hey come and get it*, he called up to us.

Cold roast beef; he was thirteen now, old enough to carve it, and I was getting hungry for potato salad, devilled eggs and buttered poppyseed rolls. We were ready to come down and dig in when a car pulled up, more guests, Dad's friend Eddie and his family, the genial commotion of hugs and backslaps, a huddling of men, a murmuring that drifted into silence.

Then a whoop of laughter, Eddie looking straight up at the three of us, yelling up at my dad, *Glen, GLEN!*, waving a newspaper and saying, *You hear the damn thing's over?* My dad knew what armistice meant, knew about Korea, even if I didn't, and he swooped me up and said, *How about that, Sally*, lifting me high above his head because there was no gravity left in the world, no weight of sorrow and remembrance. I stretched out my arms, feeling relief in my father's strong hands, letting him spin me dizzy into green sky and blue earth until I went flying straight through his eyes, into the coastal grey of another sea, into the rain of Noah, which would fall until the death of the world — rain that, even so, had brought forth green leaves, sunlight, a safe place hidden in the trees.

Two

1953

Sally decided to become a pilot because her father had lifted her up to the sky.

She imagined herself an eagle leaping from the top of the tree-home, the magnificent fan of her wings soaring over Long Island Sound as she made a steep bank, swooping down with a leafy crash into the quiet of her woods, by the edge of her pond. She saw herself float up to the treehome, where her parents would be waiting, then down again to her brother, who'd throw some briquettes on the barbecue — *Real cool, sis,* he'd say with a whistle, and hand her a bottle of root beer frothing like the crest of a wave, and her friends and neighbours would laugh and cheer. Her mother and dad and Mike, her two girlfriends Amy and Grace, Mr. and Mrs. Nolan and Jake, two thumbs up from all of them.

She opened Mike's airplane books and looked at the pictures. Later she sat and watched as he assembled his model B-29, her eyes moving from tail to fuselage to propeller and wing. When the plane was done, its glue dry, its insignia decals stuck on, Mike let her pick it up and hold it. She didn't like the colour, glum and grey as a rat. Hers would be white, her name painted in blue on the nose.

She puzzled over the mysteries of flying, its icons and ritual objects, aware that her father, aloft in his treehome, was flight-less but serene, content. He wore a scholar's quiet look as he went about his chores on weekends, the chores he postponed in order to finish the treehome. He'd saw and plane and hammer, replacing the rickety back stairs, touching the wood as if it were the arm of a friend, a companion and not a thing for building.

Sometimes, when Sally was watching him, he would pause in his work and sweep her up as he had that July Sunday in the trees. She'd stare down into his kind, pensive eyes until she was floating over a distant sea, towards some green clump of an island coast, an unknown land. She had a premonition that her dad was going to fly again. She asked him if it were true. He told her yes.

"When?" she asked him.

His smile melted into his face. "Real soon," he said.

"You'll take me?"

He paused, hesitated. "Sure I'll take you." He touched her head, his thoughts resting there.

Glen had begun to read aerial maps, which he kept in the treehome. He'd spread them on the floor, walking over them in stocking feet, standing on a stool and looking down, as if he were up in the air. Over the next year he took a ground-school refresher course, applied for a civilian licence and insisted on taking the flying test, although they would have waived it for a veteran. He got a perfect score. He bought himself a single-engine plane, a Piper Cub, and for the first time since his days in the Pacific, he flew.

Not far, and not with his family. He'd invited Mike, who by this time was looking ahead to his driver's licence, who'd dumped his airplane models for dreams of souped-up engines. Mike had grabbed his comb, slicked back his ducktail, turned up the collar of his leather jacket, one foot out the door before Glen could ask, "What's wrong, son?" Mike said, "Repeal the law of gravity, I'll go."

Her mother seldom went near the treehome, left the room when he spoke about airplanes. "Katie, hon, don't you like flying any more?" Glen asked, because that was how they'd met and fallen in love, in the cockpit of a two-seater. She told him that her flying ended a long time ago, and as far as the past was concerned, she preferred to dwell on her painted eggs, the scenes of her girlhood in Ottawa. She placed her delicate work in a box with crushed green satin lining. "These are for you, for your hope chest," she told Sally later. "For when you get married."

"When I get married," Sally answered, "I'll fly around the world."

"What will your husband do?"

"He'll fly too."

"With those eggs?"

Sally stopped to think. "The eggs'll break if I carry them."

"You can leave them at home," her mother said.

"I'm going to live in a plane. With a kitchen and a bed."

Her mother looked annoyed with that remark. Yet she was glaring at Sally's dad, at his smile, his shrug. Sally felt the ball-lightning flash of her eyes. She wondered what was wrong.

1954

Katherine couldn't bring herself to fly with Glen. She'd lived enough of her life attuned to his loss of gravity, leaving her home and parents, who'd fretted over her marrying an American. She'd waited four years for him to return from the war, where he'd found sexual consolation and where he'd almost lost his life in battle. Now she was waiting for him to recover, adrift in the trees, unable to sleep with her, unwilling to talk about the war and what had happened.

His flying was an evasion, one she couldn't resent, one in which she had joined him once. The pregnancy had been her fault — not the sex, but the relief she'd felt in having a reason to flee her parents, which meant she must have wanted to get pregnant, must have manoeuvred him. She'd paid for this in her marriage; she'd tried to redeem her life with the painting of a half-remembered world, only to lose the fine control of her hands, only to raise a daughter tainted with her parents' restlessness.

Now Glen was flying once more. His face was full of desperation when he looked at her, as if he were gazing at her from the other side of the war, from a desolate place from which he wanted to be rescued. Even so, she was no longer sure if he wanted her. One day she changed her mind. He'd asked her for help with an order for paint, new brushes.

"Will you paint a picture on my plane?" he asked.

Katherine looked at her hands. "I can't."

He grabbed them, hard. "You can, goddammit. Please, Katie," he whispered. He turned away, his back to her, and she felt his thoughts, his grief under the words.

Katherine went to the airfield dressed in her slacks, in her silk blouse cut to look like an artist's smock, her gold brooch pinned at her breast — a brooch Glen loved to see her wear because it had been his engagement gift to her, made in the shape of an artist's palette, tiny chips of ruby, sapphire, topaz for the paints. She changed into baggy coveralls, put a floral chintz bandanna on her hair and got to work.

A northern river, a soft clump of Gatineau spruce against the white of the cockpit door; above the trees, a blur of sky, a dot of a small plane, his, when they first met. Home again, they went into the garage, cleaned the brushes, washed. Katherine felt her hands shaking as she soaped and rinsed them. Glen grabbed a towel, clasped her hands inside it, held them tight in the vise of his own. The shaking stopped.

"I want you back," he said, and he kissed her on the lips. He reached for her breasts, but she pulled away from him.

"It's over. You left me."

"Katie, I ran away," said Glen. "Then *you* ran away. Took Sally, did you forget?"

"You don't want me."

"Jesus, Katie. I *love* you."

You love whoever you imagine, she thought. She opened the brooch, then her blouse.

He touched her breasts, then fell to his knees, his hands pulling down her slacks, his tongue slipping inside her. She imagined what kind of woman he might have loved in the war, imagined herself as a blonde and fair-skinned European's wife, then as a woman with a long black braid and a steeped-tea complexion, then as herself watching him do this to each of them. She closed her eyes, came in silence, felt a small, hard knot of pleasure at the sight of Glen kneeling before her. Crouching down on top of him, she wondered at herself, that she wasn't ashamed.

Afterwards, on his knees, he took her hands and kissed them. He'd never done that before.

Katherine finished his painting. Glen christened the Piper Cub *Katie*, broke champagne over the nose. She drank with him and his pilot friends, who followed her with frank, unblinking eyes.

Late that night, when Katie and Glen came home from the airfield, Sally heard her father say, *Tell me what you like, darlin'*, and her mother answering, *Right here*, and him saying, *C'mon then, Katydid, how bad you want me?* The two of them in the bedroom, carrying on like this. Sally felt ashamed that she heard it, wondered if she should tell this in confession. The priest would think that she'd made it up, that she had a foul mind. Who would believe she had parents like this? Resigned, she said an act of contrition, adding the words *but only if it's a sin*. That night she slept with cotton in her ears.

"In marriage," Sally's mother explained as she gave her a box of painted eggs, "you do what's best for your husband, your family. In doing this, you find happiness." Soon afterwards, Glen flew Katherine up in the air for the first time since the war. As she looked down, her hands, her whole body began to shake. These were not her woods below her, not the Ottawa River and the wine-red maples of the Gatineau in autumn, not the land she had once seen from a great, mysterious height above the world. It was as if she'd believed that flying would take her home again, as if she could return to the moment before Glen pinned on her orchid, before she first stepped into the cockpit of his plane, before she realized that leaving home meant the loss of a gentleness, of a way of seeing. Katherine had no words for this.

She never flew again. She returned to one of the rigours of her girlhood, hiking through the forest and across the trails, down the slope of the island to the Sound, swinging her arms, clenching and unclenching her fists as she walked. Her feet tried to remember the old, lost ground, how to find the way back home. She spent hours hiking, walking.

"I want to take you on a trip down the coast," Glen said to her. "Island-hopping near the Carolinas, on the outer banks, Hatteras, then the Florida Keys." He put his arms around her when he said it, kissed her cheek. He didn't realize that the bed-room door was ajar, that Sally was out in the hall, that she could see her mother's face, calm and introspective, more like a paint-ing of her face. Glen was standing behind Katherine, the amber light of late afternoon painting this moment into a sad and ele-giac canvas. Their daughter was nine years old and it was the last time she would see them like this. She was too far away to hear them whisper.

"Why won't you fly with me?" Glen asked.

"I lost everything, that's why. I look down and see it's gone."

"Katie, look at me. I'm here."

"I lost you too."

🦅🦅

After that, Glen moved into the treehome.

Katherine, through with painting and in need of distraction, got a filing job at Fort Travis, working with Marjorie, Eddie Nolan's wife. The army base abutted the airfield where Glen went to practise his turns and banks, takeoffs and landings. He told Katherine that he'd never enjoyed himself more, and he smiled as he said it, a faint smile, like a path that disappears into the woods. Then he spoke to Sally, invited her up to the tree-home porch.

"How old are you now?" he asked her.

"I'll be ten in two weeks." *He couldn't forget my birthday*, she thought.

Her parents had been silent, preoccupied. She felt unhappy, not knowing what to make of their trouble, afraid to tell anyone what was going on, afraid to hurt her parents with the scrutiny of their neighbours. She was thinking this as her dad looked through the oak and tulip boughs, through the delicate leafwork, his eyes moving out across the water. He lifted his arm and pointed out to sea, like a captain in a crow's nest, sighting land.

"See that, honey?"

"See what?"

"That bird. It's called a tern. A seabird." A bird called a *turn*, that was something new to her, strange.

"You mean it *makes* a turn?"

"That too," her dad said.

Sally had an idea. "Is there a bird called a *bank?*"

"Huh?"

"You said that bird's a *tern*. Well, if there's one called *bank*, they can be *tern and bank*, like what a pilot does. You can have another one called *takeoff.*" Sally started giggling. Her thoughts began to tumble out in a giddy, chaotic dance, a reel of silly jokes and puns. She grabbed the porch rail, swung back and forth on it and laughed into the trees. Yet her father looked as if he couldn't hear her laugh at all. His gaze was fixed on the patch of sky where the tern had flown. It was as if the sky were a curtain, one beyond which he alone could see.

She climbed up on a stool by the railing next to him. He took her arm and showed her how to sight along it, as if her arm were a runway straight out over the water.

"What's out there?" she asked.

"The tern's there," he said. "And the bank."

"I can't see anything." She glanced at him, saw a hint around the edges of his mouth that he'd swallowed her laughter whole. A core of brilliance was roiling away inside him, ready to spill right out of his eyes in a swirling eddy of light.

"'No eye has seen,'" he said, "'and no ear has heard. Nor has it entered into the heart of man.'"

Sally felt impatient. "Seen *what?*"

"Well, it's from the Bible," he said. "So no one knows."

"You always say that thing. 'No eye has seen.'"

"What would *you* like to see?" he asked her. His voice was quiet.

Sally looked away. Her dad knew what she wanted and it made her shy, his seeing into her.

"For your birthday," he said, "I'll take you flying."

"Does Mom know?"

"Yes, sweetheart. She knows."

In his voice, his words, she felt her parents' sorrow, felt it the way you feel a sad song that gets stuck in your head, one you could shake if you knew all the words and could just sing it once. Like one of her mother's war songs, those melancholy tunes she still hummed while she did the dishes, about lights going on again and peace ever after, as if the war had never ended.

A week later, her father showed her a book called *The Airman's Almanac, 1954*. He let her look at it, even though she could made no sense of what it said. "For flying on a clear day, you fly VFR," he explained, pointing to the letters on the page. "Visual Flight Rules." She took that to mean that her birthday would be sunny. He explained that when she was old enough, he'd get her a book like this.

Sally asked her father's permission to play on the treehome porch. There she pretended that his home was a plane and she could fly it. Feeling the lift of this lovely shingled contraption, she imagined disentangling it from the leaves and branches where it had been stuck too long, guiding it above the forest, across the Sound, then out to sea, away from the pull of gravity, the grave. What her father had wanted all along, why he had built the treehome in the first place. She realized that later, when she'd grown. Couldn't see it as a child, not then.

🕊🕊

1995

In Jake Nolan's archive is a newspaper clipping, a profile of Glen Groves, war vet and family man. *Former Airman's Weekend Flier Now*, the headline reads. It was published in the spring of 1956, shortly before Sally's tenth birthday. Accompanying the article is a photo of a smiling Glen Groves, his wife and children, all of them standing alongside the plane. The photo was taken by Lorne Winter, a college student hired for the summer at the *Banner*. In this photo, Sally and Mike are casually dressed but tidy in crisp summer shirts and shorts. Mike's shirt is white and Sally's is printed with poodles. Katherine's sundress is a cotton pastel, a pale colour, impossible to guess. Mike smiles with his eyes and Katherine with her mouth alone. Sally's eyes are high beams on a country road. They sweep the dark in front of them, they warn.

Three

These are my recollections of the day my father disappeared. Written in his memory, fifteen years after (Toronto, 1971).

On June 17, 1956 (my tenth birthday), we set out for Travis Airfield, the picnic hamper in the car. It was pleasant weather, fair and breezy, the day before the annual air show, the bleachers and reviewing stand already in place, draped in bunting, red, white and blue. The airport officials knew Dad well, and they invited Mom, Mike and me to sit in the stand, as if we were dignitaries. A few of Dad's friends came along, including Eddie, his cigarette bobbing like a tiny flare, Eddie's wife, Marjorie, their son, Jake, a few other pilots and a photographer from the *Banner*, looking for shots for the Weekend Outdoors page. I had invited two girlfriends, Amy and Grace, and their parents to watch me fly for the first time, up in the air with my father, into the wind.

A dozen or so of us, an audience for my dad, watching as his little Piper got fuelled up by a monster truck with a yellow Shell decal on the side, its long snout plugged into the plane's rear end. "Plane's gonna get pregnant," Mike said. My mother shushed him and waved at Dad, who'd just left the hangar and was walking towards us. Right then, the man from the *Banner* ran up to him, grabbed his arm and pointed at something behind the plane, as if he wanted a picture. My dad spoke with him, then came over to me.

"That man wants to see the smile on your face when I fly," he said. "So I'll go up first. Then I'll come back for you."

The fuel truck unhitched from the plane and Dad got ready to taxi out onto the runway. He was going to be a one-man air show.

He would fly across the airstrip, show off his turns and banks, do a spin around the island, then return. About a half-hour, he told us.

We watched as he taxied out, then halted, waiting for the tower's signal to roll forward into the wind. And away he went with the soul of me; I felt as if my body were a plane, I was rolling straight down the runway, the wind like a pair of hands lifting my wings, and I was above the ground now, up, up above the tiny people waving hands and the rows of bleachers stacked like twigs in a robin's nest. Higher than any of this I was, floating, gentle as a scrap of paper on a breeze, and, with a tilt of the wing, turning and banking. Ahead of me the treetops, soft green clumps; beyond them the Sound, a glittering bracelet of water.

Only now I was watching from below, a tangle of cardboard and string calling my eyes back. "Lookit Sally," Mike said, and I stared at what everyone saw unfolding from the tail of the plane. "Mom," I gasped, and she said, "I know," and smiled, her hands folded in her lap, her eyes gazing not at the plane but at a vanishing point in the distance. She looked attentive to some invisible sight, yet in a state of rest, as she used to look when she wanted to paint without disturbance. Mike didn't notice her. "It's the plane's dick," he told me. "Michael, watch your mouth," Mom answered, the sound of the words like thin ice cracking.

The jumble unfurled, a web of string and letters spelling HAPPY BIRTHDAY SALLY. We clapped and cheered. Mike had a bag of confetti, and he tossed it up in the air so that most of it drifted down on top of my head. *Dead M&M's*, he called the bits of colour. From somewhere to the side of me, a camera's shutter opened like a door to an unknown room, then closed with me inside it.

Dad did two loops around the field, tilting his wings at us as he made his pass, the lovely net trailing behind, the letters of my name tossed into the air, floating into a word. I felt immortal, as if my name were in a book, on a page of blue sky. I waved. Dad jiggled his wing at me, then banked as he headed over the trees at the edge of the field towards the island coast and the Sound, the plane with my name for a tail growing tiny, black, like a period at the end of a sentence. Below us, in the bleachers, two pilots were talking, gesturing.

"Dad's shown 'em all," Mike said. "What an ace."

Mom put an arm around me, kissed me. "Did you like the surprise?" I smiled so hard my mouth hurt.

"I can't wait to go up."

"When Dad comes back." Mom opened the picnic basket and started handing out soda to Amy and Grace, who were brimming over with pleases and thank yous and happy birthdays and little gifts, hugging me and saying, "Oh Sally, that was so neat, with your name and all." Mom and Marjorie Nolan found a pair of sycamores, some shade from the noon heat, where they set up two picnic tables with red-and-white checked gingham cloths, cutlery and dishes. Mrs. Nolan had brought a Thermos full of lemonade and a coleslaw salad in a wobbly green suspension, a jellied ring that looked like an edible tire. My mother never made recipes from a box, and in those days I craved the novelty of jellied moulds that shimmered with food dyes and jewel-like fruit. For my tenth birthday, mom had commissioned this special treat.

While we waited for lunch, my girlfriends and I found a flat, grassy spot near the water that caught a southwest wind, a good place for jump-rope in the heat, two-on-time and red-hot-pepper. When I missed and had to turn the rope, I noticed a few of the pilots clumped together under a tree, talking, glancing out over the water, a dull grey babble of voices. Mike and the other guys were listening in on them. Wanting to fly, I did my best to listen too.

"Due east?" Eddie talking, his cigarette unlit.

Jim, another pilot, laughed. "Yeah. Quick trip to Rome."

"Roamin' to Rome on a pissload o' fuel," Eddie said. "Maybe knows a tanker hid somewhere."

"Maybe."

We stopped jumping rope. An hour passed, then two, and we nibbled some lunch, the space between minutes filled by pacing, scanning the horizon, anxious words. "We don't understand it, Glen headed out to sea," Eddie told my mother, and this was why my father's friends had clumped together like dark, nesting birds, avoiding us. *Headed out due east, should have banked, should have turned south towards the tip of the island, never did,* was what Jim said. *Just kept going, didn't say where he was headed, didn't file a flight plan, none that we know of. Knows damn well he's supposed to, assuming he had a plan in mind.*

They'd checked it out with the tower, Eddie said. The tower had tried to raise him, got no answer. *Nothing wrong with his radio, just not talking, for chrissakes. Illegal not to answer and he knows it.* Eddie chugged smoke, dropped his butt, ground it out with his foot, then lit another.

"Maybe lost his bearings," said Jim, "but how the hell could he? Perfect weather, so close to home. Had a radio, a gyrocompass, an excellent pair of eyes. Maybe, God forbid, he got sick, blacked out."

The men said these things first among themselves, then in more temperate words to my mother, Mike and me. Mom's face was as calm and pale as sand. She sat us down at the picnic table, handed us fried chicken legs as if they hurt to touch. Then she picked up a small knife and started to cut the blemish out of a peach, the knife clattering on concrete as it fell from her hands. We sat and ate in silence.

They put out an alert for my father, notified radio towers all along the eastern seaboard. You'd think it would be impossible to lose him, Mike said, only this was a small plane, no doubt flying too low to be picked up by radar. He had become a phantom, ethereal and silent, slipping through radio beacons, vanishing from the sweep of radar, escaping these frail extensions of the listening ear, of the hand reaching out to the lost.

I told myself this and believed it, more so as time went on. A search was mounted; my father was never found, nor was his plane. No one reported a crash, a downward spiral, a nosedive into the sea. No one saw fire.

🦋🦋

He'll be back, my mother told us. She went up to the treehome after work, sat on the porch, hands folded, gazing above the treetops and down to the water as women before her must have done, waiting for the return of tall-masted ships, of their men from the sea. It was a warm early summer fragrant with roses and the nervous trill of cicadas. Life seemed to hold its breath. Maybe my mother conjured up an accident, a plane falling down into the water. If she did, she never told us. "Did Dad ever fly away before?" Mike asked her, as if his disappearance were a chronic ailment, one in which the mind wandered, taking the body with it. "Yes, of course," she answered, looking out over the sycamores, the beeches. "He fought in the Coral Sea in the war. He fought in Okinawa," she reminded him. *And before that he drifted north to Canada,* my mother might have thought that, too.

One night I watched as she smoothed the wide lapel of her smock, her fingers touching her gold brooch. She opened a button, letting the night breeze cool her skin. She must have felt my father's hand there; her eyes were bright with an unguarded look of desire. Ashamed to see it, I turned my eyes away.

Friends were kind to us, offering company, bringing food. Eddie and Jake came around to give Mike a hand with the chores, and Marjorie did the same with my mother after work. Some evenings, Dad's pilot friends would come by to talk with her. "I try not to think about it," she told them. "I lived through the war." The men understood, but I didn't.

When Sister Frances came to visit, she and my mother would sit together at the foot of the huge oak that held the treehome. Sometimes I'd notice how fearful my mother looked when she wasn't trying to be brave for Mike and me. At times like this, Sister would pray, a soft murmur of Hail Marys, fingering a rosary. My mother's lips didn't move. Her hands did, quivering against the gold pin on her blouse, lighting there.

Attached to Sister's beads was a leaden cross, and when she moved in her chair it swung back and forth like the pendulum of a clock. The cross seemed to be marking off the seasons of my father's absence, swinging from her skirts through late-summer grass and autumn leaves until I felt hypnotized by time, held like a prisoner in its to-and-fro. There I waited while days slipped into each other like hands into gloves, and autumn became a winter of bone-naked trees.

It was a comfort to play in the treehome after school, even though it felt lonely and deserted, a living, grieving thing. Like my mother, I peered through the branches, the fine black mesh that was bound to catch my father's tiny plane as twigs catch sparrows fluttering through the air. We had little snow in winter on Groves Island, and I imagined that my father must have tumbled down into a soft and wintry place, the noise of his landing muffled by drifts of snow as quiet as feathers, cats, the down of goslings. He was there *on retreat*, as they said in church, in need of God, for whom another name is silence.

I thought of this, and stared into the trees.

Four

Comments by Eddie Nolan, recorded for Jake Nolan's archives, May 1995

...Do I remember the day he disappeared? And how. It made me think of the war. My buddy Glen never let go of it, I'll tell you that much. It wasn't like he thought about the bad times. It's more like he kept the war in its own little corner, kind of shored it up, the way you see kids on the beach building sand walls around a fort. Keep it hidden, *safe*, that kind of thing. He read books about the Pacific, history, aviation.... Then he started fly-ing again, which said to me the war didn't spook him any more. *Those were the best years*, he said that once, and I said, *Coulda done without 'em myself*, and he said, *We made friends, pal. You saved my life*. Used to be he couldn't stand the thought that his crew got killed, he lived.

...Now, why I think he left? Tell you the truth, I don't think he had it in mind to clear out until he was up and off the ground that day. Not with Sally's name on the tail. He loved that kid, he would've never hurt her like that. The whole idea must of just sprung loose in his head, like an errand he forgot to run. Only what he forgot was what he said to me once when he got drunk. *I should of died in the war*, he said. Thought must of stuck with him, ate at the wires in his brain till the damn thing conked out, is what I think.

The day he flew, and we were all standing around starting to get anxious, I went over to the edge of the field and stared across the Sound. Pulled out a smoke, didn't even light it. Had my old wreck of a hat on, plaid band and a big brim. So then I did this funny thing. Turned east, took off my hat and tipped it to the sea, like an old-timer talking to a lady. *Take care of the old boy*, was what it felt like. Held it over my heart, that hat. Must of known inside me he was gone. Bowed my head, like I was paying my respects. Like I was waiting for taps, for the flag to come down.

Only it hasn't. I still miss Glen, and it's like all these years go by and there's no taps, no real way to sign off. Guess that's the main thing that bothers me. Not being able to make the whole thing *end*.

Groves Island Oral History Project; Sally Groves on tape. Recorded July 1995

Jake: In your notes, you talk about "a photographer from the *Banner*, looking for shots for the Weekend Outdoors page." That was when your dad ——

Sally: It was Lorne Winter.

Jake: You two go back a long way.

Sally: I didn't know his name back then. He wanted a shot of me looking at the banner.

Jake: How do you know it was him?

Sally: (*pause*) He told me it was. He was so relieved I didn't go up. He figured he saved me.

Jake: You owed your life to him.

Sally: I felt that way for a long time. Yes.

Jake: Lorne had a thing about your dad. (*Sound of rustling papers.*) Remember the Legion Prize?

Sally: I remember this clipping (*she reads headline*): "Rookie Photog Wins Legion Award; 'It's High Praise,' says Lorne Winter." My dad handed him the plaque, that's why he liked him. (*pause*) Later on, Lorne thought he was crazy.

Jake: Did you?

Sally: *Lorne* was crazy. Except I always felt I owed him something.

Jake: That he stopped your dad from ending your life. (*A pause. Sally doesn't answer.*)

Jake: I'm sorry, Sal.

Sally: Whatever Lorne thought, he's wrong.

Jake: He thought your dad was a sick man.

Sally: How did he know what my dad felt?

Jake: I'm not saying he was right. I just want to establish what happened. Your dad meant to take you up with him. Lorne said that he felt something weird going on and he talked him out of it, right?

Sally: (*Sighs.*) That's Lorne's version of what happened.

🐚🐚

From Sally's notes: 1971

...In my father's papers, Mike and I found hand-drawn maps of proto-continents, those that predated winged insects and animals with shells, maps that held in memory ancient conifers, erupting mountains, the first hesitant flower. Only my father's drawings were criss-crossed by intersecting lines, the lines joined by dots, coordinates of latitude and longitude. These were traveller's maps, the lines marked with tiny airplane symbols, the distance for each leg marked down.

Dad had made flight plans, one for each map. Destinations, estimated times and dates of arrival and departure, all filled in with nonexistent places, coordinates that made no sense, times and dates for clocks and calendars that no one had yet invented. Or that had passed out of existence long ago. What was I to make of it? These were games of his, inventions never meant for flight. Nor were they maps of contour and texture, touch and feel, the kind that allow you to sense the congruence of mountain range and human spine, of craggy outcrop and weathered face, of lakes with the depth of eyes.

Or maybe they would lead him to these things.

I'm convinced that my father fled. As a student I did research, met people who were fliers, who told me stories I've since read, of a circle of pilots, all of them war vets who, in the darkness of all they'd endured and inflicted on others, conspired to abandon the world. A silent movement of men who drew encrypted maps, who were guided to remote communities by shadow towers, by a chain of pirate beacons, encoded signals sent on seldom-used bands, all of them belonging to a cult of silence, a fraternity of the disappeared, of men who turned up in Kazakhstan, Mongolia, Samarkand, who lived hermetic lives in mountains and deserts, men who could no longer speak our language, or any tongue; men who had found peace with themselves, and, if need be, forgiveness.

I envy my father. I'm still troubled by his silence, his back turned on us. Drawn to it, also, as if it were an aerial manoeuvre I could learn through practice. Like the execution of a skater's leap, perfection. Like the ice below.

⚜⚜

A reply to these notes. Recorded July, 1995

Sally, he was friggin' nuts.

I say that as your friend Jake, on tape and into a mike. No one to hear me but the air.

It's about these notes you passed along. Do you really think your old man took off to be some kind of monk in the Gobi Desert? *A fraternity of the disappeared?* What the hell were you smoking when you wrote that? OK, no one's ever found the plane so you can believe what you like, I guess. I don't blame you. Common sense says the plane went down. You're an intelligent woman, a pilot, you *know* that. But you've got a logical mind, and logic wants proof for everything, and there *isn't* any. But honest to Jesus, if he were my old man, I'd want him dead rather than running away from me. Why would a guy do that to his wife and kids?

It's much more likely he lost his mind, Sal. People would have let it go by, not asked nosy questions like today. They'd just been through a world war, a couple of million dead, I mean, what's another crackpot?

If it'd happened today your fairy-tale wouldn't have a chance, not with the slop-bucket of info we're stuck with. CNN, Internet, Search-and-Rescues bouncing their signals off satellites, there's sonar and bottom-crawling submarines with *wheels*, I kid you not. They'd pick up the wreckage just like that. It doesn't mean a thing, that they haven't found your dad's plane. Depends on if they think it's worth the trouble. I mean, hey, they're just getting around to *Roman* ships that hit the bricks. Sailing for *Carthage*. So what are we, Sal, compared to that, huh?

Dust out here on Long Island Sound, is all.

Wayfarers II

One

1995

Sally knew that Jake was trying to be kind. He was reading what she wrote at Mike's computer, stories she could share with him or send to Gabe. Yet writing brought her little peace. Every family had its mysteries, and maybe there was no solving her parents' disappearance, no digging for treasure when there was no tool or place to dig, when all she had was a threadbare gauze of frailty and trouble, a fisher's net of mystery, one she could describe but never unravel, taking more care with the shape of what she saw than with the darkness trapped and held there. How it was woven, its threads and ladders, nodes and intersections; how strong the shape of it was, and how enduring, this dark net of grief and disappearance. She'd forget about a central fact, a telling clue, a key that unlocked; there was none.

Maybe this was all she could manage, the best she could do.

In front of the computer screen she conjured up her father. Because she'd accepted her need for flying, she could draw as close to his story as it was possible to get. Yet she was afraid, as if her musing might cause him to return, to insist on knowing what had become of her mother. She'd have to tell him. Katherine was the completion of his story, after all. Yet she couldn't draw as close to her mother. She had to step back from the shattering of her life, speaking at a distance so that her mother's brittle sky would never again collapse on her in darkness. It would be better if she could avoid the risk altogether, slam shut a cortical grate, but she couldn't. She was dry earth, an open sluice, and the torrent of her mother was pouring down on her.

1956

Sally's mother began to vanish.

Katherine continued to work at Fort Travis, making sure that Sally and Mike were fed and clothed and off to school on time. Otherwise she kept to herself, as gentle and indifferent as falling rain. She slipped into reserve, a calm withdrawal, as if it were a new, well-tailored dress, one that suited her. Hurt by her mother's coolness, Sally assumed that she had become a burden. She offered to iron, to help cook.

"You didn't used to like chores," her mother said.

"I want to help."

Her mother looked impatient. "Then I need to know what your father told you."

"When?"

"Before he left," her mother said. "Every word."

"He asked if I wanted to fly."

"If you'd gone with him, he might have come back," she replied.

That had been the plan, Sally told her. Troubled, she went up to her room, went to the bookshelf and took down Mike's balsa-wood planes, his aviation books for boys who wanted to be pilots. She disassembled the planes, put the slats of wood in a box with the books and hid them under the bed. Her zest for flying embarrassed her now. She felt like an ugly, cast-off thing, almost an odour, a coarse boy under a girl's skin, twisted that way by a hunger for shrieking metal, crazy flying. She was ashamed, too, that she might have saved her mother grief, except that her dad had *promised* he'd be back for her. Now she was exiled from her mother's tenderness, a conspirator, the child of the man who'd done this monstrous thing. Yet her mother was her breath, her skin.

One night Sally went into her room and slipped under the covers next to her. Katherine stirred, woke up. "What are you doing here?" she asked.

"I was lonely."

"You're not a child."

Sally got up, dragging the edge of the quilt on the floor.

"Please watch the quilt," said her mother.

Sally arranged the quilt at the foot of the bed, folded herself like a limp skein of wool and slept there. In the morning when she awoke, her mother arose in the dim light, ready for her shower. Pretending to be asleep, Sally watched, dismayed by her mother's nakedness, the lustrous beauty of her breasts, by her own sorrowful longing to be held like a child. Katherine pulled on her dressing gown and left the room.

You should undress in the bathroom, show-off, Sally thought.

She spent much of that school day unable to concentrate or answer questions. After school, looking in the mirror, she wondered about her hair, her face, her slight build, her flat chest. Her lust for flying began to worry her, as if it were a genetic trait, one that had derailed her growing up, had caused her body to stumble and fall into boyhood. She thought about her school friends, most of whom were beginning to look as if small, round loaves of bread were rising on their chests. While she was grieving for her father, Amy and Grace had learned how to set their own hair and how to put on a garter belt and stockings. They could walk in heels and they knew how to dance. She still wanted her mother, whose breasts she'd seen in the soft light of morning. She'd never have breasts, she'd sleep on the floor, she'd pay for her mother's suffering all her life. Her friends would grow up, get married, leave her.

Except that in some ways she was ahead of them. A strong swimmer, she'd taught Amy and Grace the breaststroke, and with Mike's help she'd mastered the big kids' trick of sliding down the embankment, hitting the surf at high tide and swimming out. *What if you got a cramp in your leg and couldn't climb back up?* they warned her. *I'm careful,* she said. It was in her soul that she felt a spasm of grief, a fear of drowning.

Sally wished she could be small again, beloved. At night in bed, curled like a fern, she rocked herself.

❧❦

Her mother walked, often as far as the airfield. *It's good for her*, the Nolans said. *Keeps her mind together, she'll walk this whole mess out of her system.* There were trails on her property, paths at Fort Travis that curved across flat fields, down grassy slopes to the water. Sally's mother became known on the island for her excursions. The Walking Woman, some called her, or even Katherine Walker, as if she'd married again. She never walked with her children. When Sally asked to come along, her mother told her no.

On one of these occasions, Sally went into her mother's bedroom, sat on her bed, stroked the satin pillow, then held the quilt to her cheek for comfort. As she did this, her eye caught a glint of something in the wastebasket. She reached in, pulled out her mother's brooch, the gold palette. She decided to keep it, knew it wouldn't matter to her mother if she did. When Katherine came home from these trips she was calm, as still as an empty house — one she'd already abandoned.

1957

On Sundays Katherine dropped her children off at church, then hiked to the airfield, a good hour's walk. *A cemetery visit*, Sally thought, convinced that her mother prayed *for the repose of his soul*, a phrase she sometimes heard at Mass. She felt sure her dad was still alive, and her mother's mournful visiting upset her.

She knew it must trouble Mike, but he never said much, didn't hang around. He was off in his jittery wreck of a car, one cigarette after another trembling on his lips. Now and again he'd reach out and tousle her hair. *Hey, shrimp*, he'd say, or *How ya doin', peanut?* He looked sad, as if he'd never again be a man's son, a good brother. When he went out, she'd sit still, hugging herself as if her arms were his.

Their mother was working overtime. Her office pool included Mrs. Nolan, who never worked past five p.m. *Come on now, it would take World War III to keep a civilian working late at Travis, everybody knows that.* Sally heard Jake's mom saying this to Sister

Frances, her voice dropping when she saw her.

A soldier — an official from the airfield, maybe a part-time pilot — noticed her mother alone on her lunch hour, kept her company, maybe even grew fond of her, but Sally had no way of knowing the details. Too young to follow what was going on, she heard the edge of it in neighbours' voices, the edge of a blade trying to cut to the core of her mother's life.

❦

Curious, she skipped school, following her mother out to the airfield, taking the bus most of the way, walking through the woods to the chain-link fence, as close as she could get without being seen. Crouching down with her father's binoculars, she looked through the fence, feeling like a spy. *Dad used these during the war.* Her hands shook. She saw her mother sitting in front of the hangar, eating her sandwich, and then she heard the *whoosh* and rumble of a little plane headed for the runway. Sally turned her binos on a two-seater, white and pretty as a seagull.

Her mom was smiling, standing up, laughing, her lunch forgotten, hopping up and down like a kid and waving at the pilot, and Sally could feel her own heart pile-driving right through every bit of hard-rock sense in her brain. *Dad's come home. It's a surprise.* Sweating with excitement, grubby in the June heat, but today her mother wouldn't notice, wouldn't care. *Maybe he was on a secret mission.* The man climbed out of the plane, smiled at her mother, took her in his arms. *I'll tidy up the treehome,* Sally thought. *We'll have a party.*

The pilot kissed her mother on the mouth. When he moved away from her, Sally glimpsed a stranger's face. Disappointment crushed her like an asteroid slamming into earth. She put down the binoculars, sat in the weeds by the fence and wept. Then she stood up and gave the fence a good, hard kick.

❦

In the treehome, Sally distracted herself with an album of news-paper clippings, photos and articles from the *Banner*. There was Glen Groves in his Piper Cub (*Former Airman's Weekend Flier Now; "Nothing Beats The Thrill," Says Groves*), and the yellowed write-up with the family photo from the treehome picnic, from the final day of the war in Korea. She heard footsteps on the out-side stairs, her mother's hand opening the door. Katherine glared at Sally. Her face was as pearly as a cold day's sky.

"Sister Frances called me at work. Why did you skip school?"

Sally hesitated, lowered her eyes. "To find out what you were up to."

"What I'm up to," she said, "is earning a living."

"I saw that pilot come for you," Sally replied. "I thought he was Dad."

Her mother took a deep breath. "Oh?"

"Do you think Dad's dead?" Sally asked.

"How would I know that?"

"Well, if you don't," said Sally, "you should both fly off and look for him."

Her mother was taken aback. When she spoke, her voice was like coal dust, soot. That soft, that dark.

"You have no business following me," she said.

"Yes I do. You've got a boyfriend. I saw you smooching him."

Sally knew it was wrong to spy on them. Maybe this was her mother's excuse for doing what she did, for striding right up to her and slapping her face with a blow that was hard yet almost inadvertent, like the crash of a flying bird against a window. Yet it was her mom who withered, her face wearing a look as feature-less as a desert, as if an invisible wind were blowing away the folds and contours of a human gaze, a mother's for her child. After her mother left, Sally felt broken.

She went out on the porch, felt the salt of the ocean on her skin, noticed the trees that were in leaf and bud, took comfort from these things and wept. She wondered how it was that her beloved forest, her dogwood and lilac, her mother's estrangement, her father's disappearance, a spring day as sweet and ripe as a melon on the vine, how could the basket of life hold them all with so much equanimity, so much room? Nothing made sense any more, not even goodness. Not when her mother had harmed her.

Still clutching the album, Sally found her dad's book, *The Airman's Almanac, 1954*. She thought about Mike, how he'd taken their father's maps to his room so he could mull over them late at night. Not for comfort, *nah, sis*. Just to give the maps a look while he listened to Elvis, his new LP. Over and over again the same two songs, *Rip It Up* and *How Do You Think I Feel?* How he'd sit and listen, slumped over, his face in his hands.

She'd take the almanac to bed with her. Like her brother, she couldn't bear to be alone, bereft.

Two

A week after the incident in the treehome, Sally came home from school to find a note on the kitchen table. *I've gone looking for Dad, as you suggested, Sally. Thought it over and decided you were right, thought it would be easier on you. Please be good. I will be in touch. Ask neighbours for help, names in my address book. Mike, please attend to the envelope. Kids, I love you.*

On the envelope she'd written *For Groceries, Phone and Electric.* Inside there was two hundred dollars in small bills. When Mike came home, Sally showed it to him. He didn't say anything at first. He felt around in his pockets and pulled out a crushed and flattened pack of cigarettes. Lazy as a tomcat thumping his tail, the way he took his time tapping a weed from the pack, putting it in his mouth, striking a wooden match on the sole of his shoe.

"Some wad o' bills," he said. "Mom playing the horses?"

"You're going to smoke in here, Mike?"

"Mom's not here to know." He paused. "You won't tell, huh?"

Sally said she wouldn't and he patted her head, lit up, drew a deep and extravagant breath into his lungs. It reassured her, his worry that their mother would find out, as if to say she'd be back for sure. He finished his smoke, ground it out, walked into the pantry.

"It's dinner out of a can tonight," he said. He fixed them soup and tuna sandwiches while Sally sat at the table, her head bowed. *I've gone looking for Dad, as you suggested, Sally.* It was her fault, she had told her mother, *You should both fly off and look for Dad.* She took a bite of her sandwich, put it down.

"What's wrong, sis?"

"I made her go."

Mike put a hand on her shoulder. Now he was her family, all she had. "She'll come back, Sal," he said.

"I got mad at her."

Mike put his arm around her shoulders. "I'm scared, Mike, I'm scared," she wept as he took her in his arms and rocked her back and forth. *So am I*, sis, his silence answered. His body like a strong young tree, a sapling bent with grief.

❦❦

Sally followed her mother's story in the *Banner*, read the head-lines. *Missing Mother Puzzles Police*, and worse. *Groves Car Found Abandoned; Police Won't Rule Out Foul Play*. They said on TV that her car'd been left near Peeksgill, miles from home. There was word she'd been travelling with an unidentified man. *Gossip's a sin*, said Sister Frances. *Don't listen, dear*. All the same, Sally heard Mrs. Nolan whispering on the church steps after Sunday Mass, *They say she went looking for a doctor*, which made no sense at all, since she hadn't been sick. Yet it felt wrong to ask Mrs. Nolan what she meant.

In school, she heard voices drop and soften when people spoke to her, as if she were a library or a church. No one said too much about her mother, no one came close to her dread. Amy and Grace stopped asking her over to watch *American Bandstand*, as if they were trying to show respect for a mourner. Sally didn't care, didn't want anyone near her.

❦❦

She did her homework with the radio on.

*More tips on Katherine Groves, now missing three weeks....
Police say she's been seen hiking down country roads and
along the shoulder of the Interstate. A pretty woman, five
foot three, weighs one-twenty pounds, has neat black hair*

pinned up, blue eyes. She left home in a blazer and jeans. A woman meeting Mrs. Groves' description has been spotted walking as far north as the Canadian border. By whom, Sergeant Preston? Cut it out, folks. This isn't funny.

Police say the large number of leads reflects the concern of many onlookers for the mental state of Mrs. Groves, the mother of two teenage kids. Less than a year ago, her pilot husband, Glen Groves, disappeared on a short flight. He is presumed dead.

Sally turned the radio off. Her father was *missing*, not dead. Her mother was gone.

Mike was almost eighteen, army age.

Her family was collapsing on the fault line of a massive earth-quake, plaster and roof-beams crushing her, pinning her down. She should never have told her mother to go. They'd put her in jail if her mother died. Her heart felt caged in her ribs, shaking the bars.

So let them. She kicked at a chair hard, knocked it over.

I'm sorry, she whispered. *Please come back.* She went into her mother's room, saw herself reflected in the mirror, felt the touch of her mother's hand, heard her voice: *It's all right, Sally, I haven't left you.*

Please don't go away.

Come closer, dear. She did.

Two clenched fists in the mirror, angry, threatening. She'd hit as hard as her mother had done when she'd struck her in the face. This time it was a glass face full of sorrow, and she hit it with a stone fist.

Three

Sally couldn't remember who had brought her to the hospital. *Why did you do this?* asked the doctor. Convinced they were going to lock her up, she felt sure it didn't matter what she said or didn't say. She didn't know why she had done it. *How old are you, dear? Eleven.* She stared at the doctors and nurses, saw in their eyes that she was too young for so much trouble. She didn't feel young. She thought that if you had no parents, you weren't a child any more.

They were ghostlike in their white shoes that squeaked like mice on linoleum, tiptoeing around her as if she were asleep, as if she were a hibernating bear who might awake and take a hungry swipe at them. *You'll be all right, honey* — kind words pressed into their jigsaw-puzzled faces. They brought her orange juice and Cream of Wheat. They combed her hair and dressed the wounds on her hand, her arm. *Look at me, dear.* Ashamed, she tried and couldn't.

Mike sat with her, his hand stroking her hair. *Sis,* he kept repeating, *sis.* He patted her bandaged arm. *It's gonna be all right, huh?* He'd brought her a copy of *Modern Screen* with a write-up on Elvis, shots from his new movie. He'd take her to see the flick, she'd feel better then.

But I don't have parents. Where will I go when I leave here?

Sister Frances arrived to take her home.

She'd just become principal of Holy Rosary School. In the corridor you'd hear her coming, staking out her new turf, her white habit swishing floors, rosary beads clattering, sounds that made Sally think of feathers, talons, a great winged bird of a woman collecting her young. Every few days she stopped Sally to ask her how she was doing, and Sally would say, *Fine, thank you.* If Sister asked if there was word about her mother, Sally would shake her head no, and scurry off, her heart full of inarticulate shame.

Now she took Sally's hand and held it. She told her how concerned she was, how sorry that she and Mike had suffered so much.

"It's my fault," said Sally.

Sister Frances listened, her eyes grave with worry. "Your mother decided to go herself," she said. "You didn't make her."

"They're going to lock me up."

"What do you mean, Sally?"

"My mother's dead." Sally started to cry.

"No, child, she's not dead. Both your parents are lost."

How could grown-ups get lost? Sally felt despair at the thought of it, felt Sister Fran scoop her up in her arms, in her long serge robe, into the clean, starchy smell of it. She held her inside the rattling of her beads and crucifix, as if she knew that Sally was in danger, leaning over a precipice, wanting to punish herself and jump. *Pray to Saint Anthony,* Sister said to her, and gave her a handkerchief to dry her eyes.

Talk about kid stuff, talk about sneezing in a hurricane. Patron saint of lost trivia, misplaced pencils and copybooks. Saint Anthony, a balding, puppy-eyed monk in brown robes, depicted holding a lily and the Christ Child. He was too gentle, hardly up to this assignment, no match for her parents' madness. Sally felt desperate.

Saint Anthony, help me to find my parents.

Lost they were. All of them, lost.

Four

Fran Winter's recollections, taped for Jake Nolan's archives, 1995

Fran: ...In a boarding-house in Poughkeepsie, they found her. Twenty miles from where she left the car. They sent her to the Oak Valley nuthouse. Electroshock was the *best* they had.

Jake: Did she know what she was in for?

Fran: Who knows what she knew? Jake, for heaven's sake, she was pregnant.

Jake: She didn't tell them at the hospital?

Fran: They told me when I went to see her. You'll pardon me, but I hate that place. Those doctors had it in for women.

Jake: How do you mean?

Fran: What they claimed she was up to. Four months pregnant and hemorrhaging. They said she'd done it to herself. She died before I could talk to her.

Jake: Jesus.

Fran: If they'd wanted to, they could have helped her. They kept going on about how she broke the law, the mess her landlady found her in. Katherine would never have gotten rid of her child. What rubbish.

Jake: Poor Katie.

Fran: Electroshock could have caused the miscarriage.

Jake: Those were the days. Don't ask, don't tell.

Fran: Later I found out they dumped her in with a roomful of loonies and head-bangers. Now, I hate that kind of talk, but it's how she must have seen them. They just left her there, no one bothered to check on her. She must have been frightened to death, poor Katherine. Her sheets were soaked in blood.

Jake: Reminds me of the war. Sorry, Fran, but I'm losing it. (*Sound of the machine being turned off.*)

"Fran," Jake said afterwards. "Do Sally and Mike know this?"
"About the room where their mother died?"
"Yeah."
Her eyes met his. "Sally knows everything but."

Five

This is for you, Gabe, to read one day. It is written in memory of your grandmother, Katherine Groves.

...The island has no burial ground, so my mother was laid to rest on the mainland, in Westchester. Gate of Heaven Cemetery, Hartsdale, I think that's the name, the place. My brother Mike has tended her grave, including the plot beside it, which waits for my missing father.

I remember the funeral Mass, the comfort I received from the simplest thought: that Mom had died in the hospital, in a safe and dignified place, in a bed, as if this in itself were rest and benediction. I must have sensed it could have been worse. She could have died in the bushes, with some guy's hands all over her, or in a heap of metal at the bottom of the sea. A grace that, after all her peregrinations, Mom died in decency. This brought me peace, the only thing that did.

There were many mourners, people whose names I didn't know. Among them were two foreign visitors, slight and elderly to my young eyes. Marie-Claire Duval was dressed in high-collared, stiff black lace, her white hair covered by a veil, on the arm of her husband, Henri, in black suit and vest, carrying his hat, his cane. It felt as if I'd imagined them to life, my grandparents from Canada. Foreigners in an American town, old-fashioned in dress, smaller of stature than the other adults, as if grief had made them spare and more compact, somehow, had crafted them out of a different sort of clay. When *Grand-mère* lifted her veil to kiss me, I could smell lilac on her damp skin. My grandfather had been weeping. He patted my head.

All my classmates came to the funeral Mass, and afterwards Mrs. Nolan served a buffet lunch. Ladies with veiled hats and gloves offered condolences, parishioners who remembered a shy eight-year-old girl in a flowered pinafore serving sweets as Katherine poured tea, a child who'd vanished with her. How grieved I was by knowing this, how tainted by my mother's death. It felt like my funeral also.

Lunch was cold cuts, ham and roast beef, rolls and jellied salads. I couldn't eat and neither could Mike. He stood in the corner, ducktailed, leather-jacketed, chugging smoke like diesel exhaust, chatting with his buddies. Later he tousled my head, told me he was going for a drive. He didn't say it would take him the rest of his life, that drive, but I must have known. He'd just turned eighteen, had just been drafted. We would say goodbye that day, and we would never share a home again.

It was in 1964, when I was about to leave for Toronto, that I learned some of the facts surrounding my mother's death. Sister Fran felt she ought to tell me what little she knew. Only she didn't know when my mother became pregnant or who the father was. Nor did she know why he'd abandoned her (or been asked to leave). She never learned why my mother left her car in Peeksgill, unless she thought a strenuous hike might cause her to miscarry. Maybe she'd figured out that a trip to the nuthouse would do that also, only Sister Fran was too polite to mention this.

I couldn't absorb it. *It doesn't mean she didn't love you*, she told me, but I didn't explain that my love for my mother had been broken by a slap, that my eyes still saw the wind of a desert crossing her face. If my mother had loved me, it had been a strange and otherworldly love, one I could never aspire to give or receive. I told Sister Fran that I would never understand her leaving us. She asked me not to judge my mother, to leave that to God. She held my hand in both of hers as she said this.

Before I left home, we went to visit the grave. I sat beside it and couldn't move, as if I were sinking into the ground, as if the grave wanted me too. Sister Fran put her arm around me. *Remember something good*, she said. I tried then, and I'm still trying. What come to mind are frail and brittle things, painted glass, the frost of her breath as a girl in Ottawa, the soft *shh-shh* whisper of her skates.

She left me these memories, and they are hers. Yet my mother is a more substantial thing than memory. She is weight and gravity and rooted branch. I carry her, I know this. Some days I sit, as I did by the grave, unable to move for the weight of her in me.

From a letter: 1995

...Gabe, I have travelled light in this world, except for these memories of my parents. It's how it is, we nest inside each other, can't get free. We are what families are; a layering, tree growth, rings inside of rings. Concentric circles; grandparents, parents, you in the centre. We have engraved ourselves on each other even in absence, exile. Yet, at the same time, things pass through us like a running stream through the fingers of a hand. Nothing is ours, no child or parent, nothing we have been given belongs to us, only to the mystery of its own life. We are mute as a forest in the face of this.

❧ Lorne's Effects I ❧

One

Gabe read Sally's letter. How little he knew about life, he thought.

By the time she got to be my age, she had no parents, she'd lost her man in a war, she'd given up her kid, left her country, got herself a pilot's licence and set up camp in the bush, not something women did back then. No whining, no complaints. Here I sit in front of my computer in Toronto. I was born here. I swear at missing documents and stuff that won't print out. I watch TV. One day I turned it on and saw my father die, me and half the planet. Even then, Sally had it worse. He jumped from her plane.

I'd like to give her something good for once.

Gabe was thinking this at his computer, pointing and clicking at the highlighted words, somersaulting from text to text, from node to node in the criss-cross of the Net. His acrobatics made him think of flying, of his grandfather Glen, of what he'd like to find out about that missing plane, what little Sally'd told him. *Sally would croak if she knew what I was up to.* Only it wasn't Glen who was pushing him; it was Lorne, his plane, his fire. Glen was just easier to take than Lorne.

His grandfather was hope itself, a man whose body had never washed up on any shoreline, virtual or real, who might have become a spectre abiding in a home page where there was no such thing as *lost* or *missing* or *presumed dead*, only a misplaced dot or squiggle in an address. Anything was possible now. Glen could be resurrected through a hotlink, a search string, a point-and-click, suspended in a weird sort of eternity where nothing and no one disappeared. And what about Lorne? The thought shook Gabe's hands on the keys. He was beginning to feel that, if he looked long enough at the screen, he'd see Lorne's face rising to the surface like a drowned man's, pale and limpid, a cloud's reflection floating on the surface of the water. Tired, he yanked off his glasses, sat slumped over, his face in his hands.

He couldn't concentrate. Not on this, not on his *Weekly* column — not when Lorne's death had come crashing through his life like a huge branch torn from a tree by a hurricane. Stuck now sweeping up debris, he had found a lawyer for the complicated stuff, had learned that, as Lorne's only kid, he'd been left everything — no small reason to repay the favour and put the man's life to rest, sorting through files, closing bank accounts, telling *The Globe and Mail* that they had one less subscriber. *In any case, you're his executor*, Dawn kept reminding him. *You don't have a choice.* She had her own work and wasn't here with him as often now.

Gabe had decided to move into Lorne's condo for as long as it took him to sort through his effects. He felt Lorne everywhere, as if he were alive and he himself were part of the junk to be sorted. A terrible weariness took hold of Gabe, as if he were being eaten by a parasite, one he was too exhausted to resist. Most times, if he wanted to sleep, he did. *I miss you, Lorne, you bastard*, and he curled up like a snail on the couch, his back turned, his fists, his damp face crushed in the pillows.

Sometimes, when he felt grieved to breaking, he'd sit up all night with Dawn. Otherwise he'd hunt down a drinking buddy or write to Sally. There was also the Net, the world clicking open like a lock on a safe. Yet he was afraid to fiddle with the combination, to find in written or spoken words the reason for his father's death. He'd begun to feel that burning might have been some sort of camouflage, as deceptive and hidden a thing as Lorne's life, an event the media had followed like a duck drawn to a hunter's wooden decoy, to a rifle hidden in the thicket. Not danger, just an image to trouble his mind, a flash of light, a lost bird tumbling through a crack in the sky.

His grandfather Glen was the chaser for too much Lorne — a computer game, a problem that intrigued him. No, he was history, part of a family. His. *Safecracking, here we come.* He grabbed the mouse and pointed at the screen.

The guy would be pushing eighty now, Gabe thought. There must be notes somewhere, records of his plane, the traffic controller's report for the FAA. Scribbled on a form, banged out on a creaky old manual typewriter with three carbons, stuck in a binder, shoved in a file drawer, info as lost and useless as a single sock, totally unplugged from any kind of network with a decent search string, facts wandering off like stray cats. Junk stuffed in manila folders — you'd hardly call that *knowing* anything, you couldn't even *find* it, never mind make sense of it. What did they do before computers, before the Net, everything and everyone not just alone but totally alone, so goddamned easy to lose? They didn't have e-mail then. When you were gone, you left no footprints. Gabe sat down at the computer, tried to think.

He'd been looking for stuff in Canada too, planes fallen out of the sky, into snowbanks on the sides of mountains. Skiers and wilderness nuts kept finding them. You'd hear it on the news, like the one they dug out of a mountain pass in British Columbia, a whole fucking *airliner*, missing thirty years. Things happened, people vanished, stuff got lost in Canada. It was like having too many pockets, too many rooms, too many files in your hard drive, a few good people rolling around in a big and lonely country. Lorne had been one of them. He'd got lost, flown north of Timmins, burned to death.

Forty years earlier, in his mother's country, Glen had flown east to the sea.

Gabe was tired, too tired to continue. He leaned his head against the computer, imagined himself curled up and asleep in the Net as it tossed itself across the darkness, rocking him.

☙ ☙

Gabe would have called Dawn, but she was working late. He hated sacking out alone, thought he'd watch Ella on TV. He clicked her on, the camera hugging her face in a close-up shot, spreading it across the screen like butter on a slab of bread. *Dysfunctional families*, she said, *are everywhere. Imagine the plight of children forced to witness....* Gabe yanked off his glasses, which sometimes had the weird effect of blurring his hearing as well as his sight. It didn't work. He went in the kitchen, opened a beer, stood leaning against the living-room wall, watching. '

Kids exposed to depravity and abandonment end up.... Christ, Ella, don't. He picked up the remote, clicked her off, glugged down the beer. He'd like to see her, find out how she was doing. He knew she had lunch hours booked more or less until the year 2000. Sometimes he got her when he phoned, most times he listened to her voice-mail message and played with the buttons, punching them all at once, getting the squawks and beeps, the robotic voice intoning, *Screw off, dickhead*, or words to that effect. These days he saw her on TV, watched as if he were waiting for her to speak to him. *Shock*, he thought of her calm, impassive eyes.

Gabe had been ten years old when Lorne had left, and ten years later he had been old enough to pack his bags. *You're on your own*, Ella had told him, a fledgling booted out of the birdhouse, flapping his wings. From that point on, no bugging him, no nagging, no why-don't-you-show-your-face. *I won't be that kind of mother, you don't have to worry*. She gave him some household stuff for his digs, some furniture and kitchenware, a TV. She gave him Lorne's address. Then she looked him in the eye and wished him well.

"We never thought we'd be parents, Lorne and I," she said.

Gabe shrugged. "Hey, you did all right."

Ella took a deep breath and handed him a package of condoms. Gabe pocketed them, clicked his heels and saluted. *Marching orders, yessir* — he wanted to pull out a rubber and blow it up in her face like a balloon, but it was pointless. Ella was so serious, she'd probably nail him for wasting latex. *You should be recycling those*, she'd say. *Rinsing them out*. He threw up his arms in mock horror.

"Are you saying I'm *irresponsible?*"

"I'm saying your parents were," Ella replied.

"If they'd used one of these, I wouldn't be here," said Gabe.

Ella smiled, bemused, a smile without the energy of laughter. Gabe had wondered who the hell would be so desperate that she'd give a kid to Ella and Lorne, and he pondered what favours they might have asked in return for taking him. He felt ashamed of himself, playing around with a dead rat of a thought, when what he felt in Ella was a pustule of bitterness, swollen, about to burst.

"She paid for it," said Ella.

Gabe told her he had work to do.

Two

It was an ignition key, Sally's remembering her past for him, and it sparked his mind, moved it like a tractor in reverse, rolled it right back into a field of buried questions. Gabe recalled that around the time he'd turned eighteen he had begun to dig and hoe, to loosen the soil around his American roots. He knew he was adopted, and yet he wasn't ready to find out more about his real parents or the circumstances of his birth. In his room were books about the social unrest of the sixties, albums of Bob Dylan and Phil Ochs, posters for *Platoon* and *Full Metal Jacket*. With these in mind, he began to shape his father and mother out of the molten lava that still bubbled up from the cracks and fissures of those years.

One by one he recalled the slain heroes of that time, wondering if any of them had left a woman with a child. R.F.K. shot in '68 — now there was a possible contender, except for the fact that Gabe had been born in the gentle spring of 1967, a year before the hell of My Lai and the convention in Chicago that ended in chaos; three years before the Kent State killings. He couldn't recall anything cataclysmic that had happened in the few months before his birth, any gunned-down martyrs for peace or civil rights who might have left a newborn kid behind.

More to the point, he'd been born in Toronto, in a time of serenity and celebration. Four months after his birth, Canada had turned a sweet one hundred, the whole country like foam over the brim of some huge invisible beer mug, and everyone had been *young* then, *happy*, said Ella. She always remarked on this with sorrow in her voice, as if, after the summer of 1967, youth as a stage of life on earth had perished, as if they'd exhausted the world's reserves of fun forever. Gabe thought of the two of them, Lorne and Ella, as lively as a batch of fresh cement. He couldn't imagine them laughing.

Ella told him that, in a rare moment of sentimental excess, she and Lorne had taken him down to city hall for Canada's centennial, for his first skyful of Roman candles and giant exploding chrysanthemums. There was no room in the square and they ended up behind the provincial courthouse, in a giant concrete flying-saucer flowerpot, wrecking the petunias, rolling joints, singing mock verses of "God Save the Queen" and staring at the giddy lights above them. Gabe dozed while Ella plucked a flower and pinned it to his shirt with a tiny Canadian flag. Just four months old, the youngest flower child, his sleepy head lolling in a wreath of fumes.

Twenty years later, Gabe went to see *Platoon*. He wheedled the poster off the usher at the Carlton Cinema, took it home and hung it on his bedroom wall. Then he tried out his grunt scenario, sprawling on his bed, staring up at the two huge dog tags dangling from the chain, imagining the whistle and thunk of mortar shells as his poor dad might have heard them, waiting for the one with his name on it to come crashing through the roof of the townhouse east of Avenue Road. Sometimes he would imagine that his father had saved a buddy's life, tripped on a mine to save him. *Dear Annie*, said the letter found in his duffel bag, *I love you and miss you. Send me a picture when the baby's born.* The shell whined, struck its target, exploded into a knock. A soft voice, Lorne's.

"Are you awake?" How Lorne paid visits, just showed up. Gabe asked him in, followed his eyes to the dog tags dangling on the poster.

"Good God," said Lorne.

"Bad taste, you mean."

"*The Globe and Mail* says it 'stinks with verisimilitude.' I would drop the last two words," Lorne remarked.

Gabe sat up. "I'm into my *roots*, dude."

"I noticed." Lorne said it as if he had, his voice quiet. He gazed out the window at a point so distant that it might have been light from another galaxy, a vanished place. He seemed to become a young man once again, his eyes clear and intent, his calm Grecian statue of a face etched in thought — what Gabe called his Elgin Marble face, lost and imprisoned in a Lorne-museum; his exile face.

"I went to Vietnam, you know," said Lorne.

Gabe stared at him. "You were in the Marines?" he asked.

"Good Lord, no," said Lorne. "I was on a film shoot. *Sowing the Wind.*"

"That's *your* film?"

"You've seen it?" Lorne asked.

"Not yet. You're on my course next term."

Lorne's documentary had been shown on TV in 1966. It was a counterculture icon in Canada; everyone over the age of forty had seen it. Critics said it exploded on the screen, a cluster-bomb of a film, *an independent view of Vietnam*, one reviewer said (meaning it wasn't American). Just the same, it had been nominated for an Emmy and had later won some arty citation at Cannes. Its closing shot was supposed to be the kicker, not the bombing scene, the camera's eye in the cockpit, the quick, ugly streaks of phosphorus and napalm. What grabbed the TV audience was a long and very slow pan across a forest of bone-bare trees grey and matted as spiderwebs, and sick with infestation, the calm voice of the pilot explaining that pesticides were used here to deprive the enemy of cover. *Woods don't burn in Vietnam*, the pilot said. *The trees have the wrong kind of resins, there's too much rain.* Gabe had seen the stills of this shot, had heard that the Americans threw everything they had at this forest: farm chemicals, gasoline, fire. Viewers in this northern country of dry prairie and wilderness were stunned. *The crop-duster scene*, they called it. They'd have to take that shot apart in film class.

Lorne never spoke about *Sowing the Wind*, never bragged that it was his. Maybe it was because he no longer worked in film, or maybe it was modesty about the prizes it had won, or boredom with the whole thing, or just that they didn't see that much of each other, he and his dad. "Hey, dude, you're famous," said Gabe, but Lorne told him, "It wasn't for me, that kind of work," and he looked away with troubled eyes.

Gabe realized that he must have known the film was Lorne's,

must have heard him mention it before. There he was, his mind as porous as a sponge, mopping up his dad's history, wringing it out and sloshing it around in the big bucket of his own imaginings. Not some made-up father, Lorne in Nam. It was just too strange, the whole thing.

"I was only there a few months," Lorne said.

"You'll tell me all about it, eh?"

Lorne shook his head. "It's on film." He looked tired then, his usual self, sleep-deprived and raw as butchered meat. His eyes were fixed on the poster for *Platoon*, his hands were clenched one inside the other, and Gabe felt for him because he'd been courageous once, nuts enough to chase a war. He wondered if his dad had flashbacks and horrible nightmares, if that was why he drank too much and slept in too many beds. He wished he could talk to him, touch him. His hands felt cold and he shoved them in his pockets.

The following day, Lorne came by while Gabe was out and left him his video. It was a sorrowful film for Gabe to watch, and afterwards he thought of his imagined father, lost there. He called Lorne and thanked him, and Lorne told him in resigned and quiet words that he'd been too old to be a hippie or a soldier, but not too old to see what was what. "The eye of the camera sees everything at once," he said. "Our own eyes shrink from doing that." Remorse in his voice, despondency. Gabe heard it even then.

Three

Years later, Gabe knew that his real father had gone to Vietnam, had more than likely died there. He wanted to watch Lorne's video again and feel both his ghostly fathers in the shadows.

He called Dawn, invited her over to watch it with him, but he couldn't find the video. He found two big 16-mill cans labelled *Sowing the Wind*, but when he opened them up he found a cache of photographs, an unsorted mess. This was unlike his fastidious dad, who packed his work in boxes and files, who dated and sorted and labelled everything. *Stuff he never got to, movie stills, who knows*, Gabe thought. Something about it felt contrived — snapshots in a film can, some phony statement, Lorne being weird. Shit, he wanted to see that flick. Gabe slapped the lid back on the can, shoved it aside, kept looking.

While he ferreted through Lorne's things, Dawn called to tell him that she had an emergency, one of her mall kids needed help, maybe he could meet her after work. It was just as well, he thought. Still searching, he opened Lorne's office closet, the shelves neat with squat cardboard boxes, each with its own hand-lettered label: *phone, hydro, income tax returns*. He shook his head. On the floor, under the bottom shelf, he noticed a green garbage bag.

Puzzled, he tapped it with the toe of his boot. It felt as if it were stuffed with newspapers, lightweight. Yanking it out, he opened the tie, dug into the bag with both hands, then shuddered at the cold, dead touch of what he felt, the celluloid cut and snipped, looped and knotted in a hundred cockeyed directions like a string of nooses, and Gabe sank to the floor, his face against his knees, because he knew without looking what it was.

He could have wept but he was sick of crying, sick of the whole thing. *More ways than one to kill yourself.* He rooted around in the bag of scraps for the leader and the credits to the film; found along with it a videocassette, its tape snarled and dangling out of the holes.

It had occurred to him before that Lorne was insane. He had to be nuts to jump into a fire, either that or high on something, but this was how insanity *felt*, a tangible thing you could pick up and hold, a thing it wasn't normal to pick up and hold, like an eyeball out of its socket or a finger severed from a hand. Gabe wondered what the hell had made his father go mad, made him cut up his prizewinning film, the only film he'd ever made. Not exactly the last copy on earth; not exactly a rational act, if Lorne was destroying evidence, say. Gabe felt bewildered.

I went to Vietnam, you know. Lorne's words, but he wasn't a vet and, besides, most vets had ended up more or less sane. *What the hell went wrong with him?* Even the question made him afraid.

ꝏ꣠

The next morning, Gabe returned to the film can and opened it again. There were a lot of pictures, some of them familiar ones that snagged and pulled at his memory like dreams he couldn't recall on waking. Other pictures troubled him more. Pornography, he thought, but he looked again and changed his mind. Nothing degrading or out of the ordinary; a series Lorne had taken of a faceless, small-breasted, boyish-looking girl; more a collection of body parts than a composite human being. *Lorne must've been into botany then* — her legs framing a soft sphagnum patch, an orchid shape. It was better than Mappelthorpe's cold white lily, this human bloom that Lorne had plucked from a body and pressed into film. Mouth dry, he imagined Dawn, then put the pictures aside, face down.

Underneath this set was one that Lorne hadn't taken, a photo of him standing at a podium with a light-haired man who might have passed for Lorne's dad. The guy was handing him a plaque. On the back of the photo, Lorne had written *Groves Island*

American Legion Award, presented by Glen Groves, 1954. First photography prize.

Well holy Jesus, there he was. His granddad, a good-looking man who stood tall, his eyes crinkled up in the corners, a high-beam power-of-the-atom smile blasting out of his face. Kind eyes, but sad too; the sad part *inactive*, as they say with computers when there's more than one window on a screen. Waiting to be clicked on, that sadness.

Lorne *knew* him.

Attached to this photo, Gabe found a manila envelope. *For Sally*, the note on the envelope read. *I meant to let you have these long ago.*

🎗🎗

Sally, I'm faxing this note through Fran because I've found some of Lorne's pictures taken of you and your family. They're yours, if you would like to have them. If this is very private turf, I'm really sorry. Death sure kicks up shit, I know that now.

These are pictures from your tenth birthday and a few shots of the plane with the banner. I didn't realize that Lorne was there, and I hope you did, so this won't be a shock. Maybe you don't want to see them. It's just that Lorne left me in charge of his stuff, and your name was on this.

🎗🎗

Gabe wondered why Lorne had left them in the can, these pictures. *Sowing the Wind.* He shivered.

There was a group of photographs with the title "Hunter's Camp," dated by year only, 1966. The studies had the bland composure of humdrum things: a tidy campsite with a tent, a picnic hamper, pots and pans, the remains of a damped fire. More unnerving was a clothesline strung between two trees, on it a pair of swimsuits, a man's and a woman's. In late daylight the shadows gave them the tainted look of decomposing flesh, a pair of carcasses strung up to dry. All of the studies played with this idea, all except for the last and the worst, the one that felt prescient, that frightened Gabe the most.

It showed a woman in a clearing, setting a picnic table. Lorne had caught her body spinning towards the camera, shock in her wild hair, the trembling plate that wanted to fly from her hand. She had a stricken look on her face, as if the camera had slapped her. The photo was blurred, a lucky accident, a mistake that worked as if the unintended movement were an act of violence, the odd camera angle knocking the woman backwards, to the side. Gabe wondered what had caused her startled look, how Lorne's camera had come to witness it. He put it down, picked up a photo of a beautiful wooden home in the treetops, a pond below, shot in the ominous light before a storm, before a wind of hurricanes and thunder. It too was dated 1966. *The eye of the camera sees everything at once.*

Sally, I was with you then.

🐦🐦

Dear Gabe,

...Yes, I knew Lorne was present on my tenth birthday. And on many other occasions, both as a reporter and as a friend. As for these and any other family pictures (or shots of me), please keep them in a safe place. I may want them later on but, for now, consider them yours.

Sally

🐦🐦

In the film can were some photos that Gabe couldn't decipher. They included several black-and-white shots of the aftermath of a fire, enlarged to various sizes and formats. Maybe more than one fire from the looks of it; some of the pages curling with age, some new. There were no dates. Gabe pulled out one of the oldest, staring at the blackened, twisted tree trunks, the charred remains of a dwelling, its beams exposed, its roof caved in, splintered debris thrusting up from the ground like the middle finger of a clenched fist, as if the ground were cursing the fire. There was ash you could feel with your eyes and almost taste, a thick grey coat of it powdering the earth like mould on stale bread. Gabe thought of *Sowing the Wind,* but this wasn't its long, slow pan across the desolation of a ruined forest. *Woods don't burn in Vietnam.* It might be another movie still, a shot of a village torched.

He was about to put it aside when he noticed that the angle of this picture looked skewed. He stared at it from a distance, then looked at it up close. It was when he stood up and tossed it back into the pile on the floor that he saw this episode of human grief as Lorne had, from the cool remove of a plane. Only this was a funeral, a burial rite of someone, something, a death that wanted more than watching, wanted someone to bear witness. *Here it happened. Remember me.* Gabe did what the silence told him, knelt down, touched the picture as if it were a face.

A Witness II

One

Sally had known Lorne Winter most of her life. A photojournalist for the *Island Banner*, he'd borne loving witness to her father's treehome, her mother's painted glass, the disappearance of her father's plane. In covering these stories, in these public acts of remembering, he had become for Sally a comfort, a healer of loss, a pair of eyes that would never stop seeing, a man who could attest to the fact that her parents had lived, that she had not imagined or dreamt them.

After Lorne's death, Sally wasn't surprised or troubled by what Gabe retrieved of her past. It was a relief to her that Lorne had saved this record of her early life, since she had lost all of her photos in the sixties fire. She had no tangible evidence that her family had existed, no photos or gifts or souvenirs. Her early life was a careless wind that would never blow her way again. Or so she had thought.

She was seventeen when Sister Frances introduced her to her brother at a parish dance. "A friend of your dad's," she explained. Lorne was standing by the punch bowl, a tall, sturdy man, his blond hair a coppery colour in the light, a fox's mane. He was no denizen of Holy Rosary Parish and he seemed amused to find himself here, sleeves rolled up like a working man's, as if dancing with young women were his trade. Lorne smiled, uncapped a bottle of beer, swigged it down and leaned against the wall with his free hand, his shoulder raised as if he were used to bearing the weight of a camera. It made him look nonchalant, that prop-up-the-wall slouch of his, too worldly for a parish dance. She felt his admiring gaze. Lorne's eyes were an ocean wave, all energy and undertow.

"Sally Groves," he said. "You've grown up." He asked her if she'd like to dance.

"I'm not a good dancer," she told him.

Lorne glanced at her long hair. "It'll dance," he said. "Come on."

It was a slow dance. As he guided her around the floor, he asked her about school and her studies and where her brother was these days. When the band stopped playing, she held onto him, as if the dance were not yet over. She hadn't planned on doing this, had no idea of the desperation lodged in the tightness of her hands.

"Tell me how you knew my dad," she said.

Lorne appeared hesitant, grave. "Only with my camera," he answered. "But I knew him well."

Sally looked into his eyes. In the moment before he looked away from her, she saw the pale blue bolt of silk that the sky had been on that hot June day, and she felt the heat on her father's shell-white plane and the shimmer of light on its wings. Lorne in slow motion floating across the tarmac, the ripple of his camera strap trailing beside him like the tether of an astronaut walking in space, Lorne grabbing her father's arm, pointing to the sign, to the picture he wanted.

"My mother said I should have flown with him," said Sally.

"God help us, no," said Lorne. He took her hand and clasped it in both of his, as if she might still fly away. His intensity stirred her. Not knowing what to say, she asked him what sort of photos he took now. He looked shy, said he made his living as a free-lance photojournalist, hoped to work in documentary film, also liked working the artist's side of his craft now and then. They danced again, and Lorne reached out and touched her hair, his hand as weightless as a leaf. She imagined floating on her back in the warm water, looking up into the sky that was his face, into his eyes as blue and serene as twilight.

"I used to love shoots at your house," he told her. "You were a wonderful family."

Sally didn't answer. Few visitors came by now (none with cameras), even when she was home from boarding school. It felt as if her parents' flight had made their beautiful woods grief-laden, no place for entertaining guests. She wondered if this might change.

"You could come visit," she said.

Lorne smiled. "I'd be coming home," he replied.

His words touched her with an unexpected gentleness, as if he were dressing a wound. They danced and, when the lights dimmed, he let his hand rest on the back of her head, so she could feel him pressing her face against his chest. She'd never been this close to anyone. He whispered *Sally* right into her ear, let it melt there, sweet as trouble.

He told her he was twenty-nine, twelve years older than she was. Something stirred in the depths of her, the light throb of a butterfly's wings. She wondered if Sister Frances was watching.

☙☙

Groves Island, N.Y.
10 August 1963

Dear Mike,

I can't believe you're in Guam, and I hope the Air Force is treating you well. My news is that Sister Frances introduced me to her brother, Lorne. I can't tell you how reassuring it is to talk about Dad's disappearance with *anyone*, let alone a newspaperman, a fellow witness. We talked a *lot*. Lorne's an army brat, he's lived all over the world, courtesy of Uncle Sam Movers. He tells me home is where he points his lens. I like that.

I told Lorne there's no proof Dad's dead, that maybe he went on retreat and became a monk, who knows?

Do you know what he said?

"He left you his beautiful mind" is what he said.

I was so touched by his kindness....

☙☙

Andersen AFB, Guam
12 September 1963

Dear Sally,

...I think about you and worry. I'm real glad you've got Sister Frances because you're still a kid and need a mother, and she's almost an aunt, but I'm on the other side of the ocean, way too far away to help you. What I'm leading up to is Sister's kid brother, Lorne. I mean, OK, if you want to be friends, that's none of my business, but I feel underneath that my sister is getting a crush on a guy who's way the hell too experienced for a teenage kid. He said some real nice things, but he could be feeding you a line. I mean, how would you know if he was for real? They sure don't teach you stuff like that in boarding school, and you've never had a boyfriend. He's twelve years older, and you're impressionable, you should start out by dating a guy your own age, so he's not too far ahead of you and giving you ideas.

Will you do me a favour and talk this over with Sister Fran, she knows him best, huh? Please don't do anything dumb, sis, you don't want to get a reputation. I'm sorry if I hurt your feelings, but I have to say I keep thinking of Mom and Dad, what happened to them. I guess I always worried they were crazy and we might inherit it. I love you, you're my kid sis and I don't want to lose you. Here's a big hug from me, OK? I feel so bad it's taken me years to say this.

Two

Lorne felt himself shudder, jittery as lightning. A warm, humid day, too warm. He sat on a park bench in Washington Square wishing it would rain.

He had saved her life.

He remembered the island airstrip, the hot gleam of the day her father had vanished. There's a white glare to this memory, a blindness, its surreal refractions of light in the mind, like film shot into the sun. His eyes could still feel the hot white dazzle on the plane, the blank white of Glen's face, the mesmerizing instant before his mind shook him loose from the grip of his eyes, from watching what he knew was bound to happen. Something — instinct or the grace of God — rattled his composure, collapsed the distance between hesitation and the reach of a hand, pushed him running out to the tarmac, his camera dangling like a broken limb, chasing Glen Groves before he climbed into the plane. "Let me get a shot of your kid, OK?"

"I'll go get her," Glen answered. "I'm taking her up." The face Lorne saw before him didn't belong to a loving father or to a demented one. It was a mirage, a strange incandescence that came and went. *Guy's hung over*, Lorne told himself, *I should lay off*, but instead he reached out and touched Glen's shoulder. "It's her birthday," Lorne said, with a nudge in his voice, and he pointed to the tangled letters hitched to the back of the plane. "She won't get to see it."

"Even worse," Glen said, "you won't get your picture." Lorne felt anxious, sick with defeat, uncertain what battle he was fighting. A moment later, Glen motioned him over to the viewing stand, where he talked to Sally and told her he'd be back for her.

Then he waved Lorne away, jumped in the plane and started preparing for takeoff.

Now Lorne wondered if he could have stopped Glen also.

Everyone had said there was something wrong with this taciturn man. Al Bates at the *Banner* thought he was still crazy from the war. "They only let him fly 'cause his name's Groves," he remarked. "Should see him," said the Legion post commander. "Flies like the Japs are still on his tail." Glen was living in a treehome, most people thought that was nuts too, but Lorne didn't. He felt it was an avant-garde statement of the anti-home, a snub to the bourgeois fifties. It was all the rest that was madness.

All the rest is gossip, said Fran. *Envy. Shame on you for listening.*

Except that he felt sure Sally was alive because he'd listened.

He'd listened because Glen had been kind to him, had welcomed him into his home. He'd been a good man with a gentle wife and two innocent children, all of it balm to a loner who came from a hundred places. It was a paradox that this shy and gifted family was news on this island, and he smiled at the memory of Katherine, who felt it proper to serve tea and cake to a newspaperman, as if in return for a kindness. He remembered the picnic when the treehome was completed, the gemlike array of casseroles and salads, how he'd taken photo after photo of that brilliant and artful treehome of Glen's. "It's the family," said Glen, "that makes it beautiful."

I belong here, lost in the trees. On the day of the picnic, that crazy thought had stuck in his mind. Later, seeing a rock by the side of the road, Lorne had kicked it as hard as he could, as if that might dislodge his idiot's notion. A rock he'd been at the tip of his father's boot, a boy to be made a man of, a child who chased squirrels and pelted them with stones. How unlike Glen his father was, a man whose power Lorne couldn't escape. Once, in the forest, he had trapped a squirrel and cracked its skull with a boulder. Afterwards he had knelt beside it until the blood dried on his hands, until he realized that his father's cruelty was also his.

He lived alone and knew he always would. The Groves' picnic had been long ago. The gentle family was gone.

Yet Sally was alive and he wanted her.

Lorne got up from the bench and walked away, kicked at

pebbles, shoved his hands in his pockets. *Leave her alone*, he thought. There were plenty of bars in the Village, signs saying *Rooms upstairs*, young girls Sally's age he could enjoy. He crossed Seventh Avenue against the light, didn't look, heard a honk, a screech of brakes as a taxi driver veered and swerved. "Fucking asshole, watch where you're going," the guy yelled. That night, in a stranger's bed, he heard the cabby curse him in his sleep.

🦉🦉

"If you come, we won't be alone," Sally told Lorne when he called.

When Sally told Sister Frances that Lorne had asked to walk with her on the beach, Sister pulled out a cigarette and lit up. Sally stared at her.

"I didn't know you *smoked*."

"Only at times like this," she said.

"They let you smoke in the convent?" Sally asked.

"I've cut down from a pack a day before I joined the order," she replied. "Just tell me where the binoculars are."

"In the treehome. Why?"

Sister took a deep drag. "Soviet ICBMs, that's why. You just never know."

It was Labour Day weekend when Lorne came, and Sally took him down to the beach below the embankment on the east side of her family's land — necking country, her brother used to call it. It was not a true embankment, not the bank of a river, but that was her dad's name for what it looked like when the high spring tides washed up to the sandy base of the slope. Eons ago, the glacier had pulverized rocks and silt, and the tides had heaped up the residue here when the ice melted back. "A ridge of dirt and sand," her father had said. "A geological junk-pile. Cape Cod, same thing. All those hilly islands, tides and wind'll get 'em all."

One day the embankment would be gone.

Sally told Lorne this, then took him for a walk down the steep path that led through the tangle of scrub brush and thistles to the water. On the north side of the beach were hiding-places, outcroppings of rocks and boulders, an isolated cove with an unused dock, nothing more than a wooden heap of splinters. Her parents had never repaired it, never made it safe. "Now it's family history," she said. "We like to keep some things as they were." She felt Lorne's gaze and she looked away. They were out of the range of binoculars here, the tree cover much too thick to penetrate. She led the way across the embankment, to the safety of Sister Fran's eyes.

At the water's edge the tide was out, and the beach was strewn with driftwood and yellow-bladdered seaweed. Her parents had never raked this beach, had left it good for combing: a trove of gleaming clam and mussel shells, wet pebbles, a gull's dredging of eyeless fishheads, delicate ladders of bones. Lorne bent down and took his sandals off.

"You'll hurt your feet," she told him.

"It's all right."

"If my mother were here, she'd yell at you. '*Maudit garçon.*'" Sally laughed, but Lorne didn't.

How odd his behaviour seemed to her. To his mind no doubt a harmless test of stamina, but her mother would have said other things, would have made her and Mike put on their sandals *right this minute, mes enfants. If you bleed, the salt is the worst.* Yet Lorne walked barefoot on rocks, on broken shells, as if there were no imprint of a mother in his soul. He seemed not to notice the ache of his feet, the swell of waves, the wheeling and screeching of gulls overhead.

"It doesn't hurt?" she asked him.

"My father was in the army," he told her. "We walked like this."

Sally went down to the water's edge, took off her sandals and waded in. The tide was out and she ran across the packed mud, the sand-spit rising under the ripple of water. Dropping down again, she felt the quick, cold hit of the sea on her skin. The salt water held her up like a pair of hands, the cool and the wet of it, the last joyful dip and lunge of her body into summer. She swam out and back, then strode on to the beach, her clothes dripping.

"You should have come," she said.

"I can't swim."

Sally was puzzled. "I've never met anyone who can't swim."

Lorne looked sad. "Did your mother teach you?"

"My parents both."

"See how kind they were, your parents."

Sally said yes, they were kind. She stretched out on a rock to dry herself, saw her own bent leg as graceful as a heron's, felt Lorne's eyes moving across her as she undid her barrette and shook out her hair. Then she remembered Sister Frances sitting in the treehome, watching. She felt relieved that she wasn't alone with the intensity of his presence, with her own desire to draw close to him.

As she thought this, Sally noticed Lorne sitting, legs outstretched, the soles of his feet scraped and bloodied. Remembering her mother, she felt Katherine's hands inside of hers as she picked up a large clamshell, went down to the water's edge and filled it. On very hot days when she and Mike were small, their mother would sprinkle their feet with water. They'd try to imitate her, filling the shell at the water's edge, toddling and spilling most of it, making her laugh. Now Sally could sense her mother in the kind touch of the sea, feeling herself as she had been then, a cleansed and grateful child. Carrying the shell, she squatted beside Lorne in the sand and poured the water over his feet.

"Your parents must have taught you that too," he said.

"My mother."

He took her hand and kissed it.

They walked back across the beach and up the embankment to the treehome. On the porch they felt like birds in a nest among the boughs, joined to all that was seen and unseen, to his unobtrusive sister in the house, the rustle of her skirts like wind in leaves.

"I remember your father," Lorne said. "Lifting you up to the sky."

"You saw that?"

"I did." His hand touched the porch fence, his fingertips resting on the grain of the wood.

"I feel my father here," said Sally.

"What will become of this place when you leave home?"

She felt perplexed, confused. "I don't know."

He looked out over the treetops. "Think of me," he whispered to the air.

The breeze caught and shifted her hair so that it blew across Lorne's face. He reached out and held it. Sally pretended not to notice how he let it brush and stroke his eyes, his cheeks, his lips, how he let it slip through his hands like parachute silk, like the strings of an elegant kite. Sally didn't breathe, closed her eyes, opened them again. Treetops above and below them, a net of green light.

Three

A few weeks later, Lorne sat alone in his Village loft, as spare a place as a barren field, a tree stripped of its leaves. He liked this space as if it were a vessel, one that held the still constraint of silence. Except for his camera and his darkroom he had few possessions, only a low ebony table, thick woven mats on the floor, a black-framed rice-paper screen behind which he slept. This was his living space and studio, high-ceilinged, vast and spotless. Its plainness was broken by tall windows, their frames making shadow-crosses on the hardwood floor, a shape that made Lorne wish for clouds, for rain.

Years earlier, before he went into the army, Fran had given him a wooden cross, a small, plain icon. Seeing that her gift was handcrafted and in very good taste, he kept it on his wall until he began to realize that its artfulness distressed him. It had the unbounded simplicity of a page that wanted writing, letting him feel and imagine too much pain. His mind played with other kinds of crosses, vertical-horizontal forms. He thought of the four directions of the compass, recalled that the British rood had started as a tree bough, imagined the sturdy crossbeams of a roof and the four bright stars that formed the Southern Cross. It didn't help. Crosshairs, gunsights, the shape was too powerful to bend out of its laden past, too redolent of suffering. He took the icon down. Banished now, it cast its shadow everywhere. He closed his eyes again.

Fran in the treehome, watching over Sally, protecting her.

"Your eyes are blessed," she told him once. "You see more than you know."

"Oh, but that's not a blessing." Life had teeth that ripped and tore at him. No sight, no eyes.

Sally, hear this. See me as I am.

On the table was a letter from Toronto. *Dear Lorne…thank you for hosting me while I was passing through. What a high — reporting the Washington march, getting to see Martin Luther King, coming to NYC. Loved the Village, loved staying with you. You told me you're restless. Come up north, try it out for a year. I can get you freelance jobs at Maclean's I have connections at the art college, the CBC…. We're "un-American" and proud of it, baby. Love you. Ella.*

A woman his age enticed him with her sheet of platinum hair, its metallic flash. A newly minted coin was Ella, bright and precious. *In here, America,* and she laughed as she pushed his head down and swung her legs wide open like a gate.

Sally was better off without him.

Fran, take care of her. No one had taken care of Fran, no one had given her comfort in trouble. Sally he'd protected more than his sister, and ever since the day Glen had vanished, he'd tried to forget this failing. Instead he'd warmed the chill, hard limits of himself with the good he'd done and was capable of doing. Sally was a candle he could cup in his hands, a soft burning light, a frail belief that he was not beyond hope.

Fran had hope, even in her time of desolation. Eighteen years old, locked in her room after she came home one night, her blonde hair dishevelled, her clothes torn and bloodied. Her mother, face as pale as bread flour, told her that young ladies never drank or smoked or took rides in convertibles, that she had to be more modest in dress and never flirt with soldiers. "I didn't," Fran wept. Her father left for the officers' club and slammed the door behind him, leaving his wife to deal with it. "It just isn't possible," their mother said to Lorne. "Fran has to be lying." She handed him a skeleton key and told him to lock his sister in her room. Lorne did. Fran kicked and pounded on the door.

There were three men. She was *accosted* — her word for what they did to her. Lorne, her jailer, felt her helplessness, felt weak with excitement, then remorseful, sick. He shoved a note under her door. *Point the soldiers out to me,* he wrote. *I'll hunt and shoot them down.*

Fran sent the note right back. *Liar. Coward. You'll open this door first.*

How ashamed he was.

Yet Fran had dug and scraped at the hard root of hope, had yanked it up from the cold ground, fought hard for this meagre scrap of food, for the lost, sweet taste of living. She had been a friend to Sally and her mother, their confidante in suffering. He glanced at Ella's letter. *Dear Ella, I will come,* he'd write, and she'd answer, *Fuck me, America,* and laugh.

He felt so little hope. He shut his eyes, saw gunsights, crosshairs. He tasted the salt on his lips.

Oh but Sally.

Four

New York City
10 October 1963

Dear Sally,

I am enclosing with this letter something I feel you should have. Here are copies of the original photos of you and your family, taken on the day of your father's disappearance. Accept these as a token of respect and friendship. Your father was a remarkable man, and I greatly admire his wonderful treehome. I hope school is going well for you. Any thoughts about college yet? Don't forget to talk to Fran about your future. As you know, she's very fond of you, as I am.

Your friend,
Lorne

Greenwich, Conn.
14 October 1963

Dear Lorne,

Thanks so much for the photos. I showed them to your big sister and she told me you're a very gifted man. In spite of your different callings, the two of you are much alike. You're both alive to what's in people's hearts.

As for college, I'm thinking about going to Canada, my mother's country. I like nature study, and Canada is pretty well all nature, the way my mother described it to me. Most of all, I want to study flying. Sister Frances would like me to get a degree first. *Your father set up a trust fund, he meant for you and Mike to study, dear*, she said. (Study as opposed to ripping up the sky, I heard that in her voice.) It would be nice to live near Algonquin Park, in Ontario. My mom painted its trees and wildlife on glass bells *so that you could hear the glitter of the snow*, she'd say. My parents flew over it when they were young, and I long to be close to their youth.

Peace, and write soon.
Sally

New York City
20 October 1963

Dear Sally,

May I recommend Toronto? I know the university and I've toyed with living there. It's only a few hours' drive from Algonquin Park, and I share your love of that beautiful place.

I read with misgivings your comment about myself and Fran. My sister and I are not alike. Her goodness is the real thing and she's always been this way. Same set of parents, same string of moves all over the world, but life has somehow taught her different lessons. I don't know why this is. All of us receive our parents' traits, but we're more than film, mere prints and replications of our families, at least I hope we are. You're more than the child of your parents. And so is Fran. I must decide if the same can be said of me. Meanwhile, your friendship gives me hope that it can.

Take care,
Lorne

Five

Lorne came to her in dreams.

Sister Frances will smell it, she'll see right through my head, she'll go and have a nicotine fit. Sally wondered what Lorne dreamt, the man who in her dreams undressed himself, then asked to brush her hair. *It's not your fault what you dream,* she had heard a priest say once. *No snacks at bedtime, they'll give you nightmares,* her mother had said long ago, which would have made those dreams her fault, so she didn't snack. She drank warm milk, prayed for a clean heart and dreamt Lorne naked anyway. She tried not to worry. Dreams were symbolic, and there were messages and prophecies in dreams, she'd heard that too.

Sally concluded that she was in love, and love was a gift from God, one it would be rude and unseemly to reject. Yet if this was love, it was not romantic, not as personal a thing as she'd expected. It felt inexorable, a law of physics, as if she were a moon and Lorne were a planet and they were leaning into the sun's gravity as reeds bend into wind. Love was a mysterious yearning, a tugging at the body's core. Sally wondered if Lorne felt this.

It was November and this was Greenwich, Connecticut, and she sat on the old wooden bench inside the station. It was warm for this time of year, a bright autumn day, and she wriggled out of her school blazer, folded it into a neat rectangle, placed it over her arm and watched the afternoon sun play on the window. She was waiting for the New Haven train, the 2:55 for Linden. A weekend home to visit with Sister Frances; she half guessed why the woman wanted to see her, and she was nervous. Later she recalled that it was early to be out of school, that Maryville was having a field day for the junior grades, that most of the Friday classes had been cancelled. Sister Peter had told her she could leave early. She'd even found a parent to drive her to the station. Fussy Sister Peter, her face as red and pointy as a lobster's claw, remarking on the sassy tilt of Sally's navy wool beret, *A lady always wears a hat, but ladies aren't sailors, dear, now are they?*

Sally had been standing in the hallway, straightening her beret under the watchful principal's eye. Sister Peter; in an hour or so her voice would become a ship's rail in a rocking storm. Stern guardian of Maryville's reputation; *A lady on a train never smokes,* Sister said, *never raises her voice, always takes a seat, and not on someone's lap, good heavens.* By the end of the day Sally would be glad for the old woman's life. She would remember the porter who lifted her suitcase onto the train, she would honour the ticket collector, she would be grateful for passengers, for Sister Frances, for the invisible presence of everyone on earth. Yet, at the time she boarded the train, she was thinking only of Lorne.

Seated by the window, she watched the train chug out of Greenwich, then pull into Port Chester. It was only as they crossed the bridge into the white-clapboard town of Rye that Sally realized that the conductor had not come around for tickets, had not even bellowed, *Passengers on at Greenwich, have your tickets ready,* echoing another of Sister Peter's dictums: *A lady hands her ticket over promptly.*

The world was not right. She was the only passenger in this car. It was as if she were riding the last train on earth.

She wondered if anyone had gotten on at Rye, then turned to see the ticket collector standing alone near the entrance to the train. The man didn't seem to care about her ticket. He didn't even realize she was here. He was leaning his arm against a billboard, his blue-capped head resting on it, and he was sobbing, tears etching lines in his face like the veins in a brown, fallen leaf. Sally went over to him and asked him what was wrong.

The man found his handkerchief and dried his eyes. Then he stuck his hand in his pocket and pulled out a small transistor radio, holding it out like a book in which she could read the thing that troubled him.

"The President's shot dead, miss."

Sally couldn't breathe.

"I took his ticket once," said the conductor. "J.F.K. Right here on this train."

She felt Sister Peter tapping her arm. *Courtesy, girls, is the beginning of compassion.* She held out her ticket.

"Would you like this, sir?" He thanked her, and his eyes filled with tears again. He told her the world was a terrible place. She told him how sorry she was, just as if this man had lost a loved one. Which he had.

Sally took her seat again, pressed her face to the sunny window, but she no longer saw the sun there, only the stops clattering by, Harrison, then Mamaroneck. She watched the blurred images before the moving train, watched as her father's plane vanished into the sky while her mother turned away from them, walking north towards her country and her death. She pressed her face so hard into the glass that she felt she was weeping rain, a smudge of passengers, dark skies, the flags at half-staff, this sorrowful river flowing through her body.

People were getting on the train now, talking, panicky, *Who the hell would do a thing like that?* She was weeping all of them out of her, she was turning into rain and grief. In the cool glass she felt her mother's cheek against her own. For a moment she could not recall who'd died.

ᔕᔕ

When Sally got off the train, Lorne was there to meet her. She hadn't expected him and she saw that he was pale, haggard. "Sally dear," he said, and took her in his arms.

Stunned by the news, he couldn't work, he told her. There were traffic tie-ups downtown, windows open, people hanging out like wash on a line, in a flap, in a crow's chatter of questions. *Who did it? What the hell happened?* He knew he shouldn't ridicule the same grief he felt himself, but at times like this he couldn't stand incessant talk, he couldn't.

Knowing she was here for the weekend, he had decided to

drive up to Linden, chance it, try to meet her train. Cars were moving off the East River Drive, the Cross-Bronx, the Hutch; people hurrying indoors as they do in a sudden downpour, turning on TVs and radios for news, but he felt their panic and wanted to flee. He had come straight here, pulled his car into a shady cove of beech at the far edge of the railroad's land where no one would disturb him. There he sat with the radio on. He told Sally this as he walked her out to the car, as they turned on the news and listened.

"His poor kids," Sally whispered.

Lorne's head slumped into his arms on the steering wheel. "I don't know why I'm so upset," he said.

Sally thought of the conductor. She told Lorne that he'd wept, and that he could also.

When Lorne sat up, he didn't turn from her gaze, and she saw that he was bereft, just as she'd been for much of her life. It felt to her as if a hurricane had struck the world, had levelled mountains into plains, had made rubble of his age and worldliness, had cast these ruins in a field of desolation, the same barren field as hers.

"What's left that's good in this world?" asked Lorne.

He took her hands in his, pressed them against his damp cheeks, and then his lips. *You, that's what*, he whispered as he kissed her mouth, and she felt the light touch of his hands on her skirt, then underneath. Time dissolved and melted into a cry of pleasure, into blackness. Afterwards she stirred as if she'd been asleep. Lorne stroked her hair.

She couldn't look at him, afraid of what he'd unearthed in her. How the truth had fluttered awake, how she'd let him do this.

"What a sad day," she said.

"Yes," said Lorne. "Yes."

He reached in his pocket for his handkerchief, then dried her cheeks, her eyes.

❧❧

Lorne dropped Sally off at the Linden ferry dock, waited with her for the boat and then drove back into the city. AP had work for him, the funeral in Washington on Monday. At home he thought about Sally, what an idiotic thing he'd done to her. He turned on the TV he kept hidden in the closet. Over and over they showed the slo-mos of the shooting, the President slumped over in the back of the car, his Chanel-suited wife crawling up over the trunk, pulled up by a Secret Service man, God knows what for. He looked away.

Why had he added to the world's grief?

Sally's still a child, she's still at the airport, staring up at the banner.

On his table was the letter from Toronto, still.

Lorne went for a walk, stopped in a bar on Seventh Avenue, bought a drink for a young girl with long hair who took him upstairs. "Let me call you Sally," he said. "Tell me you want me," and he paid her. In his dreams that night, the walls collapsed on him.

In the morning, he wrote to Ella. *I'm coming north,* he wrote. *My country is dying.*

🦜🦜

That night Sally watched TV with the Nolans, but found she had nothing to say about the darkness that had fallen on the world. No words could hold the President's death, its terrible vastness. She sat in the living room, her face in her hands, long past weeping. Mrs. Nolan put her arm around her and made her some camomile tea to help her relax. A sweet and wistful scent to it; Sally had never had it before, and she knew she'd never drink it again without tasting the sorrow of that day.

While they had tea, Eddie Nolan told them that he'd gone down to the Legion Hall and lowered the flag to half-staff. That night Sally dreamt that Mike came home in his Air Force uniform, took a flag and hoisted it upside-down in front of their house. When she asked him why, he said, *It means distress, mayday.*

The following morning, she went to visit Sister Frances.

She took Sally into the convent laundry, as far from the TV room as they could get. She wanted to fold sheets. Sister Fran said she had the heebie-jeebies from too many hours in front of the tube, from the bad news, from the prayers for the dead at vespers. On the floor in front of her was a basket heaped with laundry. She gave it a steel-toed kick and sent it skidding across the room. It stopped in front of the folding table.

"I'm sick of crying," she said.

She told Sally to grab the end of a sheet. The two of them pulled it wide, gave it a brisk snap, then drew it together at the corners for folding. Sheet after sheet — the work had a rhythm and grace that made Sally think of dancing. She told Sister Fran this.

"That was how you met my brother. Dancing."

Sally felt uneasy. She got started on another sheet, mentioned that Lorne had met her at the station.

"Lorne's too old for you."

Sally felt like a sailboat hitting a rough wind, a squall. She was grateful that the sheet almost hid her face, sure that anyone could tell from her look what had happened. Sister Frances took the sheet, put it down on the table, then put her hands on Sally's shoulders.

"Dear, listen to me, I can read your mind. It won't work out. You've both suffered too much."

Sally looked away. "I'd like to be his friend."

"He's had too many girlfriends as it is."

Sally knew sex was something Sister would never discuss unless she had a pack of cigarettes and time to smoke them all. Meanwhile she should at least feel that what she and Lorne had done was a sin. Except that it felt too large a thing for sin or forgiving. What had happened was like the day itself, terrible and speechless. Sister Frances put a hand on her arm.

"You're as lonely as your mother was," she said.

They went back to folding. Sheets everywhere now, on tables and chairs, in baskets, on top of the washers and dryers, lighter-than-air sheets bleaching, drying and folding themselves, impossible in their whiteness.

"I should be a nun too," Sally remarked. "I'd be safe then."

Sister Frances laughed until she wept.

New York City
1 December 1963

Dear Sally,

You've been on my mind because I'm afraid that I may have hurt
you at a painful moment when we both needed comfort. No, I
don't think we did anything wrong, but I feel that I want you as
a friend who's simply a friend, and not meant for exploitation or
pleasure, do you know what I mean? I hope I haven't encouraged
you beyond this.

It was an awful trip, covering the funeral in Washington. I
should have been thrilled. Imagine, my photos in *Life* and *Paris-
Match* and the London *Times*. It seems there's money in this
business of documenting tragedy, in making it comfortable, even
redeeming, for people to watch the grief of others. I photographed J.F.K.'s family, printed the pictures and saw terrible
things in the eyes of Mrs. Kennedy and her children, things too
intimate and painful for the world to see. Yet I sold those pictures
and I was paid well. I have no more principles than anyone else,
and if I were religious I would have to ask God's forgiveness on
the scant hope that he hasn't abandoned us. Some days, Sally, I
don't know where to turn.

I'm enclosing a picture by way of explanation. I apologize for
this depressing letter. I'm writing to tell you that I've decided to
move to Canada. I've been thinking for a while that I have to
begin again in a quiet place, a country that's too young for this
kind of memory. If anything, this event has forced me to ask
myself if I can do more than record the world, if I have some
visual comment to make about its condition. You're a dear friend
to me, Sally. And if you call this friendship, you have mine.

With all best wishes,
Lorne

1995

In that autumn's gusts of bewilderment and pain, Lorne's letter had calmed and relieved her. Sally recalled mulling over his thoughts, honoured that he'd think her intelligent enough to share them. She had no idea what had become of the picture he'd sent. No doubt Gabe would come across a copy in Lorne's effects. The photo was a famous one. It had been published in books about the sixties and a print of it was hanging in the Smithsonian. It was characteristic of Lorne's work, shot at an angle, slightly off-kilter, a distance created between the subject and the eye, as if he'd zoomed in from a rooftop. It was, however, a truthful picture, one that should have given Lorne some relief, some peace.

The photo showed Mrs. Kennedy at the burial ground. A Marine in dress uniform was handing her an American flag folded into a triangle, the flag that had covered the President's casket. What was most telling was the look on her face. It was unguarded and registered deep shock. She had just felt the window of her life slam down, her hands were wrapped and bandaged by this flag, she was in agony, the funeral over, the crowds gone. The chill rest of her life started here, witnessed by the last of the cameras, Lorne's.

Her face showed no forbearance, a word Lorne hated in this context. *What we wanted her to bear for us.* Maybe this was why the photo had never become one of the icons of that time. Missing was the rectitude of the widow's veil and the riderless horse, the accessible sorrow of John-John saluting. It was beyond everything, this darkness.

Lorne's Effects II

One

So why the hell did he jump into a fire?

God, the talent, the way he could see with his camera, did he ever see inside me like that? Gabe thought he should let himself cry and be done with it, but he didn't want to wreck the photograph, and his grief was so hard and long he'd need a goddamn storm sewer to handle the fucking flood. The thought got him out of his rotten mood and almost made him laugh.

He let his hand rest on Jackie Kennedy's face. His dad had lived through a calamity, couldn't have caught this moment if he hadn't come through the dark side of *something* in his life. Christ, Lorne was *young* then, twenty-nine, not much older than himself. Once he'd been a photojournalist, and after the film in Vietnam he'd started to edge away from what he called the mean and bitter world. In his mind Gabe saw Lorne's back turned, a move you make when you're too upset and you can't stand someone to see your face. Good old Lorne; over the years he got more and more artsy and abstract until, by the time he died, no one understood him and everyone thought he was brilliant. He put the photo of Jackie down. Dawn was sitting there watching him. She was off to Edmonton and had come to say goodbye. She looked at the photo.

"Now she's dead too," said Dawn.

"My old man went to the funeral."

"Whose?"

"Kennedy's."

"My folks told me all about him getting shot," she said.

"So big deal, everybody dies," Gabe said. "Or hits the road."

"I'm only going to *Edmonton*," she said. "Come on."

"Polar bears'll eat ya."

Dawn promised him e-mail twice a day. She gave him a bright blue T-shirt with her website stencilled on the front. Then her eyes locked into his, so hard he could almost hear the click-snap.

"Lorne's eating you," she said. "Bury him."

After she left, Gabe sat hunched over, aching, sure the ache would never stop, sure the knotted muscles in his shoulders and back would have to loosen up and start forgiving Lorne before the rest of him could, all those tight mean muscles that should fucking well relax and let go of that jerk. Then he thought of real catastrophes, Vietnam, Bosnia, Chernobyl, and he started to wonder if all those hurt people had to forgive the shits who had fucked them over. Not love them or anything. Just *forgive* them, put the whole damn mess aside. He thought of his J-school buddies, none of them with functioning, in-house parents, all of them hatched and fledged like himself, more than a few from places torched to the ground or pocked with bullets. *Like dirty laundry, is what it is. Shit piles up all your life.*

No choice, dude. Let it go.

He sat down at the computer, his hands trembling, the keys clattering under his fingers like tracks against the wheels of trains. He was going to get rid of Lorne, dig his grave, buy him a ticket to oblivion. He started to write things down: whom to talk to, where to dig. What he needed to find out.

Find out why the man died. Find out what the Jesus *happened*.

Two

That evening, Gabe bought a *Star* for one of its front-page stories.

POLICE THINK FAX HOLDS CLUES
TO DEAD MAN'S JUMP

New York (CP). Police here are questioning a New York-area reporter who received a fax from photographer Lorne Winter the day before his death. Earlier this week, Jake Nolan, a former newspaper publisher and owner of a cable TV station, turned over a copy of the letter to local police in which he asked Winter if he had information on the recent history of Groves Island, New York. In his letter, he requested shots Winter had allegedly taken of a local fire there almost thirty years ago. Winter had faxed the letter back with a negative reply.

Dawn, Gabe thought, *forgetting's so much easier said than done*. He thought of a note he'd received from Sally. *I don't know why Lorne died*, she had written. *I only know that the dead live inside us, Gabe, and we can do nothing about this, except to remember that they are as dead as we want them to be*. Right she was. He wasn't a survivor but a witness, Lorne's son, a human roll of film, his father burning inside him.

❦❦

In Lorne's things, Gabe found a copy of *The Varsity*, the campus paper at the University of Toronto — a parchment-stiff rag, Ella's picture on the front page. *February 1965. Why the hell did Lorne save this?* For all the celebrity mugshots, that was why; for all the future lawyers and judges and provincial politicians shown at their embarrassing worst, pissed and marching with the engineers in the Lady Godiva parade. Others were already staking out careers, running for student office, sleeping on the sidewalk of the U.S. consulate in the angry days of Selma, Vietnam.

Lorne had saved it for Ella's mug. Gabe turned the pages. The issue was full of hotshot journalists like her, their first bylines in *The Varsity*, their campus-radio voices crackling through the high-tension wires of the sixties, most of them working in the business now. They all knew each other back then, the whole roiling mass of them congealing at the U of T, big-banging their way into the wired cosmos. *You don't believe it, check this out.* There was Ella sitting with a male student, his face as round as a hamburger bun, a radio guy with a headset and mike. *BODAN THE MAN talks Vietnam with reporter and activist Ella Rhodes on Campus Radio Watch tonight....* He folded the clipping and put it aside. Jim Bodan, CJQT Radio, Timmins-North Bay, the morning man in the cockpit. He wondered just how small the world could get.

❦❦

On the TV news the Conlin fire was still wild and terrible, was part of the worst fire season in memory, of a spring and previous summer without rain. It was the greenhouse effect that kept the forests burning; it was human carelessness; it was the natural cycle of lightning and rebirth. It was all of these and none of them. It was, it was. Gabe turned the TV off. He pulled out a few maps, started to look at cottage country, the roads into the bush where Sally lived, places that had not been touched by fire.

189 🦚

Three

Gabe faxed Sally, got permission to borrow her cottage for a week.
He headed north, a day's drive, and by a rutted maze of dirt and
gravel roads he reached her digs on Gold Dust Lake. He wasn't
sure at first if he'd found the right place. The lake water didn't
look clean. There was a decrepit dock that creaked and groaned
with every nudge and slap of a wave, and a rusted-out motorboat
flipped wrong side up like a dead fish. Behind a shed were a few
old tires, bald and useless. Sally's property looked as if it might
have been a landfill once. Here and there were ragged scraps of
tin, bits of tarpaper, plastic containers and glass; a mournful neglect, as if the land deserved no better. This was Sally's home,
Gabe thought, and that was the biggest puzzle, the worst surprise.
Quiet here, clean air at least. He opened her door and went
inside.

Sally's place was very small, clean and antiseptic. It reminded
him of a room in a boarding school, a barracks, an orphanage.
Her only furnishings were a Goodwill metal-and-Formica topped
table, kitchen chairs and two fake-leather loungers. Garbage
bags on pickup day looked better. Gabe cleaned his glasses,
looked again, yanked off his baseball cap and scratched his head.
He didn't get it, not at all.

A pilot earned a decent salary; she could do better than this.
She was too hard on herself, he thought. No — depressed, the
nineties version of the neighbourhood eccentric, collector of
rusty tins and splintered boards and newsprint, harmless. Maybe
she didn't want more. He looked around the place again. She
had a nice TV and VCR, a radio, a fridge and stove, a good bed.
Nothing else, though. No Ontario cottage kitsch, no frivolity, no

beer bottles or bullfrog planters or throw rugs. No Chinese-food and furnace-cleaning ads stuck to the fridge door with plastic magnetized bananas, no tacky paving-stones for the yellow brick road through life, nothing that would point her out as, well, hey, *human*. No sign that anyone had touched her. Ever.

Gabe went into the bedroom, dumped his pack, then noticed the framed photo on the bureau, the only decoration in the house. On its white lower margin he saw the tight, thin wriggle of Lorne's signature. *Algonquin Park*, he'd written next to it. *In memory of 9 February 1965*. It was an eloquent shot of the woods, one felled tree on top of another so you could just about feel the roughness of the bark against your skin. Looking again, he felt Lorne's hand in it, a young hand, an intimate and gentle touch, his soul in his eyes. Between camera and viewer there was no distance, and in Lorne's small replication of the earth, eye to the wood and tree on top of tree, nothing was separate from anything else in the world. *Fucking genius*, Gabe thought. *What a goddamn fucking waste*. He turned the picture face down on the dresser top, was about to shove it away in a drawer when he stopped.

When the hell did he give her that?

Gabe slipped the photograph out of the frame and turned it over. Scribbled on the back was a note:

Sally, remember Algonquin. Let it remind you of life in another forest, and how innocent we were before the fire. I ask no forgiveness that I love you still. As ever, Lorne   June 1995

Baffled, Gabe read it again, wondered if he could write and ask Sally about this. Then he imagined talking to her on the phone. *Like, uh, Sally, I just happened to take apart the only picture in your house, yeah, right, and I found a note to you from Lorne, yeah, no kidding, scribbled right on the back of the photo, oh, you mean you haven't read it yet.... You didn't know it was there....* Gabe sighed, exasperated.

You are one dumb shit, he said to himself. *MYOB. Forget it*. He sank down on the bed, as tired as he'd ever been.

Gabe pulled out his *Varsity* clipping, picked up the phone and dialled. Timmins-North Bay, Radio CJQT put him on hold, thumping him with a message tape. *Get news, get WIRED — I'm Jim Bodan the Morning Man weekdays six ay-em to nine....*

"Jimbo here, g'day."

"I'm not on the air, am I?"

Jimbo grunted. "Not at this hour. Christ, it's time for lunch."

Gabe told him whose kid he was, that he knew him from the coverage of Lorne's jump, that he knew Sally Groves.

"How?"

"She's my real mother."

Jimbo paused. "Jesus. Forgot she had a kid."

"Lorne adopted me."

"Christ, I'm really sorry, Gabe. Something I can do?"

Gabe asked if he could come by, find out more about Sally and Lorne.

I want to see where Lorne jumped, Gabe thought. *You gotta take me there.*

❧❧

Jimbo looked worried, his brow more furrowed than a wheatfield. "Sure, kid, will do." He patted Gabe's arm. "Conlin fire's still burning, though. I can only get you in so far." Gabe had a reason for wanting to see the ruin of the forest, knew but wasn't saying what he wanted to find out. He thought Jimbo sensed this, hoped so. The man lit up, ground out his smoke, said, "Friend of Sally is a friend of mine," lit up another smoke. "Some background first, I'll tell you what I know about Sally. Take you up then."

Gabe pulled out the clipping from *The Varsity* and Jimbo grinned. "That was me, all right, with your mom, Miz Rhodes, the mayor's kid. No, that came later. Rhodes was a city councillor then." He pulled out an ancient reel-to-reel tape and slipped it into the machine. "Wanna hear a real live sixties demo? Good old uptight Toronto, couldn't even scream a lousy slogan. Listen up."

There was noise, shuffling feet, voices mumbling. Jimbo's young voice: "Why are you here today, and what do you plan on doing?" The next voice was Ella's. "We're protesting the bombing of North Vietnam, the escalation to full-scale war." Her voice had been a beautiful instrument even then. Jimbo turned the tape off.

"Got arrested," he said. "She ever tell you that?"

"Don't think so."

"There was a scuffle, cops made a sweep, she got pulled in with everybody else. Then Ella fainted. We all thought she was going limp like Martin Luther King. No one had ever done it in TO, cops were gonna drag off this gorgeous gal like a sack of potatoes, and her old man on council, too. Big news in Hogtown."

"I just can't imagine Ella fainting," said Gabe.

"Yeah, well. Sixties diet, cigarettes for breakfast. None of us were health freaks then." Jimbo looked as if he was trying to figure out how to make some harsh thought gentle, how to sand down the rough parts of what he wanted to say.

"You lose your old man in Vietnam?" he asked.

Gabe told him yes. "Never knew him," he said.

Jimbo looked at him, his eyes intent. "You want to know when Ella got arrested?" *You should, it matters*, was how he said it. Gabe was about to reach for the clipping and check the date, but Jimbo pulled it away.

"It's why I asked about your dad. Dates count for a lot in this world. I'd hate it to be the same date he died."

"Wouldn't know."

"I'm a sixties freak, I know all the dates. Ella got arrested eighth of February '65, day after the first big bombing of North Vietnam. Retaliation for a VC ground raid, States bombed a little burg called Dong Hoi, more or less kicked off the air war."

Gabe felt a fault line shift and break inside him. "Was Lorne on this march?" he asked.

"Nuh-uh. Sally was. That's where I met her."

"You're kidding."

"She ran away when the cops came."

"Where'd she go?"

"Home. Went north next day." He looked sombre. "Sally was a wreck, poor kid. Her brother was headed for Vietnam."

"Did she go alone?" Gabe asked.

"Up north?" Jimbo looked away. "She went with Lorne," he said. Gabe shivered. Jimbo put a hand on his arm. "You OK?"

Gabe didn't answer. He couldn't talk, couldn't string words together because he didn't know the meaning of what he saw. In his mind: Sally's photo of Algonquin, the felled trees where she and Lorne had been when, half a spinning earth away, houses caught fire, whole towns began to burn.

Four

Jimbo had a friend, a bush pilot who flew the route north to Conlin region, guy who subbed for Sally on the news chopper. He was headed way north in his float plane to pick up some fishermen on a fly-in. "Make a nice day trip," Jimbo told Gabe, "get to see where the fire was, part that's burned itself out, at any rate."

Gabe sat up front with the pilot. It was his first time in a cockpit, and he found himself staring at an eyeful of dials and switches and blinking lights, wondering how Sally could stand this cooped-up space, day in, day out. He thought of his grandfather flying over the Coral Sea, then vanishing over Long Island Sound, likely ground into dust by the racket in his ears. This plane was the fucking noisiest place he'd ever been in his life. The pilot had to wear a headset with a mouthpiece to talk to the tower. Gabe felt cut off from everyone, lonely as hell.

He saw Jimbo nod, mouthing words over the roar of the engines, *Coming up now*, his eyes glancing downward, his finger pointing. Gabe looked. He had a good view, front and side, just under the struts and the leading edge of the wing. He looked and didn't know what he was seeing: ash so thick his skin could feel the sting of it, charred stumps of trees — *They're giving God the finger, Dawn would say that*. He felt Jimbo's tap on his back.

"Right about here's where it happened." Jimbo had to shout the words.

And what's here that's different, what? It's not TV, is what, Gabe said to himself. *It's not the video at the north end of the mall*. Blackened threads of branches sticking out of the jack pines like burnt-out filaments of lightbulbs in a lamp. *Lorne's buried here, is what's different.* Gabe was frightened. Nothing he could explain — just that he felt Lorne's eyes inside of his, as if he were Lorne seeing the ruins of fire from the air. He was watching a very old photograph developing itself in darkness, he was inside a bomb shadow flash-burned in the heart for all time, he was inside Lorne Winter staring through the lens, down into the dead ash of another forest, a devastated city, a terrible catastrophe, a blinded insult to the light of day.

What Gabe saw was the picture he had found in Lorne's things, the one he had knelt and touched, its ash as human as a face. *Here it happened. Remember.* He felt a strong hand pulling him back.

"Enough, pal," Jimbo said. "You've seen enough."

☙☙

At Gold Dust Lake that evening, Gabe called Dawn, told her he'd flown up to Conlin, to the ruined forest where Lorne had died, where part of the fire had gone out. It felt as if someone were there, he told her, and she said no doubt it was Lorne, his spirit was on the loose, what else could it be? He reminded her of the old unlabelled photo he'd found, told her it had felt the same way. Lorne had printed and catalogued his stuff — names, places, dates — but on this one there was no note. "Maybe there's no such thing as time," said Gabe. "Maybe the picture is of now."

He thought about the other photo, the one Lorne had given to Sally before he died, how it had come to mind when Jimbo had told him the date of the bombing, the date when Ella had been arrested. Important, but he didn't know why, didn't know how to connect these facts to what he'd felt in the plane as he looked down on the ash of Lorne's fire. Only that his dad had been driven to photograph forests, living and dead. It puzzled him.

"I think I need to see Sally's woods," he said.

"What for, Gabe?"

"I started out there. With Sally and that soldier."

"It's weird," said Dawn. "Both your dads were in Vietnam."

Woods don't burn in Vietnam — why the hell did those words stick in his mind, the pilot's words in *Sowing the Wind?* Again he remembered Lorne's unmarked photo, the woods so badly charred that it was impossible to guess the types of trees or where the hell they were. It might have been taken during the war, not forest but underbrush, the torched remains of a village. For sure the photo was Lorne's work, his style. *The eye of the camera sees everything at once,* Lorne had said of his film. *Our own eyes shrink from doing that.* Gabe told Dawn how sorrowful those words of his had been.

"As if he died there," she said.

Gabe felt shaken by her insight. He knew there was such a thing as truth upsetting the order of the world, knew it was possible to reimagine Lorne. Maybe he had the guy all wrong. He could have been a man who was too old for Sally and knew it, who hated the war, who adopted a soldier's kid, whose own dad was a soldier. A troubled man — a vet himself, when it came right down to it, one of those who couldn't make his life work out, a media vet who held the war inside him as an urn holds ash. He was a man who looked out from a chopper over a burning forest, seeing desolation, thatched roofs, a curl of blue smoke. On the day of his death he forgot the name of the country where he was.

🕮🕮

Still puzzled, Gabe locked up the cottage and went home.

In Toronto, once again sorting his father's folders, he found a note that an American reporter had sent to Lorne. Standing and stretching, he pulled it out of its envelope, scanned it. *Some TV guy wants an interview, yeah, right.* Gabe was tired of all this, sick of crouching over file drawers and boxes stashed in corners. Sure that his vacation had ended much too soon, he dreamed of another break, another trip up north, the warbling of loons at nightfall, the dunk and splash as he jumped from Sally's dock into a less than pristine lake. *Lorne, old buddy, you sure screwed up my summer,* he thought. He trolled around in his mind for epithets he hadn't yet thrown at the man, gave up because he no longer had the heart to curse the poor guy out. Then he looked at the name on the letter, remembered something, went searching through his file for a clipping from the *Star*. The same guy, Jake Nolan, who had written a letter to Lorne, then given a copy to the police in the States. *That* Nolan.

He had the original letter, right in his hands.

As you'll recall, the letter read, *there was a fire*.

Felled Trees

One

1964

Two years before the woods burned, Sally left home for her mother's country. At Lorne's suggestion she chose Toronto, reserved and cultured and very English, a place that at first appeared as bland as an invalid's diet. The university was built around Queen's Park, a bucolic space framed on its north end by the squat pillars of the legislature. A polite murmur of a city, and yet, in this home of propriety and silence, she felt a staid kind-heartedness and mercy. Lacking passion, Toronto would never breed people like her parents. For now she'd be happy here.

Besides, Lorne was close to her.

Six months had passed since he'd left for Toronto, and she felt grateful for the space between them, sure that Fran was right, that their closeness had been a mistake, that Lorne was an ocean with a riptide, a hidden danger. Even so, he seemed different. When he met her at the airport, he looked younger, more relaxed, as if the light in Toronto cast its shadows differently and took away the twelve-year distance of his age. His ruddy blond hair had grown almost to his shoulders, and he wore slacks and a loose-fitting woven tunic. Jewellery, too, a brass medallion of the sun. His eyes seemed softer and more amused by life, and Sally saw less of their mischief, detachment, pain. He looked as if he was enjoying Toronto, she told him. *Yes*, he answered, *yes, Sally*, and his voice was gentle, tentative almost, as if he was more used to awkwardness and sorrow. He took her to see his flat on Brunswick, the top floor of a gabled house. Sally surprised him, handed him a gift.

Lorne sat down and unwrapped it, pulling from the tissue paper a single glass teacup and saucer. On them were painted impressions of the flowers of Algonquin Park, in mauve, pink and green, and Sally could sense that this was a familiar lightness floating in his hand. He lifted the cup to his lips, letting them rest on the rim, hovering like a bird on the edge of a fountain. He put the cup down, looked at Sally.

"Your mother's," he said to her. His eyes were gentle, grave.

"You photographed it once," Sally answered.

"Are you sure you want me to have it, Sally?"

"Yes." She felt stirred, as if she were the cup and his lips had touched the rim of her, as he stroked its painted surface with his fingertips. Then he put it down on the table, his eyes lowered.

"I'll never fill this cup," he said. "It was made full."

Sally could almost taste his words.

"My mother loved the wilderness," she said.

"I'll take you there," said Lorne. He put a hand on her shoulder.

The buzzer rang and Lorne got up to answer it. At the door stood a tall woman dressed in black. She had a strong and square-jawed face, pale, translucent skin, long blonde hair with a sheet-metal gleam, dark eyes. Ella Rhodes was her name, and her voice was as rich as the weight of gold coins, their clink and sparkle in the hand. She was dropping off a draft of an article she'd written for *Maclean's*, one for which Lorne was taking photos. Sally wondered if they were a pair. Lorne had mentioned someone named Ella, but she could feel nothing between them.

Sally asked her if she was a reporter. Ella pulled out a magazine, showed Sally her byline. "In Bed with a Brontosaurus: What's Ahead for Canada If Goldwater Wins?" It showed a cartoon of a dinosaur, an American flag draped across its tail. It was grazing on a clump of vegetation labelled *Canada*.

"Vietnam's next," said Ella. "That Tonkin Gulf mess, any excuse for a war."

"I hope not," Sally answered. Mike was headed for Vietnam, he'd told her.

Ella made her think of a TV weatherman holding a pointer to a map, tracing isobars, describing the movement of a warm air mass, with a voice uncoupled from the terrible storm of its words. She felt Lorne's eyes on her, a compassionate gaze. "Sally has a brother in the service," he said.

I can't wait for some action, sis, Mike had written.

"Did Lorne tell you he's going there to film?" asked Ella.

"It's not definite," said Lorne. "Depends on funding."

"Depends on war breaking out," Ella retorted.

Sally was too afraid to speak.

❧❧

"We've been together off and on," said Lorne. He looked pensive as he walked Sally home.

"Will you go to Vietnam," she asked, "if there's a war?"

"Ella should not have mentioned that," he said.

"Will you?"

Lorne paused. "Yes."

Ella, Sally realized, was terrified for Lorne. Fearing for Mike, afraid Lorne might also die, Sally told him how dear a friend he was to her, how friendship was a mysterious thing, a force of nature: one that began as a shift in the earth's crust and ended with the raising up of mountains; one she could sense inside herself as he raised the cup to his lips. How frail a thing life was, how easy to break; didn't he see this? Lorne looked at her with kindness. He didn't touch her shoulder or reach for her hand.

"How we redeem ourselves," he told her. "I need to find that out."

She said good night, unsure what he meant.

Two

The conflict had begun in August 1964, almost a month before Sally left the island. It had begun with skirmishes, confusion. A troublesome place in the South China Sea, the Gulf of Tonkin; two American destroyers shelled, one named *Maddox*, the other *Turner Joy*. To Sally's ear, the last was an innocent name. She thought of the waters of Long Island Sound, the tern her father had showed her flying there. *The Ballad of the Turner Joy*, maybe Ella could write a poem, could read it with her beautiful voice. To Ella's mind, the U.S. Congress wrote a resolution, opened a sluice, broke a dam that would flood a generation and destroy it. She called Sally a few weeks after they'd met at Lorne's. "Just wait," she said to her.

Flyers began arriving in Sally's mailbox: *End Canadian Complicity. Teach-In at Convocation Hall.* On them were notes from Ella: *Maybe you'd like to join us.* Sally went to some of these events, and Ella introduced her to her friends, each time repeating, *Sally's-brother's-over-there*, as if this were her name. Sometimes Lorne would come, taking pictures, making notes, doing research for his film. He'd sit alone.

"I love Lorne so much," said Ella. She spoke the words with such passion that Sally wondered if she meant them for her ears. Yet how drawn she felt to the gravity of these words, in them a truthfulness sturdy enough to embrace Sally's own affection for the same man. "It's why I'm fighting against the war," Ella said. "So he'll come back alive."

"Then you'll get married," said Sally.

"I wouldn't hold my breath," Ella replied.

Sally looked at her. "Aren't you two —?"

Ella hesitated. "Now and then," she said in a quiet voice. "Now and then."

☙☙

Sex. Sally was afraid to breathe the word.

She had a roommate named Riva with black braided hair, a fine, calm, introspective face, blue-green eyes with a shell-like iridescence. Riva chain-smoked, wore hoops in her ears, read Marx, spoke three languages, had lost her parents in the Second World War. She read Ella's piece in *Maclean's*, "Canada's Uncle Sam's Lackey," then tossed it in the garbage.

"Bourgeois nationalism," Riva said. "She has the IQ of a cornflake."

Sally wondered if Lorne agreed.

My daughter, said City Councillor Caspar Rhodes, *is a Communist dupe.* Riva read his quote in the *Tely* and guffawed. It was February 1965, and on the other side of the ocean the U.S. airbase at Pleiku was smoking, burning, the families of ten Americans were in shock, American bombers were cracking the sky, heading northward, some of them flying from a carrier named *Coral Sea.* Sally couldn't eat or sleep. *Bad timing,* said the Toronto *Daily Star.* What about China, the Soviets, the Bomb? *What about Mike?* She tried to relax by walking, swimming. Lorne called. "I'm looking for appropriate escape," he said. "This is the beginning of a war." Sally wept.

"Don't cry," said Lorne. "I didn't mean to scare you."

"Mike's going over," she told him.

Lorne listened. "We haven't been to Algonquin yet," he said. "Let's get away from this."

Yes, oh yes.

"Ella's going mad," he added. "She finds the war exciting, I'm afraid."

"She's worried about you, Lorne." He didn't answer.

Mike doesn't deserve what's in store for him, said Ella.

I can't friggin' wait, Mike's letter said.

Lorne was going to Vietnam in the spring. He'd follow the bombers over Northern villages with names like Vinh Linh, Dong Hoi; maybe as far north as Haiphong and Hanoi, where nothing had been put to the torch, not yet. "If they try it, I'll meet them when they come," said Lorne. "The bombing has given me a focus for my film" — as if he'd been peering at life through the lens of this conflict, adjusting the ring with the featherlight touch of his hand, at last seeing things clearly.

Sally went to his apartment, showed him the letter Mike had sent her, asked if he'd write down Mike's mailing address, his unit in Vietnam. "He could help you with your film," she said. She wanted Lorne's eyes on him, those same eyes that years ago had taken her photo on the tarmac, that had saved her life.

Lorne read the letter. *I'll carry your picture, sis. You bring me luck.* He looked at Sally.

"I'll carry your picture too," he said.

He put his arms around her, held her, stroked her hair, but he opened inside her a vast cavern of loneliness, a wordless, unbearable ache. *You're as lonely as your mother was* — she recalled Sister Fran's caution. Yet it was a loneliness as wrenching as a limb ripped from the body, a sense of irreparable loss that Lorne touched in her and perhaps in himself. "You've both suffered too much," said his sister. Yet Sally wanted him in the mindless and stupefying way that trees want rain, wanted what she saw in the pale blue of his eyes: the gentle lift of her father's plane, her mother's glass in its ephemeral beauty. He held them as he held her, and in the embrace of that truth she felt no jealousy of Ella or of any other woman in his life.

"You're my hope," he said. "My dearest friend."

"And you're mine," she replied.

He kissed her forehead, held her hands and kissed them.

She felt comforted, at least for now.

Sally hadn't seen Ella for a week or two, only her signs on hoard-
ings all over the city: *Stop the Bombing; Yanks Out of Vietnam.*
After a while Ella called, sounding tired, saying she was under
the weather. "Come to the march," she said. "Do it for Mike."

Sally felt ill at ease around the brusque edges of politics and
marches. She told Riva that Ella was overdoing it, that she
looked pale, exhausted, an angry dullness in her eyes like the
steel glint of an overcast day. "That bug everyone's got, well, I've
got it," Ella told her.

"You sure this is flu?" Riva asked Sally. She looked bemused.

"What else could it be?"

Riva smirked. "Guess."

"Cramps?"

"Maybe she *didn't* get cramps."

Sally looked out the window. "You're being mean."

"It's not mean, Sally. There's nothing wrong with giving life.
You should read Emma Goldman, the great anarchist. 'The pas-
sionate defiance of motherhood,' her phrase."

Sally asked if she could bum a cigarette.

ꝕ🖎

"I'm fine," said Ella on the phone. No, she'd never heard of
Emma Goldman. She herself was a cautious, practical sort, no
radical. "Have you heard from your brother, Sally?" She would
write a poem at the end of the war, not now.

Three

On the day of the march, Sally met Jim Bodan for the first time. She was a shy eighteen to his twenty, bewildered by his male plumage of mike and headset and tape machine. Bodan the Man on Campus Radio One, a big bear of a guy in a parka who ambled through the crowd towards her. She glanced at the U.S. consulate, a formidable, black-doored building with an eagle on the Great Seal above the entranceway. The bird glowered, arrows in its talons, as if it were waiting for a chance to nail the marchers in a sneak attack, to punish them for defiance. *They'll never let you go home again. The CIA'll take down your name.* She wondered if she alone was afraid. *You think like an American, Sally* — Riva's words. Yet Riva, a refugee, was afraid of the police. Now Sally stood alone, apart from the line of marchers, wondering what to do and whether or not she was safe here. She noticed Jimbo approaching her.

"Excuse me, Sally Groves? Ella Rhodes said I should talk to you, that your brother's in the war."

Sally took off a woollen mitt and pulled it down over his mike.

Jimbo grinned. "Nice windsock," he said.

Sally was puzzled. She thought of windsocks at airports, wondered what he was talking about.

"Keeps the weather out of my tape. You've got a future in radio, kid."

"I don't want to talk about my brother," she said. "I'm sorry."

"It's OK. Maybe just say why you're here."

"Then I'd have to talk about my brother."

Jimbo nodded, handed Sally her mitt; held her tote bag while she put it back on.

She looked at him. "Is it safe here?"

Jimbo paused. "Safer than Vietnam," he said. He patted her arm. "Hang loose, kid. We'll get your brother home for you." She could feel the amiable chatter of a deejay in his words, *Come on over to the station, show you around.* His kindness distracted her.

Sally joined the demonstrators circling in a long loop around the sidewalk. Chilled, she rubbed her hands together, shoved them in her pockets, wondered where Ella had gone in this crowd. She stepped out of the line to look for her, noticed Jimbo striding along, mike in his hand, scooping up the sound ahead of him. Sally could see an untidy knot in the long rope of protesters strung across the sidewalk. A parallel line had formed opposite them, hecklers waving signs, yelling, *Go back to Moscow.* A placard struck a head, a fist crunched a nose; Sally saw blood and was afraid. She heard shouting and the mournful howl of sirens in the distance. Police showed up like bad weather, all at once. They started grabbing people, cuffing them, shoving and pushing. Jimbo climbed up on a car roof, miked the crowd. There were TV cameras, sound trucks, a paddy wagon, Sally couldn't tell one from the other. She began to think about Riva's fear of the police.

Then she saw Ella. She was lying on the sidewalk, wan as a dead moth. The police came over, grabbed her under the arms, started to drag her to the cruiser. Jimbo ran up to a cop. "Excuse me, officer, she fainted." The cop glared at him, beckoned to another officer, and the two of them pulled Ella, lifting her up against the side of the car.

Sally stared in horror. Ella's coat had opened and there was blood spreading across the front of her jeans, an angry blotch making its way down her pant-legs. Sally felt for her, exposed this way before so many men. No, this was worse — a dark gash of blood, as if she'd been shot. Her eyes were fluttering open, and she looked at the cop as if she couldn't remember where she was. Just as he pulled out handcuffs, Ella collapsed, crumpled up as limp as a bedsheet. "Somebody call an ambulance," Sally heard a voice yelling. Cameras were nudging at Ella; crowds of demonstrators, reporters. Someone held a coat in front of her.

Ella's going to bleed to death. Afraid, she turned and started to run, brushing by surprised protesters. *Don't be crazy, it's her period,* but she felt terror slamming in her chest. A block away she saw a phone booth.

She felt as wild as a blizzard. *What the hell am I doing here?*

Her hand shook as she dialled Lorne's number.

When Lorne answered, she told him that Ella had fainted but she didn't mention the bleeding. It seemed embarrassing, too personal a thing. Instead she wondered aloud if Ella had skipped breakfast.

"She was too exhausted to march," said Lorne. "I told her that."

The day before, Ella had dropped by his place with the contents of her fridge — a stash of fried chicken, bread, cold cuts, apples and a head of lettuce. "You might as well eat it, Lorne. It's going to go bad if they lock me up," she'd told him.

They took her away in an ambulance, thought Sally.

"Ella looked tired," she said.

"She's anemic," Lorne replied.

She should tell him that Ella had been bleeding. No. This was something she wasn't supposed to know.

Lorne sighed. "Come north with me, Sally. The cold'll clear our heads."

In his half-whisper, its tingle in her ear, Sally felt his touch on a sad November day, his lips on hers, his tongue, the slow movement of his hands in her hair. Feelings she'd pushed aside erupted into longings that panic made intense. She didn't understand this, didn't care, only wanted relief. She told him she'd go.

Four

At sunrise the following day, Lorne and Sally drove north. He'd borrowed Ella's camper and they drove in silence, the chill air frosty with his breath, his hands tight on the steering wheel. She sensed his troubled mood as they drove up Highway 11 and over to 60, until they made it into the southwest corner of the park.

"If you knew," he said, "how I've wanted this break."

"Are you tired?"

"Things pile up," he said.

"All this snow," said Sally. "My mom would be so happy that I'm here."

Lorne parked the camper, then turned the engine off. "Sally," he said in a hesitant voice. "You should know that Ella and I have not been lovers for a while."

"Yes, I understand."

He took her in his arms, kissed her mouth, then drew away.

"I wanted you to know before I did that."

"I would have let you anyway," said Sally.

He helped her down from the camper, and then he raised the hood of her parka, straightened her muffler around her neck. He kissed her again.

"You taste like apples," he said.

Sally thought of Ella. *I do love Lorne* — the bright coin of truth she'd given her in friendship. *We are lovers now and again*, Ella had said, as if love drifted through their lives with the same gentle indifference as a breeze through an open window, one that would leave and come again. It surprised Sally that she rather liked this thought, of stealing in unnoticed when the breeze stopped. It made her feel invisible, fleet-footed, owing nothing to anyone.

Here in the snow, in the lightness of her own step, she could feel her mother walking.

"Does it surprise you," Lorne asked, "that I mentioned Ella?"

"No," she replied.

"I told her it was over," he said.

Is that why she's sick? Sally wondered.

They walked. Algonquin — Sally had seen nothing like it before, and could make no sense of this surreal and brittle place. Snow glittering, its chill white sleeves hanging in rags from spruce boughs; Sally wondered at their iciness, their needle tips incapable of stitching or mending anything, and she felt that Lorne had taken her to a place inside himself. *Ella's sick and he knows it*, she thought. *Is Ella going to die?* It was the same wilderness where her mother and father had found solace once. Yet the terrible cold of it was Lorne's, was hers.

She couldn't be dreaming the crunch of their boots in the snow, or the shadows of massive evergreens, spruce and pine. Maybe she was seeing through Lorne's bleak gaze into the sorrow where he would lead her. Would she follow? They were surrounded by trees that were like the enormous struts and joists of a house, white with ice, bone-cold. She remembered the warmth of another forest, spying on her mother, seeing her lips on the mouth of a strange man. She turned to Lorne and kissed him.

"This is what my mother loved," she whispered.

"What, this place?"

"Yes."

"And more than that, I'm sure."

Lorne kissed her hard and she felt alive with danger, as if she were about to step into a snare. She had stumbled upon her mother's wilderness, the same awful yearning into which she'd fled. Had Ella felt like this? She remembered her bleeding, as if she had been wounded, and she understood what must have happened to her. Snares were dangerous things. Women froze and died there. She thought of her mother and she shuddered. She'd have to be careful.

"Are you cold?" Lorne asked.

He put his arm around her. Sally wanted him, longed for a warm and sheltered place, and then she felt an inexpressible awe as they made their way through this solemn forest. It was like a church; they ought to cross themselves, rather than defile this place with longing. Yet it also felt as if time had come to an end and God had fled. Lorne didn't seem to notice the strangeness. He had his eye on something in the distance.

"That's odd," he said.

His hand gripped her arm and they walked until they stood before a very large stand of spruce, some of them dead, many of them bent and broken at crazy angles, frozen in their lopsided tilt, as if the struts of this gargantuan house had been caught in the act of collapsing, had been iced into this terrible moment forever. Next to them, in a clearing, there seemed to be some huge object, ill-defined and all but hidden, the shape of it curved and softened by the drifting snow.

"Fallen trees," said Lorne. "They weren't here a week ago."

Sally ran up to whatever it was, and began to brush the layers of snow away with her gloved hands as if she were frantic to rescue an injured child, an earthquake victim of centuries past. Under her fingers was a monstrous fossil of a thing, a primeval wreck that seemed to be neither wood nor rusted metal, her fingertips blurring the roughness of the one into the other, her eyes bewildered at the sight. Lorne stared at it, covered his face with his hands, warmed himself before he looked again.

"Where the hell did this come from?" he said.

Sally thought it must be a plane, a very old one. Had she slipped into dreaming awake? One much larger than her dad's single-engine, a wreck of a thing, the markings rusted, no call letters under the wings. Lorne turned to her, his soft words drifting into her ear, *No, Sally. Ottawa knows when a plane comes down. They don't just fall from the sky*, but she couldn't remember whispering to him *A plane*, wasn't even sure if what she heard was his voice or the whisper of his thoughts. Maybe events moved out of sequence here. Maybe this plane or this tree or this crossbeam of a mighty house had not yet landed or fallen or been put to the torch by lightning. Maybe she was sleeping, dreaming this. Maybe they had not yet come here.

It didn't matter. She had found her mother's hiding-place. She sensed her father in the broken woods.

Lorne sank down on the trunk, the fuselage, the roofbeam, the dark wings of the shadow of death, sat on whatever it was, his face lost in his hands. He seemed to be pondering something, trying to make a decision.

"It's going to be OK," she said.

He looked up. "What is?"

"Everything. I'm where I belong."

Lorne caught her between his knees. "Sally, I love you. Do you know that?"

"Yes."

"Only you. No one else."

Just hold me like you're doing now.

Lorne took her down the path back to the camper. He asked her to put her mouth against him, and she felt her head pinned by his hand. *I love you, Lorne. I love you.* It was very slow, what he did to her; pleasurable the way she held him, the way she collapsed into a point of energy, a match-head struck on flint, over and over, until she drew him into her and heard the relief of his crying.

Afterwards Lorne dried Sally with a towel and helped her into warm clothes. Then he brought out his basket of chicken legs and apples, poured her a mix of tea and whiskey, honey and lemon, but her hand was shaking too much to hold it. He put his arm around her, took the mug and held it to her lips as she drank. Then Lorne opened the picnic lunch and stared at Ella's food.

"She wanted me to have it," he said.

They ate.

Five

"Ella's been trying to reach you," said Riva when Sally returned.

"Is she OK?"

Riva smirked. "Must be. She's looking for Lorne." She told Sally that Ella was resting at home, that some lawyer friend of hers had got her out of the hospital, out of the hands of the cops. "Before anyone could guess the truth."

"Huh?"

"Good heavens, Sally. It's *illegal* what Ella did."

"What, the sit-in?" Sally knew as soon as she said it what Riva meant.

"That wasn't her period," said Riva.

"How do you know?"

"She said it wasn't. I asked her."

❦❦

Ella had left her front door unlocked, and when Sally came in she was sitting by the fire. There was no sound from her, no greeting; no *hello* or *come in*. What appeared to be Ella might have been an effigy of some kind, a pile of crocheted afghans, quilted blankets. Her long hair was pinned up and her face seemed paper-flat, as if levelled by the shock of her affliction. Sally felt her eyes as she met her gaze.

"Lorne called me after the march," said Ella.

Sally had had no idea they'd spoken. "I told him you were ill," she said.

"I told him why," said Ella.

Sally felt afraid. "Are you OK now?" she asked.

"I'll never have kids," said Ella. "I had a hack job."

Sally offered to make her tea. While she was in the kitchen, she scrubbed and rinsed the dishes, then Ella's soiled cutlery, and she found herself thinking of incisions, blood. Ella could have been butchered. Sally's hands were shaking as she poured the tea.

"Lorne found someone to help me out," said Ella.

"Because he's going overseas?"

Ella said nothing, broken as a stopped clock.

🐦🐦

It was over between them, as Lorne had said. Ella had wanted a child, but it wasn't responsible, he had told her, not when he was going away, not when he couldn't be sure about their future. Now Ella couldn't bear the thought of having sex with him, and so he'd ended it, regretting that he'd caused her so much anguish. Yet as he'd made love to Sally, he'd whispered in her ear, *It was always you I wanted* — as if he'd gotten rid of his child to have her. She'd admitted how much she'd wanted him, stirred by the risk he was willing to take for her. Later she'd draped her hair across her breasts, and then she'd taken his hand and drawn it down, moving it against the silk of her hair. She had felt as if she were dreaming, half asleep.

Just the same, he'd go soon, leave her.

🐦🐦

Toronto
10 April 1965

Dear Sister Fran,

...after all your unanswered letters, I am shamefaced because I couldn't bring myself to tell you the truth, and then you tried to call me tonight and I wasn't home, and so I know you must be worried. The truth is, I got involved with Lorne. It turns out that his friend Ella was pregnant, they got rid of the baby and now she can't have kids. He's off to make a film in Vietnam, and Mike is off to fight a war. I'm terrified I may lose them both. Maybe you could enlighten me as to why God bothers with us, if He does.

Sally

Groves Island
15 April 1965

Dear Sally,

I'm not going to lecture or gloat at this distance, or even to your face. You are not responsible for what Lorne and Ella did. Stay out of it and try not to judge them. Life will take care of that. As for your involvement with Lorne, I will say no more. You have said it all yourself.

Now, why does God bother??? I guess for the entertainment value, although I sometimes wonder what He finds amusing. On the other hand, the world is full of goodness, but you don't earn it. It's free. So that's how God "bothers," but why is far beyond us. So don't quote me, Sally — this is not advice to the lovelorn, or Holy Mother Church rapping knuckles. This is untidy rambling, dear, which is more or less the way the world is laid out for us.

Love and prayers,
Sister Fran

❧⅍

Sally ended up in the back of a dark church where she was a stranger to the priest who heard confessions. She talked into a void, her own. *Are you sorry?* She was. She told him she was afraid for her brother, who was going to war; afraid she'd be punished with the loss of him because she and Lorne had not cared enough about Ella's plight. *You don't need penance,* he told her. She explained that she was far from home, that she had no parents, no family. *Even so, you're a child of God,* he said. *Is there something you could do to make amends?* She thought about this, her hands touching the fringe of her hair. Then she told him, yes, there was.

Six

After Sally finished her exams, Lorne called to say goodbye. "I want to give you a gift," he said, but she was afraid that if she saw him she'd dissolve in grief. Even so, she went to his flat, tiptoed into the hallway, found Lorne sitting on the bare floor. He reached up, took her hands, pulled her down next to him and embraced her. Then he handed her a manila envelope. In it was a photo of two massive trees that had collapsed across each other. Their huge, rutted trunks were suffused with warmth, as if death had honed and shaped them into another form of life. She remembered this strangeness, knew where Lorne had found it.

"Everything started there," she said. "And now it's ended."

"Sally, I'll be back."

"Aren't you afraid?" she asked.

He looked troubled. "Yes," he said. "But nothing's ended."

He reached behind her, loosened the barrette that held her hair in place, pulled her long hair forward like a cape around her shoulders, as if he were trying to keep her warm, to protect her from harm and trouble, from her fears for his life and her brother's. She shivered as he buried his face in her neck.

"Sometimes I think I'll be punished," she whispered.

"For wanting me?"

"Yes," she said, but she was remembering Ella.

Lorne took her face in his hands. "Sometimes I feel I deserve to die," he said.

Sally wept as Lorne kissed her tears, his tongue on her cheek, then in her mouth. She knew her sorrow moved him, her tears stinging his tongue. Aroused by his guilt, she felt his remorse as he entered her, as if she could have borne for Ella the quick twist of a knife scraping her insides, the warm, thick rush of blood.

🐦🦋

Sally fell asleep, dreamt that Mike's fighter-plane exploded over the South China Sea.

🐦🦋

As if she were still dreaming, as if it were the only way to rouse herself, she got up, found scissors, went into the bathroom and stared at herself in the mirror. Then she took a clump of her lustrous hair and hacked it off. *A haircut like a Marine's. They can shoot me instead of Mike.* She cut off chunks of her hair, chopping it helter-skelter, slicing at it until it was stubble, wild and unkempt. Then she gathered up a clump of it and walked into the front room. Lorne was awake, staring at her, his face white.

"Sally, what in God's name?" he whispered.

"I don't feel right about us. I want to end it."

Lorne turned his back to her, went to the window, gripped each side of the frame with his hands. He didn't want her to see him weep, she knew this. "Sally, Sally" — he kept whispering her name as he stared out over the city, as if he were watching her fly away from him.

"Ella will forgive you, Lorne," she said. "Just ask."

He turned around, fear in his eyes. "Don't leave me, Sally. Please."

"I have to. Don't you understand?"

He looked puzzled. "No. What?"

"Ella. How my mother died."

"Will you goddamn drop it?"

Lorne turned to her with a stone-hard face. He gripped her shoulders until they ached, shook her hard, shoved her against the wall. She started to cry.

He let go of her, turned his face to the wall, his head in his hands. Then he took a deep breath, turned around and saw all the way into Sally's eyes, two shattered windows, as if her sight had been blown apart by the force of his anger. He reached out and stroked her bristled hair, brushed back a clump that had fallen across her forehead. He kissed her eyes and held her. That was all.

Lorne's Effects III

One

1995

Gabe returned home from Gold Dust Lake to all the things Lorne had left undone. In his hand was the letter that Jake Nolan had copied and left with the police, one he couldn't bring himself to read. Instead he sat and stared out the window, glancing at the Eaton's box in the corner, his mind's eye lifting the lid, his careful thoughts like hands resting on the things he and Dawn had found — snapshots of Sally Groves, an American flag, a cigarette lighter, a plait of hair. It felt wrong, his having anything of Sally's, indecent, as if she were the one who was dead, as if Lorne, still alive, had refused to bury her remains. Gabe felt sad. Hair at least could be recycled in a bin with shredded leaves and grass and rotting wood, things that would decompose into a rich, dark soil that would one day nudge a garden into bloom. Dawn's parents had one of those backyard bins, and the thought of it made him feel better. The rest had no life left in them, were better off buried in the ground, like Lorne.

He returned to the letter.

...As you'll recall, Jake Nolan had written Lorne, *there was a fire in 1966 in which a man lost his life fleeing the blaze that destroyed the Groves' family home. Next year will mark the thirtieth anniversary of the fire, a noteworthy event in the history of this island. I am now the owner of Island Cable 10 (and the former publisher of the* Island Banner*) and I hope to produce a documentary on this subject.... I would welcome the chance to interview you as a photographer who gave evidence to the police at that time...we understand you have*

archival material, photographs of the ruins. On the bottom of this letter, Lorne had scribbled, *Nolan, I have nothing you would want.*

Gabe closed his eyes. Once more he was flying north to Conlin, his body throbbing with the racket of the plane. A photo, a face in the ashes. *Lorne, Jesus.*

He read the letter again.

※

Gabe went into his bedroom, yanked out a suitcase, started rolling up T-shirts, stuffing in underwear and socks. *Kiss that northern lake goodbye,* he told himself. *Time to check out the ocean.* What the hell, he should pick up the phone and call Nolan first, fax him. He glanced at Lorne's boxes, felt his leg aching to give them a kick, his fists wanting to tear them apart. Instead he tried to imagine Jake Nolan, what he looked like, who he was. Having done this, he sat at his computer, keying in words with a gentle touch, as if Jake were his only friend.

I am the adopted son of the late Lorne Winter, and I have just found a letter you wrote him asking for an interview.... You requested archival photos of the Groves fire, and I think I may have found some in Lorne's effects. Unlike his other work, these photos are unlabelled.

※

Ten minutes later, Jake called, offered Gabe condolences and told him that, even without Lorne, he meant to tape the TV show. Why not come to New York, he said. Dig into the *Banner* morgue, learn your family history. There was more than enough about the fire, most of it inconclusive. As for Lorne, he wasn't prepared to say much of anything, not yet.

"Bring those photos, anything else you've got," said Jake.

"Lorne left me a lighter, too."

"A *what?*" Jake's voice snapped in his ear like a rubber band.

"A cigarette lighter," he answered.

"What kind?"

Gabe paused. "The army kind. Belonged to my real dad."

"Bring it. We'll talk when you come."

The man was like a motion sensor, bawling at stray cats and burglars alike; anything about the Groves archives put him on alert. All the same, Gabe understood that he mustn't ask too many questions or press Jake for details. That troubled him, as if Jake were both uncovering things and burying them, at once.

"Jake, I have to ask you something," he said. "Just a simple answer, yes or no."

"Nothing's simple. I don't do simple."

"Lorne's plugged into this somehow. Right?"

"Plugged into what?"

"The fire."

Jake sighed. "Gabe, believe me. Nobody knows."

"Does Sally know more than she's telling?"

Jake paused, took a deep breath. "Sally doesn't know what I know," he said.

Two

Two weeks before his conversation with Gabe Winter, Jake Nolan had driven up Sally's road and parked his truck near the swamp, not far from where the treehome used to be before the fire. What had been a pond was wetland now, stalked by a marshy stretch of sedge and rushes, grass and water willows, their slow movement forward as inexorable as time. They would reclaim their lost terrain, while the wetland, left to its own, would return to forest. As the property's new owner, Jake Nolan had it in mind to stop this.

He got out and looked around, staring into what was left of the pond. In the shallow water he saw a thick bed of sediment, murky brown with weeds and algae. He knew the pond had been dug by Mike and Sally's granddad, knew that it must have rained into this crater in its first spring, and that the pond began with the end of the rain. In a matter of days the water would have oozed and skittered with life: with peepers and water-striders, whirligig beetles, dragonflies and flowers, seeds and eggs and spiders, algae floating on the surface of the water in a pale green echo of the forest. And it would happen again when his work was done.

He'd taken a few days off work to get the land in shape, to dig, to ponder what he was trying to do, to find. Like Sally, he wanted something here. The difference was that he knew it and she didn't.

Jake drove his truck around the dry path at the edge of the marsh grass, over to the embankment that dropped down to the beach and the Sound. This side of what had once been the pond was thick with sedge, the tapered grass as sharp and pointed as bayonets. Early morning and hot it was, cicadas buzzing like chainsaws, driving him nuts. Before the sun burned a hole in the sky, he'd work.

Jake would dig with simple tools: a pick, a rake, a shovel. In his truck was a copy of the original survey of the lot, along with Glen Groves' aerial photos of the pond taken in 1953, the year the treehome was completed. There was also a clipping from the *Banner* with a diagram of the Groves fire. Along with these things, Jake had what he carried in his heart, what he remembered.

Near the pond boundary, he found a remnant of the old footpath that led up the embankment and down to the beach. He'd brought some measuring tools, along with notes he'd made comparing the old survey and the coastal land, how the tides and weather had shifted and shaped it over the passing years. With this in mind he dug and probed, got down on his knees, pulled aside roots and muck with his hands, took his pick and began to hack away, a slow and careful troubling of the ground. A prospector mining for a precious gleam in rock, a botanist in search of a rare bloom; he would be this patient as he worked his way up the ridge overlooking the beach and the Sound.

For a week Jake Nolan continued to dig. As if he were dredging memory itself, he felt a reverence, a solemnity, his hoe unearthing the war, when he had stood at attention for flag-wrapped bodies, for choppers knifing the air. Jake's stomach shifted like a huge crashing wave about to break on the rock of those unhappy times, and then he gripped his shovel, took a long and steady breath, reminding himself what year it was, what place. And having turned the war over like a clump of dirt, he tried to put it out of his mind, to work with attention to the present, to the task at hand. It was out of respect for a dead man that he had bought the place.

Until the moment when something caught the edge of his pick, the slight, dull clank of metal. He crouched in the grasses, dug and scooped it out. The small, rectangular object was rusted, inscribed with a name that was barely legible, enough like an army dog tag to make Jake think it could have been a soldier's once. Or a fashion knock-off, or a father's wartime booty passed to a son with the same name. Years ago, Jake had never known which it was, had never much cared. Now it might be authentic, all he had left of his friend Tim, a thing as precious as a strand of DNA, a metal shard from which to construct the memory of a lost man.

A chain around his buddy's neck — Tim Gabriel back from the war and he about to leave for it — 1966. Here on this beach, Jake had been strumming his guitar, he and Tim shredding the air with the sharp edges of a grisly song, when his eye caught the glint of the tag and the peace medallion, and the sorrow on his buddy's face. Jake was sure it couldn't have been an army tag, not on Tim, not then. That scrap of memory, jammed all these years in a crevice of his brain like a stuck quarter in a pop machine, it bounced out now, as if he'd kicked it loose. Only Tim was gone, and none of it mattered to anyone but him. And Sally.

Jake hadn't expected to find this pendant, and it wasn't the sole reason for his coming here. He had needed a ritual of simple work, a decent end to the past before the backhoe came and the serious dredging of the pond began. He wanted to kneel before the face of suffering, Tim's face. He had to remember the dead.

Jake pressed the rusted object to his cheek, didn't care if anybody saw him. *God, you know the truth, what happened here.* He stood still, head bowed.

𝕽𝕸

Climbing the embankment, Sally noticed Jake, wondered what he was doing. Bronzed as a cattail swaying in the breeze, poking around in water gone to marsh, a clotted thatch of reeds. He glanced up, looked rueful, stuffed whatever he'd held to his face in his pocket, waved her over.

"Pieces of eight," he said, and smiled. "Used to be pirates here on the Sound."

"Stealing yachts, huh?"

Jake didn't answer, his eyes as warm as a kettle on the boil for tea. He went back to shovelling, digging in hard to the muck of the ground. *Make it as good as new* — his words. *Bring back water plants, birds, the whole ecology. Whole damn pond'll come back.*

Sally picked an iris, yanked at the sedge. Jake asked her what was up.

"Gabe," she said. "He flew up north where Lorne died."

Jake shrugged. "He'll make a good reporter."

"How do you mean?"

"He's on the trail of something, huh?" Sally nodded. Gabe on the hunt all right, poking and sniffing around like that damn dog of Jake's. She'd just received a letter in the mail, she'd read and reread it, felt her eyes stare out the window and accuse the forest as if it were to blame for Gabe's meandering through sentence after sentence. Blame the trees. Blame wood turned into paper for his letters and faxes, blame life for setting a match to things that burn. She handed Jake the letter.

...it was as if Lorne were there in the ashes, only it made me think of Vietnam and how he hated that war. Also Lorne filmed it. That was a very depressing experience, he told me that. He left me a note saying my real dad was in the war. So I guess it all adds up, and maybe the Conlin fire brought the whole thing back to him. Maybe he jumped because he was confused, didn't know what year it was, or even who he was.

Jake grimaced. "What the hell's he smoking?"

Sally looked away. "It's called shock."

"Yeah, right."

"He doesn't know about his dad," she said. A terrible hazy crack in her voice, like flying a bad sky.

Jake eyed her. "Does he have to know?"

"He's got it so wrong, Jake."

"Later, you tell him. It's too soon."

"I'll tape it for you," she said. "He can listen."

"No video?" asked Jake.

"No."

She'd told him video made her think of Lorne, how his careful eye had observed every nuance of her family's life. Relieved that he'd saved these pictures, she also felt that he'd trapped her life like bits of a fly inside a string of amber, in the late daylight of elegy and sorrow. *I need to have you listen, Jake. Not to have you watching me*, she'd said that. He looked at her with kindness now. "We'll talk. Maybe before you leave, huh?"

She told Jake yes, told him that it felt as if she'd flown Lorne over a devastating fire that, unknown to her, had gone on burning for a generation, that the fire in Conlin was real and at the same time a shimmering illusion. It hovered above another fire, the one that had destroyed her forest, the one she had never put out. *It got Lorne, it could destroy me too*, she thought this. Since Lorne's death, she had been afraid that she couldn't escape a horror that would never end: that everywhere she went, the fire was waiting, above her head, below her feet, all around her, in a dizzy corona like the sun in eclipse. As if she herself were the darkness.

Sally watched Jake work, glad she wouldn't be here to see the pond come back, bearing its store of memory and sorrow, hers and Tim's. Mike had felt the same, had been overwhelmed by the ruined forest. *As if the war went and followed me home*, he told her. He had left the broken trees to nurse their wounds, let time turn the pond to a bog, and when he was ready to sell the place, he didn't bother listing it. He called Jake Nolan, family friend and keeper of its ghosts.

Jake Nolan was a busy man. Sally knew damn well he had better things to do than pick up a shovel and root around for God knows what scraps from the past. Maybe that was why he did an abrupt and sudden thing, thrusting his shovel deep in the ground, as if at that very moment he too had seen the folly of wasting time with this slow and mindful work, with the tact and reticence it asked of him. He was a reporter, after all, a man of frank words. His expression had changed from calm to irritation and she saw a glint of trouble in his eyes.

"I've been digging, Sal," he said.

"Yes. I see."

"No, I mean in the *Banner* morgue," he explained. "The police records."

Sally felt chilled in the heat. She could sense Jake's insides in a rolling boil from that distant fire. He took a deep breath and folded his arms across his chest.

"Lorne told the cops you were nuts," he said. "How come?"

"What are you talking about?"

Jake gripped the shovel handle, yanked it out, thrust it into the ground again. "Did you burn down your woods or didn't you?"

His bluntness was a slap. Sally didn't answer.

Jake persisted. "You wrote a confession to the police. Did you forget?"

"I wrote that I did it by accident," she whispered.

"They didn't believe a word of it," he said. "Cops never thought a girl would start a fire, not back then."

"Jake, I don't care."

"Well, I do. Lorne told the police that you were a troubled kid and Tim was a radical, deranged from the war. Cops thought Tim was out to burn Fort Travis, at the other end of the woods, and he died with that smear on his name. Did you know that?"

"What's it matter now?" asked Sally.

"That Lorne lied?" said Jake. "It matters to me."

"Tim and I were sleeping," she said. "An ember floated up into the trees."

"How would you know that, if you were asleep?" Jake's voice, so abrupt, stopped. Sally hid her face in her hands. She felt his arm around her, and the awkward solace of his words. "God, I'm so sorry. I shouldn't have brought it up, Sal. You're the one got hurt, not me." Words tinged with smoke, as if the woods were burning still.

❦❦

Sally knew there was more than this to say, that she and Jake were both afraid. "Me and my big mouth," he said. "Just blurting out stuff, but I'll cool it Sal, I promise. Little by little, the story will come out," one layer of telling on top of the next, as if they were painters, sketching first, then adding hue and depth as they came to understand the inner life of what they saw.

It upset Jake, Lorne's accusations levelled against a man who never got to defend himself, and Sally understood. Yet it had happened so long ago, he told her, and if he weren't a local history buff and a family friend he'd drop his TV project, his compulsive ferreting for information, his off-the-record swipes at his own unhappiness and hers. Sally told him not to be hard on himself, he'd done her no harm.

Jake dug into his pocket, pulled out a rusted rectangular object and handed it to her. It looked like a piece of ID. Puzzled, Sally held it, squinting as she tried to read the numbers. She realized what it was and where he'd found it.

"Pieces of eight, huh?"

"Tim's," he said.

Sally took the tag and pressed it into the palm of his hand, then pressed his hand between both of hers. "Will you keep it, Jake?" she asked.

"You don't want it?"

"Right now, Tim is very close to you," she said.

She tidied the kitchen while Jake sat on a stool and watched her, his eyes as sad as rain. In the awkward silence, Sally asked him how he was and he shrugged. He couldn't complain, he said. His daughter in Boston got straight As, Sarge was at the vet's with an ear infection, his gal, Carla, was home on leave, got herself a promotion, be brass before you know it. He laughed a little, played with the tab on the beer can, looked at his shoes.

"She's lucky the Cold War's over, huh?" asked Sally.

"She's jealous of Vietnam. Says the boomers got all the lucky breaks."

"Kids."

Jake helped her rinse the dishes. "You like the north, Sal?" he asked.

"I got to like it."

Jake offered to put everything in the dishwasher. Sally sat on the stool and finished her beer while he stacked the plates, inserted the cutlery in the baskets, cursed under his breath when the forks fell through the holes, then poured in the soap. Quick, brusque. Sally no longer liked dishwashers, didn't care for this machine. In the north she enjoyed the peaceful routine of sudsing dishes, the comfort of warm water on her hands, the reassurance of their endless making clean, her working alone in the silence. As she was thinking this, Jake stood up straight and looked at her.

"Still bugs me, all of it," he said.

"You mean, about Tim?"

"And you. You suffered more than anyone."

"It's a long time ago," Sally answered. "Time's passed, Jake."

"I was overseas, I wasn't here to help." Jake said it as if he hadn't heard her. He slammed the dishwasher shut, turned it on and headed for the door.

"What could you have done?" she asked, but the full-cycle load was chugging and swishing and she couldn't hear if he answered.

Fire II

One

1966

A few months before Jake left for Vietnam, Lorne Winter was resting in Toronto, trying to recover from the war. He was alone, having lost both his memory and the love of Sally Groves. Yet he still felt touched by her graceful presence, a gentleness he'd never know again. She'd drifted away, left him, but no, he had fled in search of some crazy redemption in a violent place. It was his own fault that images of terror made him sleepless with fear of how the night air felt, raw with the screech of car wheels and slamming doors. Hot Toronto, summer rotting like bad fruit, a whole season drenched like a hooker in cheap perfume. He sat on the tiny upstairs porch of his house, squeezed in under the gables, his body incandescent, lit with pain.

Lonely, he'd been passing himself around like a canapé tray at a party. Yet he was the one who was hungry, who couldn't be satisfied by sex, who felt or remembered nothing of what had attracted him to slight figures in white boots and too-tight skirts from Carnaby Street. He smoked hash, went back to sleeping with Ella, laid the blame for all of this on high humidity and grief. "Have you thought of air conditioning?" Ella remarked. He already had a three-speed fan, a southerly breeze, a ledge to which he could cling in case he got stoned and fell from his third-floor balcony; more than that, a name, address and phone, a driver's licence with his date of birth, his landed immigrant's papers, an old U.S. draft card from 1952. Every day he looked through them, reclaiming the history of who he was.

Late last fall, he had returned to Toronto from his shoot in

Vietnam. He had called Sally first. "Will you see me?" he whispered into the phone. "Your brother is well, he thinks of you always." He took a deep breath. "How is Ella?" he asked. "Much better," said Sally. "She recovered from her depression, she's going to be OK, *Maclean's* let her have her old job back." Sally paused. "She'd love to hear from you. She knows you've had a rough time, she understands." Lorne said nothing. "Are you all right?" she asked him.

"Took one hit, shoulder grazed," he said to her. "I'll live."

He had got his footage and he had been ready to come home, except that he had felt harmed by what he'd seen, unfit to return to his former life. It had occurred to him to stay in Vietnam, to cover the war, until the war had come whistling through his skin. After this, he had begun to forget what had happened.

Dread had overtaken him, like a sheet pulled over a dead man's face. There was a ghost whiteness to everything, human shapes bleached out of their colours. When he returned to Toronto, it was as if that city were nothing more than film overexposed, all of its subjects losing definition. Yet it was Vietnam that began to evaporate, to disappear from the world.

He couldn't compare this to anything he'd experienced. It was like waking up in a tenth-storey room with a wall gone, the bed jutting out into the sky, being forced to sit on a chair with dissolving legs, to eat on a floating table that refused recognition to a knife, a fork, a plate. Later he understood that there were no containers for his experience of the war, no beds on which the whitened sheets would fit, no walls to enclose it in safety, no domestication of the terrible things he'd witnessed. Words broke apart and wept when he thought them, and the memory of what he'd seen collapsed around him like a ruined city. Only his camera remembered it. He told Sally that Vietnam had slipped through his hands like water, that he couldn't talk.

He'd sent his eyes to Vietnam, had left his body home, wasn't that it? Except that he'd bled.

His hands flay the air, on the chopper stairs he hears the whistle, teeters, ducks too late. I'm going to die, he thinks, relieved at the sting of pain, the wet heat of his own blood. Hoping there is a God who'll weigh his life on the scales, judging how light it is against the rock-weight of desolation burning in his camera, in the world.

"Lorne, are you all right?" Sally asked. She'd agreed to meet him in a Bloor Street café. His coffee sat untouched.

"I'm sometimes afraid," he answered.

How thin he felt, as if he were spectral, returned from the dead. His body like some gangly plant in search of light, all trailing vine and pallid leaf, too rambling to fit into the measured proportions of this city. Everything made him edgy — the sudden opening of a door, the waiter handing them menus. He looked at Sally.

"At night I hear things," he said to her. "The walls dissolving."

"'All that is solid melts into air.'"

"It's like that, yes. Not as poetic."

"It's from my roommate. She likes to quote Marx."

The quote is, if nothing else, exact. A terrible death dissolving into light as over and over a filmed soldier draws a pistol, shoots the man, who slithers to the ground in a thin, dry heap of bones. That poor dead man, no more than a ghost of a creature; likewise that soldier torching the thatched roof of the man's home; both composites of light and shadow, nothing more. What has become of the solid weight of them? What did I do with the memory of their lives?

"Who were you reaching out to, Lorne?"

He looked away. "Someone who melted into air. I don't know who."

Sally, he noticed, had a new stylish haircut, filigreed earrings, a beige angora beret. On the chair next to her she'd left a matching scarf. He let his hand rest on it, felt Sally's eyes.

"From Eaton's," she said. She reached out to take it from him.

"It feels good," said Lorne. "I almost remember you."

"I don't understand," she said.

Lorne stroked the wool. Useless, he thought, like something he had dreamt and couldn't retrieve, a softness. Before him was a woman who had once given him hope. It wasn't her fault that she no longer could.

"I'm talking about how life felt once," he said.

Once before the time of Ella's loss and Sally's leaving him, before the intrusion of an image that he couldn't escape, as if it were hell, a punishment for grave wrong. Forever damned to live as a witness, to hold the camera to his mind's eye as he filmed a soldier who interrogated a slight man dressed in black, who used a telephone, a field device, a crude electrical prod. Now he wondered that he had been allowed to film this. Home again, he cringed at the range of sounds that conjured up a single shot, as he saw a dying man topple over, withered as an insect's carapace. Circumspect, a man of reticence; how artful that he, the photographer, had captured this in the slow, reluctant trickle of his blood. Mesmerized, he watched the film unspool in his troubled mind. A soldier gave the man a kick, slipped the gun back in his holster, didn't care who knew, who saw.

To live forever in the presence of this — how could he?

Sally took her scarf from him. She'd been speaking. "Talk to Ella," she continued, her voice soft.

"I'll edit it," he said to himself.

"Lorne?"

"I'm sorry."

"She'll forgive you."

He had to clear his mind of this.

*

Sowing the Wind was broadcast in January 1966. "A first...a brilliant unravelling of the hidden war in Vietnam.... Lorne Winter's point-blank TV film leaves you aghast," said *The Globe and Mail*. *The Toronto Star* added, "Hannah Arendt's phrase 'the banality of evil' might have been written with the crop-dusting scene in mind; the pilot is as calm and workmanlike as a farmer spraying for blight."

Lorne had written to Sally before he planned these shots. "I need to know what soldiers feel who have to live by instinct and a canny eye. I need to stalk, to watch.... After a while, I'll arrive at a middle ground before my empathy teeters and crashes into blind indifference. It's in that place that I'll find my story." She wrote back, "I hope the enclosed snapshot of Mike and this introductory letter will give you some 'pull' when you meet him. His unit is based in Pleiku, in the Central Highlands, I think it is.... I wrote and told him you were making a documentary and he said, 'I got a load of napalm just for him, these guys are worse than the enemy,' but he's a joker, as you know."

"We evacuate the people first," Mike told Lorne. "I hope you'll make that clear. Think of a forest of eighteen thousand acres. Back in March we had six thousand evacuees and a hundred acres of crops. Now there's what we wiped out, crops. Boi Loi was a VC hideout so we hit it with everything we had. Herbicides, diesel fuel, napalm...it's too damn humid for fire, trees have the wrong resins, they don't fucking burn. Crops withered up, though." Mike made a special trip, flew Lorne over the devastation of the Boi Loi woods, northwest of Saigon. Lorne shook Mike's hand and thanked him for his time.

Sally's brother scribbled out names and units of some friends of his: good guys, good shots. He bought Lorne a drink. Later, stone-blind drunk, Lorne said, "Sally wants you back alive, ya know," and her brother answered, "I miss my kid sis, you take good care of Sally, huh?"

In the film, Lorne didn't use her brother's name.

☙❧

"Your camera speaks," said Ella. "These are brilliant images." She wrote a feature on him for *Maclean's*, and Lorne won awards, citations. After a while, she slept with him again. Only she belonged to the world of half-formed objects bleached by light, things that no longer made any sense, a faceless shadow drifting through his walls. He awoke to nightmares, flashbacks, a month in the hospital, and Ella came to look after him. "I know what it's like," she said. "You've been through a war."

Lorne remembered nothing.

☙❧

He had made cuts in the film. Even so, he couldn't forget what he'd seen.

"You couldn't have stopped them?" Sally asked. Not Mike, she didn't mean him. "There were no people in the woods, sis," Mike had written. It was the others who got to her — a soldier shooting a villager, then setting fire to the man's house. Worse was the peasant marched at knifepoint into the woods, then handed a shovel to dig his own grave. Only then did the man break down and talk. On film, his interrogator leaned against a tree, his back to the camera, his body shaking as he retched.

"I sometimes wish I could have intervened," said Lorne.

"Someone will see your film and stop them."

"I'm not so naive," he replied.

"Don't you believe in what you do?" she asked.

Lorne didn't answer.

Two

In June, Sally returned to Groves Island for the summer. She was about to turn twenty, and Lorne sent her a birthday gift, a scrapbook containing unpublished photos of all the events of her family's life that he'd covered for the *Banner*. Accompanying them were the published stories and more of his photos, dated and labelled: her father floating his way across the tarmac with his long, loping stride and high-beam smile, the family waving from the treehome balcony the day the Korean armistice was signed, her mother's blue ribbon from the Glassmakers' Society juried competition. Over and over, her own face, expectant and joyful. In this way he'd treasured her life, saved it, given it back.

With the gift was a note explaining that he'd be in New York City in July for the first major show of his work, and for a restful assignment, taking photos for a book on Long Island Sound. Would she allow him on her property to photograph her beach? Moved by his gift, Sally wrote and gave him permission, asking that he come on weekdays, while she was working at Travis. She didn't want to see him there, not in the vastness of memory, not alone.

☙☙

She wanted to see Sister Fran, who drove up the Lincoln Road hill with a carload of groceries, a welcome home. A stranger leapt from the car to greet Sally, a woman as lean and angular as a sailor in a stiff wind. *Call me Fran, dear,* Fran in civvies, a navy shirtwaist dress, a tiny cross, black loafers, stockings. She had short fair hair, threads of it greying like filaments of steel wool. Her gaze seemed stronger, more formidable, as if it had to carry the clout of the missing veil and habit. Her eyes were Lorne's, and they touched Sally in the same disconcerting way, claiming their right to peer inside, to avoid a gaze. *She's feeling insecure,* Sally thought. *I bet guys stare at her legs.* She asked Fran if she could bum a cigarette.

"I quit," said Fran.

Sally was taken aback. "New you. You never told me."

"Do you tell me everything?"

Sally didn't answer. Fran talked about butting out, how jumpy it had made her, how as a substitute she'd taught her fidgety hands to type, her impatient mouth to say what was on her mind, knowing she would soon become the bane of senators and congressmen.

"This war is the bottom of the barrel, dear," said Fran. "Do you pray for your brother?"

Sally told her yes. She asked Fran if she'd seen Lorne's film.

"Yes, and I thought it was a brilliant exposé."

Fran reached for a phantom cigarette, started pulling groceries from shopping bags, putting them away, opening the fridge door, slamming it shut, picking up cans of soup and beans that tumbled out of her shaking hands. Sally got down and picked up a can that had rolled under the table.

"Are you jumpy because you quit smoking?" she asked.

Fran looked annoyed. "You may have noticed there's a war on."

"Is that why you're dropping all those cans?"

"I'm worried about Mike," said Fran. "And you."

"What for?"

Fran glared at her. "What *for*?"

"Yes."

"Because God made a puzzle of your family." Sally put the rest of the groceries away, imagining herself on the back pages of *The New York Times,* a letter in a crossword, a crazy intersection of Across and Down.

"A six-letter word meaning 'demented,'" she said. "Starts with G, ends with S."

"Sally," Fran said.

"What?"

"That's not funny. You came close to ruining your life."

Sally felt a flash of rage. "You mean with Lorne?"

"You *wrote* me, Sally. It's a year now, but —"

"Lorne's off the hook, I guess. Lorne's your hero now, Saint Lorne. Never mind Ella and his ——"

"That'll be enough," said Fran.

She should have bitten her tongue, shouldn't have used Ella's suffering to wound Fran, even if the woman's judgement was unfair. Fran knew her too well. She'd seen into the depths of her, into that remorseful day when Ella hadn't mattered.

"My brother," said Fran in a hushed voice, "is trying to do better."

"I'm sorry."

Fran took a deep breath, started to talk again, more words than Sally was used to hearing from her. She said she was taking a sabbatical to study politics, to organize anti-war meetings, to help protesters who ended up in jail. A rockslide of language then, Fran's words pounding her, Sally's own thoughts crushed by injunctions as weighty as boulders.

"You know I don't mean to hurt you," said Fran. "I'm fond of you, dear. Weakness is human, I have my faults too, there's no denying it, but I think you're more troubled than you let on, especially about Mike. You should sit down and write about what's happening in your life so that you can see patterns forming from the past, things that repeat. That way you can learn to help yourself."

All these *words.*

Sally felt guilty. She had liked Fran better as the Smoking Nun, before she got political and talked so much. She had liked the distance of the veil, the crumpled packs of cigarettes stuffed in the folds of her habit, the secret ways in which Fran had been different from everyone, including other sisters, the way she had looked and acted religious but hardly ever talked it. *The written word is a form of prayer* — Fran was starting to say things like that.

"Lorne was dismayed with Mike," said Fran.

Lorne promised me he'd find him, and Sally remembered the anguish of their last night together. She looked at Fran, recalling the clean-soap smell of her skin and the starchy folds of her habit, how she'd come to the hospital to give Sally solace when her mother disappeared.

"Lorne's trying to do better, yes," said Sally.

"He doesn't blame others for his mistakes," Fran declared.

Sally got the point, heard the exit of the quiet Sister Frances, her swish of skirts and the clatter of her beads, the shortness of breath that had separated Fran from a thing or two she'd had to say. A suffering she'd buried, a humming rage that moved towards Sally and her brother like a cloud of angry wasps. As if she and Mike had it coming.

🖎🖎

Sally's family had done Fran no harm. It happened that their forest drifted into Fort Travis, which had once been part of the Groves' land, so that each property was an extension, a missing limb of the other. Maybe Fran had come to the conclusion that what ailed their family was this accident of geography, the years of wind that had carried the noise of gunfire, a sound falling like seed in their fertile woods, a thing that had troubled their dreams and driven them crazy. *It could be anything made us who we are*, Sally thought. *God or a war or the forest.*

She loved Fran still.

Fran was the atmosphere of Sally's earth, as elemental as the forest or the sky, a force indifferent to love. Yet Sally wanted Fran to love her, longed for kindness from her distant eyes. "You have a birthday coming up," Fran had said a week ago. Sally had been moved that she remembered, even though she herself hadn't observed her birthday since the day of her father's disappearance. "Oh, I don't want to celebrate," Sally had said. "Not your twentieth?" Fran seemed perplexed. "No, nothing. If it's warm, I'll go down to the Clam Shack, buy a bucket and catch the breeze." Fran had looked at her hard, then turned her eyes away. "I like your spirit," she'd said. "In any case, you can't afford indulgence."

Wondering if she was harping on Lorne, stung by the blemished truth of this reply, Sally answered, "And what do you do on your birthday?"

"My laundry," Fran replied.

Two days later, Fran had come by and given Sally a small box. Inside it was a gold cross on a chain, one that had belonged to Katherine Groves. Sally had embraced her, but Fran had pulled away. She put the chain on Sally.

"Practise restraint," she had said. "In your mother's memory."

Sally had thanked her, wondered if she could.

☙❧

On Sally's birthday, Fran went out to the Travis airstrip and stood alone with a pot of hyacinths which she placed before the stone cairn in memory of Glen Groves. Sally went there with the same thought in mind. She saw Fran and watched from a distance, imagined her standing before a grave, hands clasped, head bowed, intent on thinking her father back to life, her mother also, stitching them into the cloth of memory as if the strand of thought might break at any moment, just as the frail web of this family had broken years ago.

Sally moved into the eddy of Fran's thoughts, into her hand as it made a slow and deliberate sign of the cross. As she watched, she could feel in her own hand the shape Fran was tracing on her body, and she could sense in this movement the wind's directions, north to south and west to east. A conjuring trick, this blessing was, that was all. It would bring nothing back.

When she returned home, she took off the gold cross, hung it on the wedding photo in her mother's dusty room.

Three

It had been a warm day, and that evening Sally went for a stroll along Washington Street. She stopped for a coffee at the Hoot Owl, sat alone and let another birthday drift away from her, as each of them had done since the day her father had flown out to sea with her name in tow. As a girl she had refused to honour the day her father had vanished, preferring to say that it was her birthday that had disappeared, not him. "I don't know when I was born," she told Riva, who'd been orphaned during the war, who understood.

That morning she had got an airmail note from Mike in Vietnam. Knowing what it was likely to contain, she had put off reading it until the day's end. Now she ripped it open. *I know you find it hard, sis,* it said, *but on your twentieth I send you love and good wishes for happiness and long life. Believe me, there's no greater thing.*

His kindness seared her, stung her eyes like woodsmoke. She folded the letter, put it in her pocket. She wanted to be invisible as she meandered through strolling families out for the sea breeze, soldiers and their girls, young kids hanging out at the Clam Shack and Louie's Lobster Bin. A calm here she'd always liked, a low murmur of voices and the clank of rigging on the docks, the comforting salt smells of steamers and melted butter. Only she wasn't hungry, didn't feel like eating, didn't see anyone she knew down here. She kept walking until the eateries slipped past her and into the night, until voices softened and the only sound she could hear was the swish of water under the boardwalk.

She stood still. In the distance she heard music, the odd,

birdlike piping of a flute, a plaintive air that drew closer to her, picking up speed and rhythm with each note until she could feel it in the creak and groan of the planks under a man's footstep, a man running right up to her and grabbing her around the waist, *Hey there, sister,* the words burning her ear. For just a second he was so close that she could feel the bone of his hip through her skirt, the threadbare cloth of his sleeve against her arm, the sweet, close brush of him along her midriff, bare where she'd tied her shirt-tails in a knot. Just when her body shivered like a gull's tail-feathers in a breeze, he bounded off with his penny-whistle, right down to the end of the dock. *Stoned,* she thought.

"Wait up!" Sally yelled. She ran after him.

She wondered if she'd lost her mind. She felt as if she were tumbling downward into some hole in the cosmos that didn't even feel like this dock, this place, Groves Island. She grabbed his arm, looked into his eyes, which were dark and soft as midnight. He wore cut-off jeans as old as weather, and around his neck was a chain with two pendants, one that looked like army ID. A slim, lanky man he was, with the quiet, graceful stride of a scout. He was tall, his shoulders stooped, as if he were crouching, hiding. She looked at him.

"Why the hell did you grab me like that?"

He was gazing at the water. "The war's over," he said.

Sally took his arm. "Were you smoking something?"

When he turned to look at her, his eyes were sad. "You like asking questions."

"I don't know you, is why."

"Shouldn't be walking alone, gal. Soldiers coming out of bars, it isn't safe."

She told him she'd grown up on the island, lived near the base. She wasn't afraid of soldiers, wasn't scared to go walking alone after dark.

He shrugged, dug his hand in his pocket. "Wanna toke?"

"I want to hear you play that flute."

He put it to his lips, breathing into it a slow, quiet air.

She smiled. "Where'd you learn to play that?"

"Vietnam."

"You got the flute there?"

"All those *questions*, gal."

"Just curious."

He tapped the side of his head. "Intelligence."

Sally laughed. "Yeah. I think I'm smart."

"Nah, gal. I mean you're *gathering* intelligence. Army-style."

"You did that?"

He nodded yes, and then he began to disturb the stillness of the night again with music as he walked her from the docks to the Lincoln Road bus. When they got to the stop, he put the flute in his pocket and stood still, just looking at her. *Goodnight, gal*, he said. Then he grabbed her arms and kissed her hard, so that she could feel the salt taste of his tongue in her mouth, the sweet flipping of her heart like a pancake on a griddle. The high beams from the bus were sweeping down from the hill, towards them like a pair of nosy eyes. When the bus pulled up, Sally stepped on board, her stomach leaping and flapping like a bird. She didn't even know his name, not then.

Should have asked him his name, given him mine. Should have taken him home with me. Except that his namelessness was enticing, full of sexual danger, and last night she had felt it in the touch of him. Only now he was gone, goddammit. She was a fool.

Early morning, six a.m., and Sally could hear cicadas, the loud buzz of them, a crazy sizzle, as if the sun were talking. It had been a hot night and she'd slept in the treehome. She was thinking about the stranger who had made her insides flip like a patty on a grill, and every untouched part of her regretted the absence of his tongue, his hands. She had to go to work, she needed calm. It was early enough for a dunk in the pond, a dip in the dead-still quiet.

She came down the spiral stairs, found her way through the path to the pond, where she took off her robe and slipped into the water naked, on her back, her breasts floating white as water-lilies. How sudden it was, how unexpected, that she felt she could lie there in serenity, forgetting this man and all that had troubled her, letting the losses of her life slip away unnoticed like the dead cells of her skin, gliding like a duck past the sedge and rushes and croaking frogs, *ah, lovely*. A gift, that she felt like a water-strider, a queen in a gown of duckweed. She paddled with her hands, then shut her eyes.

In the distance she heard noises, branches giving way, the snap of twigs on the path. She splashed, ducked, drew her head up for air, dog-paddling as she scanned the grasses at the edge of the pond. Jesus, it was *him*. He was wearing jeans and T-shirt and a red bandanna on his long black hair, his peace medallion around his neck like a letter in some alphabet she couldn't read. She wondered if he was carrying his flute.

"What're you doing here?" she yelled.

"Followed you last night," he said. "Took the last bus."

"You slept in the woods?"

He shrugged. "Used to it." He was smiling, clutching something close to his body, her towel and robe. "Want 'em?" he yelled.

"'Course I want 'em. After my swim."

"How about now, hon? Otherwise I throw 'em in." He started laughing. *What the fuck*, she thought.

"That's not real fair," she said.

"Well, some point you have to come get 'em, now don'tcha?" He glanced at his watch. "Don't want you late for work."

"What time is it?"

"You come up here and find out. I won't hurt ya."

It couldn't be seven, Sally thought. Then she felt afraid, thinking of Fran's admonitions. She wondered why he'd followed her, why he was sleeping in the forest. Wary, she paddled towards the flat rocks, in sight of the clearing surrounded by a circle of small oaks where she'd left her robe and towel. The man was clutching her things, following her along the edge of the pond to the shallow spot where she'd have to climb out. It didn't matter to her that he saw her naked, only that she wanted some say over when she put on her own damn clothes. This was private property, she had a right to swim in her own pond undisturbed at any time, naked or not. He was trespassing, she'd call the police, if only she had her clothes on. Sally crouched down, still under water, thinking up a plan. *Fat chance this'll work*, she thought.

"Now you hold up the towel, don't look," she said.

The man did as he was told. He held up the towel in front of him so that it looked like one of those white-sheet screens that hospitals use for privacy. Sally walked towards him and he didn't look at her. When she reached him, she was about to take the towel from his hands and wrap herself in it when she felt it collapsing all around her, until she was enveloped in its softness, then in its warmth, then in his. She was wrapped in the towel, his arms around her, and he was holding her close, all he seemed to want to do. And he kept whispering, *Oh God, oh God, oh God,* his hand on the back of her damp head, pressing it to his chest as if she were a lost child who'd almost drowned from his neglect. "What is it?" Sally asked him. He turned away and hid his face in his hands.

"I wouldn't have hurt you. I'm sorry."

"Why'd you go and steal my robe?" she asked.

He looked up. "I don't know why. I guess I wanted to hold you."

"I would have let you. You smooched me last night, what's a hug?" She stared at him, thought of how forward he'd been, swinging her around on the dock, then grabbing her and kissing her, as if he'd never in his life strolled through the sweet in-between of courting a woman. It was like watching the jerky motions of a film run at twice the normal speed, as if everything had to happen now, as if there were no time in life to get to know someone before you loved them. Maybe this was the agitation of the war in him. She took his arm.

"I'm real sorry," he said.

"You tell me your name now."

"Tim Gabriel." He looked stunned, contrite, his head bowed, his voice as tired as that of a captive who'd been questioned by jailers for a night and a day. He told her he'd been three years in the army, one of them in Vietnam, a sergeant, when he'd taken the troubles of the war to heart, enough to quit the career he'd wanted most. He said that he came from Linden, that he knew of her family. Everyone did.

Sally looked at him. "Why do you talk like that?"

"Like what?"

"Like I'm gonna shoot you if you don't."

He smiled. "Dunno."

Sally told him that he might enjoy hiking on the trails in her woods, as long as they didn't remind him of the jungle. "It's not jungle," he said, his voice very soft, and then he tapped the side of his head. "The jungle stays in here."

There was coffee on the go in the treehome, Sally said. She took him up the stairs and they stood on the porch, looking down at the holes her father had cut out of the floorboards for the huge boughs, thick green leaves, a slight breeze nudging them apart, light sifting through them to the ground below, the picnic table still there with its echoes and voices. Tim Gabriel's voice was as soft as one of these memories.

He reached up, touched the shingles on the roof, and then he went inside with Sally and ran his hands over the polished floors, the windows, the bevelled wood on the frames, the sturdy door, the crossbeams on the ceiling, until she began to feel that he was gathering into himself the moment when the glass and the wood of this building had been glazed and stained and hammered, lathed and polished and sanded down. She thought of her father's strong and careful hands. Tim's hands were finer, more hesitant.

"I can feel your dad here," he said. He paused when she didn't answer. "I'm sorry. You got no folks, Sally?"

"Just Mike."

"You got a boyfriend. Sure you do." His voice was kind.

Sally lowered her eyes. "Did."

Tim lifted her chin and turned her face towards him. She turned away, went to pour the coffee.

"He was twelve years older. Just too fast for me, was all."

Her hand shook, spilled coffee on the table, and Tim jumped, grabbed a towel, mopped up the mess, put a hand on her arm. It was his own fault, he said, his bugging her with questions. He pulled his chair close to her and began to stroke her hair with a slow and awkward touch. It was as if gentleness was a thing his hands were trying to recall, like the resting of fingers on piano keys, their graceful lifting out of music.

"Over thirty's way too old," he said.

"He didn't think so."

"Who?"

"Lorne." Tim's hand stopped moving. Sally looked up.

"Lorne from here?" he asked. "The camera guy?"

She nodded.

"He was in Nam," Tim said.

"You met him?"

Tim looked away. "That damn camera. Kept my back to him."

"You didn't talk to Lorne?"

Tim shook his head, and for a minute he said nothing. When he spoke, his voice was soft with regret.

"That stuff's for God to hear. No one else."

He began to stroke her hair again, and then both his hands were touching her shoulders, her neck, the back of his hand across her cheek so that she could feel the hairs on his skin, and on her lips the tug and pull of longing. She shivered, pulled herself away.

"Why don't you go have a swim?" she asked.

"You don't want that," he whispered, and maybe it was the mention of Lorne and trouble that brought on desire, as Tim took her in his arms and kissed her mouth, her neck, her breasts. Quick and sweet the whole of it was, and afterwards Tim went down to the pond and Sally got ready for work, just as if their encounter in the trees were a normal thing, one that might happen again. Knowing she'd be late for work, Sally watched from the treehome porch as Tim slipped out of his clothes and splashed in the water. She wondered then what had become of that early morning, of the soft air and the cicadas, of that moment of grace in the water when she was adrift in the hands of the day, as pure as a flower, a newborn cleansed of sorrow.

Four

He was company, Tim Gabriel, a watchman in the forest, and after a few weeks Sally let him set up camp. Only then did she admit how lonely she'd been. Having lived away from home since her mother's death, she had few ties to the island with her family's name, only the friendship of the Nolans and Sister Fran. Now there was Tim, who had grown up along the same stretch of wooded coast. His divorced parents had moved away. He wanted to be home by the Sound, and in return for a summer camped in Sally's woods he did chores for her, then picked up a delivery job at Island Grocers on the Shore Road. In the fall he was going to college in New York City, hoping to major in history or psych. *I want to know what the hell happened to me and why*, he'd say, and Sally could feel inside his words the low, steady humming of the army and the war. Sometimes, in the evening, she'd hear his flute, his pale, distant music of regret.

In the early mornings Tim would swim in the pond, and Sally found his caution surprising as he glanced through the sedge and cattails, then out to the opposite bank, as if he were new to the water and trying to figure out how deep it was. Like a scout, too; careful, listening. Sally thought of him snitching her robe, wrapping her up in a towel, holding her, and she still wondered that he didn't just say, *Sally, will you be with me? Will you let me hold you?*

Tim was no longer so abrupt, so afraid. He'd take her in his arms and hold her with a protectiveness that felt contrite and tender all at once. They were drawn together in silence, held in the intimate web of loss and regret. Apart from sex, there was little to be done or said between them that could touch the depth of this knowledge. Tim was awkward with words, with gentle questions. Something left over from the war, Sally thought; something not quite right in him.

It was a hot Friday when Jake Nolan dropped by Island Grocers and ran into his old buddy, Tim. "Hey pal, welcome back," he said. "I'm headed where you came from." When he heard that Tim was camping out in Sally's woods, he said they should hit the beach that weekend, bring a six-pack, reminisce about their high school swim-meet days, "and Sal's no slouch in the water," he added. Tim said he'd noticed that.

On Saturday morning, Sally dragged the treehome phone outside so Tim wouldn't miss Jake's call. He sat at the picnic table, looking pensive as he stared at the black cradle, the receiver, the long wire looped around a tree branch. At last Jake called to tell them he was heading for their beach. A few minutes later the phone rang again. Tim answered and the air crackled with a man's voice, *This is Lorne Winter*. Sally heard it.

"I'll take that, Tim."

Tim gripped the phone as if he couldn't let go. Sally heard Lorne's voice again. *Who am I speaking to?*

"Tim Gabriel," he said.

I know your voice from somewhere. Have we met?

"You goddamn following me?" Tim slammed the receiver down.

Sally ran over, yanked the phone away from him. "What the hell d'ya do that for?" she asked.

Tim hid his face in his clenched fists. The phone rang again and Sally answered. Lorne didn't say hello. He lowered his voice to a whisper, each word pronounced with care so that she had no trouble hearing. "I know Tim Gabriel, I got his name from Mike," he said.

"He told me he met you."

"Whatever he's doing there —"

"Visiting."

"— is none of my business. Just be careful." Lorne hadn't called to check on her, he assured her of that. He only wanted to ask if he could use the treehome to photograph her beach at dawn. He promised to be discreet, as Fran had been years before with the two of them. Since Tim's arrival Sally had felt free of constraint, of the chance sweep of anyone's eyes, but even so, she told him go ahead, any morning was fine. When she hung up, she realized how much she wanted someone to look in on her. From time to time she felt uneasy, alone with Tim.

She tried to put the thought out of her mind. Tim seemed dazed as he bent down and picked up the cable, looping the long black snake of it around his arm. His eyes were drifting into shock, into some fear he couldn't escape, and she thought of Lorne, how frail the war had made him.

"Winter's making a movie," Tim said.

Sally was puzzled. "He already has," she replied. "It's done."

He turned and glared at her. "You get him off my fucking tail."

"That's not why Lorne's here." Sally felt afraid.

"Guy's a shit. Know what we do to shits?" He grabbed the cable as if it were rope, a noose.

"Tim, stop."

"Wrap it around his nuts and plug it in." He threw the cable down, then slumped forward, his head on the table.

"Tim, what's wrong?"

"Fucking heat, is all."

Without warning he leapt up, ran down to the edge of the pond, towards the steep embankment to the water.

🌿🌿

Sally had started running towards the embankment, picking her way through the tangle of beach-peas and thistles on the downward slope to the water. It was the same wild place where she and Lorne had gone walking three years back. Crouching on the rocks, hidden by brush, she saw Jake come walking up the beach from the road, striding along, a rolling sailor's gait, as if the whole world were a ship's deck on a rough sea, but he'd be fine, she could see it in his grin. Dusty brown hair to his shoulders; Jake was as laid back as a pair of old shoes. He had on his swimming trunks and John Lennon T-shirt and he carried a towel and guitar case. Whistling a Beatles tune, he was a man full of rhythm and music — different from Tim, who seemed to walk in silence on his toes, a deliberate and graceful step, like a deer's.

She watched Jake embrace his buddy, pull back and take a good hard look at him, his hands gripping Tim's arms as if he knew there was something wrong. They talked but the south breeze carried their words away from her. Tim was starting to look better. The two guys took off their T-shirts, skidding into the water like a pair of clumsy penguins. Then they got serious, beginning their crawl out into the Sound as if they were still in high school meets and swimming against each other. And it seemed they swam until they were as distant as the moon.

Sally watched them dipping in and out of the waves, then turning around and crawling back towards shore. In low tide the two strode up onto the beach, arm in arm, looking relaxed. They dried off and Jake grabbed a few beers out of the cooler, pulled out his guitar and began to strum. He sang, his voice soft at first, and from what Sally could hear above the shrieking gulls and the waves, he had a nice voice, sweet as melted caramel. Real campfire stuff was what he sang, "This Train," "Oh Freedom," "Five Hundred Miles." He sang other songs that Sally could remember her mother humming, getting more boisterous and hokey, knocking off one beer after another, schmaltzing it up with "We'll Meet Again" and "Lili Marlene." Tim, on his third beer, listened.

"Now it's my turn," he said, and he staggered to his feet, dragging Jake up, "Awright, Nolan," he bawled, "here's what you're in for in Nam. Now lemme hear ya yell it out!" Tim started to march in place, shouting a rhyme, stomping the sand. Sally couldn't hear the words, and then she did.

> Napalm, napalm sticks like glue.
> Sticks to women and children, too....
>
> Children in a schoolhouse trying to learn.
> Drop that napalm, watch 'em burn.

Sally wished she hadn't come. *He's plastered, he's got to be.* She could hear a cry smashing through the din of the waves as if they were rolling into Long Island Sound straight from the South China Sea. *Will you fucking shut up!* Jake's voice.

Cobra skimmin' over the trees
firin' rockets at the refugees.

We don't care 'cause the ammo's free
and napalm sticks to kids.

We don't CARE....

Tim screamed it out as Jake grabbed him and slapped him hard across the face. Backwards he stumbled, fell in the sand, his voice fading. Jake helped him up and led him to the blanket, talked to him and tried to calm him down. Tim sat with his face hidden in his hands, the two of them still as a snapshot, a picture without the sound. Sally imagined the waves repeating, *See, the war is with us already. See how all bodies of water are the same.* Then she watched as Jake dug into his guitar case, pulled out a cloth bag and some papers and began rolling a joint. He lit it, took a drag, passed it to Tim, put his arm around his shoulder as he smoked. Tim passed it back to Jake. As quiet as a lit match was how they were. Friends in the still moment before the tide rises and the wind blows out the flame.

Five

Tim came back and apologized to Sally. He took her hands in his and kissed them, said it was the shock of Lorne's voice coming through that damn phone that had rattled loose the screws and bolts of his brain. After this, and with almost no preamble, Sally and Tim grew very close. It felt as if they were both at war against some unnamed danger. Much that could not be said, they understood; much that might have taken time to grow bore fruit in an overripe summer, as if time were moving faster than it should towards hurricane season and fall.

Sally neglected the rest of her life, her unanswered mail. Riva was vacationing in Montreal (*chère amie, are you well?*) and Jimbo wrote from his summer deejay stint in Saskatchewan, a place about as real to her as her father's proto-continents. *Prairie's as flat as an LP, we spin 'em night 'n' day. Call in your requests, eh? Luv ya.* A month home on the island, and she hadn't written to anyone but Mike, whose war lay in the pit of her stomach like a rock-heavy meal. Every day she thought of him, fearful as she was of the speed at which bad news travels: letters, telegrams, a too-insistent ringing of the phone. Her mother, she remembered, had suffered her father's going to war, had lived four years with dread like this.

She told Tim her mother's story, and one evening she took him into the sunroom where Katherine had painted years ago. Under her work-table was a lone corrugated box. Sally pulled it out and opened it. Inside were broken chunks of porcelain and glass, finished pieces that her mother's trembling hands had dropped and smashed by accident. Sally had forgotten this box, couldn't remember why they'd saved it. She told Tim about her mother's misfortunes, showing him some of her fragile bowls that even now seemed to hover on shelves like butterflies. He picked up a bowl and touched it, his touch lighter than breath.

"Nothing's broke for good," he said.

"I should dump that box."

"No way. Stuff you can fix in there."

It was too fussy, not worth his time; Sally told him this, but Tim insisted, talked about glass and china adhesives and how you'd hardly see the cracks when he was done. He improvised tools to apply the glues, got fine sandpaper and a magnifying glass; set himself up in the sunroom. Sally watched him, observed his careful hands applying hair-thin epoxies, then gentle pressure as he made and held the join in place. "Glue says ten minutes I gotta hold it," and she found him a radio to make the time pass. It was like watching a movie in reverse, the shards of her mother's life flying back together, the breaks and fractures healing at a surgeon's touch. Her mother, alive.

Sally left him to his work, went in the living room and turned on the TV. In the news was the bombing of Haiphong Harbour, the outskirts of Hanoi, the biggest conflagration of the war since the march when Ella had fainted. Sally heard them talk about F-105s, the plane her brother flew, and she watched every newscast in the hope of seeing him. Instead she saw aerial shots of burning cylinders, oil tanks etched in fire. Distressed, she went back into the workroom. Tim was holding together a porcelain bowl, finishing up. "It's all right, Sal," he whispered. "Means the war'll be over soon," but she was unconsoled.

"My brother likes what he does," she said.

Tim put the bowl down, held her. "He don't *like* it," he said. "Just *does* it."

"Mike says it's more than a job. It makes him happy."

"Liar," Tim said. "No it don't." He let go of Sally, picked up the bowl he'd just restored, his eye on its pattern of flowers, invisible cracks.

❦❦

Fran Winter was also on TV. That hot July, the news showed her irate and striding across the George Washington Bridge in a sign-waving file of nuns and clergy. Waiting for the cameraman to stop in front of her, she quoted Robert Kennedy, his words of condemnation. Sally watched her while Tim, oblivious, was working on his seventh piece of glass. He began to find shards that didn't seem to belong anywhere, and with these he started to experiment, creating strange, angular mobiles, found art: teacups with bottlenecks for handles, candle-holders from the stems of shattered goblets.

Sally called Fran, told her she'd seen her on TV. She told her about Tim Gabriel, waiting for a lecture that didn't come.

"At least he's learned from the war," said Fran.

"Lorne met him there."

"I know," said Fran. "The man with the phone."

Sally remembered Tim's slamming down the receiver, felt annoyed that Lorne had relayed the incident to her. "Tim's sorry," she said.

"The sorry ones suffer most," said Fran. Her voice was as tart as a green apple, a hard crispness to each word. Sally went along with it, allowing herself to see in her mind the harm Tim might have done in the war: women fleeing a village put to the torch, clutching their fatherless children.

"Worse than that," said Fran.

"Huh?"

"However bad you think it is, it's never bad enough."

Cynical, thought Sally.

"Even so, I'd like to meet your friend."

Yet Fran's voice was chilling in its echo of Lorne's, how it touched the air and made it strange with a quiet that was almost a sound, a low murmur of foreboding. In the flapping of gulls by the seawall, Sally could sense the telling of secrets, whispers she was not to hear in the to-and-fro of the sea.

Six

On the day Tim mended the last of the glass, it began to fall apart
in his hands. Not the objects that Katherine Groves had made
and broken, but the things he had formed out of mismatched bits
and shards, what Sally insisted were teacups, candelabra. To him
they had always been tormented shapes, no more. Yet once they
began to fall apart, he became afraid that everything he touched
would break. He knew what he'd inflicted on the world, knew
the collapse of what he'd fashioned was more than his lack of
skill at design, his faulty judgement of balance and weight. He'd
see tortured faces in the broken shards, hands tied behind backs,
feet marched into the woods, hands digging graves. All of them,
sooner or later, breaking.

Tim delivered groceries, loaded the truck, spent time feeling
the heft and weight of solid objects: cases of beer, crates of
peaches, steaks wrapped in butcher paper, packed on ice. He
swept up his shards of glass and threw them out. He mended a
shutter on Sally's house and replaced a broken lock, swam every
day and sprinted with Jake. After supper, Tim played his flute
alone in the woods. In his sleep one night, the war began again.
He watched suspects crushed under the weight of too many questions, found himself as hard as a stone. He cried out in a blue
flash, woke up.

He looked around, saw that Sally wasn't in the tent, knew he
wanted relief and had to have her. She'd gone swimming, he
guessed that, and he went to the pond, crouching like a spy in
the tall grass, feeling the sun about to roast the world on the spit
of a scorching day. He'd watch Sally take off her robe, still and
naked, pretty as a heron. He'd chase her down and have her

then. Stretched out in the rushes, cattails, marsh grass, he felt rock and stubble scratching his face, his skin. He shut his eyes and drifted into sleep.

He was hiding from the snap and crunch of heavy boots, of bullets clattering loud as freight trains skipping tracks and smashing over trestles. He heard screams for help, a village in the crackling heat of fire. Shut up, his nerves yelled, and he ran to the water, where he saw Sally naked and swimming towards him, and he prayed to God, Don't let me hurt her, please, and he lowered his eyes, took her in his arms and wrapped her naked body in a towel, knowing he should have prayed like this sooner, knowing it was too late and he was dead. He felt the sting of tears and he was startled awake by an apparition, by the sudden knowledge that God didn't want his life, not yet.

He opened his eyes. Sally was standing at the edge of the pond, naked, her back to him. She slipped into the glassy water, a gentle splash like a dabbling bird's. She'd come here to save his life: a small boat adrift on her back, her white breasts floating like a pair of buoys.

☞☜

From the middle of the pond, Sally could see the red splotch of Tim's headband in the reeds. She swam to shore, found her robe and towel, dried off and went to him. Tim gripped her and pulled her down in the grass.

"Dreamt you come to save my life," he whispered. "You can't go running off on me like that." He kissed her on the mouth.

"I went to swim," Sally told him.

"I woke you up, right? I yelled."

She shook her head, no.

"Come on, Sal, tell me. I said something that scared you."

"No."

"So how come you look scared?" *Tim, what are you getting at?* She felt afraid, as if his dreams had shaken his good sense, leaving a bitter relentlessness she'd never seen in him.

"For chrissakes, Tim. You were sleeping when I left."

"You heard me in my sleep. Come on, gal, tell me."

She wondered if he'd been smoking something bad. She felt alarmed, scared of his gentleness, of his touch saying, *Please Sally, don't be scared*, as if he were tending to a wounded thing, as if he might harm her in order to have a wound to bind, a way of showing how kind and good he was. She looked at him and tried to hold his gaze.

"You were yelling in your sleep."

Tim's eyes hardened. "Told me I wasn't, now I was. Which is it?"

"*Here*, you were yelling. I heard you."

He looked afraid. "What did I say?"

"I don't know," Sally answered.

"I'm gonna tell you."

He grabbed her arms and she pushed him away, but he was larger than she was, stronger. He pinned her down, his tongue in her ear, *I'm telling you now, hold still. Feel good, don't it? Don't it?* Tim was laughing, his tears on her face.

🐚🐚

Neither of them sees who is coming.

A man has parked his car along the road, and he's walking up the winding stretch of driveway. The man is Lorne Winter. He's dressed in tailored but casual clothes, the strap of his camera hanging from his neck. He'd come at daybreak to photograph the beach and the embankment, and he hadn't planned to look for Sally. Walking at a distance from the pond, his view of it blocked by the forest, he walks with the light feet of a cat as he climbs the treehome steps in the morning silence. It doesn't surprise him that the door is unlocked. Sally wants his presence here, he could sense that on the phone. Needs it; that too. His mouth feels dry.

Signs of her everywhere; her tie-dyed T-shirt, one she used to wear on warm days in Toronto. Lorne picks it up, presses it to his lips, his cheek. This is the closest he's been to her in a year of senseless loss and he feels her warmth. *Sally, oh God*, he thinks, as the salt tide of bitterness ebbs away from him. He's suffered enough; even Ella's said this, when she has had reason to hate him. He sits on the couch, his face in Sally's shirt.

When he sits up, he spots a pair of binoculars on the desk, old ones, no doubt her father's. They're lying on top of what looks like a map of Sally's land. Remembering his closeness to her family, he picks it up, folds it and puts it in his pocket. Taking the binoculars, he goes outside on the porch and lets his gaze meander through the leaves. He wishes he could pry them loose from their branches, wishes he could snap the branches off the trees. Sally — he should have known he'd be flooded with her presence, as if she were a high tide that would sweep away all thought of the beach. No, he has to see her, except that these are dense, protective woods and from this vantage-point it's hard for the eyes to grab light, to bend and twist it as they will, to see. *She needs me watching her, she does.* He knows there's a better view in the direction of the pond, the embankment, the beach he's come to photograph. He tries, scans, he's trembling, as if the thought of her were a chill, cold thing. He finds an opening, a dead oak branch bare of leaves. Looks there.

In his binoculars he sees Sally standing by the edge of the pond. Beside her is a lanky young man with long black hair, a red bandanna and an olive-drab shirt, a brusque man who's gripping her arms as she struggles, who's pushing her down to the ground. He's sure it's Tim, and a shadow falls over his thoughts, the knowledge that he wants to see him overpower her. He's inside this man, he's part of the war that's infected everything, that's leached through the porous skin that separates sanity from madness. He puts down the binoculars, lifts the camera to his eye, focuses the telephoto lens. *Sally, oh Sally.* His own body collapsing into hers.

Lorne runs back into the treehome, throws the binoculars down on the desk. About to leave, he notices a phone with a long cord and, on the floor beside it, a tool chest. It's the juxtaposition of the two that chills him, the sense of what these harmless objects are about to become, as if he were looking at ordinary clocks in the last ten seconds before Salvador Dali got his hands on them. He opens the chest, finds wires and cutting shears and tape inside, Tim Gabriel's name on the lid, and it feels as if the air itself could ignite from fear. *Snap out of it,* Lorne tells himself. He slams the lid down.

Feeling sick, he leaves the treehome, runs back to his car, crosses the ferry to Linden, speeds down the Hutch, then the East River Drive to the Village flat he's borrowed from a friend. There's a darkroom here. He breaks open the canister of film, sets the timer, waits in the red glow for a face to emerge in the bath. Later he prints all the photos, enlarges only the man's face. Tim Gabriel; in Vietnam he filmed his face only once. Tim threatened to smash his camera, to kill him. After that, Lorne shot him from behind. Until today.

So I caught him. What a pair of shits we are.

Lorne stares at the picture of the lovers. He wants to talk to Sally, to make his lonely confession of enjoying what Tim did to her, of putting it on film. He wants to warn her that Tim's no good and he's no better. He feels as he did when he returned from filming the war, when tabletops vanished from under plates of food and he woke up floating in the blue air. A luminous body, an organ of sight afraid of what it's seen. More than this, afraid of what it wants.

He wants what Tim wants, *it's what happens when you see too much*. He's film and light is burning Tim's image into him. Like a cruel death it's happening slowly, he's smouldering like the long ember of a cigarette, he's Tim and also his victim, he's going to die. *Sally*, he whispers. He'll get her alone, tell her to stay away from both of them. Take her hands in his, beg her to listen.

Seven

Sally left Tim in the tall grass by the pond and ran back to the camp in the woods. She found her clothes, got dressed, kept running into the deep forest, feeling scared, injured. More than this, she had fears of her own. Today was two missed periods. Distraught, she ran into a part of the woods she didn't know well, as if she might find some answer there, a lost path.

She ended up on a shadowy trail bristling with pine, staunch with walls of grey beech, a path leading out from it to a sunlit clearing, a patch long abandoned to a wild meadow of vetch and clover. She didn't feel safe in the open, surrounded by forest. *Sally!* She turned, saw Tim running towards her on the path. Behind him rose a tangle of dead branches, as if he were dragging behind him a train of shadows.

"Why did you run off, Sal?"

She looked at him and saw madness. Shadows lay dead where he stood, the leaves were flickering with eyes, the trees were sticky with resinous blood as fire hit a thatched roof and rippled through a house of air. Tim looked exhausted. He had his knife in a sheath on his belt, and that frightened her.

"I'm sorry how I treated you," he said.

He took her in his arms, but Sally pulled away, turned and started to run from him, afraid of something she could sense but couldn't name. Running, she tripped on a rock, fell to the ground, knew she had fallen into a lost part of his mind where nightmares would happen forever. She felt his hand on the back of her head as if he wanted her face in the gravel and dust. Turning to her, he touched the dirt and tears on her cheek.

"Did you hurt yourself, Sal?"

She shook her head. "I could see your dreams behind you. Like fire. So I ran."

"Only once I did it. Torched a roof."

"Someone's house?"

Tim bowed his head. "After we used the phone," he whispered. "After we got 'em talking."

Wrap it around his nuts and plug it in. Sally recalled his savage remark and began to shiver in the heat. She remembered Mike's military trivia, things he'd said about battlefield equipment. Field telephones had generators, wires with power to shock. Sally wished she didn't know this. Some terrible moment had sprung loose from the war, an ugly thing unfolding into a home movie that only Tim could see, one that was invisible unless you'd slept with him and slid behind his eyes, one of those stories too terrible even for God. Tim looked away.

"Someone else turned on the juice."

She tried to shut out his words. *Please God, no.*

"I got to enjoy it," Tim said.

She looked into his eyes. "You couldn't have. You left the war."

He shook his head. "Nothing leaves you."

He looked beyond grief or shame as he gripped the handle of his knife and yanked it out of the sheath, looked as if he might hurl it into the arid ground or thrust it into himself. *It would hurt less than what he's feeling, wouldn't it?* Sally grabbed his wrists as tight as she could, so that the knife fell out of his hand and clattered on the stones at her feet. She didn't let go. She held on to him until she'd broken the spell he'd cast, so that he couldn't reach for the knife or hide his gaunt and tired face from her. And as she stared into his eyes she remembered her father, who had sat in her kitchen and grieved for Korea with his knuckles pressed into his forehead, his pain pressed into the skin of time, so that she held in her flesh, and felt in Tim's, the marks of his suffering still.

"I wish I could have told them I was sorry," he told her. "I couldn't."

"Why not?"

"Some of 'em I shot dead afterwards. I should be dead."

Sally let her hands rest on his shoulders, knowing it was not in her power to forgive him. Tim wept at her touch, her gentleness. Even so, she couldn't take him in her arms. Not yet, not then.

Eight

Hoping Tim would relax, Sally brought him up to the treehome, where they sat on the porch and caught the cool breeze blowing from the Sound. She spent the evening easing his thoughts away from the morning, musing on when they should visit Fran or have Jake over for a beer. Tim said he'd like to see Jake, and got up to call him. He stepped inside, didn't move.

"My tool chest. Shit." His screwdrivers, hammer, pliers and a box of nails were dumped on the floor.

"I should've locked the door," said Sally.

Tim was bewildered. "Who the hell broke in?"

Sally felt sure it was Lorne, but why had he wrecked Tim's stuff? She noticed her dad's binoculars, wondered if Lorne's eye might have scanned the woods, might have stumbled upon the two of them. Only hadn't she wanted him to watch her? She felt remorseful. It was her own fault, letting Tim come on to her in the first place. She felt chilled with fear at the scattered tools, at how little effort Lorne had made to hide his presence, as if he'd found it impossible to fix some broken thing inside him, as if he no longer cared who knew it. Including Tim.

"Following me, that bastard," he said under his breath. He put a second lock on the door. Uneasy that night, they both slept in the treehome. *I'll kill you*, Tim muttered in his sleep.

In the morning, Sally noticed Lorne Winter's car parked near her bike-rack at the end of the driveway. She walked towards it, feeling like a dim-witted rabbit about to be caught in a snare. Lorne stepped out, looking hesitant, grave. Ill, in fact, and she wondered what was wrong.

"Sally, are you alone?" he asked.

"Tim's around." She glanced at the woods.

"I have to talk to you," he said.

He looked as she remembered him in Toronto. Lorne, a man blinded and without so much as a cane, his hand reaching out to the fender, the handlebars, the air, sensory stimuli that meant nothing without someone to guide his hands through the first touch of darkness. *I'm the guide*, she thought, afraid. Gripping the handlebars, she pulled her bike out of the rack and into the driveway. Lorne blocked the way.

"Lorne, I have to talk to *you*," she said. "Were you up in the treehome?"

"I was," he replied.

"Were you watching us?"

Lorne hesitated. "I saw you," he said.

"But were you *watching* us?"

He paused. "I was. Yes."

Sally realized how ashamed he was, knew there was truth in his warning about Tim. Yet she felt wary as he took a step towards her.

"Will you come for a drive with me, Sally?" he asked. "There's so much needs saying."

Not with a guy who spied on me, she thought. *No thanks.* "I'm off to visit Fran," she said.

She gave the kickstand a hard boot, swung her leg over the bike and was about to pedal off when Lorne grabbed the handlebars and swerved the front wheel hard. She lost her grip and fell to the ground, but not before she caught his astonished look, as if aggression was the last thing on his mind, as if desperation had bullied its way past good sense, had overtaken him to the point where he couldn't stop what he started. He kicked the bike aside and grabbed her, dragging and pulling her across the driveway. She started screaming.

"I'll drive you to Fran's," he said. "By the long route."

"Tim!" she yelled. Something had gone awry, she could sense that Lorne had never meant to do this, that he was aroused by what he had set in motion, as he yanked open the front door on the passenger side and started to shove and push Sally onto the seat. His hand grazed her breast; she was halfway in, kicking and screaming, his other hand grabbing her shorts. She was trying to keep him from slamming the door and locking her in, trying to fight a reflex of her body that teetered on the edge of longing. All at once he let go, his torso wrenching backward as he fell. Sally wriggled out of the car. Tim had come running and jumped Lorne from behind. With one arm he had Lorne's neck in a grip, and with the other he held the point of his knife to Lorne's chest. He wrestled him to his knees.

"Say your prayers," said Tim. "I'm gonna kill you."

Sally was crying. She stared at him in horror.

"Pervert," said Tim. "You know what's in those woods?"

Lorne didn't answer.

"A big fucking hole your size, is what," said Tim. "Waiting for you to dig it."

Lorne was white with shock. Tim laughed. "Got ya scared, faggot?"

"Tim, enough." Sally moved towards him, but he brushed her away. "I got a shovel, too, and a lot of rope. Get up, asshole."

Lorne stood up, his knees shaking. Tim still had his arm around his neck, the point of the knife at his chest. He made Lorne stand and walk in front of him, hands above his head, the tip of the knife against his back. Sally thought of grabbing the weapon out of Tim's hand, but she was terrified that he'd turn his rage on her. As for Lorne, once she'd freed him, he'd be ready to kill Tim.

"Please," she wept.

The men disappeared down a path into the woods, Tim's words fading into the darkness, *Gotcha shitting bricks, huh?* Sally heard sounds that felt shameful, too private, worse than peeing in the woods when they were kids. A few minutes later, Tim marched Lorne back into the clearing. His belt was still unbuckled. Sally looked away.

Tim stared Lorne down, told him he wouldn't waste his knife on a coward's shitty hide. He had his licence number, he'd have the police and half the army on his tail if he didn't do what he told him to and beat it. He marched him to his car, made him get in, watched him drive off. Then he put the knife back in its sheath and turned to Sally.

"You should have gone back in and called the cops."

"I didn't want my name in the paper."

Tim looked upset. "Small price, to get him in jail."

"Tim," she said. "Lorne might call the cops on *you*."

"Let 'im," said Tim.

"You don't think you went too far?"

"Nuh-uh. I shamed him good. He won't tell."

She was in shock, cold as breakers in April, feeling Tim's arm around her. At his camp in the woods, he put his knife aside, made her hot tea and whiskey, drank down a shot straight. Then he took her in his arms, rubbed her back and stroked her hair. Yet she felt uneasy with his deft prying loose of a man's fear, his knack for humiliation. He was shivering worse than she was.

"Bastard, poking around here," said Tim. "What the hell's he looking for?"

Tim wrapped her in a blanket, and she closed her eyes and slept. When she woke up, she told Tim her dream. *For forty days, it rained and we were up in our treehome, safe. When the rain stopped, you could hear Ella's voice, half speaking, half singing. "God gave Noah the rainbow sign/No more water but fire next time."* Sally paused, wondered aloud where the words came from. Tim said he didn't know.

Nine

It was a terrible thing he'd done, a compounding of guilt, a making worse of what had been bad enough already. Lorne poured himself a Scotch, his second, downed it from a plastic cup from a bathroom with a pull-chain toilet that stank of disinfectant. A dive near the docks, a window fan chugging a slight breeze in from the sea; he had meant to bring Sally here, but only if she consented. It was true, he should have left when she declined his offer of a ride, but he had had to touch her. She wore the invisible clothing of his past, and he was naked, in prison. He'd hoped she'd draw him back into life, but the war was running loose in her woods, how could she? In any case, it was too late now.

He sat up, poured another drink, looked around at the faded quilting, the peach *faux* satin spread, the scoop in the mattress, sex beaten into it. Tim Gabriel had pulled a knife on him. *Say your prayers, I'm gonna kill you.* In the woods Tim had watched him crap, the knife still pointed. *Fair's fair, pervert*, was what he'd said. Lorne drank down his Scotch, sat bent over, crushed by a rockslide of shame. He felt destroyed, knew he had to fight back, knew Tim mustn't get away with it. He drank another glass of Scotch, his stomach tight with rage.

The phone rang. His clumsy hand groped for it, knocked it out of its cradle.

"I heard all about it, Lorne," said Fran. "You owe Sally an apology."

"Like hell I do," he said. "That bastard threatened to kill me."

He heard Fran's pause, her taking in of breath. "I think there's more," she said.

"There sure is." He told her everything that had happened.

Fran listened, paused before she spoke. "You were both wrong," she said in a weary voice.

He thanked her for listening, hung up, slipped to his knees, let his head rest on the cheap satin quilt. Fran knew a thing or two about men who grabbed for sex, but she didn't know about humiliation, what men inflicted on each other. *Fair's fair, pervert,* Tim had said. *I agree,* thought Lorne. *Just wait.* His eyes were full of tears but he was laughing.

❦

15 July 1966

Sally, I am writing to ask your forgiveness. I regret what I did to you, that I was so cowardly and disrespectful, that I lost control. I wish I'd behaved differently. I meant to share some of my life with you, I've been unwell, but that doesn't excuse what I did. Nor does it excuse Tim's threats and crude behaviour. If that man gives you trouble, don't be afraid to ask for help. I'm still fond of you and I will still be a friend to you in whatever way I can.

Lorne

❦

Lorne mailed the letter with shaking hands, imagined them tightening around Tim Gabriel's neck, around the last expulsion of his breath. Only he knew he'd never do this. While he was here, he'd have to stay calm. He studied the map of Sally's land, then called friends of his, wealthy New Yorkers who understood discretion, who found him a detective to record her movements and Tim's. Lorne had no plan in mind beyond the need to assert himself, to recover his dignity. An overview, a means of rising above the wretched nightmare of Sally's forest, the crummy particulars of Tim's behaviour — that was all he wanted. At least for now.

He learned that Tim had set up camp in Sally's woods, that

since the knife-wielding episode Sally had been spending nights at Fran's, that Tim, unarmed, had agreed to guard her treehome. He'd done intelligence work in Vietnam, had been assigned interrogations, had become sickened and quit the army. He smoked dope, played flute and enjoyed a campfire. Both Tim and Sally were on the premises at suppertime, and on weekends Sally spent the night in his tent. Lorne knew the property, knew the back roads into the woods, knew that, from his perch in the branches, Tim couldn't see his own tent through the thick layering of trees.

Ten

Sally would have to tell Tim what was troubling her.

She counted the days on her calendar, marked the absence of her periods, fearful of disturbing Tim, who'd been sombre, gentle, since his confession to her, as close to peace as she'd seen him. One evening he borrowed her father's binoculars and stood with his arms around her. She watched him as his eyes glanced upward. "Straight up, Sally, I want to show you something," and he pointed out the three bright stars of the Summer Triangle, showed her how to find the North Star from the Dipper and how to scan the meandering river of the Milky Way. Still, it was; vast, mysterious, a serenity her father would have loved. For a while, she forgot what was upsetting her.

"Did they have these stars in Vietnam?" she asked.

"Some and more," he said. "In spring you could see the Southern Cross."

"Must be beautiful."

"When there's no bombs going off, yeah."

He took her in his arms, stroked the back of her head, pressed her face into his chest, told her he'd been wanting to show her something pretty, told her that he loved her more than anyone, that she gave him hope. He kissed her forehead, her lips, the tears on her cheeks.

"Why're you crying, Sal?"

She looked at him. "Because you might change your mind."

She told him what she suspected, and was stunned by the meditative look that softened his face, his eyes. He took her hands, raised them to his lips and held them there.

"Marry me, Sally, huh?"

"I don't even know if I'm pregnant."

Tim embraced her. "Doesn't matter," he said. "I owe the world a kid or two. Kids'll come."

They started to talk about the future, to imagine life in her family's home, in the coach house when Mike returned, then on their own when Tim finished college. He'd take her to meet his parents soon, in Maryland and Texas, and she realized that marriage meant she'd have relatives. She was about to end up with a family, the last thing she'd expected of her life, its barren ground.

Out of his pocket, Tim pulled a cigarette lighter, flipped open the lid, sent a flame shooting up, then slammed the lid down. He pressed it into Sally's hands and folded her fingers around it. Sally noticed an inscription on the lighter. She read it, frowned.

"'Nothing's as sweet as the smell of death in the morning.'"

"I'm giving you my bad dreams," said Tim.

"How come?"

"Because I trust you with every word I've told you, everything I've done," he replied. "Including my fucked-up fight with Lorne."

"You're sorry for what you did to him?"

"I'm sorry."

Sally touched the lighter. "I'll always keep it."

"Pray over the damn thing. Hide it," said Tim.

"I'll find a place."

"Far away. Where only God sees."

Sally touched his damp cheek. "I will," she whispered.

🪶🪶

"A Nehru suit with a boutonnière, why not?" said Sally. She wanted a tie-dyed gown, a wreath of lilies in her hair, guitars in church. Tim smiled, said he just wanted her. "A little party, huh?" he said. "For us getting engaged, for Jake's shipping out." He said he'd cook and get the place fixed up, as if it was the least he could do.

A ring, also. They took the ferry to the mainland, the train to Manhattan, then found a cut-rate jewellery store on the lower

East Side, one Sally's parents had known. The original owner was still there, a Mr. Stein, who recalled her mother and the painted glass that he had sold on consignment, who took her hands and said, "Sally, how you've grown, and who's the boy?" Tim bought her a ring, a thin wisp of a gold band, a hint of diamond. "How proud they would be, your parents," said the jeweller. Standing before the old man, Tim put the ring on her finger, and Mr. Stein clasped their hands as if to bless them.

"Let's for an afternoon be young," said Sally. In the East Village she found a white silk Indian gown embroidered with flowers. Tim bought a powder-blue Nehru suit. Uptown, they fed nickels and dimes into the chrome slots at the Automat, the glass doors opening wide to cold chicken salad and lemon meringue pie. In the clatter of trays and cutlery, the warmth of voices, they sat and ate in silence. "Mike used to bring me here," said Sally after a while. "When our parents left us, he'd try to cheer me up with egg-creams, and now I can't look at them, they make me sad." Tim bought her a root beer instead, noticed some men in uniform standing in line for food. In a bright flash, time cracked the air with a coil of smoke and a man fell dead at his feet. He left his lunch unfinished.

Too blemished for the flowers of Rockefeller Center, too weary of heart for Saint Patrick's Cathedral (or for any church); even so, they felt better as they strolled north on Fifth Avenue and found a small theatre where *A Man and a Woman* was playing. During the film, Tim stroked Sally's leg, kissed her neck in the cool dark. "Life don't have to be sad, see?" he whispered. She nodded, pulled out some Kleenex, dried her eyes, passed one to him.

After the film, they took the subway back to Grand Central. As they sat waiting for the train to pull out, Sally held her parcels on her lap and touched the ring on her finger. Tim took her hand and kissed it. They talked about Mr. Stein, the jeweller who remembered her parents. "What a sweetheart," said Sally. "Yeah, a groovy guy, felt like your uncle," Tim said. They both enjoyed the movie, and Sally followed most of it in French. Both of them were proud of themselves, that they worked so hard to have a good time.

Neither of them thought to buy a paper, so they missed the review in the *Times* of Lorne Winter's opening, missed a multitude of other things in this crammed-full city, including a black limousine inching along like a dark clot through the bloodstream of traffic, trailing behind Manhattan's yellow cabs and lumbering trucks and buses. Neither of them realized that they had been followed for hours by a cab, by a man on foot. *East side, west side, all around the town,* Sally hummed the tune all day as they walked and rode, as a stranger hid in the shadows.

Eleven

Parked at the edge of Sally's woods, Lorne sat at the wheel of his car, smoking a joint. She and Tim were on the mainland, he knew that and more. He finished his smoke, left the car and made his way through the forest with his camera, observing the delicate etching of sun, the blotchiness of late noon shadow. On a clothesline strung between two oaks, a pair of swimsuits were drifting in the breeze. In the falling light they looked like half-formed bodies, carcasses. Lorne felt giddy as he touched her swimsuit, then held it to his cheek. He knelt and raised the camera to his eyes.

He knew what he was after, but it wasn't this.

Walking over to the tent, he pulled aside the flap, knelt again, felt the groundsheet where they slept, then a T-shirt and a pair of shorts folded beside a pillow. Ordinary things — he touched them as a blind man would, with puzzled hands. *No. Not here.* Near the tent he spotted Tim's duffel bag, a skillet, a small camp stove folded up in its fireproof case. He opened the latch on a metal bin and his hands shook as he fingered small, domestic things, the stove fuel packed and sealed away, cutlery, cooking utensils, dishes; a rolled-up hand towel, a pink one with flowers, Sally's. It felt heavy with something and he unrolled it. There it was — a rather ordinary cigarette lighter and a note in her writing: *With our engagement, may this be cleansed of suffering, hidden and never used again.* Army issue, dime-a-dozen shit from Nam, flame-throwers. Lorne knew what dreadful thing he was holding in his hand because he'd filmed it, because his snoops had said he'd find it here. He shoved the lighter in his pocket, rolled up the towel, put everything back where he'd found it in the chest.

When he returned to his apartment in Manhattan, he pulled out the lighter and flipped it open, horrified when the flame shot almost to the ceiling. He slammed it shut, adjusted the flame, rolled another joint and lit it, this time with care. He didn't close the lighter. He stared at the fire until everything else receded from view, until it was all he saw.

Twelve

"You two are engaged," said Fran. "This is sudden."

Sally fingered her mother's gold cross, felt Fran's eyes drawn to it, then away. *Don't try to butter me up* — she could almost hear the woman's thoughts. She remembered the warmth of the jeweller in Manhattan, a man she didn't even know, and she wondered if it was too much to ask that Fran might take her in her arms, might wish her well.

"We're not getting married tomorrow," she said.

"Thank God," Fran remarked. "Your mother married quickly. She came to regret her haste."

Except that she was pregnant, Sally thought. She felt her cheeks burning. Fran shoved her hands in her pockets as if she was looking for a smoke.

"She had to leave her country," Sally said. "That's what she regretted."

"Even so," said Fran. "You hardly know this man."

"You'll like him, though."

Fran looked at her. "I know Lorne misbehaved himself," she said. "Nonetheless, he says ——"

"Lorne should mind his own goddamn business."

Fran grabbed Sally by the shoulders. "You listen to me, Sally. Lorne knows more than he should."

"Lorne's *jealous*, for chrissakes." She pulled away from Fran.

"Sally, Tim's a danger."

"Just leave me alone, will you?"

"Gladly," said Fran. Her face was cold.

Sally lowered her eyes and was silent. Then she apologized. "I don't want you to leave me alone," she said.

"Don't be ridiculous, child," Fran answered. "Of course I won't leave you alone."

Yet in the cool metallic ring of these words Sally heard a coin, a price, an I-will-have-my-day, and she felt a stirring, a wondering when and how that day would arrive. She puzzled over what the coin was, how high the price would be, why it would have to be paid, how she might bargain for mercy.

Thirteen

In the morning, Lorne called an acquaintance with a private plane. He wanted to complete the aerial shoot for his coastal book, and they arranged to meet at LaGuardia Airport for a flight over the Sound and the east beach embankment of Groves Island. Airborne, Lorne thought of Glen Groves disappearing over water, of Mike poisoning trees from the sky. Unlike the men in Sally's clan, he wanted no more than a view of the forest, one that would help him rise above the indignity he had suffered there.

"Waddya looking for?" the pilot asked.

"Good coastal shots," he answered. "Woods, too."

The throbbing of the engine shook him, rumbled loose a troubling thing or two. He should have seen this coming. He'd been smoking up too much, the only reason why, on this warm day, he recalled the snow, a dizzying whiteness, a ghostly shape in the northern forest. The derelict plane that Sally imagined, the felled trees, pain that lodged in his throat like the delicate bone of a fish; he'd never lost the memory of that day. He'd lost nothing of the past; it was his own deception that he had. He should have known that forgetfulness was nothing more than a stuck door to hell, and all it needed was a good push. Now he had to see Sally's forest, as if the sight of it might banish what he'd remembered.

He asked the pilot to head out to Groves Island, to the green-clumped northern slope of Sally's land. "Pretty thick canopy" — the pilot's voice shouting over the cockpit noise.

"Buzz the place," Lorne told him. The pilot grinned, his thumb in the air.

Lorne hadn't planned this, any more than he'd planned his foray into the treehome. He'd wanted an aerial view of the forest, and now he began to see why he needed it. Swooping down over the treetops, he could see a woman standing at a picnic table, setting out a tablecloth and plates; Sally at peace in her contemplation of a simple life, of marriage and home in the years to come with Tim. Of all his photos, this would be the most perfect, the most eloquent. It was how he wanted to remember her.

"Friend of yours?" the pilot yelled.

"Let's say hello," said Lorne.

The plane made a steep bank, then its pass, shearing the treetops, snapping off branches. Lorne took only a few photos. Sally had run away, frightened.

Looking down, he saw villages on fire, Tim's war about to end. In his pocket he felt something cold, metallic.

"I'd like to finish this shoot," said Lorne.

"No beach?" the pilot asked.

"Only the woods, if you don't mind." Calm as a windless day, he felt. That still.

Fourteen

You are invited to an engagement-and-goodbye-Jake party.

Sally wrote this in India ink on each of the blue-green tie-dyed cards she had bought in Greenwich Village. She planned an after-work barbecue: burgers and buns, salads and corn on the cob. Jake's mother, a vegetarian, offered to bring a lemon-custard layer cake, and in return Sally made her a no-meat dish from the *I Hate To Cook Book*: Chinese noodles, peas and carrots baked in condensed mushroom soup that wobbled right out of the can. "Cream of concrete," said Tim when he saw it. "Eat it before it hardens."

Tim put Sally's bicycle pump to a dozen balloons, and he and Jake looped crepe-paper streamers from the treehome porch to the trees below. Together they strung up Japanese lanterns that glowed in the boughs of the giant oak that held the treehome. Sally set the picnic table in the clearing, ironed her mother's pink damask cloth, filled one of Katherine's hand-painted vases with a huge bouquet of day lilies, black-eyed Susans, chicory and daisies. Tim got the charcoal started, and the Nolans showed up with an ice barrel and a case of beer. Some friends arrived from Fort Travis, others from Holy Rosary Church. Fran brought a large box of chocolates.

A froth of conversation, a sweet lightheartedness; everyone except Mrs. Nolan ate everything. Jake's mother complimented Sally on her culinary prowess, while Tim gripped his stomach and pretended to be sick. Tabs popped off beer cans almost by themselves. Jake was chugging lemonade. Tim swigged a beer back, elbowed his buddy in the ribs.

"What's this, Kool-Aid?"

"Hangover cure." Jake crunched ice, slurped on a lemon rind.

Tim puckered up his face. "You won't get scurvy, soldier."

"No scurvy and sober as a judge." Jake had his mouth open, the big rind covering the space between his lips as if his whole mouth were painted yellow.

Mrs. Nolan glanced up, dismayed. "Jake," she said, "you *are* what you *eat*." He nodded, bowed in silence, plopped his empty cup down on his head, picked up three peaches from the bowl and started juggling them. Everyone laughed. Jake noticed Sister Fran chuckling over his schoolyard tricks, and he caught her eye and winked. *Christ, she looks like her brother, the cameraman. Could be twins.* Later he remembered thinking that.

"Welcome to Uncle Jake's circus." He took a bow.

"Uncle Sam'll love it," said his dad.

Jake Nolan toasted the happiness of his buddy Tim and his good neighbour Sally. The two of them thanked everyone for coming, wished Jake well in the army and gave him a photo album with autographed pictures of all those present. Jake and Sally sang duets, Jake on guitar and Tim playing his flute: campfire songs that everyone could sing, songs older than everyone there.

"I've never heard you sing, dear," said Fran to Sally. Mrs. Nolan dabbed at her eyes.

Guests began to leave, and Jake asked his parents if they'd take his guitar since he meant to walk home by himself. He wanted to hike the long beach route that loped along the eastern edge of the Groves' property, right down East Shore Road and into town, then grab a bus up Lincoln Road to Sycamore and home. He'd been walking two miles a day all summer, hoping that, along with swimming, the hikes would keep him fit, give him a leg up on boot camp. His folks were driving Sister Fran home, so they didn't mind leaving without him.

Later Sally forgot it all. Jake, who hadn't been drinking, remembered everything.

☙ ☙

This is the weight of evidence, built up like layers of sedimentary rock; Sally remembered most of what happened after the party, but not all. On the whole, she had been an accurate reporter, sometimes inventive through no fault of her own, losing track of minutiae that later became important, inventing facts that blurred into illusions that drowned inside each other, converging like the waters of a flood.

Earlier that evening, Lorne had driven up Sycamore Road, parking his car near the westward path into the Groves' forest. He knew Sally and Tim were planning a party; knew Tim's camp was invisible from the clearing. He smoked a joint, felt better and strode into the woods.

Tim's camp had been left in disarray. They must have slept late, had no time to clean up. Lorne noticed the unwashed frying pan, dishes piled in a bucket, the portable stove, an ashtray with a pair of roach clips. As he glanced at the stove, he remembered seeing a can of fuel on his last foray into their camp. His hands gripped his arms as he rocked back and forth like a rowboat on a gentle swell. It would be easy, what he had to do. The world was beginning to disappear beyond the narrow horizon of the present moment, of a lit match and its vast power to re-order everything. Nothing beyond this single thought, nothing at all.

Except that he didn't want to hurt Sally. He wanted to give them both a scare — no, more than this. Something inside him was burning, a spinning vortex of need and desire. A match struck and lit with yearning; the thought of fire felt like that. He started to laugh, but laughing made him want to weep. He got on his hands and knees and started to search.

Half hidden behind Tim's rucksack was the metal chest where he'd found the lighter. Lorne opened the lid, pulled out a squat can with a handle. He unscrewed the cap, sniffed it, screwed the cap back on. It smelled like kerosene. How careful they'd been with the stuff. In that chest, they'd sealed the can itself away from air. They were prudent, as he was. In his own car he always

kept a spare gallon of gasoline, a habit from driving on wilderness
shoots in northern Canada, where it was easy enough to get
stuck in the bush, then freeze to death at night without a fire.

He squatted, unscrewed the cap and began to pour, watching
the volatile liquid oozing onto Tim's plates, dripping on tent
flaps, soaking undergarments, seeping into towels and a tablecloth and napkins — Sally's. What frail and simple possessions,
these everyday things, dry and absorbent as candle wicks. *You can
smell kerosene a mile away. Never mind, they won't come around.
Not after the party. It'll be late.* He tossed the can into the woods
as he walked back out to his car on Sycamore Road, remembering what he always carried — warmth in an emergency — and
he opened the trunk of his car, hauled out a large metal can and
made his way back into the woods, sprinkling here and there like
a priest at benediction, blessing the earth.

He should light a match, do it now. No, it was still daylight,
too risky. He'd head over to Sally's beach, snoop around, make
sure they meant to stay put on the other side of the woods. After
dark he'd come back here to finish what he'd started. Only he
realized he didn't want a conflagration. He wanted to watch a
sinuous fire lick at their clothing, slither through their intimate
things. The slow ruin of what little they owned, a quiet act of
revenge.

Everything he touched would burn.

❧ ❧

Lorne drove east towards the Sound, parked in a secluded spot,
walked towards the beach and the embankment. He would keep
vigil in an isolated nook, a clump of rocks. It had been good hash
he'd smoked; the tide was lapping music on the sand and his
spine could feel the *ping* of notes like tiny hammers on a xylo-
phone. Tired now, he thought of Ella, to whom he had done
irreparable harm, for which he had been punished. He kept on
making the same mistakes, he did not learn.

Leaning back against the rocks, he shut his eyes, felt euphoria
ebbing away. He drifted into the memory of the day he'd come to

speak to Sally, then lost control and made a grab at her. In his half-sleep Tim pushes the point of the knife into his stomach in a slow and careful excision of his life. *You asked for it, buddy.* Lorne opened his eyes again, sick at this unravelling of himself. It would be easy enough to end his life, to float out like driftwood in the rising tide and drown. Easy but unneeded. In his pocket was Sally's lighter. He felt like Aladdin, but he couldn't remember the story. *Rub the lamp and make a wish, was that it?*

I wish to make a pyre of their belongings.

I wish for oblivion.

Is that one wish or two?

He longed for those spirituals that Ella and her friends would sing, a medley of songs; he ached for the rich gold amber of her voice. A litany of fire and rainbows, of melting rocks and boiling seas, a bleeding moon. *Oh, sinner man, where you gonna run to?/All on that day.*

He rolled another joint and laughed.

Lorne dozed, slept on the embankment. Half awake now, he imagined he could hear the party's dying sounds, the crunch of the Nolans' car on the gravel road. He climbed up on a few rocks, and from his vantage-point he could see the last of the headlights fingering the dirt, the shadows of Tim and Sally cleaning up and lighting cigarettes, oblivious of the dry, brittle trees and cooking embers and the night wind from the sea; touching and fondling and fooling around. He felt something pull and tense in his stomach, a hard fist of grief. He touched the metal in his pocket.

Make a wish.

He heard Ella, her voice on the waves. *Run to the sea, sea won't you hide me?/All on that day.*

He'd lost his hope in living; Lorne knew it as he climbed down the embankment. He realized he was crying as he walked south on the beach to his car. *It's time*, he thought. It was less than a mile, the drive westward, back to the woods.

❧❦

Tim rolled a joint, lit up. He and Sally stretched out under the oak tree, and she felt so relaxed that it was as if she'd dreamt the woods, the party, the man beside her. Tim passed her the joint.

"It's real nice stuff," she said. "But I've sworn off."

"Huh?"

Sally patted her stomach. "Just in case." Tim smoked the joint alone, put his hand on her breast.

She laughed. "You're a real bad man, Tim Gabriel."

"Got hash in the tent'll make me worse."

Sally put her mouth on his. "Couldn't."

"Sure it could. Where bad comes from, there's always more."

Sally glanced towards the woods, wondered out loud if they should sleep in the tent. Tim looked at the sky.

"Just saw lightning, babe."

"Wait for thunder," she said. "You can tell how far away the storm is." Neither of them heard thunder.

Tim sat up. "I saw lightning."

Sally believed him. She glanced up at the treehome, told him she didn't want to sleep there. For two days she'd lived in terror of the plane that had shaved the trees and left broken branches all over the roof. It was an omen, she was sure of it: a vast and terrifying blackness, the memory of her father's flight, his shadow rushing towards her.

Tim held Sally, rocked her back and forth and stroked her hair. Comforted, she slept in his arms. Tim leaned against the oak and fell asleep.

In her dreams Sally saw choppers dumping canisters of napalm, fires torching the roofs of huts. Until minutes had passed, hours, she didn't know which; until, dreaming herself into wakefulness, she fought back, grabbed the flame-thrower Tim had given her and lashed the trees with fire. Then she heard screams, Tim's shouting, he had his hands on her shoulders, shaking her. She woke up to find herself right in the middle of the war. Tim's face was lit with fright.

"Fuckin' woods on fire!"

"What?"

"I must've lit a spark. Look!"

How, Tim, how? she thought. Not fire; lightning, it had to be. A bolt of it jumping from the earth into the clouds (but wouldn't lightning do the reverse? Or even both?) Or maybe it leapt from her fingers, a pillar shooting ten feet into the sky. The glow of it, red in the deep woods, and while they slept time had slowed down and speeded up, lazy seconds unfolding, hours crushed together by the brutal hands of a clock. All in a circle, flames grabbed hands and started to dance around the heads of every oak and beech and sycamore in the clearing. Danger was pummelling her heart, collapsing her breath.

"I'll call in an alarm," Sally told him. She was about to run upstairs to the treehome when Tim grabbed her arm.

"You can't. You could be trapped. Over to the house. Come on." Running west, she felt as if her legs were refusing to move. "Tim! Wrong way!" she yelled. "It's coming from there!"

The forest was spattering like a griddle full of frying grease, like popcorn with the lid off. She remembered screaming, but not the sound of whatever word she said, remembered only how branches flashed into big strings and ropes of cracking flames, sheets of fire flapping across them in the rising wind — *like wash on a line*, Sally thought that crazy thing, couldn't remember what she did then.

They had to get inside the house, call the fire department, but the front door was blocked by a mean, hissing little groundfire sneaking its way to the back. Sally was going to go inside, but Tim grabbed her arm. "Sally, run, it isn't safe!" he shouted.

They tore off, back towards the clearing and the treehome, east towards the safety of water, the pond, the embankment, the beach and the route to the main road, help there. *How did it happen? It all went up like a torch, but how?* Flames like curtains blowing in a hurricane, flames like flags snapping on twigs, *how the hell long were we asleep?*

It could happen. Almost a month of days over ninety; almost no rain. Heat lightning, spontaneous combustion, sparks from the barbecue, a fire she hadn't put out, her forest running a temperature, a burning fever known as July. August now, still hot.

She should have thought of this, no one had told her to water the woods. Too late now.

They were running down the path to the pond, the whole shoreline of sedge and cattail writhing in flame. Beyond them a clump of slender oaks was lit up from behind, the place where Tim had taken Sally's clothes, where he'd wrapped her in a towel, crying out, *Oh God, oh God*, or was he saying that now? They ran down to the water, and just as Sally was about to jump in she looked back and started to scream. Tim ran up to her and grabbed her arm.

"There isn't time to look, babe. Come on!"

He pushed her into the water, but not before she saw her father's treehome torn into pieces by a sleeve of fire that went roaring right up that huge split oak and under the porch. Glen Groves' retreat, the whole thing sheared in two by a knife of flame; the treehome swayed and cracked and fell apart, and the slatted staircase that was like a ziggurat came tottering down in a flaming spiral; down came the porch railing with the yawning creak of a capsized ship, the shutter slats and roof tiles spat out across the forest by a crazy centrifuge of heat and wind; glass exploding out of the windows, teapots, flowerpots, a pyre of her father's maps and books and papers. Sally saw this, couldn't remember when she stopped screaming.

"There's no time, babe, there's no time!"

Time, like everything else, was over.

Tim's voice. "Charlie Cong is after me!"

He's stoned, he smoked something bad, he lost his mind — no time to think this. The two of them jumped into the pond, which was lit up by the fire and lay before them shimmering like the wax of an enormous candle. Rushes standing straight as wicks, dangerous; Sally felt this, kept swimming alongside Tim. On the other side of the pond was the embankment. They could see it ahead, a dune that rose some ten feet up, then dropped straight down to the beach, a slope covered by a tangle of grasses, thick shrubbery, broom-sedge, beach-pea, clover. There was no fire here, and wouldn't be, *please God*, Sally thought. Tim took her by the hand, helped her out of the water, up the slope.

Dark out here, the climb through the scrub brush lit by the

orange flicker from the opposite end of the pond, the only sound the crackling of fire and the crashing of the forest to its death. Sally clawed her way up the hill, didn't stop to look back again. She was scraped from brush and debris, black with soot, didn't notice her ruined clothing or the places where she bled. At the top of the dune she couldn't see in the dark, tried to push through shrubbery knotted tight as a barbed-wire fence, tried to find a path down to the beach. Maybe the fire's reflection would light a path for her.

And then she realized that Tim wasn't there.

He'd been up ahead of her, and now he was gone, like that. "Tim!" she called, but there was no answer in the dark, the light of the fire throwing shadows large as trees. "Tim! Tim!" The sound didn't carry; his name vanished into the world, into its fine threads unravelling, into the crash of tree limbs flying everywhere, into the dune and its shrubbery thick with ash, branches glowing like cigarettes, and the roar of the wind in the trees.

They had been safe, she thought. He had got her into the water, swum with her to the other side of the pond, grabbed her hand and pulled her out of the brackish scum and up the embankment. He was here on the dune somewhere, in a sheltered place; he'd gone to find a path to the beach. Sally stood on top of the slope and screamed his name.

Was that the wind, or was he calling out? Was he afraid he'd lost *her*?

And then the dune-brush lit up like a match in the darkness.

How long was she standing on the dune, screaming? How long before she heard the whistle of fireboats, felt firemen dragging her down from the flaming embankment to safety? Maybe just minutes before a rescuer came to carry the slight young woman in his arms, across the beach to the boat. Kept saying, "All right, honey, you're safe now," kept trying to console her. Only she kept on crying, "Tim!" and then "Tim Gabriel!" as if she were hearing trumpets, as if this were the Final Judgement, as if she thought she were dead and confronted by the burning face of God.

THE ISLAND BANNER
August 19, 1966

FIRE RAZES GROVES' FOREST
Some Damage to Travis; Extremists Suspected

"The Forest Went Up Like a Bomb," says
Witness to Violent Blaze

Groves Island, N.Y. (AP) Arson is suspected in last night's fire that destroyed twenty-five acres of forest including the island's first heritage home. The historic premises belong to long-time residents Michael Edward Groves and his sister Sally Marie. Miss Groves was present at the time the fire broke out. She escaped with minor injuries. A Vietnam veteran is missing and presumed dead.

Fifteen

As Tim clawed through the underbrush at the base of the embankment, he knew what had happened, knew damn well who'd done it. That prick, if he saw him again he'd kill him. This time, no mercy. *Bet he booby-trapped the path down*, knew that was the war in him talking as he climbed up the embankment, stumbled and tripped, grabbed at the brush to right himself, felt the stab of pain from a twisted ankle. He glanced ahead in the flickering light, wasn't surprised when he saw Lorne Winter crouching by a boulder alongside the path, rising to his feet. *That shit's gonna get it*, he thought. Tim's heart pounded, cold and hard, a fist in his chest. He knew how to stop Lorne, what he was going to do to him.

❧❧

Lorne returned to the north end of Sally's embankment, ahead of the blaze. What a fool he was. He should have realized he couldn't contain this fire, should have remembered the gasoline he'd spilled along the path. His small blaze had ripped through Tim's tent, had hit the trees, and then he'd understood that what was dreadful could only get worse.

So burn it all.

Dazed and exhausted, his string of fires chasing him, he'd fled to this place near water. He'd hidden in the brush, jarred into alertness by the sight of Tim Gabriel groping his way towards him down the steep path, falling, unable to rise. So he'd escaped. The man looked up at Lorne, his eyes steel-cold. Lorne felt chilled, afraid.

"Where the fuck's Sally?" he asked.

Tim looked at him, his gaze full of contempt. "Sally's dead," he said.

Lorne felt his knees grow weak, felt sure he'd collapse.

"Fucking burned to death," Tim said.

Lorne felt in his pocket for the lighter, knew at that moment that he'd forfeited his own life. He turned away from Tim, started down the slope, heading for the thickest, driest patch of brush. He was stoned enough that he wouldn't feel a thing. Then his mind cleared and he realized Tim hadn't told the whole truth. *He killed her, that sonofabitch. Otherwise he'd be screaming, crying. Out-of-his-head nuts.* Tim was trying to get back on his feet as Lorne, well ahead of him, hurried down the slope to the base of the path. *Didn't I try to warn you, Sally? Didn't I?* Plenty of dry brush, tinder here. He flipped his lighter open.

🖙🖎

Walking home, Jake Nolan thought about Sally. *Strike while the iron's hot,* his dad had said. *She's gonna be hitched real soon, you watch.* Mike's little sister, grown up now. He shrugged. He hadn't wanted a woman in his life, not until he was out of the army. Maybe his caution had been a mistake.

Pensive, he walked towards the beach. Two miles of East Shore Road, a south breeze off the water, a good stretch. Jake was in the mood for night and the sea, for a dark sky where the cat's-whisker of a moon had set. It was his last walk along the beach where, a few weeks back, he had gone swimming with his buddy Tim, where Sally, too shy to join them, had hidden like a squirrel in the brush and watched. *Goodbye* — he said it first with his heart, then with his lips. When he returned, he'd come back as his father and Sally's had, changed by war, gazing on his familiar home with the weary eyes of a stranger. Glancing back at the curve of the beach, he felt pained at the idiocy of taking things for granted. His eye caught a red sky, a bloodied flicker of light. He looked again.

Sally's woods are burning, Jesus Christ! Flames in the trees, a mile or so away; he should call in an alarm. Only there were no alarm boxes on this road, it was another half-mile into town. Someone must have called by now. What the hell could he do? His feet started running back the way he'd come. The rest of his body followed, his brain bringing up the rear.

Gone was his sense of time. Inside him a metronome, a beating heart, the rhythm of his running stride along the shore road to the beach. By the time he got near the Groves' embankment, the forest sky to the west was lit like a foundry. *Christ, the whole thing went up fast.* He thought of his dad, a safety freak, warning his mom that the woods were too dry for a barbecue, the kids might smoke and get careless, and his mom's reply, *But there's no telling Sally, she has her heart set and you know that, Ed.* Now he realized his dad was right.

Then what the hell had happened?

Jake began to climb the embankment, got himself a foothold on the rocks, grabbed at the scrub and looked up. From where he was, he could see the crackling and spitting of fire in the clearing, the gutted ruins of the treehome dangling from the oak like an eyeball out of its socket. *We were partying there — Jesus!* His stomach shifted, turned like sour milk, and he started to make his way back down. This was no place for amateurs, he shouldn't even be here. Damn noisy, the hiss of the blaze; but he could hear fire trucks clanging, way the hell off on the west side of the woods, by Sally's house. Then a few hundred feet ahead he heard a sound, and looked. Two forms in the shadows, two men in the brush — who?

One of the men lost his footing on the rocks and toppled over; the other moved towards him. Jake wasn't close enough to see their faces. "You all right up there?" he yelled, but they couldn't hear him over the roar of the conflagration. He got closer. In the light of the fire he saw a silhouette, a tall man making his way down the slope.

"Hey, you! Jake Nolan here!" he shouted.

The man turned his face towards him, a slow turn of the head, so that Jake would never forget what he saw.

It looked like Sister Fran's brother. It *was* her brother, had to be. Eyeless was how the guy looked, two black holes in a concrete face. It was as if he'd lost his face, as if the expressions and the contour, the warmth of human flesh had been seared away, as if Jake were looking at the scaffold of a man in the moments before God came and hung a soul on him, except that he had it back‑wards and he knew it. There was no soul here, not any more. Was the photographer here on a shoot? Years ago he had been the *Banner* man at every Groves' occasion, always behind the camera lens. Only he had no camera, he'd been ravaged by the fire, he looked as if he'd lost his sight. *He heard me, he turned his head. Did he see me?*

At the base of the path Lorne Winter stooped and lit the brush, and the flames rushed up the slope, swallowing the man who couldn't get up, the man who was screaming. In the light of the blaze Jake saw Tim's face for the last time.

Winter, what the fuck, you've gone crazy!

He started running towards them, saw his path blocked as the brush went up in flames.

🦢🦢

Lorne was exhausted, unable to move.

He'd run with his back to the wind that had dragged the fire southward. Ahead was a hidden cove, a sheltered spot at the north end of the beach. There in the sedge and grasses he found the ancient pier that Sally had shown him the first time they'd walked here together, a rickety pile of slats and nails where, she told him, she hadn't been allowed to play. *It's family history. We like to keep some things as they are.* Too late for that, but the pier had survived, and next to it an outcropping of rock, its centre hollowed out like a cave, a boulder upended by some cataclysm long ago. He sat in the shelter to wait out the night.

Earlier he had heard sirens, seen the guttering blaze in the dis‑tance, the charred stumps and claws of trees, the end of the for‑est. Now he felt his wretchedness opening all around him like an ugly, night‑blooming flower, a massive jungle florescence with a rotten stench. *Sally, oh Sally.* Like the day he'd made a grab for her — what had he set in motion, what had he done? He had set the fire but he'd never meant the two of them to die. The world was made of fire, after all, and one day fate would set a match to him. *Burn it all.* The damnedest thoughts were starting to torment him, the heat of Fran's voice: *A day will come when you will say to the mountains, "Fall on me"*...she'd loved the remorse of that Gospel quote, good old pious Fran, and wasn't there more to it? Words for Sally that made him want to weep. *For if this is how you treat the green wood, what will you do with the wood when it is dry?*

Ask Tim Gabriel, Lorne thought. Icy cold, he started to shake. What a coward, that he'd go on living. He left his shelter for the water's edge, where he cleaned the soot and dirt from his clothes, his face, his hair. It was too late for the ferry now, for the trip back to Manhattan. He'd have to stay on the island. Looking at his watch, he realized that he couldn't read the time, couldn't make sense of the numbers or which hand told him what.

He strode along the beach, past the markers where the fire department had cordoned off the embankment. A dark night, the moon gone down; he was hidden. The water was still, almost becalmed, as if the fire's cyclone had sucked away the last soft eddies of the wind. He could smell ash, acrid and bitter; more than that, he could taste it, as if he himself had been consumed by fire and was about to crumble into blackness.

He found his car off East Shore, on a quiet, wooded street, and he drove towards Lincoln Road in the eerie darkness. At the foot of the island, the bars were packed with soldiers and locals, with the crisp electric static of their voices. *You see it go up? Jesus Christ, the whole fucking woods! Now they're talking sabotage at Travis. You ask me, they should fry 'em all, string 'em up.* Lorne nodded. He had one drink, then another, then found company in a stranger's bed. "They're wrong about the fire," said the woman. "What started it."

Lorne froze. "What are you talking about?"

She looked at him. "Lightning. I saw it hit the woods."

Lorne could have wept.

Heat lightning. Not even rain.

Sixteen

Sally couldn't speak. It was as if she'd dropped her last dime down a sewer grate, the coin she needed to call for help. She'd lost everything in the fire, all her clothing and possessions, all of Mike's belongings, her mother's glass and French-Canadian pine, her father's library of maps and books, the house, the treehome and the forest. Fran and the sisters gave her clothing and a place to live, a quiet third-floor room with a dormer window and a view of sky and trees. Sally was grateful but silent. She sat straight, knees together, hands folded in her lap, as she had been taught to do in school. She didn't move.

In the hospital after the fire, she'd dreamt that the periods she'd missed had returned, that blood was pouring out of her body. Convinced that she was pregnant, afraid that the shock of the fire would cause her to lose Tim's child, she'd decided to do whatever she could for this tight little fist of a life inside of her. She rested, drank milk, ate fruit and vegetables, meat and eggs, recalled her fortunate good health, her physical strength, the swimming prowess that had saved her life.

Tim will be back, she thought.

She stared at a crucifix on the wall, at a calendar with a lithograph of Saint Anthony, brown-robed and humble as porridge. She didn't hear Fran sit beside her, didn't feel her take both her hands.

"You've been so still," she said.

Sally looked away. "I have something to protect."

"What's that, dear?"

"My sanity."

Fran put her arm around her, brushed aside a strand of hair on her forehead. She told Sally to rest for now. She'd said the same to Lorne, who was distraught, grief-stricken, a strobe light flashing with agitated talk. When she'd told him Sally was alive, he'd wept.

Sally Groves' "confession" (a letter mailed to Sgt. Mike Blanchard, Groves Island Police Special Investigations Unit)

25 August 1966

Dear Sgt. Blanchard:

The fire at my family's house was my fault. I should have banked the barbecue fire properly and I should have doused it. We had a few beers and we drifted off to sleep while we were smoking. I also left a lighter and some kerosene at the campsite of my fiancé, Tim Gabriel. No doubt you recognize his name because Sister Frances Winter (my guardian) tells me there are rumours circulating about Tim's involvement in the fire. It's said he set fire to himself and to the forest to protest the war. This is untrue. Tim took pride in the fact that he served his country in Vietnam. If you like, I can provide you with character references to clear his name.

If you find Tim Gabriel, please don't harm him.

I take full responsibility for the fire.

Yours sincerely,
Sally Groves

Fran put her arms around Sally. "Can you look at me, dear?"

"I'm praying for Tim," she said. "I feel him inside me."

"Sally, Tim's dead," said Fran. "They checked the dental records."

"Not dead," she answered. "Lost."

Seventeen

Fran brought her food, encouraged her to eat. Sally did, but she found it impossible to speak. It was like sliding on snow, a down-hill slope and she was clumsy with the poles and skis and intri-cate trails of a sentence through the whiteness.

"You don't have to use your voice, dear. God can hear you."

What will I do with Tim's child? she thought. *I owe the world a kid,* Tim had said. He was here with her; he had given her this thought, these words.

"Would you like me to read to you, would that help?" asked Fran. Beginning with the mail, a letter from Toronto.

Dear Sally,

I am writing to express my sorrow over your terrible misfortune. It has forced me to realize how sorry I am for the suffering I've caused you. One day, Sally, I will make amends. I hope you will rest and recover, and I know that Fran will do all she can to help. If there is anything I can do for you, please tell me.

Lorne

"Can you ask him for Ella's address?"

Fran said yes, but Sally felt the woman's eyes prodding her, an impersonal prying open of a shell, a knife shucking a clam. *She sees through me, she knows,* Sally thought. She sat with her hands on her stomach, her head bowed.

❧❧

The following morning, Sally got sick, couldn't keep down her breakfast. The next morning also, and the next. Fran took her to the doctor for tests. Before they went, suspecting what the problem was, Fran prayed alone.

Eighteen

The bristle of the doctor's voice against her ears: "You're in trouble." Sally didn't answer.

"And what will become of your child?" asked Fran.

"It'll *live*."

"Surely not with you." Fran's voice was a gale, a slap of raw wind. In it was an unspoken thought: *Tim was brave. Now you be.* Sally forced the words out, slow, hard words.

"Ella ought to have a child."

"Yes, indeed." Fran paused. "I would say that's fair."

Fran took in a great, deep breath and it seemed to Sally that she was drawing in noxious fumes that made her eyes red. There were fine creases worn into the hollows of her face, as if from tears that had dried long ago. Fran, she realized, had always looked like this.

Only Fran didn't weep. She breathed out, expelling the thing that for years had tortured her.

"Katherine all over again," she said. "Sally, I cannot be with you."

"It's all right."

Fran took a deep, impatient breath. "It's not all right. You're in trouble."

"I'm not in any trouble."

"What would you call it then?"

Fran was drilling at a sickened root, an aching nerve, causing her terrible pain. Even so, Sally folded her arms and stared her down.

"This is Tim's child."

"Does that make you less responsible?"

"No."

"Men cannot help what happens," said Fran. "Women are the only ones who can."

Sally glared at her. "I bet you told my mother that, too."

"Drop it, Sally."

"I won't drop it. I bet you drove *her* away."

Fran got up, strode out of the room.

They never spoke about her mother again.

⚐⚐

Sally was exhausted, without resources, and she left Fran to sort out her future. She'd made her point, and that was enough. Tim's child would live beyond the fire, and she would give birth, as her mother had been unable to. Whatever Fran thought, this wasn't atonement, wasn't the healing of her mother's wound or Tim's or even her own. Nothing could heal these things or return what the fire had taken away. All that was left was her body's urge to finish what it had begun.

Fran would take Sally to Toronto, but not to university, not this year. There was a job waiting for her in a private girls' school where no one knew the name Groves. Once the child was born and adopted, there would be money for her in the family trust, enough for Sally's education. How fortunate that she had friends in Toronto, that she was blessed with ambition, a good mind, knowledge of French. Now she would have the refuge of Canada, her mother's country, a place as vast and sturdy as a giant pair of hands, the kind that tend to injured birds, releasing them later to the wilderness. "Canada's all about flying," said Fran. "All sky." Long ago, these words had been spoken by Sally's father, and Fran had written them down.

"You are very much your parents' child," said Fran.

"So I guess I'll stay there."

"You have nowhere else to go," Fran replied. "And I won't be with you." *And no one knows if or when Mike will return.* Sally heard ashes in her voice, her soul laid waste.

⚐⚐

Autumn, and the leaves were bloodied and crisp when Fran drove Sally through upstate New York, then across the Canadian border. "A decent country," Fran remarked. "They welcome refugees. Kids your age are coming here, hundreds of war resisters." Fran had said little on the trip, preferring the radio, CBC News, the Canadian take on Vietnam. "At least they don't talk about 'the enemy,'" she said. Sally, half listening, couldn't focus on the words. She tried not to speak, to think, to face the enormity of her loss. In the motel the night before, she had written a letter to Riva, telling her everything that had happened. She had had trouble composing the letter, had forgotten to include a return address.

"I don't want Mike to know," said Sally. "Or Jake."

Fran was driving, looking straight ahead at the road, impassive. "Jake won't know," she said. "I told the Nolans that you're off to college." Sally thanked her. "You're most welcome, but they happen to think I'm a Communist," Fran retorted. "When they find you've left your country, I'll get blamed, not you."

None of this bitterness mattered, Sally knew.

As if her child were swallowing her, she had begun to lose words, time, sequence. On the journey north, she felt the softness of her mother's cheek, the solace of her father's hands holding her up, the sweet touch of Tim's lips, without the words that named these things. She was content, resigned, but had no sense of these words either — only the warmth of the car window, heat pouring from the round bowl of the sun and into her body, bloating it like the seed pod of a plant. Before she had left the island, realizing that there was no escape from exile, she had thought of her father, of flying to him. She had waited until the sisters had left Fran's house for the day, and then, taking a sheet, had stood on the bed and looped it around her ceiling light. The ceiling was low, the fixture too flimsy to carry her weight. Later, in Toronto, she could try again.

"We're close to Queen's Park," said Fran. "I'd like to see your campus."

Sally glanced at her. "Please let's not," she said. "I wouldn't want anyone to see me."

Fran ignored her, kept driving up University Avenue, past the

Fran ignored her, kept driving up University Avenue, past the massed beds of chrysanthemums on the boulevard, past the United States consulate, where, almost two years ago, Jimbo had shoved a mike in front of her and Ella had collapsed and fainted. "No one will notice you, that's not the point," said Fran. "It's *you* who'll notice *them*."

Fran was right. Toronto was a large city, and she'd be invisible here. As they drove around the great curve of the crescent, Sally felt Fran driving her through the passing away of her youth. Jostling students, a crisp autumn's gleam to them in the bright sun, talk she could almost taste about their profs, their books. She had walked to class with Riva like this, passing the lunch-hour workers quick on their feet to the sandwich trucks, to the park benches under the trees. Yet, in its order and serenity, the scene before her was a paradox, was madness.

In a look, a glance, her terrible summer disappeared. The scene before her erased everything, bore witness to nothing, made her feel as if she were still a student and had never met Tim. Yet at the same time she felt as if she had never seen anything as senseless and as disconnected from the tumult of her life as the meandering and gentle scene before her. Or maybe this was tragedy's extent, that, five hundred miles from her devastated forest, the fire had reached out to destroy this serenity too.

"It makes no sense," said Sally. She told Fran what she felt.

"Of course it makes sense," said Fran. "The world doesn't turn around you. Or me." Sally didn't answer. Fran said no more for the rest of the trip.

At night, when she felt most desperate, Sally imagined God's listening to the whisper of ash, to the part of her soul that the fire had destroyed, that human words would never touch again. Now she wondered how she was going to survive, and as they drove across the campus she found herself thinking of Ella and what she had suffered at Lorne's hands. Ella had written back: *How generous, thank you, Sally*, and then, *I'm engaged*. Sally didn't ask more, didn't want to know, suspecting who the man was by the moodiness and distance of Fran's eyes. Yet in this she had found some hope, and that was all that mattered.

With her hand on her stomach, knowing that Ella must have

done this also, Sally found herself talking back to the fire and the darkness that had overtaken her. She imagined that she was carrying a son who would grow one day into a lanky, dark-haired kid, the likeness of his father. *One day, Sally, I will make amends*, Lorne had written. For the rest of his life he'd have to live with Tim before his eyes, and he'd face in his child the human frailty of the man who had perished in the fire.

If there is anything I can do for you, please tell me. She'd ask that they give the child Tim's name.

Wayfarers III

One

August 1995

Gabe Winter arrived on Groves Island on a fry-it-on-the-sidewalk kind of day, and he thought about Sally, who lived in a cabin by a northern lake and shovelled snow in October. How the hell did she stand this heat? *Grew up here, dummy.* A ferry dock, a ramshackle heap of wood-frame houses and restaurants and clam shacks — stuff you'd recycle in a nice neat city like Toronto, where crummy little dives like these were bundled up and left by the curb. Friendly down here, though; no snotty Queen Street types in undertakers' black. Unhip, uncool and so damn close to Manhattan, how did they get away with it? There was salt air he could taste on his tongue, his first time close to the sea. Yet in the banter and racket there was something unnerving, a stillness.

A space he heard in talk, in the clank of rigging and the rattle of bikes and cars as they rolled off the boat, in the gull's cry that was a black stroke on a vast white sheet of silence; maybe just his mood. He picked up his backpack and set out to walk along the dock, imagining that Sally and his father might have ambled along here in the sixties, a slight young woman in a tie-dyed dress, a man his height in a Che Guevara T-shirt and cut-off jeans, the two of them sitting on the edge of the dock, rolling joints and waving at the moon. *Innocent kids, they couldn't see what was coming.* He stopped and thought. After that, his dad had been sent to Vietnam. Not much over twenty when he died, probably got his ass blown off, a really undignified way to go. *Boy, am I Canadian, or what?* "Undignified." *Where's my Yankee*

DNA? Gabe paused. *I'm twenty-eight years old and I've lived longer than my father.*

All those years Sally's lived alone. Never married, never had any more kids. He felt this loneliness of hers, an ache she'd swallowed all this time, felt it tight in his throat. Strolling from the docks up to Washington Street, he passed a store window, saw reflected in it a tall and lean young man, a shock of black hair, a baseball cap on backwards, a tired, angular face.

Gabe found his way to Jake Nolan's office, and later that day Jake took him for a walk around town, pointing out the Groves' woods, its young trees like sentinels on the high point of the island. Aloof it was, a hibernating stillness that had its echo in the smaller silences that Gabe had heard, a place that wanted to be left alone. The hilly land between the forest and the docks was stylish now, a glossy fold-out of condos with Jacuzzis and central air. "They want to forget about the fire," said Jake. "Those who were here then."

"Do you have a photo of my dad?" Gabe asked.

Jake looked at him. "Try a mirror," he said. Patting Gabe's shoulder, he promised to look.

Jake was single-minded, sitting at the computer screen, tapping away at his keyboard, coaxing out facts from a database with the old-time grit of a prospector picking at hard rock for gold. He had that look about him; you expected boots and a hard hat, a big belt loaded down with miner's gear. Only he was no miner. He was a wanderer home for good, like Ulysses, the Trojan War vet. Groves Island, Jake's childhood home and Sally's. *An answer to a question, that's what home is.* Jake's words.

Jake told Gabe he had lots from the morgue, stuff he had dug up for the special. He sat at a terminal, his hands picking at the rich lode of what he had to find until Gabe's fingers ached to do the same. Jake had the CD-ROM up, the Groves Island fire, 1966.

"Have a read," he said. Gabe sat down beside him.

Timothy Aaron Gabriel, presumed dead. Gabe was puzzled by the name, and then Jake explained to him that Tim Gabriel had been his father. Not an invention, but a real man whose flesh and bone were his. Gabe looked away.

"He didn't die in Vietnam."

Jake shook his head. "In the fire," he said.

Gabe turned in his chair, looked at him. "Does Sally know he died here?"

"I'm sure she does, yes." Jake's eyes were sad as he said it.

"Lorne and Ella?"

Jake paused, folded his arms over his chest. "I don't know what they knew," he answered.

Gabe heard a door slamming in his head, Jake's door bolted shut, locked with this remark. It was the kind of comment a reporter makes when instinct tells him something he's not saying, some wild intuition that the facts at hand don't fit. Gabe wanted to prod Jake but he wasn't ready to find out more. Instead he glanced at the date of the fire, started counting on his fingers — started feeling queasy, as if he'd spotted a red light flashing, the cop car, *Hey, this means you, buddy, pull over,* that feeling. Jake looked at him, perplexed.

"Sally was carrying me," said Gabe.

"Fucking miracle you made it through."

"Yeah. When my own dad didn't."

"I'm sorry, Gabe," said Jake. "Tim was my buddy, but I had to go to Nam. I had to leave the whole thing." For a minute he sat, his head bowed, as if he wanted forgiveness.

☙ ❧

Jake Nolan's remarks on tape: 23 August 1995

...Sarge, allow me to pour myself a beer and confide in you that I never had a chance to tell the police what I saw on the way back up the beach. I went home that night and all I could think was *believe me, God, I saw it. If I'm lying, give my life to Charlie Cong.* Early next morning I was off to Benning and a few weeks after, I shipped out to Nam. Years later, I go to put my buddy Tim to rest, I collect all kinds of tape for the special and then Lorne Winter faxes that idiotic letter, *Nolan, I have nothing you would want.* Then he kills himself. Christ, was it my asking made him do that?

I mean, what the hell could I have done to him? What could I have proven? Would anyone have paid attention to the accusations of a media crank thirty years after the fact? Maybe they would have, and maybe Lorne knew that and I didn't. Maybe I was too successful, bluffing Lorne. Maybe he thought I knew something when I didn't have the facts pinned down. I had a hunch, an educated guess, an adding up of two and two, and it turned out I was right. Only nothing added up until he jumped. And even then, who knows what grabbed his mind and twisted it like that? Could have been anything made him kill himself, but Jesus Christ, he didn't have to jump into a *fire*. Poor pathetic fucking bastard, it was no way for anyone to die. Not even him.

Except that, in Nam, I'd shoot and think of Lorne. A bullet moving towards him all those years.

🐦🐦

Sally, Jake thought, *it is time I told you.*

🐦🐦

Jake got on the phone. "Gabe's in town," he told Sally. "He's closing in on more shit than he knows."

"I don't want to see him," she said.

"I've got him in tow, it's OK. Just one thing."

"What?"

"He's dug up most of the fire from the *Banner* morgue. They got it wrong."

"So who got it right?" Sally asked.

"You did. You're the only living witness. Your word should stand."

"On tape," she said.

"For all time," Jake replied. "You said you wanted to do that for Gabe. Remember?"

She hesitated. "Yes."

"Gabe brought aerial photos," said Jake. "Courtesy of Lorne's estate, taken after the fire. I want that mike on when we talk." Jake took a deep breath. "I was there, Sal. I want our words to last forever."

Two

Jake on tape: (25 August 1995)

...To the best of my knowledge, this is the only eyewitness account of the fire that exists. Let it stand as an act of witness, as the fire continues to turn to ash the voices and memories of all of us.

Sally: Did Gabe give you this picture?

Jake: Gabe found it with Lorne's stuff. Said it wasn't catalogued like the others. Now he thinks he knows why. He decided to see if it was an aerial photo of your woods. So he went and got this (*rustle of papers*) from the New York State survey people, a topographical map of the island. See, here's your place. Kid even found a topographer to help him read it, match it up with the photo, also with an aerial survey, photos your dad had done. It's shot over a ridge of some kind, right near the edge of the Sound, is what she told Gabe.

Sally: It's where we escaped.

Jake: Sally, did you know I was down on the beach that night?

Sally: You saw all this?

Jake: I was walking home, remember? I was halfway down the shore road, almost into town, when the fire broke out.

Sally: All I remember is Tim smoking up. He had a match and lit it. No, that's not right. Tim had a lighter, he gave it to me as a gift. What the hell did I do with it? It was, what do they call those things, a flame-thrower. I never got the flame adjusted right, that must have been how the fire started. We fell asleep. When we woke up, the woods were burning.

Jake: That lighter. Gabe has it, did you know that?

Sally: (*her voice weak*) He said Lorne left it for him.

Jake: And how the hell did Lorne —

Sally: Someone must have found it and —

Jake: It wouldn't have survived the fire. Whoever found it picked it up where you dropped it. Not on the embankment, and not that night. It would have been sopping wet from your swim.

Sally: I was so sure I had it.

Jake: Sal, you didn't have that lighter. I read your confession. You told the police you'd left your lighter at the camp site. The lighter was stolen, but not that night. How do you think Gabe ended up with it?

Sally: Are you telling me Lorne stole it?

Jake: Stole it, and put a tail on you. Him and some private detective. Gabe found some old receipts of his.

Sally: That's nuts.

Jake: Point is, I saw Lorne on my walk that night.

Sally: But he wasn't tailing me. He had some photo project. I let him walk on the beach.

Jake: He didn't have a camera, Sal.

Sally: Jake, stop.

Jake: I saw what I saw in the brush, on the north end of the embankment. A nice, secluded spot, necking country. Right down near the beach. Right where you tried to escape.

Sally: Please don't tell me you saw Lorne there.

Jake: I saw Tim running. There was hardly any moon, so I saw him but he didn't see me. He must have stopped to wait for you. I heard him holler, *Sally!* — must have got lost in the waves. And then the second fire broke out. Just went and hit the air like you said, a flame-thrower. Tim was screaming, scared fucking shitless.

Sally: Don't tell me any more.

Jake: It wasn't Tim who had the lighter.

Sally: Jake, stop it.

Jake: Please, Sal, you've got to listen. The police were into
          radicals and arson. Morning after the fire I was off to
          Uncle Sam. I never had a chance to speak. Meanwhile
          Lorne went and told the cops that Tim had set the fire
          and they bought it. Tim died alone. I'm the only witness.
          Even in Nam, dead guys had buddies who could say, *I
          saw him die*, and say how he got it. But right in my neigh-
          bourhood, no. I had to walk away.

Sally: You never spoke to anyone?

Jake: I tried. By the time I got back, I was in lousy shape and
          you were gone. So was Lorne. No one would tell me
          where you were or how to find Tim's parents. No one
          would talk about the fire.... Thirty years, Sal. God's the
          only one who knows.

Sally: It's OK, Jake. I'll listen.

☙☙

Dizzy with dread, Sally heard Jake's account of what he'd seen
that night. She was remembering a drive from Timmins Airport
to Gold Dust Lake, Lorne in her jeep, moody and pensive, his
fine hands gripping his camera. It was late spring by the calendar,
and along the sides of that wilderness road were patches of snow,
pine and spruce that for all their dark solemnity felt frail and
naked to their bones. Lorne had asked to visit, had wanted to
give her a gift, had come to her cottage. He'd told her how he
envied its simplicity, drunk the beer she gave him, then slumped
forward, his long fingers barring his face.

"I came to find out why Jake Nolan is snooping around my
business."

"I don't know why."

"He wrote to you, didn't he?" Accusation in his voice; fear
rumbling thirty years of solid ground.

Jake had written, yes: *I'm a witness to your family's life, to all the
misfortune that surrounds it.... I was there the day your father vanished, I was at your mother's funeral, I saw your woods burn, I and
half of Long Island Sound.*

Lorne grabbed her arms. "Sally, please tell me. Did he mention Tim?"

"Dear God, Lorne. Why would he mention Tim?"

"Answer me, please." In desperation, Lorne let go of her, falling to his knees. Yet it was hearing Tim's name that frightened her, lost in the dune-brush of the embankment burning still. *Tim! Tim!* Never again would she light so much as a candle in this room.

"Jake didn't mention him."

"Jake wants me in New York, some goddamn TV show."

"You could say no. Tell him you're busy." Puzzled, Sally took Lorne's hands and pulled them away from his face. It made her uneasy that a thing like this could trouble him so much. He calmed down at her touch, gave her his beautiful photo of the felled trees in Algonquin. Trees or a plane? — a running joke between them years ago. *What did I see then?* she'd ask.

What you imagined. Beware of false witness. She reminded Lorne of this warning of his.

"A good line for historians. I'm going to tell Jake Nolan that, *but I can't,*" he said, and he was on his knees again, his head in her lap, and she held him. *Sally, Sally, I came back to tell you before Jake does. I did you so much harm,* and then a fault line opened in the Shield, in the bones of the earth, in the marrow of serenity that all these years had fed her soul and healed it, and in the dark maw that opened there she fell into the flaming embankment, the crackling heat of Lorne's words, *Sally, I destroyed your life,* and she said, *No, Lorne, no, there's nothing to forgive,* she'd outlasted any harm he'd done, it had taken her this long to accept what she'd lost. *I don't want forgiveness,* Lorne told her. *You mustn't forgive me.*

She wouldn't let him put a knife to her scars; she clamped her hand over his mouth, as if she could push the words back down his throat. *Tim Gabriel* and *fire* and *I lied* and *for thirty years I ran and then you found me.* A jumble of words, like Mike's old trick of playing albums at the wrong speed. Nonsense. Gibberish.

Hush, Lorne, stop it. Forget this. You've been drinking. It's all right.

Please don't anyone forgive me.

Sleep with me, Lorne. You'll sleep. She pulled him down on top of her, drew his tongue into her silence. She would not have him trouble her like this.

A week later, Lorne was dead.

Sally told Jake this story.

"You knew, then?" he asked.

"I thought he was high on something, drunk," she said.

Later Jake remembered that Sally wept, that on a warm night she was shivering. He found a blanket, wrapped it around her, took her in his arms and rocked her.

"Tim never got buried right," said Jake.

Sally looked at him. Her eyes glittered like broken skylights, shards of glass. "Have you told Gabe any of this?" she asked.

"You want him to know, Sal?"

"It's only fair he knows."

He felt her tears on his hand, and he hid his face and wept with her.

Three

The following day, Jake sat Gabe down in his living room and showed him his father's rusty pendant. He told him he'd found it digging on the north side of Groves' embankment. Then he watched as Gabe picked it up with careful, reverent hands, as if it were a relic, brittle and precious remains. Which it was; Jake knew this, knew what he had to say, didn't look forward to saying it. Gabe turned his eyes towards him, calm, resigned. He thanked Jake, told him he'd put these things with the rest of his collection.

Gabe dug through his backpack, pulled out the small flag and an envelope. In it were some of Lorne's photos. Jake opened the envelope, gazed at scenes full of eerie daylight, as if it were about to rain on a tent in the woods, two swimsuits on the line. For one strange moment he thought of his mother reeling in a great white gull's-flap of laundry, always minutes before the first crash of thunder. He went cold then, as if he could feel the wind.

Lorne took this picture of Tim's camp, Jake thought. He squinted as he turned it sideways.

"'Nineteen sixty-six,' it says." Jake paused. "Tim was camped out in Sally's woods. What the hell was Lorne doing there?"

Gabe looked scared. "Dunno."

"He was snooping. Spying. Going through their stuff. *Stealing*."

"Gimme a break."

"Gabe." The name snapped on his tongue. "Lorne left you what else with his stuff? You told me on the phone."

"A lighter. With a note ——"

"Your dad gave the lighter to Sally. Lorne stole it."

"Lorne was into fire," Gabe said, and then Jake saw that Gabe's face would soon grow old, too old, with the unbearable weight of that flip remark, a weight he could not yet feel. Words died on Jake's tongue, crushed into rubble broken by grief, words that were as tired as a long day, tired as forever. He looked at Gabe, at the last moments of his innocence. And then he looked away.

"Do me a favour," he said. "Get rid of that thing."

"Why?"

"Lorne defiled it."

Gabe kicked his backpack, shoved it under the table. "Don't fucking tell me."

"I'll tell you what I have to," said Jake. "The prick had no business passing it on."

"Lorne set the fire?"

"That burned a man to death."

Gabe slumped into his chair as Jake spoke: "Lorne went and told Sally just before he died."

Jesus Christ, Gabe whispered, and Jake sat with him in the silence of his thoughts. When he felt he could speak again, he told Gabe about his glimpse of Lorne and Tim on the night of the fire, how he'd had to leave for the war, how, thirty years later, he'd planned a TV special to commemorate the island's worst disaster. And this was how Jake knew for sure that, on the night Tim died, Lorne's eyes had met his as he climbed the embankment — that, all these years, Lorne had remembered who his witness was. He'd faxed Lorne and asked for his photos of the ruined forest, the ones Gabe had found uncatalogued, unlabelled. Lorne had faxed back, *I have nothing for you*, and leapt into a fire.

He explained to Gabe that he had imagined doing right by Tim, who'd never had a proper burial. He'd seen how he might assemble the photos, tags, chain, lighter and flag, shove them into a lead-lined canister like nuclear waste, sink the poison into the rock and sand of the embankment. Give or take half a million years, there would be no toxic matter left, no sorrow. Archeologists would find them, Jake said. Be as confused as we are now.

"Yeah, right," said Gabe. He dried his eyes.

"On Sally's land," said Jake. "I'll ask her."

"Without me, OK?"

"Sure." He offered Gabe something stronger than a beer, a shot of whiskey, and they sat for a while drinking in silence. From time to time they would glance at the backpack under the table, but never more than a glance. Then they would look away into the distance.

Four

Sally had begun to pack. Having found in her woods what she hadn't come to find, she was ready to return to Gold Dust Lake, to its rutted gravel roads, to wilderness.

She thought of Fran, her words the night before she'd left Sally in Toronto years ago. *You will find peace, Sally. Try to be what God means you to be.* And Sally remembered that she felt jarred by the sly, imposing riddle of these words, except that she had never seen Fran so tired, so wrung dry of life, her gaze turned inward as if she were sifting through her meagre lode of wisdom for some precious stone to leave her. She'd taken Sally's hand and held it between hers, as if she might press some counsel, some hard-won knowledge into her skin, and Sally had felt the dark heat, the intense conviction of her words. *Some troubles we are sent again and again, because we do not learn from what we suffer* — those were her words. *Believe me, Sally, I have lived through this. And you will too.*

In the north she was quiet, often alone. Maybe she'd learned from suffering, because trouble fell away from her like the weight of snow from spruce boughs, and she was grateful that she never heard her own name spoken, even by the wind. Nothing could conjure up the slight breath of her, nothing on earth. She thought of Fran's words, of being what she was meant to be, and she no longer missed Groves Island and the home from which her parents had vanished. Her family was meant to be dust and air, and that was the meaning of the fire. All her life she'd been dust, drifting away.

She was startled by the doorbell. It was Jake Nolan, and he came in carrying a strongbox, his eyes troubled as he glanced at the laundry basket, at the suitcase opened on the floor. He handed her the box, told her that these were Tim's effects, that he wanted to bury them on her land.

"Will you do it with me?" he asked.

She looked at him. "Soon. I leave day after tomorrow."

She was folding clothing from the laundry basket. Jake came over, took a blouse from her hand and looked her in the eyes.

"Sally, why are you going back?"

She stared at him, puzzled. She'd always planned to go back. At night she had dreams of the boreal forest, the Northern Ontario spruce and jack pine, their grave, mysterious silence. Yet knowing how bereaved Jake felt, realizing that this would be their last talk before she left, she began to tell him about her life in the wilderness, how she felt woven into its solitude, into its simple, almost monastic cloth of work and rest and silence: a skein of years in which she was no more than a strand. In all that time, she had flown a plane that was like a needle crossed with a thread, stitching one lonely hamlet into another, as if she were mending a fraying coat too thin for the sombre chill of life. This had been her human cloth, her work.

"You don't want anything more, Sal?" Jake asked.

"I have all I need," she told him.

"I mean *want*," he said.

She looked at him. "I just accept each day," she said. "It gives enough."

Jake glanced at the strongbox. "We'll bury this," he said, and she could feel in her throat the tight knot of sorrow he carried in his. Without speaking, they went outside and walked slowly across the swampy field towards the embankment. *Ashes to ashes, all flesh is like the grass* — she thought these words. Like a leaf fluttering, the tail of a kite adrift, she was unmoored. Death flying with her name in tow, she felt it here.

At the foot of the embankment, before they made their climb to the ridge, Jake stopped. He turned to her, set the strongbox down on a rock and took her hand between the two of his. He held it there, then pressed it against his cheek. *Sally,* he whispered over and over, *Sally, Sally,* her name drifting across his voice and into the sky, *I can't forget what happened here.* He held her hand as if he were afraid that the first strong gust of wind would lift her up and blow her away, the lone witness to his sorrow on this earth.

Five

Sally and Jake buried the strongbox in the embankment, and there she said goodbye to him.

Alone, she walked. Grains of light under her feet, and the sand was the clamshell colour of the sky, so she wondered if the sand was sky, and then she looked back and saw someone crouching in the brush of the embankment. The man was kneeling, and she knew this must be Gabe, her son. In his hands he held a clump of red carnations and a small American flag. He pushed the stem of the flag into the ground, then stood the flowers between two chunks of rock. Unaware of her presence, he took off his baseball cap, bent forward and kissed the ground. Then he sat up and, still kneeling, pulled his cap back over his head and covered his face with his hands.

She didn't want to meet him.

He had dark hair, wore cut-off jeans, sneakers and a T-shirt with *Toronto Weekly* printed on the back. His face was lowered and she couldn't see his gaze resting on the spot where she and Jake had buried the strongbox. She knew that he was here because he belonged here, and she could sense the claim that his hands, his knees, his whole body made to the rocky soil that held him up. He wasn't afraid. He knew what was owed him, a sturdy creature, a tree rooted in earth.

Sally felt as if she were floating, skittering like a leaf, falling into the hurricane of evening news, wayside shrines tossed like flotsam on the rocks of grief, greengrocers' flowers, family photos, scribbled notes to the dead. How it was done now, the world praying by the side of the road, the engine in idle, the meter running. Her thoughts dipped and fluttered, turned and banked, trying to remember her date of birth and how to spell her name. She had no weight, no gravity. Years ago she had lost it in the fire; she was a singed moth drifting forever into the light. Voiceless as a mote of dust, no words, no name.

She could run to the sea and drown.

Long ago, a knife had fallen from Tim's hands. *Who will forgive me?* he had wondered. Years later, his words on her lips.

Long ago, a lost man's hands had lifted her up above the trees like a blessing on the world before the fire. *Sally, how about that?* and she felt again, in the shape of those hands her flesh and weight and substance; felt a woman's hand smoothing her hair, handing her a painted glass brimming with light. Then gravity, the tug and pull of weight inside her body, a child's weight, herself. It was she who would be born here.

What could she say to the man before her?

You have his eyes. You have your father's limbs, as graceful as a deer's. You have patience, forbearance. Your parents are lost, not dead. You have his name.

Gabriel turned and looked into her eyes, his gaze sombre with anguish, recognition. She watched as he took off his baseball cap, stood up and walked towards her.

Acknowledgements

For historical information pertaining to the Vietnam War I made use of a number of works, including William A. Buckingham Jr., *Operation Ranch Hand: The Air Force and Herbicides in Southeast Asia, 1961–71*; Carl Berger (ed.), *The United States Air Force in Southeast Asia, 1961–1973*; John Duffett (ed.), *Against the Crime of Silence: Proceedings of the Russell International War Crimes Tribunal*; Harry Maurer (ed), *Strange Ground: Americans in Vietnam, 1945–1975: An Oral History* and Marilyn B. Young, *The Vietnam Wars: 1945–1990*. Beryl Fox's CBC documentary "The Mills of the Gods" (1965) inspired the fictional film "Sowing the Wind." For facts on New York's geology I found Chet Raymo and Maureen E. Raymo's *Written in Stone: A Geological History of the Northeastern United States* a helpful guide. Thanks to the New York Botanical Garden for Juliet Alsop Hubbard's "A Walk in the Wild: Native Plants and Their Habitat" and for the eco-tour of the old-growth forest. For a thorough introduction to forest fires, I'm grateful for data provided by John Cerasuolo of the Ontario Ministry of Natural Resources. The image of the tree-home took root in my mind after viewing a *New York Times* photo excerpt of Peter Nelson's book, *Treehouses: The Art and Craft of Living Out on a Limb*. Thank you to historian Barbara Davis and journalist Nancy Q. Keefe of the Westchester, NY *Reporter-Dispatch* for pertinent details of local history that piqued my interest and imagination.

The Canada Council and the Ontario Arts Council made the writing of this book possible, and I am most grateful to them for their generous financial support. I owe a great debt of thanks to my publisher, Jan Geddes, for her faith in my work, and to Gena K. Gorrell for her diligent editing. Thanks also to Walter Anderson, Phil Giangrande and Jack Scovil for their assistance and encouragement, and to Bev, Kate, Beth Ann, Janis and Brian for the warm hearth of friendship.